THE SECRETS OF ETERIN
BOOK ONE

A FORGOTTEN LEGEND

To my little brother who inspires me everyday with his strength, resilience, and kindness.

This book contains depictions of
- **Violence**
- **Physical altercations and gore**
- **Explicit language**
- **Sexual innuendo**
- **Death**
- **War**
- **Sexual assault/rape (mentions of)**
- **Self harm**
- **Abuse (physical and emotional)**
- **Parental death**
- **Child death**
- **Suicide**
- **Genocide**
- **Derealization**
- **Mental health struggles**

Please proceed with caution and be sure to take care of your mental and emotional wellbeing while reading this book.

PROLOGUE
557 YEARS AGO

It had been only days since she had escaped into the capital city with an army on her heels. Only days since she escaped the heat of the flames that annihilated everything in her life. But now, it appeared, the army had followed her up into the mountains and through the city gates.

The first thing they'd burned was the schools. They slaughtered the teachers and killed the students. They went door to door to homes, piling books on the streets in a sickening bonfire of shriveling pages and burning inks.

Of the priestess's students, she was one of two that escaped the city and made their way through the mountain pass to the capital.

When she had woken in the alley behind the capital city's library this morning to the sound of screams and the crackle of burning wood, she knew they had broken through the gates just like they did in her hometown.

She stood now in the middle of the street, watching the flames devour the city's library. The fires roared in front of her, the library completely engulfed by red-hot inferno. Shadows of people she didn't know danced around the building, pouring buckets of water on the fire to no avail.

Screams and clanging metal invaded her ears, rattling her mind. She let a shaky breath loose.

They're close.

She gripped the strap of her satchel tightly as people spilled onto the streets, running from some unseen enemy. In this bag was all that was left of the priestess: two books and a dagger.

The girl looked around wildly as people ran past her, screaming, bleeding, their faces twisted in pain and horror. The library came crashing down behind her, sending pieces of flaming wood and ash onto the ground. Whistling sounded behind her, people rushing past her from the direction it came. She turned to watch them run, her heart thumping in her chest as she clutched the pack she carried.

Her eyes settled on a boy in the crowd. He was familiar, her classmate, a few namedays younger than her. It seemed so long ago now that they had been with the priestess in that room with blood on the walls, when they had run from the death that plagued their hometown.

The whistling got closer, louder, an almost joyful playfulness in its tune.

She burst into a run toward the castle in the distance. Sweat beaded on her forehead as waves of heat from the flames tore through the streets. As she passed the boy, she grabbed his hand, the other still gripping the satchel for dear life.

The boy wailed in agony as they sprinted, ducking below adults running in all directions but she didn't stop. She couldn't stop. The tower was right there; she just had to get there.

The girl wove through the crowds of people, tugging the little boy behind her. Sweat dripped off her forehead, clouding her vision as her breath heaved. Through the smoky haze, a door came into view. She pushed herself harder toward it.

Her body slammed into the unforgiving wood, a dull pain shooting through her shoulder.

She pulled at it, her muscles screaming as her fingers clamped onto the metal handle. It came open slowly, carefully, barely moving due to its weight. She squeezed herself inside the small gap then turned and pulled the crying boy into the tower.

The whistling behind her crescendoed again over the screams and crackles of fire. Turning toward the long hallway in front of her, she reached one sweaty hand into the bag she carried and wrapped her tiny hand around the hilt of the dagger, the rubies embedded in it pressing into her skin. Then, taking the boy's hand again, she sprinted.

Blood spatters decorated the walls of the castle as they ran down the stairs, the red glow of fire highlighting the bricks. Bodies lay strewn across the floors like her dolls at home, their limbs bent at odd angles as they laid motionless, dark liquid spilling from their wounds. But she couldn't focus on that. She jumped over one, a woman about the age of her mother, ignoring the cries that reached her ears. The door was just up ahead.

They were almost there.

She clutched her knapsack tightly, her fingers gripping the boy's hand as she pulled him through the thick smoke. Her feet ached, screamed at her as she ran but she didn't stop, she couldn't stop.

The children ran through the doorway into the room, and she let go of the boy's hand, falling to her knees in front of a far wall made of large stone bricks. With shaking hands, she grasped the dagger in her hand and started chiseling at the furthest bottom brick's grout with the blade. Her heart pounded in her ears, fear overtaking her body, as another scream cut through the silence like a knife.

She glanced at the stone doorway behind her, smoke filled the hallway, reaching toward the two children like fingers of an ancient monster.

Hurry.

Her hands shaking, she tuned out the sound of everyone being butchered in the castle walls of Teveban. She focused on the dagger in her hand, the task, her hands refusing to do anything else.

The boy slid next to her, his eyes wide with fear and she gulped.

"I know!" she squeaked out, swallowing hard, trying to stop the realization that they were going to die from paralyzing her.

Screaming got louder, closer, and the sounds of clanging metal and muffled cries overtook her. The smoke poured into the room, blocking her sight as heavy footsteps echoed down the long hallway toward them.

Throwing the dagger down, she pulled desperately at the heavy brick, pleading with it to abandon its resting place. She gripped the rough edges, the jagged stone tearing into the flesh of her palms.

"Help me!" she said to the boy and two shaky hands quickly became four, pulling the stone brick from the wall.

She grunted with the effort, blood pouring between her fingers as it ripped her skin open. The footsteps got louder, closer; a faint whistling sound echoed through the hallway.

"Close the door," she whispered to the boy, his young face twisted in horror as tears welled in his eyes. "Hurry!"

He jumped to his feet. With a grunt and a loud slam, the stone door fell into place and the whistling became muffled.

He ran back to her and together they pulled at the brick with all the force they could muster. Her heart pounded as the whistling sounded again. They were almost here.

Frantic now, she planted her feet against the wall and pushed hard, pulling on the stone brick with every bit of strength she had left. The man outside whistled louder, banging on the door with something metal. With one last desperate pull, she fell backwards, her head bouncing off the floor.

The boy's hands pulled her back to a sitting position, tears freely streaming down his face but with a slight smile. Her eyes darted to the brick in her hands, and she set it aside, digging in her knapsack as hope filled her. She did it.

Her bloodied, trembling hands pulled out a stack of books. She threw them into the hole in the wall haphazardly as the banging on the door got louder, heavier, rattling her very bones.

"We have to put it back!" she whispered, her hands pulling at the brick on the floor, staining it with her blood.

His feeble, shaking hands gripped the side of the stone and with a grunt, they lifted it, her muscles burning from the effort as the whistling gave way to yelling, demanding to let him in.

The children replaced the brick, and she pushed with her feet, kicking it all the way back against the books, even with the rest of the wall. She ran her hand over the floor, clutching the dagger as her bloody fingers found it.

She jumped to her feet and grabbed the boy, adrenaline pumping through her body, and dragged him through the room and into the one next to it, pushing the wooden door closed behind them and turning the lock. She glanced around frantically, a table, chairs, and barrels. A storage room.

The stone door in the room behind them gave way with a *boom*, pushing them both to the floor as horror filled her body. They were going to die. They were going to die.

"Open up!" a man's voice roared from behind the wooden door, banging his fist against the old slats as the wood began to splinter. "I know you have it!"

The girl pushed the boy toward a barrel in the corner, pulling the lid from it. "Get in," she whispered as he shook his head, hands clutching her arms.

"No!" he said, the sound of his voice filling her with dread.

The wood splintered more, the sound of laughter coming from outside it. "We're gonna kill you," a man said in a sing-song voice.

"Please, get in the barrel," she pleaded with the boy, trying to lift him into the air and shove him within the mead inside. "Please."

He shook his head again, and she picked him up and shoved him inside, his sobs muffled as she replaced the lid. She ran to the other corner, pulling the wooden lid from the top of the barrel and jumped inside, the liquid enveloping her. She pulled the lid over her head, descending into darkness. Her small hands clutched the dagger as the alcohol burned her nose and eyes. She squeezed her eyes shut as the door gave way, hooting men bursting into the room.

Their footsteps pounded through the room, each step, each clang of their armor squeezing her eyes shut tighter. She shook hard, the liquid around her jostling from her body's tremors, burning her cut-up hands. She pleaded with the Goddesses, begging that the men wouldn't hear her.

A pang shot through her heart as a man spoke out from nearby. "Over here!" he beckoned the others, and she grasped the dagger, ready to poke and stab at their fingers when they lifted the lid.

A piercing scream reached her ears, and she jumped, the liquid sloshing around her. The scream sounded again, and she realized what it was.

The boy.

"Where is it?" a man demanded.

The boy sobbed in response, his agonized cries bringing tears to her eyes. She sat paralyzed, unmoving as she listened intently.

"Where is it?!"

The boy cried louder, screaming for his mother. Tears fell down the girl's cheeks as she tried to block out his pain, praying to the Goddesses that they wouldn't kill him, that they'd just leave, that this wasn't happening at all. The boy screamed and screamed and screamed and then didn't.

A soft thud reached her ears, and she clasped her hand around her mouth to muffle her cry of shock. She squeezed her eyes shut, tears pooling around her bloody fingers.

"Stupid little rat," a man said, exasperated, footsteps moving away from her. "Everyone, search the rooms! Rozien's orders!"

She sat paralyzed, silent tears pouring down her cheeks as rustling, clanging, and banging sounded in the room nearby. She dared not move, lest the liquid around her alert them to her presence. Blood still trickled down her hands, combining with her salty tears and landing with soft plops in the mead she sat in. Her skin burned beneath the alcohol, her hands screaming with white-hot pain, but she dared not move.

After an agonizingly long time, the sounds stopped, and a man spoke out. "It's not here, boys. Move on."

Relief washed over her, her hand still clutched around her mouth, the taste of her own coppery blood filling her mouth. The whistles started up again and slowly, surely, faded from earshot.

She sat there for a long time more, whether it was minutes or hours, she wasn't sure. She waited and waited, half expecting the boy to come and open the top of the barrel. But he never came, and she sat, in the darkness, tears streaming from her eyes. She clutched her teacher's dagger, the only thing left of her anymore and pushed the top of the barrel. The light stung her eyes as she climbed out, like she had just stared at the sun for too long.

As her eyes adjusted, the room around her came into focus. Barrels were strewn about and tipped over, the mead within them soaking the stone floors. In the very center of the room was the boy, blood trickling, mixing with the mead.

She climbed off the barrel, moving quickly through the liquid on the floor toward him. She dropped to her knees, her wet body landing with a soft splash. Her heart pounded as she focused on the boy, on the deep slash running across his neck, blacks and deep reds and white fat all blending in a gruesome painting of death. Bile rose from her stomach, and she swallowed hard, pushing it down. She pressed her trembling fingers to his tiny, bloodied wrists, her own heart pounded louder than ever. She found no pulse.

Another tear spilled from her eyes as she rose to her feet, backing away from the boy's body. She wiped it quickly and rushed away, toward the priestess's hidden journals. She burst into the room, her eyes darting across the bottom of the walls until they settled on one at the bottom, the grout around it chiseled away. The stone was still in place in the wall, untouched.

She sighed, moving into the hallway beyond the stone door. She raised one hand as she pushed the stone door into place and focused on her breathing, saying a silent prayer to the Goddesses above, offering her body to be used for their magics.

The girl thrust her hand toward the door, her fingertips barely touching the stone's smooth surface. Her arm went numb, a tingling feeling spreading from her lungs to the tips of her fingers. A loud, dull boom came from the door, sealing it shut with the warding of the Goddess, the way her teacher taught her.

As she watched the white sparks spread around the edges, she began running, her dress sticking to her legs with the moisture of her sweat and the mead. The warding wouldn't last forever but it was better than leaving the knowledge unguarded. Her feet thudded against the floor as her thoughts wandered back to the dagger in her hand, the priestess's.

Was that what they were looking for? Or did they want the journals? Or both?

She swallowed hard, wrapping her fingers tighter around the priestess's dagger. The journals were hidden. And deep within the furthest reaches of Teveban tower they would stay.

She didn't know when the journals would see the light of day again; she didn't know if she would be the one to dig them out; she didn't know what the future held. But with those journals surviving and this dagger in her hands, by the mercy of Chistah, the truth would be found out. Maybe not in her lifetime, maybe not in several lifetimes, but the truth would come to light.

One way or another.

CHAPTER ONE
LISYNIA

L isynia moved silently through the woods as she approached the river. She had to be silent. The river roared in front of her, the sound deafening. The light of day had long since faded from this side of Eterin, leaving her utterly and completely in the dark.

Each step she took was a risk—a risk of being caught, a risk of being hanged for the treasonous crimes she had committed. But when the rule of law puts down her people, treason was the only answer she could live with.

She walked along the rushing river and raised her head, peering with the light of the moon at the mountains in front of her. A wall stood behind the river, the stone bricks matching the gray stone of the mountain exactly. So exactly, in fact, that if you didn't know where it was, it'd be next to impossible to make it out. But Lisynia knew it like the back of her hand.

She steadied her breathing as best as she could, her chest heaving, up and down, up and down, a rhythm she found strength in. Turning her eyes downward, she stepped carefully over the muddy riverbank toward the water. Droplets splashed against her hands and face as she approached, rolling down her skin. She studied the water before settling her eyes on the out-jutting rocks, flat on their tops from years of rushing water over them. Taking one last deep breath, she steadied herself and jumped.

Lisynia skidded across the top of the rock, grappling for any semblance of balance she could muster. She waved her arms wildly before regaining her bearings and standing upright. She let out a breath and turned her gaze toward the next rock.

She jumped again, and again, and again, making her way slowly across the river that separated the lands of the Southern Coalition of Andyse from the Davegu Kingdom. Getting caught crossing would mean certain death by order of the Davegu King Tovik.

But she was going to kill him herself.

She swore that long ago.

With one last jump, she rolled into the mud of the bank, the grime clinging to her wet skin. Raising herself to her feet, Lisynia spit the mud from her mouth and moved her gaze to the wall again. Within its confines, barely protruding from the height of the wall, one solitary peak stood, its roof faltering from years of negligence. The sight of it in such disrepair just motivated her to move quicker, more intentionally through the muck.

Lisynia trekked through the mud and up the hill, toward the sewer grate that ran out from the side of the wall. The smell was nauseating as she advanced toward it; human waste mixed with the coppery scent of blood, from the last execution no doubt. Still, she moved forward and wrapped her hands around the topmost portion of the grate. It shrieked as she tugged it along the rock. Lisynia cringed at the sound, turning her head wildly, prepared for someone, anyone to ask what she was doing. But no one did. She was still alone in the darkness.

Her muscles burned as she dragged the grate open wide enough to slink herself through, plugging her nose with one hand as the stench grew in strength. With her other hand, Lisynia pulled at the metal behind her, covering her tracks from any watchful eyes. People didn't normally come here—no one was allowed outside the walls—but she still didn't want to take the risk. Not after all the work she'd put in.

Lisynia clung to the short walls of the tunnel, stepping close to the side to avoid the stream of fluids that flowed in the middle. Her mind wandered in the monotony of the long, dark cavern to all the memories she tried so hard to forget.

Her twin sister swung from a rope in the town center. Her eyes bulged from her young, purpled face as a slight breeze swayed her lifeless body back and forth like some sort of sick, gruesome ragdoll.

The gallows were a typical sight, a warning to any dissenters. And Catina was a dissenter in the eyes of those that mattered. Even at just fifteen namedays old, she was not innocent to them. No one within these walls got the luxury of peace.

Lisynia gagged, a combination of disgust from the human waste flowing beside her assaulting her senses and anger. She was always angry now.

The end of the tunnel was in sight, a pinprick of warm light in the far distance. The urge to run the rest of the way nearly overpowered her common sense as the glow crept closer. But she stayed at her same pace, slow, methodical.

She approached the mouth of the tunnel, listening intently for anything above at the surface level. A horse neighed but everything else was silent. The guards were not on this section of street, at least not yet. She wrapped her hands around the grate, doing her best to ignore the mush that squished between her gloved fingers, and pulled hard. It came free of its confines with a squeal of metal against cobblestone and she faltered, stumbling backwards from her own force.

The metal was heavy, weighing her down, and she dropped it on the tunnel floor where it landed with a slight splash.

Now for the hard part.

Lisynia gripped the sides of the hole and heaved herself upwards, toward the street. As her head reached the surface, she paused. Her arms struggled under her own weight, shaking slightly as they grew tired, but she closed her eyes and focused on her breathing like her mother taught her, in and out.

Like a hot flash of burning fire, heat spread through her veins, pulling her upwards.

In and out.

The fire within her blood gave her the oomph she needed to pull herself the rest of the way, landing in a strewn-out mess on the cobblestones above.

She opened her eyes, and the heat dissipated from her body. Lisynia peered around; the empty streets were lined with downtrodden houses. They were once great homes, built of stone and hardwoods, their architecture the marvel of the world. At least according to her mother.

But now they were sullen and broken down, the stone stained with blood that flowed through these streets so freely now and the wood half-rotted away leaving only the shell of a once-great people.

Her people.

Lisynia took a deep breath, the smell of the sewer fading from her nostrils as she took in the cool mountain air. Despite all the horror that happened here, she couldn't help but feel slightly at peace. She broke into a run through the street, headed for the solitary peak in the distance, the castle's tower. Inside, Otto would have a group gathered, the next ones to leave this forsaken kingdom.

Her blonde hair whipped in front of her eyes as she ducked into a nearby alley. Her legs pounded on the cobblestone, a feeling of warmth, of happiness, of *hope* spreading through her body as she ran. One thought stayed with her as she approached the door to the tower:

She would change it all.

CHAPTER TWO
TIVEA

J ust like every day, Tivea woke before the sun's first beams crept through the cracks in the old wood of the walls in her father's longhouse. The only light she had been privy to upon waking over the last nine years was simply the dull embers that danced in the firepit from the night before and the few feeble candles that burned through the night.

She inhaled deeply, taking in every bit of the frigid autumn air as she methodically rose from her bed. And just like every morning before, she cloaked herself in the same animal hides, slipped the same worn-down leather boots over her feet, packed the same hide knapsack with the same old journals and charcoal she'd had since her twelfth nameday— the day her mother began her training—and slipped over to kiss her father's forehead as he slept. She'd be gone by the time he woke. Just like every morning before.

Absently, she ran her fingers through her thick dark brown hair, weaving it into a tight braid as she began her daily trek toward the tree-line in the distance, the light of the sun caressing her back, giving her ever-so-slight warmth in the cold morning air. Tivea followed a small, thin path through the plains, one she and her mother created themselves from the long years of walking it nearly every day. The only sound that reached her ears as sleep wore off her senses was simply her own footsteps and soft, even breathing.

Whether it was five minutes or an hour of walking, she did not care. Tivea had reached the treeline now and all that mattered was the pure bliss she felt wash over her as she reached for the familiar bark of the trees at the very edge, their branches twisted together just enough that they seemed to form a portal into another world. Tivea shivered as her fingers made contact on either side, pressed against the rough edge of the doorway into what she considered her true home.

She kept her hands pressed firmly into the bark as she stepped between the two trees and into the safety of the forest.

This part of the forest was old, even the younger trees reached far beyond the top of her head, the lowest branches gently cascading over the top of her hair. The leaves hanging down, the moss on the bark, the ferns beneath her feet all a brilliant, deep green. Even before she knew the truth, the power of these beings, when her mother would bring her to these woods to forage for mushrooms, there seemed to be a magics here. To Tivea, and her mother before her, this forest was alive in more ways than one.

She let her mind wander to her mother as she walked, something she only ever allowed of herself when she was amongst the trees. Her mother, now gone, snapped from her life one day like she never existed, was a talented woman. The journal within her pack was proof enough of that. There was not a single thing Tivea had come across in the world that her mother could not make listen to her, respect her presence. Her magics, a magics now passed onto Tivea, was a dying one but one that Tivea loved with all her heart.

She took a deep breath, breathing in all the crisp forest air. The sight of her mother's face was faded within her mind, but her legacy lived on within the trees.

The path she walked through the forest split into four, all zigzagging in different directions from this fork. Here she paused, the cold of the still air now creeping below the animal hides. The trees around her seemed to shiver in solidarity, many of them beginning to show signs that the nights were getting colder. Leaves shriveled on decrepit branches, a few already having started to cover the foliage below. Tivea sighed. Winter always meant more work for her in camp and less time in the forest.

She took the path headed southwest, toward the southern river. She had taken this path many times beforehand, always alone except for the notebook and charcoal tucked in her satchel. The cold of the morning air was unrelenting, seeping into Tivea's bones. The thin animal hide covering her shoulders did little to shield her. And yet, despite the cold, her breathing was slow and steady. Even the cold was peace to her if she was out here.

She drew a deep breath, feeling every part of her body welcome the chill that followed. Out here, nothing could reach her. Here it was not like the bustle of camp, with people surrounding her wherever she went and the fires crackling deep into the night. There were no expectations of Yidenu's daughter here. It was simply her and what she loved most—the magics of the forest.

Halfway down the path, after walking for at least half an hour, she glanced up toward the mountains in front of her, the wind blowing down the peaks throwing the few strands of her deep brown hair that escaped the braid in front of her eyes. And just like always, a decrepit peak of a building between the mountain tops looked down on her. The shingles were falling off the frame, a thin layer of white snow misting over the very top of the roof. No matter where she stood in this clearing, no matter whether she gazed upon it from the top of a tree or the forest floor, she had never quite been able to make out what hid beneath it.

Over the years she had been studying out here, the building did not fall into further disrepair as something clearly and utterly abandoned would. Rather, it stayed just the way it was now, old and slanting, with roofing missing and its fair share of holes but in a sort of limbo that suggested at least some care and attention given to it.

Every time she had questioned her father about what that building was and why no one else in camp would admit to seeing it despite many people walking in these woods over time, he shut her down quickly and easily with a simple 'do not speak of it'. Coming from such a man, this struck a chord with her. So, she obeyed and buried the curiosity.

As she let her gaze linger on the leaning tower that peeked ever so slightly above the trees, an odd feeling washed over her. A chill, almost, but quite unlike the chill in the air that reached the tender flesh of uncovered skin. Rather, this was a deeper chill, one that caused her body to shudder uncontrollably as if she had jumped into a freezing lake to gather the lakeweed under the surface. There was something untold up in those trees. Something that hadn't quite yet been fully uncovered. For her father to shut down any mention of the building...

When she first started coming into these woods alone a few years back, her first theory was that it was some type of fortress of Xienee's people. After all, Xienee did dislike her father and wouldn't balk at much. With some thought, though, that theory didn't make the most sense. Xienee and Yidenu had come to an agreement over the years. A tense, fragile agreement but one that had been ultimately upheld at the risk of the destruction of both of their homeland of Andyse. And the building sat nestled in the furthest south reaches of Yidenu's land, so south in fact, that it nearly sat in Davegu territory. Xienee's armies in the north would have a tremendously difficult time navigating even that miniscule sliver of Yidenu's land unseen. Not to mention the Davegu king, with all his spies and surveillance would rather brutalize both Yidenu and Xienee's people than allow even one of them to taunt his power and authority in such a blatant way as having an outpost within two days walk from Oshgor.

It wasn't Xienee's. It also wasn't Tovik's, the Davegu king, but he certainly knew about it, however impulsive and rash he may be, he wasn't oblivious. Whatever it was, it seemed to almost stare back at her as she allowed her gaze to focus on it. And once again, that deep, over-whelming chill caused her body to tremble. Perhaps, one day, that chill would begin to fade and maybe, just maybe, she would have the forti-tude to find out for herself what lay isolated beneath its decrepit roof.

But today was not that day.

She was not an adventurer. She was a student. The only thing happening with her today was the usual studying and, if she was lucky enough, time to work on her *clorhestas,* control over nature, the magics passed down from the woman before her.

She sighed as she lowered herself to her usual seat on this path, a smooth rock with a perfectly curved spot for her to cross her legs and hold her journal in her lap. The forest was beginning to come alive around her, the soft sounds of birds chirping from within the branches of the trees around her soothing her nerves further.

But even as she scratched the charcoal across the paper, her body tensed again; hair on the back of her neck raised toward the canopy that blocked out the sun. Her breath quickening, she slowly raised her head, looking over her shoulder. She stared at the trees and for a quick, unsettling moment, they almost seemed to stare back.

The sun set over the forest, casting the world in brilliant shades of orange and pink, the color of her mother's old dress from before she married her father. She tried to find comfort in the peach shade of the fading light as she ran through the trees, bounding over the fallen logs. Tivea gripped her mother's old journal tightly in her hand, loud crashing following behind her.

The stitch in her chest grew tighter as she sprinted over the foliage, the sound behind her getting louder, closer. Her heart thumped in her ears, the blood rushing through her body. She jumped over another tree and turned quickly on her heel to look behind her.

Peering around the forest, she searched for the source of the crashing, the clanging of metal. Someone was in the woods with her. Tivea's chest heaved, trying to catch her breath as a silence now surrounded her. Not even the forest was speaking. Frantically, she turned her head at the snap of a branch in the distance. But nothing more reached her ears.

Her eyes looked to the peak in the distance as a cold wind blew through the trees, hugging her skin with icy fingers. The peak was barely visible over the mountains and trees, the rocks of the mountains blocking most of her view of it. But something was there, looking— watching her. Tivea took a shaky breath, the journal nearly slipping out of her sweaty hands.

Her heart pounded in her chest as the rustling faded away, not leaving the edge of the forest. She glanced over her shoulder, her hair flying into her eyes as it escaped her braid. As she scanned the forest, there was nothing. Just the familiar shape of the twisted trees and the swaying of the branches as a slight gust of wind tickled her skin.

But something was there.

She knew it.

CHAPTER THREE
RAUNA

The woman's voice warbled pleasantly as Rauna dunked her hand into the dingy water of the bucket beneath the counter. Her hands, cracked and chapped from endless work, burned as they entered the dirty water and pulled a washing cloth from the bucket's depths. Rauna sighed as she swished the cloth along the wooden counter, the sound of her exhaustion drowned out by the cheers of this night's patrons as the singer finished her song, holding a steady high note in the air delicately. Men's voices whooped and cheered, asking for an encore, their hands slapping together in praise.

Rauna raised her head, stopping the rhythmic movements of her chores and turned her attention toward the bar beyond the counter she stood behind. It was a worn-down, beaten place, the faint smell of mead and last night's vomit hanging low in the smoke-filled air. Wooden tables and chairs were spread over a dirty stone floor, filled with men and women in rich garments. Though it was in the more affluent southern edge of Lasari, Bottom Mountain Bar looked identical to the bars in the northern parts of the city. Just richer patrons.

In the far edge of the bar, there was a small stage with a three-legged stool atop it. Sitting on the stool was a woman, well, really a girl, no older than eighteen, her feet barely reaching the raised platform beneath her with long, curly, red hair and a soft face. The woman was clothed in rags, much like Rauna's own and a far cry from the expensive garb the patrons wore. Her eyes shifted once again to the girl's feet, boots skimming the platform with little kicks of her feet.

Rauna shook her head in amusement at the sight, a small smile pulling at her lips. The girl raised herself from the stool, her hair bouncing with her movements. She flitted through the crowd like a bird before landing at Rauna's counter, a wide grin on her face.

Releasing the rag, Rauna reached out to the girl's hand and took it in her own with one hand and with the other cupped the girl's chin. "You did well, Gaabi. You always do."

Gaabi laughed softly and closed her eyes. "You're only saying that because you're my sister."

"You may be right," Rauna stated simply, pulling her hand from Gaabi's and going back to wiping the counter. "But you still did great."

Her sister's smile lit up and a warm feeling came over Rauna at the sight of her joy. Gaabi followed her as she moved along the counter and leaned toward her ear. "Thank you for letting me come tonight."

"Of course, you're doing well in your studies at Valetu, even got a special assignment," Rauna said.

Her sister's training at the most prestigious healer school in the Lupegi province was not cheap; they weren't from a rich family or a noble background. But it was a way out of the poverty they lived in, at least for her sister. And that was worth more than all the hours Rauna worked to pay for it. "You deserved a night off."

A giggle escaped Gaabi's lips. "Thank you, Rauna. It's nice to take a break."

Rauna's smile grew at her sister's words, and she pulled her eyes from the sticky counter back to Gaabi's face. She opened her mouth as if to speak but the sight of movement behind Gaabi caused her to pause.

A man approached, stumbling as he walked toward the women. He was dressed in the ornate silver and purple tunic and chainmail of the soldiers from Timestone, a Sevensguard. Why was he this far north? The

Seven never left Timestone and rarely did their guards. Rauna's throat went dry as he crashed into the wooden counter, waving his hand for another drink.

Turning to her sister, she gave an apologetic smile and moved toward the drunken man, desperate to keep his eyes on her. She swallowed hard before she spoke, eyeing the sword at his waist carefully. The Seven's soldiers were not known for being particularly kind to women in these parts.

"What can I get you, sir?" Rauna asked in the sweetest voice she could muster, forcing a large smile onto her face.

The man hiccupped loudly and ignored Rauna's question, turning his leering eyes toward Gaabi to his side. "Well, aren't you a sight, girl?"

Rauna fought the urge to smack him upside his head as his eyes moved hungrily over her little sister's body, lingering far too long on her chest. Gaabi sucked a deep breath through her teeth, backing away. Rauna's heart pounded in her chest, an ache growing in her body. Moving quickly, she shot her hand up from beneath the counter and clasped his hand in hers.

Slowly, his eyes left Gaabi and turned to her, blood rushing through her ears as her body shook. A large toothy smile appeared on the soldier's face. Out of the corner of her eye, she shot Gaabi a look, one she hoped she would understand and as her sister moved toward the door, a wave of relief rushed over her. She didn't need to see this.

"You're a pretty little thing too, ain't you?" the man said, his hot, reeking breath hitting her face like a brick.

Rauna gritted her teeth, moving her hand from his to grab another mug from beneath the counter. "Thank you."

"I love you northern women," the man rambled on, his eyes boring into her like a hunter staring down his prey as she poured him another glass of mead. "Them southern girls are so... prudish. Don't like to have any fun at all."

She grimaced, watching her sister pull open the door and exit into the night. All this talk she got from these soldiers, they never seemed to realize she and Gaabi weren't native to the north. Quickly wiping the disgust from her face, she forced another smile, sliding the mug across the counter toward him.

After serving him yet another mug of ale and dealing with his grotesque attempts at flirting, he hiccupped and flagged her down again.

A small curiosity pulled at her mind. If she was going to deal with his drunken advances, might as well satiate her questions. "What *is* a man of your position doing up north?"

The man took a long swig from the fresh mug and let loose a long belch, slamming the mug back onto the counter. Liquid sloshed from the glass, right onto her freshly cleaned counters. "Didn't you hear, girl? The Seven are sending us into Andyse again. That Andysi bitch is acting up."

A shock shot through her body. It was suicide, going into Andyse, but The Seven wanted their slave labor and the Northlanders neutralized. She took a deep breath, erasing the look from her face. "Oh, just The Seven's army, then?"

The man guffawed. "Nah, there's some runts from that healer school coming too. Jovan's orders. They're rounding them up now."

Rauna's heart dropped. Her throat went dry, blood rushing to her head as the world around her started to blur. The special assignment.

Gaabi.

Raising a hand into the air, she shouted above the raucous sounds of drunken men. "Everybody out! It's closing time!"

Protests reached her ears, but she didn't care, her body moving without thought to clean up as dread filled her. People began filing out of the establishment through the rickety door into the streets beyond, grumbling all the way. Rauna tried to quell the fears in her mind by stacking the empty glasses from the countertop and tables in her hands. She dumped them into the washing basket and turned back around to the soldier.

Grabbing the mug from the counter, she pulled it from the soldier's grasp, and he shot his hand out, his fingers firmly holding her in place by her wrist. The soldier leaned over the counter threateningly, his face mere inches from hers. She could taste his foul breath. "Closing up early to spend more time with a Lupegi hero, are you?"

"Let me go," she warned, her voice low and steady as pain pulsed through her arm from his grip.

Her heart pounding, her eyes flitted around the now empty tavern. Everyone was gone. The man pulled her closer, tightening his grip on her. With her free hand, she reached into the pouch she kept at her belt and her fingers found the hilt of the small knife within it. Her hands shook as she clenched it firmly in her hand, the man ignorant of her plan in his inebriated state.

It was treason to hurt a soldier.

But she had to keep Gaabi here. And that's all that mattered.

Rauna twisted hard, pulling back from the counter and freeing her arm from his grasp. The soldier crumpled as he flew halfway over the counter, anger flashing across his face. His grubby hands clamped in the air to grab her again and she raised the knife, the lantern light glinting off its metal edge. His groggy eyes settled on the blade, and he retreated, landing hard on the stool below him. He mumbled under his breath, rage etched onto his face as he glowered at her.

Ignoring the grumbles, she twisted the knife in her hand and moved it quickly, her hands quivering as she pointed it right at his eye. He gulped loudly, eyeing her with fear instead of anger now. Her body shook, like she was outside in the deepest winter without furs. Whether it was from the adrenaline of taking on a man twice her size or the fear of losing her sister to the wilds of Andyse, she didn't know.

"When are they leaving?" she demanded, almost choking on her words.

"Now."

The walk to her place was not very far, only about twenty minutes, but at a run she could make it in ten. Rain pelted her, soaking her clothes, her skin, her soul. Her legs trembled under her weight as she sprinted through the grimy streets toward the northern slums her and Gaabi resided in, but she barely noticed. It didn't matter. None of it mattered.

The cobblestone gave way to mud, splashing up her legs as she ran through the alleyway near her room. She relied solely on memory at this point, the lanterns were only for the wealthier areas. Her dress was solidly stuck to her legs with moisture as she threw open the rotted door to her building.

Up the stairs. Through the hallway. She fumbled with the key, banging with one fist on the rickety door to her room. She turned it and burst inside. "Gaabi!"

No answer.

"GAABI!" she screamed, her voice raw with desperation as her chest heaved.

Still no answer.

Rauna's chest tightened. She couldn't breathe, couldn't think. Tears streamed down her face, cutting through the heat in her cheeks. Her dress dripped muddy water onto the creaky wood floor. She was gone. Sent on a fucking suicide mission to Andyse!

She threw her keys against the wall, resisting the urge to scream, to rip her fucking hair out of the ratty bun she threw it in this morning. She rustled through the room like a madman, grabbing every ounce of food they kept and packed it haphazardly in a pillowcase stuffed with the only other clothing she had, an old pair of pants and threadbare shirt.

The money from today's work and the keys that hung on her belt were left on the bed as she tore out of the door once again. They could find another room if they needed.

What the fuck were they thinking, sending the students? Gaabi was top of her class.

A dark thought burst into her mind.

Gaabi was poor, Gaabi was dispensable.

Anger seethed within her as she walked back into the rain and headed further north, to the city walls. Her dark hair stuck to her forehead, obscuring her vision as she traveled by the light of the moon, but she didn't care.

She could've walked for mere minutes or hours; she lost track. She even stopped noticing the men jeering from the alleys or the pack of dogs that prowled behind her for a street or two before being chased off by a patrolman. She barely even noticed as she walked out of the city gates and followed what little remnants of the path she found in downtrodden grass, heading up to the mountains.

The exhaustion, the pain, the jeering of the men, all of it was but a distant, far-off feeling to her now. She was going to find her sister and she was going to bring her home.

CHAPTER FOUR
MOLAC

The dim light of the dying lantern outside his holding cell swung slowly back and forth. Molac sighed, pressing his head back against the wall. It was just his luck, getting thrown in here. He was in training to be a diplomat like his father before him. His family's money had given him the means to avoid the mandatory military service the rest of the Davegu were subjected to. Now that was all gone. He was going to die.

He wasn't known around Dhunviro as the town coward, the weak one, for no reason. He had no stomach for the types of games that the rest of the Davegu seemed to go berserk for. He had no stomach for cheering as another man was gored and strung up on the grotesque display that decorated the castle walls. Molac was not a fighter of any sort; that was the reason he had been thrown in here in the first place. It had been a very, *very* long time since someone had failed out of the most basic military training, especially at the age of twenty-four namedays. He was a coward and in the Davegu Kingdom, that didn't stand. King Tovik didn't allow it to.

Weak, soft, cowardly. He was every name in the book. And therefore, he was dangerous. A man that refused to lower himself to the filth everyone else groveled in and beg for a king's blessing was indeed a man that needed to be silenced. *He* would be the man gored and strung up if the king and his bitch had their way. A lesson to the other aristocrats was all Molac was to them now.

Far off footsteps broke the unending silence he had lived in for days now. A guard approached, decked out in the garish armor of the Kingsguard, blackened chainmail overlaid with a woven tunic of interlacing strands of red, orange, and yellow. He wore a helmet, obscuring his eyes from being anything more than slight pricks of light behind the darkened steel.

"Get up," a gruff voice barked out from behind the mouth visor.

He obliged, a low groan escaping his mouth despite his best efforts to prevent it. "Is it time?"

The guard did not answer. Molac watched his hands as they moved to unlock the cell door; they were tan and muscular, a side effect of the rigorous training befitting a man of the Guard. They weren't even shaking as they opened the door and sent a once-respected aristocrat to certain death.

The sunlight blinded him as the door opened to the arena of the Cruor. The crowd beyond roared with excitement, an insatiable beast that took a unique form. They craved blood and violence and death. Anything less was simply unacceptable.

The peasants are sure to love the fact that a Kludishav is going to die today.

Molac's eyes adjusted, painfully, as a hand shoved him forward and slammed the door behind him. His legs buckled as an unfamiliar feeling swelled in his chest, tightening it, strangling it. He fell to his knees, the dust kicked up tickling his nose in a way that made him cringe. He raised his eyes from the ground and the crowd came slowly into focus—large masses of people screaming, jeering. Colors from across the rainbow mashed together, jumping every which way.

He had been to exactly one of these arena games before, a part of the beast himself that day, a warning from his father to keep power lest he found himself in the sand below.

He gulped, his throat raw. His legs shook uncontrollably, protesting his movements. In what could've been a lifetime of seconds, he stood, back against the wooden wall, begging his legs to muster up the strength to stay standing.

Just stay upright. Just stay standing.

The crowd roared with laughter as tears began to stream from his heavy eyes. They jeered and mocked. Even the children were screaming.

Then, the jeers become cheers. The beast roared with pleasure at the door across the arena flinging open. The knot in Molac's chest gripped tighter as a burly figure sauntered out of the darkness, arms raised, reveling in those horrid screams and cheers. The man stepped fully into the light, revealing a face marked with scars so prominent they were acutely visible from forty paces away. He held a short sword in one hand and pounded on his chest with the other. The beast around them responded with a resounding scream of excitement. The man standing across the arena smirked and screamed himself, the roar of it sending chills down Molac's back.

But still he stayed still, back pressed firmly against the wall. His opponent began bounding toward him, screaming, sword raised in all-but-guaranteed victory.

Pick up the sword.

The man drew closer.

Pick it up.

The crowd jeered from the stands.

PICK IT UP.

Molac bent down, raising the sword from the dirt. The man's blade hit the wall right where he was standing, splintering the wood.

"Please," Molac squeaked out of his raw throat, barely audible. He gulped again, dodging a fist as the man wrestled his blade free. "Please!"

"What? You don't wanna die?" the man mocked, his hand pushing Molac roughly toward the wall again. "You wanna get out of here?"

Molac's eyes clouded with tears as he raised his own sword to meet the man's. The fighter pushed, Molac's muscles burning from the effort of holding it back. "Please."

The blade inched closer and closer.

The crowd got louder and louder.

He ducked, twisting his arm as he ran. Every muscle screamed as loud as the crowd, the shakiness in his legs bringing him to his knees again. With the last courage he could muster, Molac turned toward the man, his footsteps thudding into the ground beneath him.

The man raised his sword and Molac covered his face with his arms, swinging the sword in his hand and squeezing his eyes shut, preparing for the blow that would end him.

Except it never came. The crowd was silent; the world was dark, but his own breathing rattled his chest.

Molac gingerly opened his eyes and struggled to take in the scene in front of him.

The man laid on his back, hands grasping his abdomen as blood poured from a slash to the stomach, his breathing strained and gasping. Blood dripped into the sand from Molac's sword as it trembled in his hand. He made his way back to his feet, dropping the blade from his grasp. The crowd around them watched in awe, slight whispers rumbling through the stands.

He killed him. He killed a human being, a person, a living creature.

A mistake, an accident, the blade in his hand slashing the man's stomach when he threw his arms up.

He killed him.

He did it. He actually fucking did it.

And the crowd roared once again. And Molac's shock kept him still. And men rushed out from the arena doors, overtaking him quickly as he sat motionless, staring at the man in the sand, a halo of red surrounding him.

Chapter Five
Lisynia

1 50 men and women marched through the western woods of Andyse, squeezing as close to the jagged, rocky Malcier mountains as possible for a force this size. They were lightly armored, leather and linen serving more for protection from the cold than from blades. That wouldn't matter though. They only had a few more hours before they reached their destination.

Lisynia let the sound of their footsteps, of their swords and bows clanking in rhythm with their movements, serenade her with its sweet melody. As she let it sway her into a trance, she gazed in awe around her. She had made this trip many times to bring more of the soldiery to Ryrie fortress in the north but the soft swaying of the trees in the wind, the sound of leaves crunching beneath her boots, amazed her every time.

So different from the city streets of Teveban.

She ran her hand absentmindedly around the hilt of her dagger, tracing the intricate carvings and the outlines of the rubies embedded within it. Her eyes scanned the woods, her head on a swivel, as she searched for any sign of recognition of what was happening here. She almost begged for someone to show themselves and prove her suspicions right.

But nothing jumped out. Nothing gave signs of anything out of the ordinary. Her scouting missions had always said this part of the woods was largely devoid of people. But it never hurt to be careful.

She turned slightly, peering over her shoulder at the people marching with her into the unknown. Her chest swelled as she saw faces full of awe at the place she had brought them. These faces showed joy, toothy grins as far as she could see, murmuring amongst themselves as they too looked at the landscape around them in astonishment. They were following *her*. After hundreds of years, she was the one to get them beyond the walls and ready to finally fight back. She was the reason for the pure joy on their faces.

Turning back toward the woods in front of her, she let a small smile cross her face. Her chest swelled with pride. This was the last group to bring to Ryrie, at least for now, making the total of her soldiers 650. They were so close. So close, in fact, that the outline of the entrance began to take form beyond the trees.

Ryrie was an old fort built by the Tevebrisians of times long ago according to the archives she found stuffed deep in the Teveban castle library. Built into the side of a mountain, it was nearly impossible to find if you weren't looking for it. There was one door. Easy to defend. The brick was old and matched the color of the stone of the mountain exactly. As they got closer, she had to resist the urge to run forward and deep within its walls.

But instead, she turned again, stopping in her tracks thirty paces away from the door. She pounded her dagger hilt against her metal canteen to draw her people's attention. "When we enter, going to the left and up the stairs will bring you to the bunks. Choose any free bed you please and meet back in the foyer in ten minutes."

A collective nod of acknowledgement followed her words, accompanied by barely suppressed grins of excitement.

"Well," she said, "let's get you all inside and out of this cold!"

With that, the soldiers sprinted toward their new home.

Lisynia stood at the top of the grand staircase in the foyer, watching her people mill about below her. Laughter rang from the bunks, echoing as a cacophony of happiness through the halls. Within these walls was a force of 650 waiting for training and direction.

The new arrivals slowly trickled back in from the stairs to her side, lantern-light dancing on their faces as they turned toward her. She had been at this for years, planning, moving the rebels into Ryrie, playing submissive to those who wished for her to be as powerless as they led her to believe she was. But despite all the times she had given this exact speech before, the gravity of this moment was never lost on her. She fidgeted with her dagger's hilt again.

She swallowed shakily as she opened her mouth. "Today we stand together, in the fortress of our ancestors, of our forefathers and fore-mothers. For hundreds of years, we've lived under the thumb of those who wish to see us fail. We will not anymore bow to those that have poisoned us, erased our history, killed our children!" Her throat grew ragged, torn. "Today we stand together, ready to fight for our families, our brothers and sisters, mothers and fathers, our children, and their children after them!" Lisynia's face burned with righteous anger at the image of her sister, Catina, swinging from her neck in the town center. "Everyone around you has lost, has suffered. We stand here to say 'no more! We are the descendants of warriors that gave their lives for us!'" She unsheathed her dagger, raising it above her head. The crowd below her roared, raising their own weapons, a sea of steel and tears glinting in the light of the lanterns above them. "We will bow no more!"

She roared with them, an orchestra of pain and sadness and suffering. Her heart wrenched at the sound of so many people in the crowd sobbing as they pumped their arms, the faces of those so young filled with so much pain. She would punish every single person that spilled a single drop of Tevebrisian blood. They would pay for the sixteen namedays old, Ason, who lost his mother in a book raid, they would pay for the thirty-nine namedays old husband whose wife was gutted by a soldier for not giving him bread she needed to feed her children, they would pay for the twenty-six namedays old woman who was forced to watch her daughter be brutalized and raped by a group of soldiers. They would pay for her own twin sister, Catina, fifteen namedays old and sentenced to death for knowing the truth.

No more. "No more!" she screamed, the words coming out choked and raw.

"No more!" the boy, the husband, the mother, the whole crowd screamed with her, their pain visceral.

Her chest heaved for several minutes, the crowd still chanting, screaming, pleading for vengeance. She let a choked sob out of her mouth. And they sat there, 151 people, beaten down and battered, but refusing to allow it to continue.

As the crowd calmed, Lisynia directed them to the mess hall up the grand staircase to join their fellow soldiers for the last meal of the day. She maneuvered through the empty halls toward the general's quarters. Sobs racked her body, the grief and pain of everyone in this fortress tugging heavily at her mind as soon as she left their direct sight. She stopped quickly at the sound of footsteps running toward her from behind. She wiped her tears swiftly, her calloused hand stinging the raw skin of her face.

The footsteps grew closer. She pivoted on her heel, unsheathing her dagger once more, arm outstretched toward the corner.

A man rounded it, disheveled and sweaty but large in stature, dwarfing even her. His face was red from running, his ashy blonde hair slick with sweat. But she knew him. She smiled. Otto.

Her old childhood friend, the first person that joined her after Catina's death.

She quickly stowed her dagger back at her hip and straightened her back. "Otto, what is it?"

"Lisy, there's a group up north. About forty strong."

Her face flushed; there's no way they knew already. "Xienee's?" she asked, hoping it was the commander's people instead of the alternative.

He shook his head. "No," he swallowed loudly, still catching his breath, "Lupegi."

Her chest tightened at his words. "Thank you," she choked out herself, throat still raw. "Get some rest, you did good."

He nodded this time, lifting his head and giving her a slight smile as he spoke again with slight playfulness. "Go get 'em, General."

They moved through the forest as silently as possible, a group twenty-five strong. Lisynia positioned herself solidly at the treeline, crouched behind a fallen tree as she surveyed the scene in front of her.

About forty Lupegi and twenty horses sat in the plains after the treeline, setting up temporary shelters from branches and leather, roasting rabbits on spits over the large fire in the middle of their encampment, or sharpening their weapons on stones they took from the nearby riverbed. They outnumbered the group she had accompany her by about fifteen people but they had the element of surprise.

A woman inched up near the tree Lisynia had settled herself behind. "What would you have us do, General?"

Lisynia mulled it over for a second. These people were heavily armored. They carried flags of war, hoisted high in the sky. Half of them didn't even seem to be worried about a possible attack, laughter rang out in droves from their encampment. But this was not their land. This wasn't even her land. This was Xienee's and the commander had a very specific way of dealing with those that tried to take what was hers.

Lisynia needed Xienee and she knew that. There was one way to ensure that Xienee and her people would march with her. And she'd be lying if she said she didn't want to do it either. She smiled, the anger from before fueling her thirst for retribution. They would know what it means to bleed.

She pulled her dagger out, the only weapon she would need. The woman next to her unsheathed her own sword. Lisynia turned around, raising herself above the tree now. She let out one sentence to the group that watched her. "Kill them all."

CHAPTER SIX
TIVEA

For the past week, Tivea dreaded her usual trips to the woods, through the portal into her own personal paradise. Something changed that day last week. She no longer felt alone in her preferred solitude. Something seemed to always be watching, hungry for something she didn't quite understand.

When she mentioned it to her father this morning upon questioning why she wasn't off studying yet, he glanced with a knowing look in eyes toward the old peaks in the distance, poking ever so slightly above the treeline. His worry was potent, hanging thick in the air. She knew better than to ask for answers though. The old man had wisdom seeping out of his pores but there were things he did not share.

He swallowed slowly, looking at her with a softened expression. "I wish I could tell you, blossom," he used her old childhood nickname, "but I can't. Not yet." His eyes flitted away once again, so quickly she could've blinked and missed it.

Tivea sighed dejectedly, fiddling with the braid in her hair. She wanted to ask him to tell her everything, to answer all her questions but to this day he still wouldn't tell her the details of her mother's death. He certainly wouldn't tell her this.

He reached his hand out to hers, taking it gently from her braid. She glanced back at him, staring into the eyes everyone said she had herself. "Your mother used to do that too you know," he said, smiling, though the pain shone in his eyes. "You remind me so much of her."

She sighed softly, grasping his hand back. "I miss her too, father."

Tears began to well behind her father's eyes, one escaping and marking a shiny path across his face. "I know you have a lot of questions for me, and I promise I will answer them," he said, his voice choked. It had been years since she had seen her father cry. "But right now, you need to go back to the forest. She always wanted you to be there with her in the trees. If you're in the trees, you're not ever alone."

Tivea nodded, tears starting to burn behind her own eyes. This was the most he had talked about her since she died all those years ago.

He grabbed her journal from the entrance table outside their long-house, reaching to her other hand at her side. "She'd be so proud of you, Tivea. I'm so proud of you." With this, the tears sprung. "When you get home tonight, I'll tell you more about her, more about you."

She nodded, a lump in her throat preventing her from speaking as she gripped the journal in her hand. Her father pulled her toward him, embracing her in a tight hug, the kind that made her feel like a child again, running to her father when she had a nightmare.

He pulled away after a few seconds, gazing into her eyes again.

With a quick nod, she turned away and began walking her typical path back to the woods, to the spirit of her mother. She let the tears flow freely now.

The walk was harsher in the mid-morning sun, the warmth beating down on her shoulders like the pulsing heat of a fire when you stand too close to it. But still, she walked toward the trees, inching ever closer. As she reached the treeline, a strange noise from behind her gave her pause. She turned, inches away from the twisted trees.

No.

Off in the distance, flames rose high into the sky, faint screams coming from pinpricks that moved in every direction. She threw her knapsack through the trees behind her and ran. As she got closer, the screams only got louder, more desperate, pounding through her skull.

She paused a few hundred paces away from the camp as the scene in front of her came into focus. Armed soldiers sporting Davegu armor ran rampant on the camp, torches thrown into buildings, into her own longhouse. The putrid smell of burning flesh and blood reached her nose. Her legs shook beneath her, her heart screaming in her chest.

The soldiers cut down every screaming voice they heard. One soldier held up the head of the wild dog that hung around asking for scraps, cackling.

Her breath quickened and she keeled over, heaving up every bit of her breakfast she had eaten this morning. It came up raw and acidic, burning her nostrils.

Against her better judgment, she raised her head toward camp again. *We were at peace. We did everything they asked.*

But no more.

As her life burned away in front of her, a group of Davegu soldiers roughly pulled people from the one remaining longhouse, all bound and bloodied. The woman that made the best stewed venison you'd ever taste, the children that played in the mornings, the man that helped her learn to sharpen a knife. And one more figure, his face swollen and shiny with blood almost beyond recognition.

Her father.

It took everything in her to not raise herself to her feet and rush the soldiers, screaming, begging them to spare her father. Her sweet, kind, smart father. The man that held her hand through every sobbing fit she had, the man that always kept her fed, the man that made peace with his enemies to protect his family.

But instead, she screamed. Her life was gone. Her home was gone. Everyone she ever knew, gone in an instant.

As the sound ripped through her throat, the soldiers turned their attention her direction and Tivea's blood ran cold. One pointed to her and shouted to the others who pulled the bound group toward the horses.

Pulling herself together as best she could, Tivea raised herself to her feet as the soldier rushed toward her. Her heart pounded as she took one last look at her father, his face bloodied by fists and swords. And then she ran, faster than before, she ran.

She reached the treeline as the soldier trailed closely behind, weighed down by his armor and weapons. Bending down, Tivea grabbed her bag and rushed into the woods. North at the fork, toward Xienee. All she could hope for is that she'd lose him in the trees. She ducked and wove expertly through the woods as he barreled through the underbrush behind her.

"I'll find you, just come out now!" he roared, gaining on her; she could hear his thundering footsteps now.

Her hope of losing him waned, a dread settling over her rushing mind. Then an idea burst into her brain.

Tivea ducked behind a tree, crouching as close to the ground as she could. She reached quickly into her bag, grabbing her journal. Trembling hands flitted through the pages as the soldier crashed closer and closer.

A disbelieving smile came across her face as she found a page, written in her mother's neat handwriting. The soldier came closer and closer and closer still, now only about twenty paces away. Tivea popped up from her sitting place and focused on the vines around her, trying to block out the man rushing toward her, sword raised.

Will them, with everything in you, will them. Her mother's voice came back to her.

She let herself go numb, reaching an arm up above her head and closing her eyes. She clenched her fist and yanked the air downwards, willing the plants around her, pleading with them to listen and oblige. Her fingers went numb, her mind going blank.

A choking sound reached her ears, and she opened her eyes. The man was tied to a tree in a sea of plants, the vines constricting his movements as they tightened around his limbs. His hands, the only area of bare skin visible, shook and then dropped his sword.

More crashing and voices reached her ears, far off in the distance and she jumped to her feet again, willing herself to stay upright as she grabbed the soldier's sword and her knapsack and ran again. She could lose them easily in the forest that they didn't understand or respect. The forest would hide her. And she would use that protection to head north, away from the soldiers for long enough to figure out how to get her father back from Tovik's clutches.

CHAPTER SEVEN
HANUE

Hanue stood in the forge bought and paid for by The Seven themselves, specifically for him. *Clang, clang*. His hammer thrusted down on the hot metal in a familiar rhythm. He focused on the sword blade in his tongs, blocking out any other sounds. Not that he'd hear anything over the roar of the fire anyway.

Clang, clang.

The sword started to take a solid shape now, the blade itself long and sharp, the length of his entire arm. He dunked the hot metal in the water to his side, relishing the feeling of the water jumping out of the pot at the sudden intrusion and hitting his bare arm.

He grabbed the gemstones he'd gotten from the market from a shelf built into the rock face and twirled them in his hands. They rolled like marbles, small and spherical, deep red colors.

Like blood.

He smiled to himself slightly and it was at this moment that a hand grabbed his shoulder. He nearly jumped into the fire at the unexpected touch and dropped his gems. Hanue swiveled on his heel to face the interrupter with anger.

"Don't you know how expensive those are?" he asked, his voice booming.

But as he turned, he was met with a familiar face. His sister. Anavi was sweaty, her dark skin coated with beads of liquid across her forehead. Her tight braids were pulled up perfectly from her face, tied back behind her head. She must've been training. But her face, her usually calm demeanor, seemed slightly troubled this time.

Hanue pulled from her outstretched hand and reached down to retrieve the gemstone for the hilt. "Anavi, what is it?"

She sighed, her eyes flitting back to the large manor down the hill they resided in. "Garien is here."

He gasped slightly, pausing in place as his hand skimmed the gems. He picked them up, wiping them off and shoving them into his pocket. A member of The Seven, here? The Seven were the leaders of Lupegi, gods really; every house Hanue had ever been to had a shrine to The Seven. Only a few chosen people ever saw them and Anavi, for some reason several years ago when their father disappeared, was chosen to work for them.

And yet Garien, the most recent one to join them, taking the place of his predecessor Cerue, was here, in their house?

"He came up from Timestone?" The Seven never left Timestone.

Anavi nodded. The troubled expression making sense now. "He wants to talk to us. Both of us."

Hanue nodded, mulling this over. What could possibly warrant a visit from one of The Seven themselves? Did the Davegu attack again? Everyone knew the peace was tense and wouldn't last, but now? Or did Xienee invade and attack Lasari in the north? What could Garien want with them?

His feet moved automatically under him as he followed his sister down the hill, approaching the house.

43

Hanue had never seen any of The Seven in the flesh before and while he didn't fully know what he expected, the man standing in front of him was certainly not it. Garien was young, only a few namedays older than Hanue himself, probably in his late twenties. He was tall and lean, muscles rippling under his sleeves as he moved to open their door for them. He had long blonde hair tied in a neat bun behind his head, not a strand out of place. His features were sharp and defined, giving him a natural sneer to his smile. He reminded Hanue of the kids he went to school with two years ago, the children of large landowners or the nobility that resided here in Aethiel. Nothing about him screamed immortal and powerful like The Seven were.

But still Hanue couldn't help but feel dwarfed next to him despite being taller and larger than Garien. He exuded an air of competence and confidence that was unmatched in anyone Hanue had ever met, save his sister.

The group made their way through the hallway and into the sitting room. Once they all took their positions and Hanue had closed the door behind him, Garien spoke, "My apologies for barging in like this, Anavi."

His sister stood next to Hanue and gave the man a small nod.

"We've run into an issue in Lasari. Jovan wanted me to deliver this to you." He handed Anavi a small, neatly folded piece of paper which she fumbled with for a second before staring at the words.

Hanue drummed his fingers on his crossed arms. Why was he even here if it was just Anavi getting another mission? He sighed deeply, peering out the window beyond Garien and stared back at his forge up the hill. "Your grace," he said, "I don't mean any disrespect but if it's just Anavi again, why did I have to come inside too?" His sister elbowed him, her way of saying shut up.

Garien laughed slightly, the sneering smile crossing his face again. "That's a good question, Hanue. Why don't we wait for Anavi to finish reading and then we'll see."

He was exactly like the kids he went to school with those years ago, talking down on him. Garien had a slight reason to, he admitted to himself, but that did little to quell the annoyance.

Anavi inhaled sharply beside him, turning to look at him, then Garien, then back to him. "A mission in Andyse hasn't sent word in several days. They need to know why," she stated to no one in particular then she turned and touched his arm softly, "you're to come with me,"

Hanue's mouth fell open and he uncrossed his arms, barely believing his ears. "Really?"

Garien responded over his sister "Really, Hanue. Why don't you go and get packed while I talk to your sister."

And the annoyance was back. He crossed his arms again but obliged, headed quickly up the stairs. He was in no position to argue with a direct order from one of The Seven. For years he had been begging for Anavi to take him with her on one of her missions and for years the answer had been a resounding and simple 'no'. But now Jovan himself, the leader of The Seven, said that he goes with. She wouldn't be able to hold him back this time.

He imagined himself in the untamed wilderness of Andyse, a sword of his own making in his hand as he cut down enemies one by one by one, eating off the land, catching fish and rabbit and roasting them on a spit in a warrior's camp. Oh, how he had been waiting for this moment. This was the moment he proved himself to the people in school, those that spit on him in the streets due to his sister's many enemies. Now he would quell the rumors that his family just had a handout from The Seven. They were worthy!

He grabbed his pre-packed backpack and bound back down the stairs to meet Anavi in the foyer and get on the road. As he made his way to the foyer, pure, unbridled excitement replaced the annoyance from before.

He was going to prove them all wrong.

Chapter Eight
Anavi

Hanue came back down the stairs just as Garien finished explaining everything to Anavi. Her mouth hung open with the realization that this was no normal mission of hers. This wasn't a spy mission in Teveban or Davegu, or a quick assassination of a rebellion leader in Estia. This was something more, judging from the way Garien talked. Jovan wanted information this time. Knowledge, not blood. Something was different. Maybe the fact that the healers were sent? Or was the amount of people larger than usual?

He had skirted around the reasoning behind her little brother joining her and the reasoning why this mission was so important. Missions went missing all the time—Xienee was not known to show mercy to those she considered invaders. But Jovan had taken an interest in this specific mission and somehow had decided to send his top spy and decided to throw her brother into the fold. Something was up. She didn't get this far in her career without getting killed for no reason. She could read people, and as she stared at Garien, his arrogant demeanor held a secret behind it.

But it was not her place to question the will of The Seven, especially to their faces.

She turned to her brother, his face giddy with excitement. This was exactly why she didn't want to bring him with her, he was too naive. He'd only hold her back. "Are you ready, Hanue?"

"Yes," he said, turning slightly to show his backpack, stuffed to the brim with who knows what.

After showing Garien out of the manor, Anavi gathered her own supplies: food, water, blanket, throwing knives, and two short swords hidden beneath her long blouse. Then, they mounted their horses and got on the road. Going through the mountains near Aethiel was not an option, the Numor Canyon was nearly impassable except for one path. And she would not take Hanue there, so they headed toward the secret mountain pass near Lasari. Anavi slowed from her typical pace to ride right alongside her brother. They rode through the afternoon and then into the night as they finally made their way toward the city walls. She quickly dismounted and tied the horses to the back of the stables of Lasari.

They would take the hidden northern pass into Andyse that she had traveled so many times before and get within the trees by morning if they kept at this pace.

Hanue panted next to her as they walked, still giddy with excitement and now, many hours from Aethiel, she decided to speak. "Hanue," she started, waiting for him to glance over at her, "I need you to understand this so listen to me."

He nodded slightly, wiping sweat from his brow. Though it was cold, she was sweating too. "What is it?"

"I need you to stay close to me when we get there," she said. He scoffed in response, and she worked to quell the anger rising within her chest. "I'm serious, Hanue. They think Xienee killed them. If she did, she may be trying to come over the mountains soon enough. This is going to be dangerous. Everyone there will be trying to kill us. That's how they are there."

He scoffed again as they skirted about the outside edge of the city, only visible from the pale moonlight shining on his face in slivers. "I'll be fine. I don't know why you worry so much. I'm bigger than you, for Seven's sake."

She stopped in her tracks, drew her sword and kicked her leg out, sweeping his feet from beneath him. Anavi crawled on top of him as he groaned. Holding her sword pointing directly at his throat, she spoke, "Size does not matter as much as you think it does in a fight for survival. Even the smallest can take down an army if you take away their choice. Stay close and I'll keep you alive."

His breathing was rough and ragged as he pushed her sword from his neck, fear oozing out of him.

"Do you understand me?" she demanded, stowing her sword back beneath her blouse.

He nodded his acknowledgement, softly touching the back of his head where he fell. She held no guilt. This was not the time to be sentimental. It was time to be cautious and keep her head on a swivel.

Anavi got off him and extended her hand down. He took it and she hoisted him back up with a force she had never used on him before. Just one last reminder for him as he walked again, stumbling slightly to regain his balance.

Anavi exhaled sharply. How was she going to get any information with him here?

CHAPTER NINE
RAUNA

The jagged rocks around Rauna seemed to mock her exhaustion as she searched the path ahead for a place to lay down. The Malcier mountains were well known as treacherous and dangerous, especially for a lone traveler, and although she had put her warmer clothes on over the ones she left in, she was astounded at the cold that seeped through her clothing and deep into her bones. Winter was already well on its way to taking hold of the world up here in the thin air.

She panted heavily, her chest rising and falling with a quickness. Gaabi had been gone for five days and Rauna still hadn't even made it out of the mountains. Although the horses that Gaabi's group took—judging from the tracks in the snowy ground—had certainly helped them navigate through this terrain with more ease.

She cursed herself for the overwhelming tiredness that racked her body. If she wanted to find Gaabi, she had to hurry, before the Andysi leader of the Northlands killed them all. So, she kept walking.

The pillowcase she haphazardly packed with her food and clothing weighed her down despite feeling so light when she started her journey.

She'd almost finished all the food, and her muscles threatened to give out beneath her with every step she took. But she kept walking.

The light of the day faded fast as she headed further downhill, the forest below her beckoning her closer. And so, she kept walking.

After a short time, darkness finally blanketed the world around her and she let herself lower to the ground, sitting on the pillowcase to prevent the cold from chilling her any more than it already had. Rauna took the knife from its spot in her pocket and cut her last piece of dried meat into three pieces and put one on her tongue. The salty taste puckered her mouth, but she welcomed the meager portion she allowed herself. Still though, she eyed the other two pieces hungrily, her stomach twisting painfully. Surely if she kept walking, she'd be down the mountain before she slept tonight and could catch something in the morning. Surely it wouldn't hurt to just have a little bit more...

Put it away.

She raised herself to her feet, shaking her head as she shoved the meat back into her pocket. Suckling on the one within her mouth, drawing every last bit of flavor she could out of it, she kept walking.

The slight shadows of the trees were a welcome sight as she finally, *finally* made it to flatter ground hours after she had finally swallowed her rations. Rauna knew she wasn't finding Gaabi tonight so instead, it was time to let her aching body get a feeble attempt at rest before the morning sun would peek through the canopy.

Rauna walked a little longer along the edge of the mountain, never straying too far from the path she knew they had taken through the mouth of the forest. She traced her hands along a rock face feeling for an alcove large enough to fit her so she could curl up inside. After several minutes of walking south, her hand dipped into a small cave. Perfect.

Her eyelids heavy, she set up a feeble attempt at a bed by gathering the foliage around her and shoving it within the cave. She crawled into her little home for the night and, eyelids heavier with every second, grabbed her knife from her pocket, gripping it tightly.

She shivered as sleep swallowed her.

The pale morning light shined perfectly through a gap in the tree canopy above her at first light. She slowly opened her eyes, sighing deeply as she blinked sleep away.

Her neck was stiff and reacted to her attempting to look at her surroundings in the light with a quick, sharp pain through her spinal cord. But regardless of the pain, the landscape was gorgeous. She had unknowingly set up her camp near a small creek that flowed from the mountains above, lapping softly over the rocks near where she had laid her head. The trees themselves were covered in a thick green moss on all sides, broad leaves a brilliant shade of green as they undulated back and forth with the slight morning breeze. She sat for a moment, staring at the nature around her.

Something moved through the foliage toward the south, beyond the creek. Branches snapped and the few fallen leaves of early fall cracked beneath the weight of whatever moved through them. Probably a deer, a rare sight near Lasari with all its hustle and bustle. She raised herself to her sore, aching feet as they pulsed in protest to her added weight. Gingerly, she made her way toward the sound. Then it quickened. She stumbled back, hitting the rock face with a resounding *thump* that sent tingles up her back.

That's no fucking deer.

A woman was running, bounding over the foliage as graceful as could be. It was like she herself was a creature of the forest.

"Hey!" Rauna called out.

The woman paused, ducking behind a tree before Rauna could see where she went.

She grabbed her knife from her pocket and moved slowly forward, her hands trembling. "I don't want any trouble, I'm just looking for my sister," she said, her words choked as she spoke.

The foliage rustled in response.

"Have you seen her? Please, I just want to find her," she called out again.

"Stop talking!" a voice called out, barely audible over the distance. A soft rustling followed, and the woman poked out from a tree a few feet away, sword in hand.

The woman was beautiful—with long deep brown hair tied into a hasty bun behind her head. She had eyes the color of amber that stared at her with a deadly determination so strong Rauna took an instinctive step back. She was short, shorter than Rauna by about a full hand but the shiny sword of Davegu making in her hand gave Rauna pause. She wasn't wearing any armor, instead wearing a long shirt of animal furs and leathers and loose pants. The sword glinted in the light as she moved closer.

Rauna gulped nervously. "Please, I just—"

"Stop. Talking," the woman responded, her voice barely a whisper but commanding nonetheless, turning away from her now and glancing in the direction she had come from. "They'll hear you."

"What?" Rauna whispered back. "Who?"

The woman ignored her, watching the trees intently. Rauna strained her ears and stared at the trees in the distance, looking for something to come jumping out. Sure enough, there was a faint crashing in the far distance.

"Alright." The woman turned back toward Rauna, lowering her sword. "They're far enough away, I think. They'll stay away up here."

Rauna nodded although she wasn't entirely sure why as her heart pounded at the sounds in the distance. "Who are you?"

The woman sighed and chuckled a bit, a pleasant sound, very different from the harsh way she spoke before. "My name is Tivea."

Rauna stared blankly at her. Did she expect her to know who she was? The confusion must've been visible on her face because the woman took a step back.

"You're not from around here?"

"No, I'm not," Rauna responded, still eyeing the sword Tivea hadn't dropped fully yet. "I'm from Lasari, looking for my sister."

"I'm Yidenu's daughter. The commander of the Southern Coalition."

Now it was Rauna's turn to take a step back; she glanced around at the trees around her, half expecting the rest of Yidenu's group to jump out at her. How far south had she gone last night? "Why are you this far north then? Isn't this the Northlands?"

"It is," Tivea sighed, finally relaxing somewhat and tucking her sword into her belt behind her back. "The Davegu attacked two days ago. They took my father. That's who was after me."

Rauna stared intently at her, attempting to take in the information. If the Davegu attacked, the lands she and Gaabi had found themselves in were even more dangerous than she thought. Tivea's eyes glinted in the sun, watery.

She sniffled a bit, wiping her tears away quickly with her sleeve. "You said you were looking for your sister?"

Rauna nodded, her chest tight as she thought of her sister, dead, or bleeding out, a darkened figure standing over her body. "She was sent to the Northlands a few days ago. I'm trying to bring her back."

Tivea nodded. "Well, with the Davegu in the woods, you and your sister need someone that knows how to get you out of here. Plus, safer with the both of us for both of us." She stared at Rauna, waiting for confirmation.

Rauna nodded slowly, still reeling from the information she just had dumped on her.

And with that nod she was off, headed north.

Rauna trailed slowly and clumsily behind Tivea on the path they found. Tivea navigated the woods like she was a creature born of them herself. The branches always seemed to avoid hitting her and she barely made a sound as she moved swiftly through the foliage. Rauna's aching feet kept getting caught in the ferns, twisting her ankles uncomfortably as she wrestled them free.

Several times, Tivea doubled back to wait for her to catch up.

"Why are you helping me?" Rauna asked the most recent time she came back and waited for her to struggle free.

Tivea sighed deeply, mirroring Rauna's own thoughts. She seemed to pause in thought for a few seconds. "My home's gone," she said slowly. "If I can help it, you will go home safe."

The nobleness of this cause struck Rauna. In Lasari, everyone was only out for themselves. Even her. That explanation didn't seem entirely truthful, but she caught her eye on the sword against Tivea's back again and decided not to push it.

Tivea must've sensed her suspicion because she spoke again. "Plus, it's not safe for you or me alone with them in here too." That answer seemed more truthful.

Rauna finally got free of her most recent trap and reached into her pocket, taking out the pieces of meat she had cut the night before. She tapped Tivea's shoulder and held up one of the pieces. Maybe if she showed her kindness, she'd be less likely to kill her later.

Tivea took it with a small smile. "Thank you."

Rauna nodded and then walked past her, throwing her own piece into her mouth in a desperate bid to get her stomach to stop eating itself. They neared the edge of the treeline as the path seemed to split in every which way.

She heard Tivea let out a sharp gasp from behind her and turned quickly on her heel. Rauna approached where she was pointing slowly, searching for what caused her exclamation.

A person laid face down on the ground, unmoving. A strong stench of rotting meat tingled her nose.

She rushed forward, turning the person over, revealing a man with an expression of horror frozen on his face. He had a slash on his stomach several days old judging from the maggots that festered within it. The dried blood from his cut stained the ferns below where he laid. Rauna had served this man at Bottom Mountain Bar. This man was Lupegi. Rauna jumped back in shock, landing firmly on her back on the ground.

She rushed to her feet and ran for the treeline, branches smacking across her face. As she neared, the rotting meat smell strengthened, the pungent stench assaulting her nose. She plugged her nose as she ducked behind a fallen tree and gazed at the scene in front of her. Tivea quickly joined her, grabbing her shoulder, trying to pull her back.

Men and women laid splayed out in the tall grasses, red staining the ground around them. She searched desperately, hoping against hope that Gaabi was not among them for a few minutes. The telltale sight of bright red hair wasn't there though.

She pulled her shoulder from Tivea's grasp, jumping over the fallen tree and rushing into the clearing. Rauna ran from tent to tent, searching under all the blankets and packs, anywhere a person may hide or die. She threw things behind her as she moved—a pot, a rope, firewood. As she moved from tent to tent, she caught glimpses of Tivea standing at the treeline as she ran around frantically, turning over bodies, bloodying her hands with theirs. She zipped, from body to body, from death to death to death. But she wasn't there.

Did she dare to hope? Gaabi wasn't there.

She ran back to Tivea, gasping for breath. "Gaabi wasn't there; she wasn't there."

Tivea opened her mouth to speak but Rauna was already off, searching the ferns and grasses for any bodies she might have missed. She found one, then two, then three, not counting the former patron. But none of them were Gaabi. Gaabi was still alive. She knew it.

"Are you still wanting to help me find her?" she demanded of Tivea, her voice harsher than she meant it to be.

Tivea nodded solemnly then added with a whisper. "I'll help you find her. But right now, we need to leave. The Davegu are here."

Rauna peered around wildly before finally seeing a woman approach from the east, out in the plains. She wore the telltale armor of the Davegu foot soldiers, blackened chainmail with a red tunic over her chest. She held two swords, one in each hand, that glinted in the sunlight, reflecting a sharp beam of light into Rauna's eyes. Her breath quickened as she drew her knife from her pocket just in case. Tivea raised her sword, visibly shaking as the woman approached. The woman hadn't seen them yet as she turned her head, searching the woods for Tivea.

"Run," she whispered.

Rauna didn't need to be told twice; her measly knife was no match for a trained soldier. They bound over the fallen trees and foliage and Rauna pleaded to The Seven to not let her feet get caught again.

They moved alongside each other, ducking beneath branches quickly. The woman must've heard the rustling because, as Rauna turned to peer over her shoulder, she barreled toward them, determination on her face.

Fuck, fuck.

Tivea stopped in her tracks as Rauna ran past her.

"What are you doing?" Rauna hissed.

She ignored her, reaching into the knapsack slung across her shoulder and taking out an old leather-bound journal.

The Davegu got closer.

"You're going to get killed."

Tivea ignored her again, flitting quickly through the book and closing her eyes. The woman was only about thirty-five paces out and Rauna turned and ran. Behind her she heard a clashing, Tivea being cut down no doubt. But a scream sounded from further off than Tivea stood and Rauna turned toward her again.

Trees bent and contorted, vines manifesting from their leaves as Rauna's mouth fell open. Tivea stood in front of them, hands outstretched toward the growing vines. The Davegu woman screamed again as vines wrapped around her body and pinned her to the bent tree.

Rauna's breath quickened, staring wide-eyed at Tivea as she turned toward her. "That'll hold her for a while," she stated simply, beginning to run again.

She stared at the woman running past her. She had heard stories of the old magics. The way users seemed to be able to hear for miles, run faster than the deer in the woods on the outskirts of Lasari. Rauna had always gotten the sense that they were stories, myths spread by The Seven to keep people scared and stuck in Lupegi.

But there was some truth to it after all.

She jogged after Tivea, staring over her shoulder again at the Davegu woman, bound to a tree and gagged by plants of Tivea's creation.

CHAPTER TEN
MOLAC

"Get up!" a man barked as the door to the carriage was thrown open.

Molac jumped, straightening his back as he squeezed his eyes shut at the sudden burst of light. As he slowly opened his eyes, a burly man climbed into the carriage with a scowl and grabbed Molac by his bound arms.

Molac frowned, trying to make anything out in the blinding light. Two days he had been in that carriage. Two days the rope had bit into his raw wrists. Two days of squalor, especially for a man of his status. He was an aristocrat!

But as he followed the guard out of the carriage and finally set foot on solid ground, Molac's breath hitched. "Oshgor."

It was overwhelming.

Oshgor was a city he had never been to before, but he'd learned of it from his father. The city was mainly a military base, just south of the Andyse border, used back when Andysi and Davegu people were at continuous war. Soldiers marched up and down the cobblestone streets in tight formation, their swords and armor clinking as harsh voices barked out orders. Every building in sight was built with the same blackstone and dark wood that buildings in Dhunviro were built with but beyond that, the similarities were few.

Unlike Dhunviro, there were no bodies strung up on buildings, no blood running through the streets. Everything was clean, polished. People moved with purpose, barely looking at the fallen aristocrat just yanked from a carriage. The Davegu colors adorned every free pole and building face, red, yellow, orange in a tri-fold pattern.

The burly man tugged on the rope and Molac winced as the fibers bit into his wounds. The man led him through the streets, down the alley, through the tunnel, up the road.

The slack on the rope loosened as the man slowed and Molac looked around. They stood in front of a tall building, more of a tower than anything. It dwarfed them, carvings of swords and bows and daggers in the rich blackstone it was made of. The doorway was large, foreboding, like the mouth of an ancient beast. Molac gulped, an unease growing in his chest.

"I'm guessing we're going in here?" he spewed with sarcasm.

The guard responded by jerking the rope again and Molac winced.

"Not a talker, then? Got it."

He was answered with a grunt as the man pushed open the large doors and led him into the tower.

Inside was as busy as the streets outside. Men and women laughed heartily, swigging from large mugs of something alcoholic. As eyes fell upon him and laughs boomed, Molac held his head high, staring straight ahead. Maybe this was it. He didn't die as Tovik wanted him to, so he was entertainment for these beasts?

Through the sea of people, a figure walked slowly down the staircase, pushing the others out of the way. Molac blanched.

Asmuto.

Ten years. That's how long it had been since Molac and Asmuto had last seen each other. Asmuto was older now, larger. His black locs were showing hints of gray despite being about twenty-four namedays old. His skin was a dark brown, his eyes a matching hue but the whites of them were stained a sickly red hue. Unlike when they were kids and

Asmuto was scrawny but lanky, he seemed to have grown into his features now. Still tall, taller than most men Molac had met, but his arms, legs, and chest had bulked out, now a wall of muscle.

As Asmuto's eyes fell on Molac, his features hardened. "Thank you," he said assertively to the guard holding Molac's bindings. "I've got it from here."

The guard handed the rope to Asmuto and excused himself without as much as a cursory look at Molac.

And then they were there, alone in the mass of bodies, staring at each other. Molac gulped.

Asmuto yanked on the rope and Molac jumped forward, stumbling as he did. "What did you do?" Asmuto hissed.

Molac flinched but Asmuto turned on his heel without waiting for an answer and led Molac through the crowd, down the hallway, the same way the guard did; roughly and painfully. Molac tried to focus on anything else—the leering faces, the pain of the rope against his wrists, anything besides the fact that he was being yanked around by his child-hood best friend, his former boyfriend.

As the hallways became less crowded and the sound of jeering barely reached Molac's ears anymore, Asmuto shoved a door to the side open and pulled him inside. Asmuto closed the door behind them; Molac's ragged breathing was the only sound to fill the darkness.

As his eyes slowly adjusted, he gasped as Asmuto's hand gripped a knife from his hip. "No," he pressed himself against the back wall of the closet and raised his hands, "no, please!"

But instead of striking the blade at Molac, Asmuto lowered his knife and sawed at the bindings around his wrists.

"Thank you," Molac said, rubbing his raw skin.

Asmuto shoved his knife quickly back into his belt. "Don't thank me; tell me why you're here. Now."

Molac raised his eyes to meet Asmuto's but faltered and lowered them back to his feet. "Father's dead. Tovik put me in the Cruor," he said quietly. "I won."

A flicker of surprise passed through Asmuto's eyes, but he quickly replaced it with a steely expression and crossed his arms. "Do you know where you are, Molac?"

Molac shook his head, shame creeping into his body.

"Why were you even in the Cruor? I know old Tovik's going crazy in his age but it's not normal to put aristocrats in that arena."

Molac took a deep breath. Why did this have to be the first conversation they'd had in ten years? "After Father's death, Tovik put me in training, and I failed. Guess he figured the Cruor would teach me a lesson."

Asmuto scowled. "Well, I think your lesson has just begun. You're in Meluth's army now."

The blood drained from Molac's face as he searched Asmuto's for any sign of falsehood. So, this is where Asmuto went all those years ago? To become a soldier, a battlemage? Was he here to be a victim or to learn the art of death?

He weighed it over for a second and decided he didn't know which was worse.

A horn sounded in the distance before he could form a reply and Asmuto turned and left, shutting Molac in the closet alone.

The horn signified prisoners, Molac learned, overhearing the people in the building screaming about it. He did not move from the closet Asmuto had left him in though. He stared blankly at the door, pondering what would happen to him now. The empty closet gave no answers.

He shook his head and grasped at the handle to the rickety door. Just as he moved to pull it, the door flung open, revealing Asmuto.

"Come with me," he said, face betraying no information.

Molac obliged, following him closely, around corners, weaving in and out of people that crowded the hallways. Up the stairs, into another room. Asmuto shut the door behind them quickly as they entered. The room was magnificent, dimly lit and luxurious. A four-poster bed made of deep brown wood took up much of it, the curtains a deep ruby red. At the foot of the bed was a small sitting bench, tufted velvet. Candles littered nearly every free surface on the dresser and desk, crackling softly as they burned.

"Sit." Asmuto gestured to the bench.

Molac made his way to it, running his fingers over the rich fabric. The luxuriousness of the room wasn't lost on him as an aristocrat. This room belonged to someone important, probably the queen when she came to visit her army.

"Whose room is this?" Molac asked with a slight waver in his voice.

"Mine."

He jerked his eyes to Asmuto. "How?"

Asmuto sighed deeply. "I'm the general of Meluth's troops."

Molac had to hide his shock. Asmuto grew up orphaned, living on the streets of Dhunviro. How could a man of his status possibly be the queen's general when Molac, an aristocrat, was now subject to his whims?

Asmuto didn't seem to notice Molac's indignation. "General Khal, the leader of Tovik's Oshgor troops, just brought in prisoners from Andyse." Now Asmuto moved with a purpose to the desk in the corner, grabbing a quill and parchment and scribbling something down. "They brought in a man I know well. They brought in Yidenu."

Molac racked his brain for why he recognized this name. His father had mentioned it once before. Until he finally settled on it. The leader of the Southern Coalition. "But why? I thought there was an agreement of sorts," Molac asked, his throat dry.

The Davegu were going to war soon if they'd attacked Yidenu. The Commander of the Northlands would not take kindly to a provocation. She was probably marching on Oshgor right now.

"There was an agreement with the Southern Coalition. I'm the one that set it up. Me and Yidenu knew each other well. We were..." Asmuto's voice trailed off. "I'm writing Meluth right now and then," he paused slightly, swallowing loudly as he turned to Molac, his eyes intense, "we're going to talk to him."

The dungeon lived below the building in an area that was best described as a crawlspace. It was short and damp, the smell of mildew assaulting Molac's nostrils as he lowered himself down the steep stairs, following Asmuto closely like he expected something to jump out and grab him from the deep shadows that surrounded the men.

Asmuto moved skillfully through the tunnels, torch in hand. They passed one cell, and then another, all filled with people in rags, their faces bloodied and raw. They flinched away from the light as Molac stared at their faces, his stomach curling.

Finally, they reached the end of the squat hallway. It was dark inside except for two pinpricks of reflected light in the distance.

"Yidenu, step forward," Asmuto barked.

The pinpricks moved closer, the light slowly illuminating the figure of the man within. Molac inhaled softly at the sight of his face.

The man that stared back at him was about fifty namedays old, tan skin stretched taut over large muscles and sharp cheekbones. One brown eye was swollen nearly all the way shut and the other was so bloodshot, Molac could've sworn he wouldn't be able to see out of it at all. Blood, dried and fresh, decorated his face and body, cascading over his face, chest, and arms. The man smiled a sarcastic grin, revealing a bloodied, red mouth beyond his cracked lips. It was a miracle that the man was even still standing. His teeth glistened menacingly in the firelight. Then he pursed his lips and spit, landing squarely on Asmuto's face.

Asmuto grimaced, wiping away the mixture of saliva and blood. "We do not wish you harm."

"You mean any more harm than you already set upon my people? We were friends, Asmuto!" the man said indignantly.

As Molac stared in disgust at the man, this seemed a valid question. Molac could swear he was about to reach through the bars and strangle Asmuto just on principle.

"I need you to know I had nothing to do with this, Yidenu. I don't know what's going on; I'm sending for the queen," Asmuto said harshly, flicking the spit from his hand.

Yidenu shook his head in disbelief. "And did this boy also have nothing to do with my people's deaths?" Yidenu asked, turning his burning gaze to Molac now.

Molac took an involuntary step back from the harshness of his gaze and shook his head frantically.

"He just arrived today, Yidenu. We're just trying to figure out why this happened to you and your people. Did you do anything to provoke Tovik that I'm not aware of?"

Now, Yidenu roared in indignation, "Anything to provoke the death of all my people? The burning of my home? The men I saw headed to hunt my daughter down? No! I stayed beyond the river and never interfered with Tovik's missions. I kept my people in check. I traded our resources to secure our safety! I held back the armies in the Northlands! All in the name of peace with your bastard excuse of a fucking king!" He shoved his hands through the bars, grasping Asmuto by the shirt and pulling his face against his cell.

Molac found a courage he didn't know he had and jumped in, wrestling Asmuto from Yidenu's grasp. Asmuto fell back into Molac as he was released. He stumbled back to his feet as Molac pressed himself against the wall to support their weight.

Asmuto breathed heavily next to him in the dim light, feeling where Yidenu's hands had grabbed him.

"The Sisters will make you all pay for this, Asmuto," Yidenu spat out, spraying both of them with saliva. "You will pay for this."

CHAPTER ELEVEN
LISYNIA

L isynia walked through the foreign camp with her head held high. People all around her pointed and gasped upon seeing her—children pulled away from the edge of the path by their mothers and fathers. But she paid no mind. She was here for one reason and one reason alone.

The buildings around her were nothing like the ones back home, built of old bricks into the sides of mountains, their peaks towering over the streets with their decrepit triangular roofs. Here, they were wooden one-story cabins of various shapes and sizes with thatch roofs or tents made of animal skins, fires crackling softly outside their entrances. Small farms with various edible and medicinal plants lined the outskirts of the town and for a moment, Lisynia curled her lip in anger. Here, they had food. Here, they didn't depend on the Lupegi soldiers bringing them batches of old, half-rotted crops. Yet another example of the indecency the Tevebrisians had to endure.

The path through the camp was dirt rather than old cobblestone walkways and there were no lantern posts, simply a large fire pit in the very middle of the camp, wider than her if she was lying flat. She skirted around the edge of the blackened pit and continued toward her destination.

The sack in her hand swayed back and forth with her quick movement. She came bearing gifts.

As she approached the largest building in the camp, a squat but large wooden cottage, decorated with a flag bearing the words 'The Northlands', a woman stepped out from inside, a grim smile on her face at the sight of Lisynia. She was tall, taller even than Lisynia, and large. Deep scars marred her face and arms, which were large and muscular. Her hair, which she wore down, was a light mousy brown and chopped off roughly at her mid back. She was of darker skin, in large contrast with Lisynia's pale skin.

"Commander!" Lisynia exclaimed, raising the sack in her hand to the air above her head. "I came bearing gifts," she smirked as she dropped the sack at Xienee's feet and a human head rolled out, cut off at the still-dripping neck, "the head of the Lupegi settlers from the west."

Xienee smiled slightly, bending down to inspect the head. She rolled it in her hands and then nodded slightly to the door of the building.

Lisynia fought a smile as she stepped inside. Just like the outside of the building, the interior was also devoid of much character. This was more of a war-camp than a town anyway. Andysi people moved often, only little outposts here and there serving as trading hubs and their governing bodies. Beds made of animal furs lined the walls; low wooden tables filled with papers and candles stood at even intervals around the perimeter. In the very middle of the building was a table and three chairs, at which sat one man already.

"When we heard you were coming, we set aside another chair," Xienee explained, "this is Torvo, my most trusted advisor." She gestured to the man, his face shrouded from the hood he wore. "It's good to see you again, General."

"Likewise, Commander," Lisynia said, extending her hand to Xienee's, grasping at the forearms quickly, a greeting of respect.

Xienee gestured to the chairs as she lowered herself into one. It creaked beneath the weight of the muscular woman. Lisynia sat down at the table, extending her hand to Torvo as well. He did not return the gesture, instead just stared at her from beneath his cloak of darkness. She attempted to swallow down her indignation as she turned back to Xienee. "I understand you wanted a show of loyalty last time we met. Does this suffice?" She motioned to the head still in Xienee's hand.

She held it further up, grasping it by the hair, inspecting it for a minute before turning it over to Torvo. He reached a wizened, wrinkled hand from beneath his cloak, grasping it too by the hair. He traced the bloodied features of its face with another hand that seemed to appear from thin air as his cloak didn't even shift.

"Lupegi," he grunted, the word barely recognizable.

"Yes, Lisynia, I would say this is more than enough," Xienee smirked, "only thing that would've been better is for you to bring Jovan's head himself."

Lisynia grimaced at the name as it reached her ears. Oh, what she wouldn't give to be able to have his head. Xienee must've realized the mistake because she burst out laughing, a sweet sound to hear from such a serious woman.

"I'm sorry, I should've known to hold my tongue," she said, still obviously holding back laughter.

Lisynia returned her smile and let out a small chuckle herself. "No issue. We both would have preferred that, I'm sure."

Xienee nodded, suddenly solemn. "So, what do you propose, General?"

"I would like my people to train with yours," Lisynia offered. "They would all learn tactics from both of us making us the most fearsome army in Eterin, with my weapons and magics and yours joined together." Her tongue seemed to swell in her mouth despite the fact she had rehearsed this in the mirror many a time. The gravity of the situation could make or break her entire warpath. "I already have a group of 150 I brought to the fortress a week ago, all trained warriors already, all eager to join you should you allow it."

Xienee's face upturned into a slight smile and Lisynia's nerves calmed. Thank the Sisters that she seemed open to it. "Torvo, what do you think?"

Torvo was silent for a few agonizing seconds as both women stared at him, awaiting an answer. "We shall dine together tonight to seal the alliance."

Xienee nodded. "So it shall be done."

The dinner took place that night by the light of the camp's main fire. Every citizen that resided in the camp gathered closely, wooden plates of meat and roasted vegetables handed out to everyone around the pit.

Lisynia ate absently, her mind elsewhere. War plans and battle strategies and the stories of suffering of her people raced through her brain. With Xienee's people joining her, Davegu was now a viable target, even with their magics. But Lupegi? The Seven in their fortified cities and strong numbers and powerful magics would serve more of a challenge. Maybe if she got Yidenu in the south to join her?

As she pondered the next steps, the next target, she fell into a trance, enveloped in the smell of burning wood. Her vision began to sway and blur.

The world around her faded quickly away, replaced with an everlasting darkness. Her chest heaved with her futile attempt to steal breaths from the darkness around her. She was choking, suffocating. Anxiety flooded her body. She attempted to run, to move out of the overwhelming nothingness around her but to no avail. The darkness gripped her from every direction. She stood not on the ground but floating within the air itself.

A woman's voice rang out from every direction. "You have not the full story." The voice was loud, booming. It shook her to her bones as it repeated one phrase. "You have not the full story. You have not the full story. You have not the full story."

Lisynia opened her mouth to scream but nothing came out. Nothing in all directions. Nothing was everything all at once.

"You have not the full story."

The voice changed now, becoming softer, more personal and the outline of a woman emerged slightly from the darkness, a frenzy of red surrounding her head against dark brown skin. "Seek the whispers of the past in the ruins of your home. Seek the gospel of your people in the holds of your oppressors. Seek the truth from me, Lisynia."

The darkness faded as quickly as it had come, revealing the physical world once again. Lisynia's chest heaved, her body shaking uncontrollably. She turned and keeled over, dropping her plate on the ground and puking her meager meal onto the dry grass below.

A hand grabbed her shoulder. "Are you alright, General?" a woman asked with a slight laugh. "What happened?"

Lisynia turned to face this voice and was greeted with the familiar face of Xienee. She quickly quelled the nausea as best she could and raised herself back to her feet. She tried to push the voice of the red woman away, but the words echoed in her mind.

You have not the full story.

"General?" Xienee ventured with a hearty chuckle. "Overcome with the prospect of joining forces? We'll be the most fearsome army in Eterin, you needn't worry."

And although Lisynia had come here hoping against hope for this exact thing to come about, she had no joy in her heart for what was next to come. The holds of the oppressors, the ruins of her people. What did it all mean?

What was the full truth if not that which she already knew?

Lisynia nodded to Xienee. "I will send for your people within a few days. I must return to my own."

Xienee's face twisted in confusion, but she nodded, outstretching her hand once again. Lisynia took her forearm to seal the deal and then walked slowly, unsteadily toward her horse, her mother's stories of the Goddesses playing in her mind.

CHAPTER TWELVE
TIVEA

The conversations the past few days had been stilted, awkward almost. While they still tried to get to know each other, since Tivea had shown her magics to Rauna, she had caught her staring at her in a mixture of awe and fear when she thought Tivea wasn't paying attention. Tivea did her best to ignore the stares. She was used to being looked at like a commodity. A way to get food in the winter months, a way to ensure medicinal plants never ran out. Living for so long as the only user of clorhestas in the Southern Coalition had taught her to ignore it.

Her thoughts strayed once again to the last time she saw her father, beaten, bloodied, limping, as she stoked the fire at the cave's edge. She wondered if she'd ever see his sweet, kind, loving face again or if the Davegu had already strung his body up at their River Crossing Fortress as a warning...

Rauna's voice pulled her out of her thoughts. Her voice was soft, as it had been since the soldier ran up on them. "How did you do that?" she finally asked, after days of probably pondering it over in her mind.

"My mother taught me," Tivea stated simply.

Rauna stared at her expectantly, awaiting a better answer.

Tivea spoke once more, breaking the awkward silence. "We can search for your sister more tomorrow, we're losing the light."

Rauna nodded but still seemed deep in thought. "It's impressive. It seemed like second nature to you, almost. How does it work?" Rauna finally said.

Tivea raised her eyes, staring at the woman in front of her in shock. No one, besides her father, had ever really taken much interest in her studies, they just expected her to help the crops grow and feed them during winter.

Her shock must've registered on her face because Rauna's eyes got wide, and she started stammering. "I mean only if you're okay with telling me, only if you're willing to. I don't want to overstep or anything, I just—"

"Rauna, it's okay," Tivea said, holding back a laugh. "I'll explain it to you later."

Rauna sighed, a smile crossing her face that Tivea returned. "Are you hungry?"

Tivea nodded, her stomach grumbling at the mention of food. "I'll go check the traps I set up this morning. They're bound to have caught something." While true, it was more of an excuse to get some time to think.

"I'll go with you," Rauna said, moving to stand up.

"No!" Tivea said, harsher than she meant it to come out.

Rauna's eyes widened, and she lowered herself back to the rock floor of the cave.

"Thank you, though. I'll be fine."

Rauna once again did not object and Tivea stood up, handing the stick she was using to stoke the fire to the black-haired woman. Rauna took it, eyeing the sword at Tivea's hip carefully.

Tivea grasped the hilt where it was shoved into her belt and handed it to Rauna. "Here," Tivea said, handing the woman the Davegu sword. "You can probably get more use out of it than I can."

Rauna nodded slightly, her hand wavering but took the sword from her all the same.

Tivea turned her back, her chest squeezing, and walked into the darkness. Her eyes adjusted quickly to the lack of light as they had many other times she wandered the forests after dark.

She maneuvered through the trees, ducking under branches and vines and reached the few snares she set up some 200 paces from the cave. A rabbit squealed at her, its leg caught in her trap, and she quickly grabbed its soft head, twisting sharply to break its neck. Tivea undid the snare quickly, expertly and let her thoughts wander.

The Davegu had attacked, yes, they killed or captured everyone in camp. They burned her home. No doubt the Davegu soldiers that were crawling over Andyse were searching for the rest of the Coalition. But why? That was the one question she had pondered all these days now. Why would they attack? Her father had a good relationship with Asmuto, one of the generals at Oshgor. There hadn't been any issues in years and then one day they attacked out of the blue?

Maybe Asmuto was simply biding his time, waiting to catch them off guard one day. If he was, he sure accomplished that. The one thing that didn't line up with this theory was the fact that the armor these men wore, while Davegu, was not the armor of Asmuto's men. Asmuto's were lighter armored, using leather rather than chainmail. Chainmail was for the heavily armored, Khal's men, not the foot soldiers of Asmuto's.

As she struggled to make sense of the death of her people, a light flickered, high up on the side of a nearby mountain in the distance. She focused her eyes on the light. Did Xienee have troops in the mountains? But this light didn't move like a torch would, it was steady, ongoing. It gave her the same feeling she had in the forest two weeks ago. Watched, like the trees themselves were spying on her. It was the same feeling she had when she stared too long at the decrepit peak of that building in the south mountains.

A branch snapped in the distance, and though it was probably just a deer, Tivea flitted back to the cave, rabbit in hand, chest heaving with anxiety.

Rauna waited at the mouth of the cave, the sword in her lap. "What's wrong?"

"There's a light outside," Tivea said, "I think we should check it out in the morning." she said, against her better judgment. She had ignored the feeling in the forest before and look where that got her. Might as well be prepared this time. Be proactive.

"Do you think it's Gaabi?"

Tivea sighed; she had forgotten for a second why they were even traveling together for the past few days.

"Maybe," she said, shivering as the feeling of being watched came back over to her. "If she's not, we'll keep looking,"

Rauna nodded. "Is that food?" she asked.

Tivea held up the rabbit and grinned.

Teaching Rauna how to step in the forest, where to gather water, how to skin the animals Tivea brought to the cave, all the things that were second nature to Tivea, was proving to be a hard task. But Rauna gingerly took the rabbit from Tivea's hand and pulled her knife from her bag.

Tivea was pleased to see her hands were steadier this time.

The light of the first morning sun caressed her skin, ebbing her from sleep from the night before. Tivea yawned, sitting up slowly as sleep washed off her tired eyes. She reached her hand out above her, feeling for the rock she used as a pillow. But instead, her fingers trailed along cloth pants. Rauna's pants. She shot up quickly, turning to look at what she was laying her head on. Rauna's face greeted hers with a smile. She had been laying in her lap. Tivea's face blushed with embarrassment, the heat stinging on her cold cheeks.

"Good morning," Rauna said simply, moving to sit up. "Did you sleep well?"

"Um..." Tivea blinked at her.

Rauna must've realized the issue because she spoke as she made her way to her feet, dirt crunching beneath her boots against the rock floor. "You moved in your sleep, and I didn't want to wake you. It's the most peaceful I've seen you yet," she offered with a smile, the dying light of the fire glinting in her green eyes, the deep color of the mid-summer leaves, "except maybe when you're reading that journal of yours."

"I'm sorry."

"Don't be," Rauna said simply, now picking at the embers at the mouth of the cave. "My sister used to do that. I didn't mind it."

Tivea let out a small smile at the mention of Gaabi. From what little Rauna had mentioned about her, she seemed to really love her. "Are you wanting to get searching right away?" Tivea asked, her face still hot.

"Yeah, if that works for you." she laughed softly, twirling her small knife in her hands.

Tivea nodded, making her way to her feet and grabbing the sword from where she had placed it the night before. She tucked it back in her belt behind her back.

She thought back to the light from the night before, deep in the side of the mountain. "Are we checking the light first?"

Rauna nodded, throwing a small piece of cooked rabbit from last night in her mouth. "If there's a possibility Gaabi's there, I want to see it myself."

Tivea walked closer, bent down and picked at the rabbit herself, tearing off a small piece and placing it in her own mouth. The cold meat squirted out juices as she bit into it, making her cringe. But it was food. Sustenance.

Tivea pushed back her nausea from barely eating in days and walked toward the dirt floor of the forest, motioning Rauna behind her.

They walked in silence for several minutes, headed south, toward where the light was last night. Then came a small noise, a slight rustle in the leaves. Tivea's hairs stood up on the back of her neck and she pivoted quickly to Rauna, who trailed closely behind. She raised a finger to her lips, beckoning her to be quiet, and crouched down as close to the ground as she could. The ferns and grass tickled her exposed arms as she brushed against them. She searched the forest in front of her for the source of the noise and in the distance, behind a tree, a man stepped out, whistling quietly as he swung his sword.

Rustling, now from behind her, reached her ears and Rauna appeared next to her. "Who is that?" she asked, her voice barely sounding in Tivea's ears.

Tivea shook her head, silently conveying that she didn't know as she studied the man's armor. It was different from the Davegu's heavy metals, or the Lupegi that they had found dead in that clearing. They also weren't Northlanders—the leatherwork was sloppy and harsh. Xienee would never be caught dead sending someone out like that. That showed unpreparedness, that showed weakness. At least in Xienee's eyes.

No, this man did not belong to any factions she knew of. Tivea raised her eyes to the sky, searching the mountain face for the source of the light, the source of the man. Sure enough, high up on the tall mountain to the west, small holes were cut out from inside, making windows of sorts. One had a lantern swaying outside it, right where she had seen the light from. As she turned to point to the light for Rauna, another man stepped out from the woods, meeting the first one in his patrol. They began to speak, their voices barely carrying over the distance. She strained her ears and caught glimpses of their conversation

"General will be back soon," the new one stated simply, "hopefully good news."

"Then we can finally get off watch," the other said. "Have the commander's troops do it instead. These woods freak me out."

"She'll surely tell us. But I call the first training. Still can't handle this sword well at all."

The second one laughed heartily, punching the other one softly.

Tivea's heart seemed to fall into her stomach. They, whoever they were, were teaming up with Xienee?

"You're fine! You didn't seem to struggle when we took care of that Lupegi group."

Rauna lurched next to her, anger fuming off her shaking body. Tivea grabbed her arm, staring intently at the men still, hoping they didn't hear Rauna moving. But they just walked further away, turning their backs to Tivea.

She released Rauna's arm and grabbed her face, turning the furious woman toward her. Her green eyes screamed murder. "We need to go," Tivea mouthed to her, glancing at the direction of the men. "Slowly."

Rauna ignored her, moving her head back to face the men. She looked as if she was about to jump up and rush them herself with just that sword.

Tivea jerked her face back to her. "We need to run, they'll kill you," she said, aloud this time, hoping to reach the rational part of her brain.

This seemed to work as Rauna, still fuming, let her eyes settle on her own. She nodded and they retreated, moving quickly, crouched down in the underbrush.

As they got further away, both women raised themselves up and ran. Rauna crashed to the ground next to her and she doubled back, lifting the taller woman to her feet. She limped slightly and Tivea turned her attention to her feet. Rauna's foot was caught in a root and the ankle was twisted, already starting to bruise.

Just my luck.

Tivea hoisted her arm over her shoulder, her knees nearly crumbling from the added weight and jogged, glancing one last look at the direction the light was in.

"Ryrie," Tivea said as they got back to the cave.

Rauna winced as Tivea guided her to the ground. "What?"

"I think that was the Ryrie fortress," Tivea said.

There were stories in her father's camp of an ancient people's old fortress, built into a mountain in the Malcier range. She had always discounted this tale as the rambling of old fools. An ancient people, now extinct? What nonsense. But with everything that had happened in the past week and a half, she could believe it now. She groaned as this information settled into her brain.

"Said to be an old fortress belonging to a people called the Teveban. I never thought it existed but... those people, that armor, I didn't recognize them."

Tivea shivered as she thought back to their words.

The general.

Rauna blinked at her. "Do you think they have Gaabi?" she asked, wincing as she lowered herself into a laying down position, propping her foot up on Tivea's leg.

Tivea sighed, staring at the injured foreign woman in front of her. She just wanted her sister back, still holding out hope even after hearing that the group was 'taken care of'. Even in the face of all this horror and mystery, she still held onto hope.

"If anyone has her, it's them," Tivea said softly, her fingers working to unlace Rauna's boot. "Let me take a look at your ankle."

Rauna inhaled sharply as Tivea pulled the boot and sock off her foot. Tivea gulped. Her ankle was twisted at an odd angle and swelling quickly.

"How bad is it?" Rauna asked through gritted teeth.

Tivea adjusted her leg and pulled Rauna's ankle further onto her thigh. "It's not horrible," she lied. "Let me see if I can find anything for the pain." Tivea pulled her eyes from the sight and opened her satchel, pulling her mother's journal out and flipping through the pages.

Endless yellowed pages of her mother's scrawling handwriting danced in front of her eyes and, later in the journal, her own handwriting. Her mother had some healing potions in here and had documented some medicinal plants. But she knew it was futile. Rauna needed something more than Tivea could give her to set that ankle right.

Finally, she came upon a page in her mother's handwriting, a drawing of a tree with the instructions of chewing on its bark to reduce pain. That was the best she could do right now. Tivea scooted out from underneath Rauna's leg and shoved the journal back into her satchel. "I'll be right back."

Rauna nodded, her eyes squeezed tightly shut.

After a short time walking from the cave, Tivea came upon the correct tree and dug her fingers into the bark, pulling the hard outermost portion off it. As she scraped at the soft inner flesh, her mind wandered, her mother's voice playing in her head again, telling her the story of the Teveban.

An old people, a forgotten people, locked in their mountain city for their powerful magics, for their work with the ancient Goddesses themselves. Violent, raging, powerful, and bloodthirsty.

At least that's how others told it. Her mother said something different; she said they were victims of a jealous king in a war long ago, their children murdered, their cities burned until the only way they could survive was centuries of hiding from the outside world, always living under the threat of genocide if they stepped out of line.

Her mother's version seemed more like the way the Andysi lived than the way those men in the woods did.

Tivea clutched the tree bark in her hand and made her way back to the cave. Rauna was laying on her back, her hands pressed over her eyes as her breath exited her body in short bursts. Lowering herself next to the woman, Tivea pulled her injured ankle back into her lap. "Keep it elevated."

Rauna jumped, her eyes wide.

Tivea held out the bark. "And chew on this. It should help with the pain."

"You'd get along with my sister. She's always fixing my dumbass self up," Rauna said, shoving the tree bark into her mouth. Then she winced. "By the Seven, I need a distraction."

Tivea stifled a laugh. This woman had no clue how to survive in the woods but followed her sister anyway. She didn't know what noises the animals made at night, didn't know how to build a fire, but was here anyway. And for all her bravery and stubbornness, this woman couldn't handle pain. "What are you thinking?"

Rauna let another puff of air out, her voice coming out strained. "Tell me about your... what did you call it? Clorhestas?"

A small smile teased at her lips and Tivea giggled slightly. "Clorhestas. It lets me connect to the natural world. It's almost like..." Tivea paused, trying to put the words together, "it's like the plants *talk* to me. I can sense the things the plants do if they let me. I can help them grow if I show them the respect they deserve. And sometimes they help me, like they did with the vines and the Davegu woman."

As she looked up, her eyes met Rauna's green ones. The woman stared at her with a smile on her face, her eyes wide and Tivea felt a heat spread in her cheeks. "Magics then? I thought only The Seven had those."

Tivea gave a dry laugh, averting her eyes from Rauna's. "That's only what they want you to think. We're barbarians to them, remember? It's kind of magics, I guess. I think of it more as a connection. A mutual respect. The plants are almost like my friends." She cringed as she said this last part. Pathetic. It sounded pathetic.

But when Rauna spoke, there was no air of superiority or judgement. "Well, tell your friends thank you from me."

For the first time since her father's kidnapping, Tivea allowed herself to let out a hearty laugh.

Chapter Thirteen
Hanue

Hanue's legs screamed beneath his weight as they ran through the forest. His chest heaved with the effort of keeping pace, a sharp pain in his ribs making him wince with every step. Nothing about the land they were on seemed to want them to be there; the cold seeped through his clothes, and the mud kicked up high and onto his back. The trees' limbs themselves seemed to object to his presence, hitting him hard across the face with every step he took. Anavi slowed her pace just as the pain in his chest reached nearly unbearable. He stopped in his tracks, thankful for the break as he gasped for breath, hands on his knees.

His sister beckoned him forward and he begrudgingly moved the few steps toward her. She pointed silently to the treeline, pointing to a camp beyond, decorated with the bodies of upwards of thirty people. Hanue's blood ran cold as he gazed upon the carnage. One body was missing a head, a stump of sticky congealed blood left.

"I'll scout the Northlander camp in the east," Anavi started, her voice barely a whisper. "You search for survivors."

Hanue scoffed. Survivors? Xienee had killed them all, like she always did. But he didn't argue, rubbing his neck where his sister's blade was pressed against him only a few days ago. "When will you be back from your suicide mission?" he asked, knowing full well she was more than capable of making it back alive. She could probably kill the whole camp before they even knew she was there. But insulting her skill was the only way he could jab back at her for treating him as a child.

She glared at him, warning in her eyes. "Only about a day. We'll rendezvous here. Do. Not. Wander." She unsheathed one of her swords and pressed it firmly against his hand. "Take this and be safe, I'll be back soon."

And with that, she was off, quickly darting between the trees and out of sight. Hanue sighed deeply. He was twenty. Why did she still treat him as if he was weak and needed her protection?

He let his gaze wander to the bodies in the distance. Might as well humor her. Still catching his breath, he moved slowly out of the cover of the trees, swinging Anavi's sword back and forth in his hand. The camp was trashed, bodies and blood covering the ground everywhere he stepped. The tents were in disarray, the contents strewn all about the clearing. He moved methodically from body to body to body. And surprise, surprise, he found no survivors.

But as he turned over what must've been the tenth body, he began to feel the twist of confusion. Every body so far had only one cut on them. A clean slash to the stomach, not particularly deep or large. Certainly not enough to kill someone. But out of every body with this cut, they all had tendrils of black spreading from the wound. Poison most likely.

Since when did Xienee use poison? He didn't remember learning about that in his politics classes. For a second, and only a second, he let his mind wander, imagining boogeymen in the darkness, poisoning people with a simple touch to their flesh like some sort of demonic death entity. Perhaps it wasn't Xienee after all that killed these people.

As he fleshed out the demon he'd created in his mind, moaning from within the trees echoed into the clearing. He raised himself to his feet, walking slowly toward the treeline.

"Hello?" he called out, against his better judgment.

No answer. He approached the trees, peering within for any hint of life. The moaning sounded again, a sharp cry of pain following quickly after.

Hanue stepped past the treeline, scanning the ground below for anything out of the ordinary. The groaning continued in the distance, carrying ever so slightly over the foliage below his feet. He walked slowly toward it, paying careful attention to his heart beating hard in his chest.

A small creek trickled below his feet, rushing down from the mountains above him. He knelt as something caught his eye on one of the rocks on the creek's edge. Pressing his finger carefully to the substance, he inspected the fluid, red in color. Blood. He snapped his head up as the moaning got louder—he grew closer.

He searched the surrounding area for any other traces of blood, a spot glinting from the sunlight on one of the ferns in the distance.

His heartbeat took a life of its own now, pounding loudly in his ears. What scene was he approaching? Was it a survivor or a trap? He gripped the sword's hilt tightly, the wrapped leather handle cutting into his hand from the force.

Stalking through the forest, his eye was caught by a mess of red hair peeking over the ferns in the distance.

As he approached, the scene in front of him came into clarity. A woman about his age laid face down in the dirt, blood streaming slowly from a cut on the back of her arm. The black tendrils were not present on her pallid skin. She turned toward him and raised her hand into the air feebly, blood pouring quicker now from her wound.

"I'm over here." Her voice was barely more than a whisper.

He rushed toward her. Taking her limp body into his hands, he turned her over, searching her for more injuries. She had hazel eyes, clouded with pain, and red curly hair, littered with dead leaves and dirt. She had another cut across her chest, blood spilling out as it rose and fell. She was a slender figure, only a few inches shorter than him if they had stood back-to-back.

"Are you alright?" Hanue asked, his heart pounding as the blood seeped from her wounds. He pressed his hands against her chest, stifling the flow.

She shook her head slightly, so slightly that she might not have at all. "Water. Water, please," she spoke from her chapped lips.

He removed his hand from her chest, her body still laying across his lap. With one hand he cupped her head, fingers tangled in her matted hair, with the other, he removed his pack from his back, sifting quickly through it until his fingers grazed the leather of his water bladder. He pulled it from his pack, removing the wooden cap with his teeth, and raised her head.

Her hands fumbled with his as he held the mouth of the bladder to hers, trickling water onto her parched tongue. She coughed, spraying water over his face.

He winced, capping the bladder again and wiping his face. "What's your name?"

"Gaabi," she squeaked out, fighting back coughs still. She moved now to sit up, her body still in his lap, but her strength failed her, and she fell back into his waiting hands.

"Don't try to sit up yet, you're still weak," he said, pain tinged his voice as her eyes stared into his. With his free hand, he searched his bag again for something to bandage her wounds, still dribbling from her chest and arm. He bit off a chunk of his shirt and grabbed leather straps from his bag, hoping that it would work for her chest wound, at least for now. He raised her body up, still cupping her head and wrapped the leather around her torso, shoving the fabric of his shirt between the strands.

"Thank you," she said softly, her eyes becoming a little less clouded. "Can you raise my hand to my chest?"

He blinked in confusion at this request but raised her hand up with his free one, pressing it against her wound. A bright light shone from her hand and the blood stopped oozing beyond the fabric. She collapsed back into his hands, the suddenness of her full weight catching him off balance. He stared at her chest in shock. "How did you do that?"

"I trained at Valetu. I was too weak to do it before. I haven't had water or food in days," she offered in response, invoking the name of the most prestigious healer school in Lupegi. The Seven's own healers were trained there. He nodded in acknowledgement but was still confused. How did a student get here of all places?

He pushed his questions out of his mind, focusing on the girl in front of him. She needed him. "You were here with a military mission, right?"

Gaabi nodded, breathing heavily, her chest rising and falling quickly. "Yes. Sent here by The Seven themselves."

"What a coincidence, I was sent here by The Seven as well. To find you," he offered, laughing slightly as he stared at her face.

Now that they were both a little calmer, and her more stable, he focused on her face. She had full lips and large, wide hazel eyes, the color of the changing trees of fall, set upon freckled, pale skin.

He must've stared for too long because she scooted out of his lap. "Are they all dead?" she asked, tears beginning to well in her eyes.

Hanue opened his mouth as if to speak but nothing came out and instead, he just solemnly nodded. He paused for a second, finding the words to comfort her as tears ran down her dirtied face, cutting streaks through the muck on her skin. "Me and my sister were sent here to bring you guys back," he stretched the truth with this statement but for the most part, it was accurate. "You're the only survivor I've found so far. Who attacked you?" His thoughts wandered back to the black tendrils from the wounds on the other bodies.

"I don't know; they didn't seem to be Andysi. I only escaped because they didn't see me. I wasn't in the camp, I was trying to gather some water. I fell when I ran, hurt my leg, and I've been here since." That would explain the lack of poisoning in her wounds. And why she was the only survivor. Her lip quivered as she continued to recount the events that lead to the deaths of everyone she traveled with. "It was horrible, the screams..." she took a deep breath, trembling against his hand, still cupping in her hair, "they cut down everyone. And then a day or so ago, soldiers came running through near here, I heard them cutting through the vines. I tried to flag them down, but I don't think they were looking for me."

Confusion settled over him at this last detail. Soldiers from where? Did Jovan and the rest send a rescue mission before them? Unlikely. But possible, he guessed.

He turned his attention back to Gaabi, choosing to revisit that information later, out of the cold. "Well, we better stick together. Can you walk?"

She nodded. He raised himself to his feet and extended his hand, pulling her up onto her feet for what must've been the first time in days. She stumbled slightly before regaining her balance, gingerly limping toward him, pressing deep into his hand. He bent down, keeping his hand steady and grabbed his sword from the ferns below.

It wasn't the adventure he had planned, the adrenaline filled fights or the heroic tales that would have him regaled in Lupegi. But as he looked at this woman, the woman he was going to save, something ignited in his chest and for a moment, that flicker was better than what he'd hoped for.

"Let's get you home."

They walked slowly, Gaabi limping alongside him as the sun began to set on the mountains above. The cold of night settled in quickly, freezing Hanue to his bones. He held her hand, she pressed her entire weight onto his palm, and they made their way toward the rendezvous point Anavi had left at. With his other hand, he gripped the sword his sister had bestowed upon him. As they stumbled through the darkness, Hanue's indignation at Anavi had all but disappeared, replaced with a newfound wish to get the woman next to him to safety. He was going to get her home, that's what mattered. That's all that mattered.

He couldn't save anyone else in his life, but he would do everything he could to save her.

Through the woods ahead they heard rustling. Anavi. It had to be. She had most likely seen nothing of import and came back to help him search. "We're over here," he called out in the darkness. The rustling got closer at the sound of his voice, and he turned to help Gaabi make her way over a downed tree. "I found one."

The rustling did not respond, as his sister surely would and now his heart began to tighten in his chest. He released Gaabi's hand, shoving her behind him as he raised his sword. Who had he called out to? Even though it was cold, he sweated as Gaabi's heavy breathing behind him quickened. He focused on the sword in his hand. He had forged it himself, interlaid the gemstones, built it up.

Now if only he could remember how to swing it properly.

His breaths heaved in and out, in and out as the rustling grew ever closer.

Then a man rushed out from the darkness in front of them, staring at him, eyes just pinpricks in the darkness, then reached a hand out. Hanue swung the sword quickly, awkwardly, but the man moved quicker, avoiding the hit. A smirk became visible in the darkness as Hanue dropped the sword in shock.

The hand reached ever closer...

Gaabi screamed behind him and fell to the ground. He turned quickly on his heel, leaving his back exposed to the man in front of him. Another man stood behind her. Gaabi laid frozen on the ground and for an agonizing second, he thought she might be dead.

Then a finger touched Hanue's back and every muscle in his body froze. He tipped over and landed hard on the forest floor. He tried desperately to move his body, to grab the sword again, to reach for Gaabi as the man picked her up, stiff as a board and threw her body over the back of a horse tied to a nearby tree. The only thing he could move was his eyes, wide and terrified as he felt himself get lifted into the air, powerless to stop it.

"Lupegi from the looks of it." One of the men spoke to the other as he tied Hanue's motionless hands behind his back. "General just arrived back yesterday, we'll take them to her."

Chapter Fourteen
Molac

He had been in Oshgor for two days now but the experience he had that first night in the dungeon had all but left him.

You will all pay for this.

Asmuto had left after Yidenu said that, pursing his lips in thought as he turned. But Molac had stayed for a second longer, watching the hatred in that man's eyes as they stared at him from behind the bars.

What had they done to him?

Asmuto offered no answers, he might've not even had them himself and Molac made use of his time feebly attempting conversation with the foot soldiers and wandering around the building he now called home for the foreseeable future.

As he made his way to his bunk for the fifteenth time today, Asmuto appeared from around a corner. "Ah, Molac," he said, "I've been looking for you." The words fell from his mouth with ease but something in his expression, his furrowed brow or downturned lips, screamed trouble.

"Why?" Molac asked, half expecting this to be the final warning of his impending death via the king's orders. He pushed past Asmuto.

"There's a group heading out tonight. To Andyse. Tovik insists you be in it."

Molac stopped in his tracks. This was punishment for showing Tovik's champion up in the Cruor, it had to be. He was sentenced to die, just in a different way. He turned back to Asmuto. "No."

Asmuto gripped his shoulder as he turned away again. "You don't have a choice, friend. You go or he kills you himself."

Anger bubbled in Molac's body at his words. It was just like the king to do this, to strongarm and bully others to his will. That's how he got power and that's how he'd kept it all these years. He turned to Asmuto, his old friend, and scowled at him. But Asmuto didn't seem to notice his displeasure, his face far off, scrunched in concern and... worry?

The heat of his anger dissipated slightly and Molac sighed, "There's something else isn't there?"

"Yes," Asmuto said, his chest rising a bit as he wiped the odd look from his face and replaced it with the stoic expression befitting a military commander. "There's someone that wants to talk to you," he stated matter-of-factly.

Molac felt the blood drain from his face, and he stepped toward Asmuto, grazing his fingers along his arm. "Who?"

Asmuto's jaw tightened, and his gaze darkened. He shook off Molac's hand. Asmuto beckoned Molac up the nearby stairs with a wave of his hand. "Just come with me."

Molac obliged, following the burly man up the stairs toward his room.

Asmuto led him to the door to the general's room and gestured toward the handle. "She wanted to speak to you alone."

Molac gulped, staring blankly at the man in front of him. She? Could it be...

The queen herself greeted him as he pushed the door open. Meluth was tall and slender, her skin so pale it seemed to glow in the candlelight, only her lower arms visible to him. She wore a rich green gown, dusting across her feet, and a sheer veil over her face, the same deep color as her dress.

She extended a hand to him, beckoning him inside. "You are Molac Kludishav, correct?"

He nodded, extending his hand to hers and closing the door on Asmuto with the other. Meluth did not take his hand and Molac lowered it back to his side.

"You are the one my husband sent to me as punishment." Her voice seemed to not come from outside, in the room she stood in. Instead it pounded into his head, overtaking his own thoughts. The power and grace that emanated from her dwarfed him, despite him standing several hands taller.

He gulped and willed himself to speak, pleading silently for Asmuto to open the door and rescue him from her beautiful, bewitching gaze. "Yes."

"Good." She said, gesturing to the same bench Asmuto had two days ago. Molac sat obediently, without even thinking of why. "I have a task for you."

He nodded again, finding that he was rendered speechless in her presence.

"My husband has recently attacked an ally of mine. I believe you met with him yourself the other day."

Yidenu.

Molac nodded yet again, a chill spreading through his body at her words.

"Now," she started her dress swaying as she paced, "I cannot send my general on this mission as he may hold some love for my husband. And I need him here, with me. I trust that you do not have love for your king though, given the circumstance of your arrival here."

Treason to admit but Molac nodded again, unable to lie to her excellence. He could think of nothing but how utterly powerful she seemed to be, exuding confidence from every pore on her body, not even a strand of silky black hair out of place as it laid across her back, drifting out from beneath the veil she wore.

She laughed slightly, a pleasant sound but one that sent shivers down his back nonetheless, the hairs on the back of his neck rising. He trembled.

"Good man," she said. "You are going to Andyse with the king's soldiers to discover why my ally was attacked. They will be unaware of what your mission is. You are never to tell them."

Now the spell she held over him seemed to break. He frantically shook his head, still finding it hard to speak. "Ma'am, er, your grace—"

She interrupted him with another titillating laugh. "Just call me Meluth, no need for the pleasantries here."

"Queen Meluth," he corrected himself, standing from the bench as his legs protested. "I cannot go to Andyse; I have no training. I have—I have no weapons. Nothing. I will not return."

"Oh, Molac," she said, the world around him fading away as she spoke, darkness creeping into the corners of his eyes as her voice overwhelmed him. "All will be taken care of. You need simply to find out why the king has attacked and return to me here. If what I think is happening is true, there will be worse things than a death in Andyse coming."

He blinked, desperately gasping for breath as she paced, the only thing in his vision anymore. He opened his mouth to speak but no sound came out except a slight choking.

"My husband's forces will soon advance on Andyse in full force, on a warpath that is certain to lead to ruin. You will be under my protection there, you need not worry." She turned to face him and gave him a tilt of her head as the world around him faded away.

"Molac!" a voice screamed in the distance. "Molac, man, wake up!" A hand slapped his face, stinging as it left.

He opened his eyes to Asmuto standing over him.

Asmuto's face softened at the sight of his open eyes. "What happened? After she left, I came in here and you were just passed out."

Molac sat up, his body protesting the sudden movement. He

ignored Asmuto, searching beyond his face for Meluth. Asmuto waved a hand in front of his eyes.

"Where is she?" Molac asked, pushing Asmuto's hand from his face.

"She's gone, Molac. What happened?" he repeated.

Molac opened his mouth, words tumbling in his mind as he struggled to comprehend his thoughts. Nausea nearly overcame him, and he swallowed hard as he sat up from the bench. "I have to go."

Asmuto grabbed his shoulders, pushing him back down onto the bench. "Ah, man, she got you good, didn't she?" he said, more a statement than a question. Asmuto's face twisted in concern as he held Molac up. "Are you alright?"

"Yes."

"No, you're not."

"Yes, I am. I have to go. I'm going on that mission."

Asmuto let go of his shoulders and Molac stood up, walking quickly to the door.

"I'm sorry Asmuto, my old friend, but I have to go," Molac stated simply, grasping the door handle to leave. He turned it and was interrupted with a hand on his back, soft but steady. Shivers ran down his spine again.

"Just be careful, wherever you go, man," Asmuto said, a tinge of sadness in his words. "I just got you back."

Molac turned to look at the man behind him, keeping that warm touch of his hand on his back. "I will be, I promise."

And with that he walked. He walked down the stairs. He walked to the armory, leaving Asmuto behind. He walked to the door of the battlemage headquarters, ignoring the hushed whispers around him. He walked to the group, ten men strong, gathering in the foyer of the tower. He walked through the town with them, darkness surrounding him in the night. He walked out of the city walls. He walked and walked and walked north, headed to the river, headed to the torched camp. He walked for his queen, for his honor, for revenge.

CHAPTER FIFTEEN
LISYNIA

L isynia paced in her quarters, pondering the words of that night. They had seared themselves into her brain, repeating every time she had a free moment of thought. She had been back at Ryrie for nearly two full days and still could make no sense of them. Upon arriving back, she had locked herself up in her room and paced and paced and paced.

The Goddesses, or the Ancients, were an old legend told in hushed whispers, their names had been lost to time, at least in Teveban. They were four women, according to her mother, that used to shape history with their magics, their priestesses given powers beyond comprehension. Then they disappeared centuries ago, leaving the question of if they ever even existed to be pondered in dark rooms between the guard's rounds. But Lisynia could not imagine anything else that could've spoken to her in the same way as the red woman.

You have not the full story. Seek the whispers of the past in the ruins of your home. Seek the gospel of your people in the holds of your oppressors. Seek the truth from me, Lisynia.

There was something she didn't know and so she went over everything she did, searching over and over for holes in the story. The Davegu and Lupegi attacked her people over 500 years ago, trapping them in the town of Teveban, holding them there for years, centuries. They outlawed magics. They outlawed worshipping the Goddesses They outlawed books. They killed anyone that dissented publicly. Like Catina, poor sweet Catina. They had taken people as slaves over time. The Davegu and Lupegi had even gone to war on who could take more from their beds in the night.

What was she missing?

She had trained underground, her mother, Queen Nelina teaching her their ancestral magics that she'd learned from her mother and so on. Lisynia had used her hidden existence from the Davegu and Lupegi to gather her troops. She had trained her people in the same magics she knew. The power of paralysis, the power of building your own strength. She had the Commander of the Northlands on her side.

What was she missing?

She paced and paced and paced, the lantern in her window crackling as it burned.

What was she missing?

A knock sounded on the thick wooden doors, interrupting her pacing. "Come in," she adjusted her blouse, rubbing her face with the edge, hoping to cover up the eyebags.

A man entered. Otto. He was clean this time, ashy blonde hair falling over his face gently. "Scouts just brought in prisoners from near the old Lupegi camp. A Davegu soldier and two Lupegi citizens. The Davegu and one of the Lupegi had weapons. What do you want done with them?"

You have not the full story.

Well, here was a chance to get it. "Put them in the hold, I'll come down."

❖❖❖

The hold was deep below the ground level of the fortress, consisting of five cells, all dank and dimly lit, the air itself stale from lack of movement. Lisynia walked down the stairs alone to the three new prisoners. Perhaps one of them would have some answers for her.

The first cell she approached housed the Davegu soldier, a woman found tied to a tree with vines, from what she was told. She wondered why the woman was this far north, far from the nearest Davegu outpost. But as she peered into the dark cell, she saw the woman, hanging by her sheets from the topmost bar, her neck bent at a grotesque angle. Dead.

She whistled, calling for the guards as she stared at the woman's eyes, purple and red, popping nearly out of her head. Her eyes, though dead, were haunting and Lisynia quickly moved on to the next cell.

This one held a teenage girl, redheaded with pale skin that seemed to glow in the dim light of the dungeon. She gingerly nursed a wound on her arm, wincing slightly, unaware of Lisynia's presence.

The last cell held a boy, no more than two namedays older than the girl but they couldn't look more unalike. The boy's skin was dark brown, so dark it seemed to blend into the dim light around them. His face and hands were covered in dirt and grime from the forest outside and he scowled as he stared. He stood at attention, staring directly at her, motionless. His features, an odd combination of soft and chiseled at the same time, danced in the lantern's light.

"Who are you?" he demanded, his voice as rough as his appearance.

At the sudden sound, the girl next door jumped to her feet, staring now at Lisynia too.

"I am Lisynia," she answered plainly.

The girl gasped upon seeing her face, hearing her voice. "You..." she said, her voice hissing from the darkness in her cell, "you killed them all."

Lisynia smiled. So, they were settlers. "Yes, I did, little girl, and I would again."

The boy took a step back, retreating into the darkness. "Why? They meant you no harm."

"They always mean harm," Lisynia shot back, heat building in her chest from the accusation in his voice. She whistled for the guards removing the Davegu soldier's body from her cell. "I'll talk with him first," she said to the guard, motioning for him to remove the girl from the cell nearby and give them some privacy.

"Where are you taking her?!" the boy demanded as the girl struggled against the guard's hold, barely able to even hold herself up on two feet.

"Don't worry about her, she'll be fine," Lisynia said simply, pulling a chair from behind her. "Let's talk about you."

His face twisted in anger as she sat down, facing him. He stared into her eyes, looking like he would sooner kill her than give her any information.

"I mean you no harm," she said mockingly, "I truly don't. Let's start with this, what's your name? I gave you mine."

His face still contorted in rage as the girl was carried out, screaming. "What are you going to do with her? She's injured."

She sighed, raising herself from her seat and yelled to the guards. "Make sure she is not harmed in any way. And get her some medicine." She sat back down, cocking her head at the boy. "What's your name?"

He breathed a sigh of relief as the girl stopped screaming. "Hanue Sareni, son of Tanue."

Her face flushed at the mention of Tanue. *The* Tanue? The Lupegi man that her sister sheltered, the man who helped Catina find the truth of who they were? She composed herself quickly, wiping her face of emotion, betraying nothing to the boy in front of her. "Good, now you can ask me a question," she offered, her voice softer as he relaxed, "I promise I'll answer truthfully."

He stepped back, shocked at her offer. "Are you serious?" he asked, his voice trembling.

"Well, that was a question, but yes," she chuckled. "For every question I ask, you get to ask one. Now it's my turn."

Hanue nodded tentatively, staring at her, suspicion clear in his dark eyes.

"Why are you in Anyse, Hanue, son of Tanue?"

He swallowed hard. "Searching for the settlers."

Her face fell at this answer. So, the Lupegi already knew they were dead? Great. She pondered this for a moment, awaiting his question.

"Why did you kill them?" he asked, his voice softer, sadder than anything else.

She answered plainly, "I needed to get someone on my side. Easiest way to do it."

Hanue took another step back, catching himself on the lip of the step within his cell. This answer obviously shocked him and he mulled it over for a second before speaking. "You're not Andysi?"

"Ah, ah, ah, that was out of turn. I'll let it slide. I am not," she said, a small smile creeping onto her face. "Who sent you?"

He paused for a second, his face twisting slightly, weighing the risk of the truth, no doubt. "I came here myself," he answered after a long pause, the tone of his voice betraying that he was lying. "*What are you?*"

The smile on her face grew. Hanue asked the good questions, even if he was a liar. She would break him of that habit soon enough. "I am Tevebrisian, Hanue. Do you know what that is?"

"No," he said, finally stepping down the step within his cell, his face becoming shrouded in darkness.

She laughed, her voice echoing through the dungeon. "Good." She sat up from her seat, all the information she needed from him received, at least for now. "I will bring the girl back and put her in with you. You can help nurse her back to strength as a reward for this talk. What is her name, by the way?"

A wary smile spread slowly across his face at this offer. "Her name is Gaabi."

Lisynia stood from her chair, walking slowly toward the separate room the guards had dragged Gaabi to, pushing a whistle out from her lips, a signal for the guards to listen. "Put her in the cell with our other guest and make sure they have plenty to eat and drink."

The guards shouted back their acknowledgement, the sound of movement emerging from the room. Gaabi walked back through the door, escorted by a guard on each arm. They walked past her, one of them sticking their sword through the bars of Hanue's cell, pushing him even further back as his face brightened at the sight of the girl. They shoved her inside, clanging the door shut behind her. She fell into Hanue's arms, whimpering slightly as she stood on her injured leg.

Lisynia began to walk toward the stairs at the end of the hallway, light spilling from the floor above. "Hanue, Gaabi. One more thing," she said to the cell behind her. "Let's agree not to lie to each other anymore."

Hanue's face hardened.

One of the guards caught up behind her, touching her shoulder lightly. "Are you sure this is a good idea?"

She smiled and turned to face the guard; his face contorted in confusion. "Yes," she said. "Send for Xienee's trainers. And send for my mother, I have much to discuss with her."

She climbed the stairs quickly, mulling over her newfound information. As she approached the mess hall, Otto came running down the stairs. "I was just headed to find you, General. News from the south."

Poor man, always running to give her information. Even when they were kids, he'd always been the one making sure Catina stayed out of trouble. She placed a hand on his shoulder and tilted his head toward her face, offering him a warm smile. "Catch your breath, Otto, that's an order."

He nodded, smiling slightly as he stood straighter. As his breath steadied, he raised his hand to hers, the touch sending shivers down her body. Her smile grew larger.

"Davegu forces..." he started, swallowing loudly between the words, "...they destroyed Yidenu's camp. The people that weren't there are scattered across the south or heading north right now. We did not see any survivors."

The smile on her face wiped quickly off as she whistled again, stepping back from Otto. Another man approached, she recognized him as the sixteen-year-old that lost his mother, Ason. One of the people to be trained by Xienee. She spoke to him softly, his young face hanging onto every word. "There is a rider headed to the Commander of the Northlands. Take a horse and ride to him, you are to deliver a message to the commander."

The boy nodded, eagerly awaiting her next words.

A tinge of guilt shot through her heart. "Tell Xienee we march south. Yidenu has been attacked."

His face fell but he quickly burst into action, running to the stables to gather a horse.

Otto still breathed quickly next to Lisynia as she uttered one last phrase to him. "It's been years in the making, Otto. This is it. We're finally doing it."

He nodded. "I always knew you had it in you, General," he said the last word with a slight tease as he always did.

"Watch your tone," she warned. Not convincingly, judging from his snicker.

She let a small smile form on her face. Otto always kept her from taking herself too seriously. That's one of the biggest reasons he had been the first one she asked to join her.

"Well, General," he said, "you'll be leading us to war soon. You'll be leading us all into something better."

Though he didn't seem scared, the reality of the situation hit her. The next few weeks would decide the very future of her people. And according to whatever Goddess had reached out for her, she still didn't know the truth.

Her throat went dry, and she pulled Otto though the foyer, into a side hallway devoid of people. "Something happened at Xienee's camp."

His smile faltered, replaced with a look of concern. "What happened, Lisy?"

Lisynia swallowed hard, trying to put words to the feeling of weightlessness, the all-consuming nothingness, the voice that had haunted her since. "Do you remember the stories my mother used to tell us of the Goddesses?"

Otto nodded warily, reaching one hand slowly up to her shoulder to steady her shaking body.

"One of them spoke to me. Told me to seek her out. Do you remember what Catina said that night before..."

"Before everything," he sighed. "Yes. That Lupegi man had told her that the Goddesses still lived. That their power was hidden somewhere in Teveban..." His words trailed off. Otto didn't need to add the last part.

She paid for that heresy by swinging from a rope in the town center.

Lisynia hurried into her theory, trying to force her mind anywhere but her twin's death. "I think I need to find what she was looking for," she said cautiously, not daring to meet Otto's eyes. "And I think that Lupegi boy down there can help that happen."

Chapter Sixteen
Anavi

Anavi ran low to the ground, muscle memory allowing her to move quickly through the tall grass that reached beyond her head. The pale light of the sun dimmed quickly, turning the sky above her brilliant oranges and pinks. The Northlands camp had held no hints, no clues on what led to the fate of the settlers that lay strewn across that clearing, just a head of a Lupegi man, cut off at the neck, on a pike near the entrance, his face twisted in death, his eyes pecked out of his skull by vultures.

Hopefully Hanue had found at least one survivor, a clue into what befell the settlers. The Seven needed answers. Jovan needed answers. And right now, Anavi had none.

The sun completed its trek over the mountains, plunging the world around her into night. The air around her already began to bite, the cold piercing her skin. With the last light of the fading sun, the treeline in the west came into view. She quickened her pace, ignoring her fast breathing.

She crashed through the trees and underbrush, headed to the rendezvous spot she had set with her brother two days ago. He was going to kill her for being late like this. But she could usually figure out the stories pretty quickly. Something was different this time; something didn't quite line up.

She slowed her pace, her chest heaving from the exertion of running as many miles as she just had. The trees danced around her in the night breeze, freezing her skin as it reached through her blouse. As she approached the meeting spot, she turned her head to peer at the forest around her, expectantly awaiting her brother's presence.

But he wasn't there. Her heart quickened as she looked around. The dark trees around her stood silent, betraying no answers. "Hanue?" she called out tentatively, keeping her voice low, just in case other ears were around to hear her.

No answer.

Anavi reached up her loose blouse, hiking it up past her hips and her hand found the leather hilt of her sword. She unsheathed it carefully, her eyes still searching in the quickly dying light for his figure.

"Hanue!" she called out again, slightly louder this time.

No answer.

Her breath hitched in her chest as rustling sounded in the distance. She turned her attention toward it as it got louder, closer. She gripped her sword tightly. "Hanue! Come out!"

A figure came into view in the distance. But as it grew closer, her heart dropped. The figure raised its arms, a familiar *twang* of an arrow being pulled back on an Andysi bow.

Fuck.

She ducked, landing roughly in the dirt below. The arrow whizzed by, pulling her hair from her head with a sharp sting.

Another figure emerged from behind a nearby tree, moonlight glinting off metal in its hand. Her breath quickened again as she raised herself to her feet, ducking quickly behind a tree to her immediate right.

"Two on one," she whispered to herself.

She ran out from the tree, rushing the first figure, the one with the bow. A man came into focus as she approached him. He released another arrow from his bow with a *twang*.

Anavi ducked again, rolling on the ground before jumping back to her feet. The man dropped the bow, pulling a knife from his hip as she raised her sword. She twirled as she approached him, so close she could touch him. Her blade slashed across his stomach, eliciting a deep groan from his mouth.

She turned quickly, facing the other figure, his body rustling the foliage with his barreling movements. He raised his sword, letting out a cry. Anavi raised herself up, thrusting her sword to meet him and kicked her leg out behind her, sending the injured man behind her tumbling to the ground. She pushed against the man's sword, staring him in his eyes, squinted from the effort of holding Anavi's sword back. Her muscles screamed as she held back his blade. She made ground, pushing him slightly back.

She smiled slightly, her breath loudly exiting her body. They were no match for a trained Lupegi assassin. She pushed, hard, sending the man flying back. He landed in the dirt, his sword knocked from his hand.

Anavi turned again, driving her sword deep into the chest of the man at her feet, twisting it for effect. His ribs cracked against her blade. He groaned and coughed, blood trickling from his mouth in the darkness, the light already leaving his eyes.

And now she turned her attention to the one she'd pushed to the ground. She approached quickly, shoving her bloodied sword against his neck, pinning him to the tree behind him.

He breathed heavily, the stench of fear seeping off him.

"Where's my brother?" she demanded, panting heavily as she pushed her sword closer to his neck, a stream of crimson glinting at the edge.

He pushed his head against the tree as far as he could, struggling with his hands to push her off him to no avail. "I don't know. I swear," the man choked out, his voice strained.

Her eyes searched the forest floor, and a familiar glint of metal caught her eye.

Her other sword...

"He was here," she growled back, pressing her sword deeper into his neck. "What did you do with him?"

The man shook his head, or at least tried to, sending a gush of blood from his neck down his bare chest. "Please, I don't know."

She roared in anger, grabbing the blade of her sword with her free hand and pushing it all the way through his neck. He gargled on his own blood, clawing at her arms desperately as her blade moved slowly through his throat.

The sting of where the sword cut into her head just fed her anger, her rage.

It hit the wood behind his head with a resounding *thud*. She flicked her sword, sending his head tumbling into the ferns to her side. Blood spurted from his neck stump with the last beat of his heart. The liquid landed in her open mouth, and she spit, her saliva and his own blood now plastered across his chest.

The headless man fell into the underbrush as she pulled her sword from the bark. She backed away from his body slowly, her chest heaving. She wiped her bloodied hand on her clothing and, reaching down behind her, she grabbed the sword she had given Hanue and studied it. The metal edge was still sharp, moonlight catching on the edges. Not a single drop of blood, a single fleck of red, tarnished the steel.

Which could only mean one thing. He was taken.

Hanue was gone. She swallowed loudly, her heart pounding in her head as she settled the sword into its sheath, leaving one still in her hand. The copper taste of the man's blood stung her taste buds as she stood over the bodies of her foes.

Hanue was gone...

She gripped her sword tighter, steadying her shaking hand slightly. She ran toward the massacre of the settlers, leaving the bodies on the forest floor carelessly.

Hanue was gone. And she was alone.

She had to find him.

She had to find him and figure out what happened here.

Jovan would not accept her failure in this.

CHAPTER SEVENTEEN
RAUNA

Her ankle screamed in protest as she limped through the forest in the mid-morning light. She gripped Tivea's arm as they moved slowly, searching every nook and cranny they found, every possible hiding spot Gaabi could be holed up in. Rauna winced as they took another step.

"How's that ankle doing?" Tivea asked as she squeezed her arm tighter.

"Oh, just fucking great," Rauna answered, sarcasm dripping in her pained voice. "Might go on a run later."

Tivea chuckled slightly, pausing her movements. Rauna stumbled, desperately trying to regain her balance the sudden stop threw off. "Rauna, I really think we should go to Xienee. If Ryrie doesn't hold her, Xienee does."

Rauna turned and looked at her walking partner incredulously. Tivea's face twisted in concern as she hopped on her foot slightly.

"Do you think she'll just let us walk in and give us my sister? She wanted them dead just as much as those people at Ryrie did."

Tivea averted her eyes, something weighing on her. "Rauna, my home is gone. Xienee needs to know; they might be coming for her soon. Plus, we aren't going to find Gaabi out here like this." She gestured with her free hand to Rauna's twisted ankle, bruised and blackened.

Rauna scoffed, letting go of Tivea's arm and lowering herself to the forest floor. "You're more than welcome to go. I don't know why you're still here."

Tivea's face twisted in pain at this and she stayed silent. A slight guilt tugged at Rauna as Tivea just stared into the distance.

She breathed heavily, turning her head toward the sky, away from the woman that stood beside her. The trees above her swayed slightly in the mid-morning breeze, branches crashing softly into each other, a cacophony of rustling. The sun peeked through the tree's canopy, cascading on her skin with a slight warmth that caressed her body. She closed her eyes, trying to focus on the world around her, trying desperately to move her sister out of her mind, at least for a second. But as she envisioned the trees above, green leaves slowly gave way to red curly hair, the sunlight to the warmth of her touch when she curled up beside her in bed, the sounds around her to the sound of her sweet laughter. All their lives, all they had was each other. These few days were the longest they had been away from each other and, by The Seven, it was killing her.

Tivea just didn't understand.

She opened her eyes again, turning to Tivea. "I need to find her," she said to the wide-eyed woman. She fumbled her way to her feet, limping forward, away from Tivea. "I understand if you don't want to stay, but I am." But that wasn't truthful. For some reason, she wanted Tivea with her on this journey.

Tivea scrambled to her feet behind her, jogging slightly. She touched Rauna's arm with her fingertips, sending shockwaves through Rauna's body. Her breath hitched and at the touch and she turned slightly, wobbling on her one good foot.

"I want you to find her. But I need to find my father too."

Rauna stared at the woman in front of her for a second. Her brown waves fell over her shoulders, catching the light and sending streaks of red through her hair. Her skin seemed to glow in the sun, the color of the sand at the beach north of Lasari at the coastline. She wanted to beg her to stay, to help her find Gaabi. It was selfish, she knew, but she couldn't explain the peace she felt around her. Even when finding the bodies of the settlers, even when finding Ryrie, Tivea's presence grounded her. She didn't want to go it alone. She opened her mouth to explain.

But Rauna stayed silent, turning slowly away and facing the trees ahead. She wobbled ahead, dragging her foot behind her.

Tivea jogged back to her. "Rauna, I'm going to Xienee tomorrow. She's my best chance to get my father back." Her voice was tinged with sadness.

Rauna sighed deeply, her heart sinking into her stomach. She stared at the trees in front of her, tracing the bark of the nearest with her eyes. Pivoting on her good heel, she tore her eyes from the tree and faced Tivea again. "That's understandable," she said, reminding herself that her father was missing, her home burned. It was selfish to ask her to stay. But still her body filled with dread at the thought of Tivea leaving. "Will you help me search until then, at least?"

Now it was Tivea's turn to sigh, averting her hazel eyes, the same color as Gaabi's. "Yes," she said, extending her arm out for Rauna to grab.

Rauna obliged her, pressing her hand against her arm. "Thank you, Tivea."

Tivea nodded slightly, still averting her eyes. "Of course." She answered but her mind seemed far-off, wandering.

Rauna felt a stab of guilt shoot through her at the sadness in her voice.

It was selfish to ask her to stay. It was selfish. But as her hand rested on Tivea's bare arm, tingles spreading through her fingers, she wished she would. For Gaabi. But also, for her.

The sun began to set, quicker than the days before. Fall was taking hold of Andyse quickly, cold air biting at her skin, leaves twirling as they fell to the ground. Rauna shivered as a breeze hit her skin, sending chills down her spine. Her teeth chattered as Tivea guided her back toward the cave they had called home for the past days.

Tivea bent down, raising her arm up higher to offer her stability to Rauna, and picked up several twigs from the ground. She stood as both their heads turned to the light in the distance. Ryrie, according to Tivea. An ancient fortress of an extinct people. Now occupied by Seven knows who. Rauna willed it to give up its secrets, staring at the light as it danced in the distance, faint as it moved back and forth.

As she stared at the light, her mind drifted back to her sister. Her poor sister. Another day of searching and coming up with nothing. And Tivea was leaving in the morning. She sighed deeply.

How was she going to ever find her?

Tivea took a step forward, breaking Rauna from her trance staring at the flickering light. Rauna followed her lead, heading back toward the cave.

As they approached, Tivea slowly broke from her hand, walking briskly to the ash-stained place they'd kept their fires. Rauna walked slowly, only a few steps, but pain shot through her body at the slightest hint of weight put on her ankle. She winced as she lowered herself next to the stain, Tivea already building a fire to burn.

"It's getting colder," she said nonchalantly, testing the waters for conversation.

Tivea raised her head, staring at Rauna. "Yes, it is," she looked back down at the sticks she was arranging, offering no other words.

Rauna's heart panged. Even the person she was trapped in the woods with didn't wish to speak to her. "So, I've got a question," she said against her better judgment, curling her legs up beneath her for warmth.

Tivea didn't look up from her wood which now had small licks of flame in the center. "What is it?"

"You said your mother used clorhestas, too?"

Tivea sighed, still fiddling with the sticks and dead leaves as warmth began to reach the tips of Rauna's toes.

"Yes." Tivea's eyes filled with water and Rauna fought the urge to reach out for her. "She died several years back. She used to be able to make flowers bloom beneath her feet as she walked; the nature respected her so much."

"What happened to her?" Rauna asked softly.

Tivea sat back from the fire as it grew, her expression giving the impression she was elsewhere. "I don't know." Tivea's hand reached almost absent-mindedly into the knapsack she carried and pulled out the journal Rauna had seen her read through by firelight. "My father never told me. She was here one day and the next, my father came back to camp shaking and crying."

Rauna tossed this information around in her mind. Tivea had rarely mentioned her mother. Or her father for that matter. It was almost odd to see someone working so hard to get back to their parents. Rauna's parents being gone was perfectly fine with her. "You're going to get him back, you know. I'm sure of it."

Tivea nodded, the flames now dancing in her eyes as darkness settled over the world around them. "I hope so."

Rauna stopped herself from asking anymore questions, letting the silence continue after Tivea's words. Tivea moved quickly to build the fire, seeming to not want to speak anymore of her mother or her father or their fates. The tinder caught quickly and Rauna sighed with relief at the warmth of the crackling fire. Her eyes focused on the dancing flame, and her thoughts drifted once again to her sister. Where was she?

Tivea lowered herself to the ground with a groan, laying down right next to Rauna, still clutching her knapsack. She fell quickly into sleep, leaving Rauna alone with her thoughts. Her soft breathing caused Rauna's smile to deepen. At least one of them could sleep soundly.

She lowered herself to the ground, staring at the roof of the cave, pinpricks of stars visible in her periphery. Was Gaabi somewhere, staring at the same stars? As tears built behind her eyes, she turned her attention elsewhere.

Without the stress of the day weighing on her consciousness, Tivea's face was peaceful, serene, the firelight catching in the hints of red in her dark brown hair. Rauna sighed with a slight smile and softly brushed Tivea's hair behind her ear.

Rauna woke with a jolt, sitting up quickly. She muffled a scream as her ankle throbbed as if it was on fire. Shocks of pain burst through her leg, upwards toward her hips. The campfire had gone out, only embers glowed softly in the night. With the low light of the dying fire, she reached her hand to her foot, biting her lip so hard she tasted the familiar copper of blood.

Shit.

Her skin screamed at her touch and a deep moan escaped her mouth as tears welled in her eyes. She pulled her pants up her leg with shaking hands, revealing a gruesome sight. Her ankle was black, the bruising having spread, and throbbed in pain. Tears spilled from her eyes at the next jolt of pain, sending shockwaves through her body.

Tivea grumbled next to her; her muffled cries must've woken her.

"Oh, Goddesses," she said softly upon seeing Rauna's ankle, quickly rushing to sit up. "I still have some bark somewhere."

Hot tears spilled freely now from Rauna's eyes. She squeezed them shut, begging for a relief to the pain. Gaabi would be very helpful to have around right about now.

"I think we overdid it yesterday," Tivea said, reaching a handful of bark out to Rauna. But the pain was too much to even reach up and grab it. Rauna's eyes shot open as another jolt sounded through her leg, sending a burning sensation through her ankle.

Sobs racked her body as she shook. She keeled over, Tivea's hand on her back following her down. "Please don't leave me," Rauna wailed between cries, ignoring the selfishness of the request. She couldn't walk; she couldn't fight. Her sister was gone, maybe never to be seen again, and she was stuck here, surrounded by enemies on all sides that would rather kill her than help her. She clasped a hand against her mouth, wet tears spilling over her fingers as her ankle throbbed. "I'm so sorry."

Tivea's voice barely reached her ears as white-hot pain shocked her leg again. "I'll stay another day, just to get that ankle healed."

Rauna nodded frantically, a weight lifting off her shoulders. Thank The Seven. "I'm so sorry. Thank you, I'm so sorry."

Tivea pulled her toward her, wrapping her in her arms as she sobbed. "It'll be okay, Rauna."

A sigh of pain escaped her as she settled into Tivea's arms, relishing the warmth of her embrace. Nothing was okay. But at least she wasn't going to be alone.

CHAPTER EIGHTEEN
HANUE

Gaabi shivered in the far corner of the dark cell, the dim lantern light barely reaching her figure. Shadows cast harsh lines through the space. The general had come back down a few times, always asking vague questions about The Seven or life in Aethiel. Hanue always met her with one-word answers. She was nice enough, for a woman with evil running through her veins.

Hanue breathed heavily, staring at the plate of food brought to them this morning. The chicken and potatoes beckoned him, the smell of warm food making his mouth salivate. But he wouldn't eat it.

Begrudgingly, he moved back toward Gaabi, crawling on the ground. "How are you doing?" he asked, reaching a hand out to stroke her face.

She shivered violently at his touch. "I miss my sister," she said, her voice barely audible.

A pang shot through his heart as he ran his hand along her smooth skin. "I know, Gaabi. I miss mine too." He wondered where Anavi was —had she been captured by Xienee? Or worse... He pushed the image of his sister, bleeding on the ground, the light leaving her eyes, from his mind. "Tell me about her."

Tears began to stream down her face, catching the light of the lantern as they fell. "I never should've come here."

Hanue started to think the same thing for himself. He paused his movements, trying to figure out how to comfort the girl in front of him. How could he possibly make her feel okay when the same tightness weighed on his own chest? He took a deep breath, pulling her toward him. Maybe a different tactic? "It's alright, Gaabi. How are your wounds healing?"

She lifted her shirt slightly. The wound on her chest was all but healed, a deep brown scar running the length of it. But other than that, it was like nothing had happened at all.

Hanue smiled, hoping that Gaabi could see it in the darkness around them. "Good," he said. "Like nothing even happened."

He regretted the words as soon as they exited his mouth. Gaabi's face twisted and she took a deep breath in.

"Are you going to eat?" she asked quickly, sliding further into her corner.

His mind clouded at her pain, completely spacing her question. "What?"

"Are you going to eat?" she repeated.

He sighed, staring once again at the chicken and potatoes, steaming hot on the lip of the cell. "No. I don't trust them," he said, his voice low so the guard that was surely just out of sight wouldn't hear him. "It might be poisoned."

Gaabi scoffed slightly, sitting up straighter. "Don't you think if they wanted to kill us, they would've by now? We need to keep our strength up to get out of here."

Hanue pondered her words for a moment, thinking back to the conversations he had with the general. General of Teveban, she had called herself. Hanue had more schooling than most in Lupegi, but the name 'Teveban' had never come up in his studies. She had seemed steely, her stony-faced exterior only breaking once, at the mention of Hanue's father. The man had been missing for years now but Lisynia seemed to recognize his name. Maybe she knew him. Maybe that's why they were alive.

But his father had been rambling when he left, when Hanue was eleven namedays old and Anavi only a few namedays older, suddenly the head of a household. He had been rambling about 'the secrets in the mountains' and 'the people of the legends' and some old saying about ancient powers.

As Hanue remembered his father's words, the name of Teveban clicked. His father had been drunk, stupid and cowardly, muttering under his breath curses at every free moment he had on that last day. But the Teveban... Hanue recognized the name from the stories his father had told of his journeys in The Seven's armies. An old legend. People with magic rivaling The Seven, people that were barely human, their minds corrupted with greed and bloodlust. But when his father left, he didn't speak of them the same way he used to, there was almost a respect, a sadness, in his words then. Maybe, just maybe, this stony cell belonged to the 'people of the legends'. Maybe Lisynia was the general of the secrets in the mountains. Maybe Hanue's father had *found* them.

If that was the case, they needed to leave—to escape. The few rambling words that were coherent of Tanue's spoke of powerful magics, the ability to control others' bodies. Like paralyzing their victims...

Hanue jumped to his feet, his head overwhelmed with information. What the fuck was happening? The black tendrils on the bodies flashed in his mind—his father's words, the feeling of not being able to move at all with one touch. They were no match, none at all...

Gaabi spoke, breaking him out of his downward spiral. "What's going on?" she asked, fear painfully apparent in her voice.

Hanue calmed himself as best as possible, focusing on his breathing as he forced it to slow back down. "You're right, Gaabi. We really, really, need to get out of here."

"What's going on?"

Taking a deep breath, he racked his mind on how to say everything without sounding crazy. But this entire situation was crazy. "You know The Seven's magics? The way they can control light and air? How they're immortal, how they use their powers for good, for the betterment of life?"

Gaabi's face hardened at this last part and her voice came out stronger than before. "I'd say 'good' is a matter of opinion."

Hanue was taken aback and let out a slight gasp. "What do you mean?"

Her eyes stayed focused on his for a second before she spoke again. "Nevermind. What about them, though?"

Though confusion tugged at his mind, he tried his best to explain his thoughts to her clearly. "My father told me stories about people hidden in the mountains with powerful magics. Then he disappeared. I think they killed him like they killed the people in your mission, like they want to kill us."

Gaabi's eyes grew wide. "The paralysis," she said softly, "and the black wounds. I've never seen a poison like that in Valetu..."

Hanue nodded solemnly. "We're being held by the people of the legends."

They waited in the dark as the footsteps of the guard echoed down the hall. Hanue clenched his fists, ready for a fight, to pounce upon the guard's entrance to gather the untouched food. The footsteps got louder, louder, and Gaabi crouched next to him, hand on his shoulder to maintain her balance.

"I still don't think this is a good idea," she whispered, her lips pressed against his ear.

He ignored her, focusing on the steps getting ever closer. What other choice did they have? Gaabi inched forward, pressing herself against the bars, her body still shrouded in the shadows of the cell wall. What was she doing? They both needed to fight to get out.

He opened his mouth in protest as the guard came into view. She was going to make them miss their chance. Fuck this. He unclenched his fist as a sword was shoved through the bars, the guard grabbing his keys from his waist.

Hanue stepped back, rising to his feet as the guard pulled his sword and another came into view, entering the cell. "Stay back!" he barked, his voice squeaking slightly. He was young. This would've been the perfect time. Heat in his body threatened to boil the very blood in his veins as he glared at the faint outline of Gaabi in the corner.

Fuck it.

The guard bent down and Hanue jumped forward, fists raised. His stomach met Gaabi's arm and he fell to his knees with a low groan. The guard didn't even notice, picking up the food and leaving the cell, locking it tightly behind him.

Hanue glared at Gaabi as she crawled back into the light. The footsteps slowly faded as they stared at each other in the darkness.

"What was that about, Gaabi?" He wanted to scream but his voice only came out a low whisper. "That was our chance!"

She only stared in response, moving slowly into the light. Her lips were raised into a slight smirk and Hanue's anger heated up even more.

"What's so funny? We need to get out! Do you want to die here?"

"Hanue—" she started.

"We need to get out!" he said, louder than he meant to. He clasped his head in his hands, squeezing his eyes tightly shut. What if they heard him?

He paced in the cell, what little space there was taken up by his frantic movements. He needed to get to Anavi, to tell her their father wasn't crazy. He needed to get to The Seven, warn them, get her home. He needed to get out.

He squeezed his eyes tighter. Then a slight *clink* reached his ears. He opened his eyes and looked to the source of the sound.

Gaabi stood tall in the light, raising one hand in the air. "We're going to get out, but not like that." The smirk was fuller now, giddy with excitement.

He looked at her hands. In them lay the guards keyring, a mess of upwards of twenty keys. He opened his mouth in shock.

"We're getting out like this."

Apologies spilled from Hanue's mouth as he rushed at Gaabi, raising her into the air in triumph. She giggled slightly, closing her fist around the keys. "You're a genius!"

She giggled louder now, and she wrapped her legs around him, raising herself into the air. His face reached for hers, her full lips. He held her head, fingers tangled in her messy hair and...

She pulled away, dropping to the ground, a pang shooting through Hanue's heart again.

Gaabi spoke, awkwardly breaking the silence between them. "We need to wait a bit, until they settle down."

He nodded and lowered himself to the floor. Gaabi sat down too, right next to him. He opened his mouth again, but nothing came out.

They sat there, waiting in the dark, for what could've been minutes or hours, Hanue was unsure. He simply stared into the darkness, the promise of freedom tearing at his heartstrings. He was going to get out. He was going to find his sister. He was going to get Gaabi home to her own sister. He'd had enough of the world beyond Aethiel. He would go back to his forge and arm the top soldiers with his blades and never, *ever* pick one up himself again and, by The Seven, he was going to survive.

But right now, they waited, legs slightly touching each other. What did she think of him? Trying to kiss her in a situation like this? Stupid. It was stupid. What had come over him? He clenched his fist again, digging his fingernails into his palm.

Finally, Gaabi spoke, and relief washed over his body at the sound of her voice. "I think we're good," she said, opening her fist to reveal the keys. She picked through them and held the first one up.

She crept toward the cell door and reached her hands through the bars, her tongue sticking out slightly as she fumbled with the keyhole. "Damnit," she said, pulling the keyring back through the bars and carefully, silently choosing the next one, her hand tightly gripping the rest of them to prevent them from clinking.

Hanue moved slowly toward her, awaiting the lock to click open. No luck with that one either. She brought her hand back inside, repeating the previous process of choosing the next one. She stuck her hand through the bars again and the door opened slightly with a soft *click*.

Gaabi chuckled slightly, shoving the keys down her shirt and standing up. Hanue made his way to his feet, straining to see the hall beyond them. He pushed the door open slightly, sticking his head through the gap.

The hallway beyond was as dark as the cell, lanterns placed sparsely throughout it. Gray stone made up the whole thing, floors, walls, and ceiling. In the distance, at the end, a cascade of light poured down from a staircase. A slight sound of laughter reached his ears from up above them. But the hallway was deserted and this was their chance.

He opened the door slowly.

Don't squeak, please, don't squeak.

The door seemed to obey his command, moving silently through the air. With his other hand, he beckoned Gaabi to follow him out. He closed the door behind them, clicking the lock back into place.

They hurried through the corridor, hugging the edge, where the light shone dimmer. As the staircase came into clear view, voices sounded from above and his blood ran cold.

He turned back to Gaabi, her eyes wide with fear. He reached his hand out behind him and to his surprise, her warm hand slid into his, squeezing tightly.

He tested the first step with his toes, but the stone was silent. Good. He walked up the step, then the next, flinching with every step he took toward the light. They reached the top, hand in hand, and Hanue paused.

He strained his ears, listening for footsteps, loud voices, any hint of where the people above were. He waited agonizingly, his heart pounding in his chest. A laugh rang out from above, far away. He rushed up the remaining stairs and into the light.

He glanced around wildly, Gaabi breathing heavily in his ears. The foyer was massive, several staircases leading upwards from their point. The same gray stone of the cells made up everything solid but large rugs and banners flew from the topmost rocks above them, Lanterns swung from every possible surface, illuminating the whole foyer. Two small windows and a large wooden door were on the far wall, and he strained himself checking for anyone about to walk in.

No one, no footsteps, nothing. He clasped Gaabi's hand tight, the laughing coming again from a large entrance in the distance, up the largest staircase. He turned behind him; Gaabi stared at him expectantly.

He turned back to the door in front of him, only twenty paces away, and ran, Gaabi right alongside him.

He heard a shout behind him, and his pulse spiked. Then more shouts. They were so close to the door. A stampede of footsteps sounded from above, heading toward them. He reached the door, ripping his hand from Gaabi's and thrusting the handles out, revealing the darkness of the forest.

He ran, Gaabi trailing shortly behind. His feet screamed with pain as he pounded through the forest, breathing heavily. The darkness of night obscured his vision, branches whacking him across the face.

He ran and ran and ran, the sound of shouting now far in the distance. He slowed his pace, pivoting on his heel. Gaabi approached quickly, her hair bouncing as she ran.

"We did it!" he shouted.

She smiled. "We did it!" she said breathlessly as she ran past him.

He quickened his pace to match hers, a smile creeping onto his face. The pain in his chest didn't matter, the throbbing of his feet didn't matter, the fact he could barely breathe didn't matter. They did it. They got out.

CHAPTER NINETEEN
MOLAC

The darkness of night smothered him as he walked, having passed the River Crossing fort on foot earlier in the night. After two long days of continuous movement, blisters covered his feet, his boots pulling painfully at them as he took each step. He winced.

Murmurs from his brethren tore through the still air, whispers in the night. Their eyes were just pinpricks of white in the otherwise black world, soft orange light dancing on their chainmail in the distance. He followed their gazes as they all began walking once more, toward the orange light of fire.

The camp was now just ahead, the embers of the burned wood still illuminating the ground around it. The men took slow, tentative steps toward the place that was once a force to be reckoned with—the headquarters of the Southern Coalition. Molac swallowed hard, trying to quell the unease washing over his mind as they approached.

The camp was large, the entire area absolutely demolished. The smell of burnt flesh and hair still lingered as they approached. Pikes were set up at the very edges of the large camp, burnt heads on them. His face drained of blood as he stared at one, a child no more than twelve namedays old. His eyes were pulled from his head by the birds that circled low overhead even now, his face frozen in a look of pure terror and pain. Molac stared at the empty sockets, bile making its way up his throat. He swallowed hard.

He knew what Tovik's troops did here; Yidenu and Queen Meluth had both told him but there was something about seeing it himself...

He keeled over next to the child's pike and emptied his stomach, the smell of death assaulting his nostrils. It hung low in the air, infesting every living thing it could get its cold hands on. He muffled a sob, tears welling in his eyes.

Tovik killed everything within reach; Tovik's hands had grasped this camp, this child. And Tovik didn't let anything go unpunished.

"Come on, pussy, get up," a sharp command came from behind, followed by a rough slap on his back.

He winced again, quickly wiping his eyes with his hand. He thought back to that meeting two nights ago, the sound of the queen's voice, the mission she gave him. Out of everyone here, she chose him. And he wouldn't let her down. That was how he would restore his position; that's how he would bring honor back to the Kludishav name.

He steeled himself, raising back to his feet, averting his gaze from the child's empty face and his commanding officer's scowl. He had to find out why this child burned. That was why he was here, that was how he restored his position.

Molac stepped gingerly beyond the pikes, away from the other men that moved through the remains, headed into what used to be the home of a powerful commander. He unsheathed the sword as he walked on his tiptoes, stepping over blackened bones and planks of half burnt wood.

With his other hand, he plugged his nose as the smell became intolerable, trying his hardest not to keel back over again. He searched the ground, embers glinting slightly in the black of burnt grass, the only thing lighting his path on this cold night. A glint caught his eye, and he dug through the burnt wood, ash sticking to his fingers, coloring them deep blacks and grays.

The object came into view as the other men in his group hooted and hollered upon finding their own treasures. He held in his hands a piece of sea glass, words etched into its smooth, turquoise surface. It was large, bigger than his head and obviously special. Sea glass was rare in this area of Andyse. It had to have come from the seas far to the east.

Molac quickly wiped his hands in the grass to remove the soot and traced the letters so carefully drug into the glass.

> *To my daughter,*
> *Know you are always loved, always cared for.*
> *I am always with you, and I always will be.*
> *Do not forget who you are.*
> *Love, your mother*

A chill ran through him as he read the words. He took a deep breath and closed his eyes, dropping the glass onto the fire-damaged ground below. The world was silent, the sounds of the men he traveled with, the commanding officer barking orders, the soft crackling of the still burning fires, all faded away.

The pain here was unfathomable. It was palpable, hanging in the air, haunting his conscious. He *had* to find out why.

After an agonizingly long time sifting through human remains and broken homes, he left from the camp empty handed. That was besides the only intact thing he found, the sea glass with the message of love between two people that were certainly dead now. He gripped it tightly, lowering himself to the ground outside the camp's edges and sighed deeply.

What happened here?

The group of men he came with laughed and chuckled amongst themselves as they threw trinkets and knick knacks taken from the wreckage back and forth. They were careless, a trait Molac almost envied. What he wouldn't give to have the same lack of empathy. He didn't expect anything else from the peasants though.

"Animals," he grumbled under his breath as one of the men guffawed at the look of terror on a boy's rotting, chopped off head.

"Hey!" the commanding officer barked at the men. They looked up from their brutal source of amusement, standing at attention. "Set up camp, fellas, we move early."

His comrades muttered in discontent but ultimately began rustling through their packs for their tents. Molac followed suit begrudgingly.

He made quick work of the setup, faster than the rest of the soldiers by far, his fingers moving deftly as they set stakes into the ground and pulled the ropes into place. One good thing his father had done was at least teach him how to set up a tent. He meant for it to be used in case Tovik ever fell or the Kludishavs lost favor and the aristocracy had to flee.

But, in a way, that's the world Molac was living in right now.

Molac settled into the mouth of his tent, attempting to block out the jeering of the others. His eyes fell on the embers of the still-burning fires of Yidenu's camp, watching them dance on the ground.

He stared at the embers for a long time, the movement of their light letting his thoughts stray from the scene they were a part of. Exhaustion tugged at his eyelids, and he allowed himself one chance of rest. How had he gotten here?

He thought back to the man weeks ago, laying in a pool of blood in the sand. His chest filled with pride at the thought, muffling the outrage he felt at taking another human's life. He had proved them all wrong and that's what mattered. An aristocrat could play by their rules and still win.

"Now look at me," he whispered to no one, a smile plastered across his face as he averted his eyes from the death around him. He was now on a mission, from the queen herself! Oh, how the people in Dhunviro that spit at him in the streets after father's death would quake at the sight of him now—the queen's protection on him, prepared to kill.

"Get up, men!"

Molac's eyes shot open.

He raised himself to his aching feet, a newfound fire in his chest to go on, even after a restless sleep. They walked from the camp, headed north, parallel to the Malcier mountains in the west. He had no qualms about leaving the camp behind, there was nothing to be found there anyway. Queen Meluth wanted answers, not the burnt embers of what was.

Before long, the sun peeked over the east horizon, casting a soft glow on the ground around him. Molac turned, checking their progress and found he could not even see the remains of Yidenu's camp anymore. In all directions, the plains stretched out in front of him, empty, devoid of life besides them.

Molac paused.

Empty.

Not all of Yidenu's coalition had burned—just the camp, the headquarters. So where were the rest of them? He strained his memory, trying to remember seeing figures in the distance or hearing a horse's neigh. But for the life of him, he could not conjure the image of another soul since he entered Andyse, save the men he traveled with.

His blood ran cold at this realization and his breath hitched. He turned slowly, peering over the waist height grass, searching for something. Anything. Any signs of life. But only the yellow grass, swaying in the slight breeze, met his eyes.

The Northlands lay just beyond the river several miles north and Molac's breathing halted at the realization that those that Yidenu had commanded were likely joining Xienee right now. Davegu would burn, the flames coming swifter than those of Yidenu's camp if that were the case. There would be no way to restore his honor if there was nowhere left to welcome him back.

Dhunviro, Oshgor, Targiv and Mergrin would burn. Everyone he never knew, his friends would burn. The queen would burn. Asmuto would burn. What had Tovik done?

Molac's breathing returned with a sharp inhale and he began running north, his feet moving swiftly through the plains without him even giving the command. His breath shot in and out of his chest in short bursts as his feet smacked the dirt below. Yelling sounded from behind him, no doubt the rest of his company screaming at him to come back.

But they were Tovik's men. They didn't understand what was at risk.

He would plead with the commander; he would plead with the tribal leaders loyal to Yidenu. His home would not burn. Not while he could help it. Not if he wanted a place to go back to.

It was midday before he reached the river, even at the pace he had carried on. Sweat poured down his body, soaking the clothes beneath his rather ill-fitting armor. Molac panted, his hands on his knees.

He turned behind him, looking for any sign of the men he had traveled with but not a single blade of grass was out of place. He'd lost them for now, or more likely, they simply didn't care about a fallen aristocrat barreling toward his death.

The river raged in front of him, water flying into the air as it slammed into the rocks cutting through the surface. It was wide, about thirty paces at this point, and the white foam that threw itself into the air indicated it was moving faster. He glanced at the Malcier mountains in the west, the rocky peaks barely visible as they jutted above the clouds in the distance.

He sighed, lowering himself to the river's bank. He dared not set foot in the water here, the rapids would sweep him away with no more effort than it took to move a stick through the air. But pass it he needed to do.

Xienee's land sat just beyond the river's other side, and he needed to get there. The queen's mission and the sake of his homeland, his own honor depended on it. He raised himself back to his feet and began walking upstream. It was bound to slow at some point along the water's edge.

The sweat on his body chilled him to the bones as a strong gust of wind swept through the plains, the grass shuddering with him. The forest below the mountains was another half-day walk if the map he snagged from the armory was at all accurate, but he needed to get there soon. Sooner than nightfall.

He quickened his step, his aching body protesting as he pushed it to its very limit.

The sun was just beginning to set as the forest's edge came into sight. He exhaled as he gazed upon it. Tall trees scraped the sky, broad leaves on their branches. They were just now beginning to change for fall, brilliant greens with specks of yellow on some of the edges.

He slowed his pace, searching the river for a good crossing point. Up ahead, about forty paces away, a rock cut into the river's surface, smooth on the top. A perfect crossing. He rushed toward it and bound across the river. A chill overtook his body as he stepped foot on Xienee's land for the first time and the hairs on the back of his neck raised.

He was being watched.

Molac looked around wildly, searching for a person, a horse, hell, even a bird—any explanation of the chill that shook him to his bones. Then a harsh scream rang out from the trees in the distance.

Run.

Run.

Run away.

But as Meluth's words from before echoed in his mind, he found himself running toward the scream. It sounded again louder, not a scream of pain but one of rage. He picked up speed, his chest heaving as he approached the trees.

He crashed into the foliage, so different from the pine forests to the north of Dhunviro. He went tumbling down as his foot caught a root. His face met the dirt and, as he raised his head, his eyes were met with bodies. Two Davegu soldiers in Tovik's armor laying in a pool of blood. A commanding voice rang out. "Who are you?"

He raised his head, staring at the source of the voice. It was an Andysi man, clothed in a thick cloak that obscured his face. The man held a sword, the blade pointed right at his neck.

Chapter Twenty
Tivea

She tried to look at the woman in front of her with pity, or care, or sadness, or something other than anger. But she couldn't.

Rauna had now been bound to the cave for more than a day, her ankle continuing to swell as time went by. Tivea had gathered herbs and bark, made the teas from creek water and plants, everything she could to get her healthy, the way her mother taught her. But it was to no avail. She tried to respond to the wails of pain with compassion and grace like her father taught her. But it was to no avail. She was angry. Angry that this woman had prevented her for days now from leaving this cave and finding her father. She was angry she couldn't get her to leave, though she had offered to bring her to Xienee, plead her case.

And now Rauna cried quietly into her bag in the dark of night, pleading for The Seven to bring her sister back from the dead. But even in her anger, Tivea could not bring herself to leave her here. Or tell her that her sister was all but dead, being in the Northlands alone for this amount of time.

Tivea stood from her spot next to Rauna's black ankle and walked toward the mouth of the cave she had been trapped in for far too long. Her stomach grumbled, twisting inside her body. She hadn't left

Rauna's side to get food in a day now, just picking at the rabbit from days ago. "I'm going to look for something to eat," she said, hiding her mood the best she could.

Rauna looked up from her pack, tears glimmering on her face in the moonlight. A pang of empathy shot through Tivea's heart at the sight of this woman, so torn up, so out of place here. "Are you coming back?" Rauna whispered, her voice barely carrying to Tivea's ears.

Tivea sighed, ashamed of her anger as she stared at the woman in front of her. "Yes," she said, forcing a small smile. "I promise."

Rauna nodded slightly, shaking tears from her skin onto the cave floor. She sniffed, pulling herself into a sitting position, her ankle still propped up. "Thank you, Tivea," she said, her voice raw. "I'm so sorry, I really am. You can leave if you want to."

Tivea nodded, the shame growing deeper. She understood not wanting to be alone and however much she wanted to leave this cave, she couldn't help but admit she was scared to leave herself. She sighed. "I'll stay for the night."

Turning from Rauna, Tivea strode onto the forest floor, stepping on the leaves that had fallen in the winds of the night before. They crunched under her feet as she took small steps away, trying to avoid detection from anyone that may be nearby.

She took a deep breath as she ducked behind a tree, shielding her from Rauna's vision. The cold air of the fall night filled her lungs.

Her thoughts drifted to her father teaching her how to set snares in the cold morning air of winter many years ago. The smile on his face as they came across one she had set the night before, a squirrel trapped in its clutches...

No. Now was not the time to dwell on the past. She hurried into the darkness, pushing those thoughts from her mind. The snares were just up ahead.

A cool breeze swayed the trees, dead leaves falling to the ground as it swept through. She held a hand out, catching a leaf in her open palm. She sighed deeply, her mother now coming to mind, catching leaves in the early fall and making them come back to life in her hand...

No. No! She shook her head vigorously, pushing her mother's smiling face from her thoughts. Not now.

Her stomach turned yet again, cramping her torso as it protested the lack of sustenance it had to endure lately. Tivea walked quicker now, stepping over the leaves on the ferns and toward the area with the most snares. She traveled south, headed toward Ryrie and cursed under her breath. Of course she set them there.

With a deep breath, she plunged into the trees faster, headed toward the old fortress.

It didn't take long for her to reach the snares, a soft squeaking audible over the wind's cry. She bent down, observing the trap in the moonlight. A squirrel. Just like the first she ever caught. She smiled slightly as tears built behind her eyes, red-hot blood rushing to her face. Tivea reached out to grab the animal, watery eyes obscuring her vision. Her fingers made contact with its fur, and it began squealing louder, harsher. It turned beneath her touch and bit her, hard, on her hand. A sob escaped her mouth at the sudden pain, and she threw the animal across the forest floor.

It scampered into the darkness as she clutched her hand, fighting to hold back the tears that threatened to spill over. Her legs shook beneath her as blood dripped steadily from her hand. She collapsed to the ground, sobs racking her body freely now. She had no more strength to hold them back.

Everything was gone. Everything and everyone were gone. Her thoughts cycled through images of her mother, her father, the children playing, the fires, oh Goddesses, the fires. She pulled her legs into her chest, gripping them there tightly with her bloodied hand. The fires raged in her mind, a scream building in her throat.

"No, no, no," she whispered as her father's face came into view, beaming with pride. The image was soon replaced with the last she had of him, beaten, bloodied, and carried away by soldiers they were allied with. Her sadness mixed with anger and the scream gained traction.

Her mother's face, blurred in her memory, came into view, crow's feet crinkling beautifully as she talked to her, softly, sweetly.

The ferns prickled her bare skin as she shook on the ground, her face soaked with tears. It was all gone. All of it. And here she was, alone, and cold, and hungry.

The fire in her mind consumed everything she loved as the cold settled into her skin, eating at her flesh.

Pull yourself together.

She bawled louder. If anyone was nearby, they certainly knew where she was now.

Pull yourself together.

Her breathing slowed as she hiccupped, the tears taking longer to come now. For a while she sat there, in the cold with a wet face and ragged breathing, her stomach still growling into the silence.

Then she moved with purpose. She wiped her face with one hand, spraying the tears on the ferns below and with the other, she pushed into the ground, raising herself to her feet. Tivea's chest moved up and down slowly, hiccups interrupting the rhythm occasionally. Her legs were jelly underneath her weight as she took note of her surroundings. She glanced up in the distance, the light now gone.

Strange. But now was not the time to investigate. She walked briskly to the next snare, even closer to Ryrie. Another animal in this one. Another squirrel. Tears threatened to spill back over her skin as she broke its neck, blood still dripping from her hand. She disassembled the trap and reset it, pivoting on her heel and heading back to the cave that Rauna surely waited in.

To her surprise, she was glad to be headed back to her. At least she was consistent, a source of calm in this mess. She sighed, resolving to apologize when she reached the cave. Rauna was good company, even now.

Suddenly, a rustling sound reached her ears from behind her. She dropped the limp animal, reaching swiftly behind her back to get the Davegu sword. Her chest heaved as she stared into the darkness in the direction of the sound.

Then came voices. A tone of fear sounded in their voices and something in her urged her to call out to them.

"Hello?" she ventured, barely audible.

The voices stopped, quick rustling following it. She took a step forward, lowering her sword. The moonlight glinted off the blade as she lowered it and she strained her eyes, searching for the owners of the voices.

She listened intently as the trees swayed in the slight breeze. *Over there.* She walked toward the last place she heard them, following the sounds of the trees. *Behind that one.* One in the distance caught her attention and she approached it slowly.

Tivea spoke again, hope dwelling in her chest as she thought back to the woman in the cave behind her. "Gaabi?"

A gasp sounded in the silence and hushed voices followed. She walked toward the tree, stowing her sword back in her belt. She peered behind the tree from a distance and a figure took shape in the dark.

"Who are you?" a boy called out.

A smile crossed her face as another figure emerged from behind the first, a mess of curly hair on its head, shades of red catching the moonlight. This one approached, the first attempting to hold her back from coming closer.

"How do you know my name?" the girl asked, her face now visible in the low light. She was pale, so pale she seemed to glow as the light hit her skin.

Tivea thought back to Rauna in the cave and smiled. "I'm with your sister."

The figure holding Gaabi back now stepped into the light, a man, early twenties, with dark brown skin and wide eyes. "What do you mean?"

"She came looking for her," Tivea said, pointing to the girl in front of her who had a look of utter disbelief on her face. "Rauna's in a cave nearby, just that way." She extended her hand out behind her, gesturing in the general direction of the cave.

Gaabi wrestled from the boy's grip and bolted in the direction Tivea had pointed. The boy followed just after her, hissing her name. Tivea broke into a jog, confusion beginning to weigh on her. She picked up the squirrel she dropped as she jogged. How did Gaabi survive out here this long, even with someone else? The boy was not Andysi, judging by his thick foreign accent, he didn't know these lands. She kept them in her sights as the cave came into view.

"Gaabi?" Rauna's voice called out, eyes wide at the sight of her sister, she pulled herself along the ground with her hands, still unable to stand. Gaabi slid on her knees, embracing her older sister tightly. Tivea felt a smile creep onto her face at the sight as the two sisters shook in each other's arms.

"By The Seven," the boy whispered beside her as they watched the reunion. He turned to Tivea. "How did you..."

She beamed at the boy, extending her hand to his. "I'm Tivea, daughter of Yidenu." Her father's name was almost painful to speak but she did her best to prevent her face from showing that.

The boy responded in kind, reaching his hand out to hers. "Hanue Sareni, son of Tanue."

Disbelief was still etched on his face as she looked at him. "She found me," she said, gesturing to the sobbing mess that was Rauna in the cave. "We've kept each other alive. She came looking for Gaabi."

Hanue turned from Tivea, staring at the sisters as well. His mouth hung wide open, confusion plastered on his face.

Tivea moved slowly toward Rauna, placing a hand on her shoulder and lowering herself to her level. She was warm to the touch and Tivea glanced at her ankle below her. Black, with new shades of green and yellow, a deep cut running along the length of it. It was getting infected. She swallowed, not wanting to interrupt the moment in front of her. "How's your ankle?"

Gaabi pushed back from Rauna, tears spilling down her face. Her gaze landed on the bruised ankle in front of her. "Oh, Seven," she whispered.

Rauna responded through sobs, "I'm fine, Gaabi, I promise. I'm so glad Tivea found you," she turned now to look at her, "thank you."

Tivea nodded in response, concern weighing on her. Gaabi pushed further from her sister and extended her arm, palm facing Rauna's ankle. She waved it slightly over her foot, eyes closed and Tivea felt a rush in the air, like the oxygen was being pulled from it. She watched intently, her mouth falling open as Rauna's ankle returned to normal color with a touch of Gaabi's hand. The foot was still twisted but the bruising gone.

Gaabi turned to Hanue who had silently approached, standing right beside Tivea. "We need to find her a walking stick for tomorrow."

He nodded in response, seemingly unimpressed by this display.

Tivea's mouth opened. "How—"

"She's a student of Valetu," Rauna said, sighing as she spoke. "Best damn healer I've ever met."

Tivea nodded silently, reaching for the firewood she gathered earlier. A smile formed unimpeded on her face. With them here now and Rauna healed, she could go to Xienee in the morning. She could get her father back.

As she looked at Rauna, it was almost bittersweet...

Rauna looked up from her conversation with Gaabi and her green eyes met Tivea's with a smile. For a second, Tivea almost thought Rauna would miss her too come tomorrow.

CHAPTER TWENTY-ONE
LISYNIA

The horse swayed beneath her as the mid-morning light beat down on her shoulders. She stared at the men and women in front of her, their leather armor catching the light of the sun, creating a mirage of movement, almost hypnotizing her. Clanging weapons and heavy footsteps serenaded her ears, a beautiful orchestra of anger and determination. She turned her attention now to the woman on the horse beside her, the Commander of the Northlands forces that surrounded them.

Xienee grimaced as their eyes met. Lisynia returned the look.

"How long until Ryrie?" Xienee's voice rang out over the sound of the troops' movement.

"Not long, about half a day still," Lisynia answered, straining her voice to be heard.

"Good, we'll settle there for the night while you get your people ready for training."

Lisynia nodded, turning her attention back to the people in front of her, moving with purpose southwest, the front lines trailing the edge of the forest.

As the first people plunged in after the scouts that were sent out this morning, Torvo ran out from the treeline, his cloak billowing behind him, catching the attention of everyone up front. He dragged a man behind him, Davegu armor on his body. The prisoner grappled desperately with Torvo's hold on him but he thrust the man down to the ground at the feet of Xienee's horse.

Lisynia raised herself on her horse for a better view as the group came to a slow stop, staring at the scene unfolding in front of them.

"I caught him headed toward Ryrie, Commander. Must be a Davegu spy," Torvo said, his voice strong and steady despite the physical task he just performed.

Lisynia's face paled at this assertion, searching the man's face with her eyes. He had tan skin with a slight sunburn across his cheeks. Shoulder-length black hair scratched the top of the ill-fitting armor he wore, greasy and caked with dirt like he hadn't had a bath in months. Despite his roughness, he was handsome in a polished way. Too polished. The man glanced up at Xienee expectantly, shaking visibly as he cowered. He looked fucking pathetic.

The commander spoke after a long pause, throwing her fist into the air. "I'll kill him myself." She dismounted gracefully from her horse, grabbing her sword from the sheath on her hip. It glinted in the sunlight as Lisynia's breath quickened next to her.

She approached the man slowly, drawing out his inevitable death as she raised her sword in the air, a yell bursting out from her mouth.

Lisynia watched the man begin to shed tears at his impending doom. A voice rang out in her head as Xienee started to swing the blade down to meet the man's neck. *Seek in the holds of your oppressors.* Lisynia's face went cold. This Davegu man may be the key.

"Wait!" Lisynia screamed, hopping off her horse and running to the commander. The man condemned to die stared at her in shock.

Xienee lowered her sword and turned quickly, sticking her angry face in Lisynia's. She could smell the ham they'd had for breakfast on her breath. "What is it?"

Lisynia gulped, wiping her face of any emotion and staring back at the woman in front of her. She forced a cool smile onto her face. "I'd like to speak to him about why he was headed to Ryrie. That's my hold," she lied through gritted teeth.

Xienee glared at her, her brown eyes searching Lisynia's face for a hint she had ulterior motives. Lisynia forced her breathing to be even and steady, cold faced as Xienee watched her intently. "Is that so?"

It was obvious the Commander of the Northlands was not used to being questioned, her typically calm demeanor replaced with paranoia and distrust at Lisynia's intrusion. "It is. That's the safety of my people on the line. I must insist."

Xienee backed away a step, grasping the man's arm quickly. He yelped in pain at her touch. She thrust him to his feet and threw him toward Lisynia. He landed hard in the dirt, whimpering slightly.

Coward.

"Take him then. But my people will not guard him. We take no prisoners in the Northlands," Xienee growled out, her eyes screaming murder. "Don't question me again in front of my people," she added, leaning in close to Lisynia.

Her heart pounded but she nodded calmly. "Thank you, Commander." She extended a hand out to her and Xienee begrudgingly returned the gesture, gripping Lisynia's forearm with the force of a thousand soldiers. She did not wince though, staring deep into Xienee's eyes.

Xienee released her hand and Lisynia whistled, calling for a messenger as she stared at the pathetic man on the ground, still shaking violently. The boy, Ason, approached quickly from the masses on his horse. "Yes, General?"

"Take your horse and ride ahead to Ryrie and tell Otto to prepare my mother for my arrival. Can you do that?"

He nodded profusely, already starting to prepare his horse for the journey. "Yes, General. Anything else for you?"

She smiled as she stared at his young face, reminding herself of the story that led Ason to her. "Make it home safe."

He nodded with a small smile and then was off, riding into the distance alongside Xienee's people. Xienee waited already on her horse, ready to move again. Lisynia grabbed the man at her feet and drug him toward the back of her horse.

"Thank you," a small voice squeaked out and she stared incredulously at the source.

"I didn't do this for you," she said, taking a piece of rope and tying his hands to her saddle. Confusion ate at her mind as she saw the rawness on his rough wrists already, barely healed over. He winced sharply as she tightened the knot.

Xienee sighed exasperatedly next to her and Lisynia pushed her questions from her mind. She mounted her horse and kicked her heels into the ribcage of the beast as the crowd moved forward again. "Make sure you keep up, it'll hurt a lot less."

Xienee had not talked to her in hours at this point, choosing instead to converse with Torvo to her right. Lisynia focused on the fact they were approaching Ryrie now, the mountain growing ever larger upon their movements. The man tied to her horse behind her had been begging her for some water for almost as long as he had been behind her at this point and her patience with Xienee, Torvo, and him was all growing thinner by the second.

Lisynia dismounted her horse as the frontline approached the entrance. "Dismount here, stables are nearby," she said loudly.

Xienee's people did not move from their horses, instead staring at Xienee for a command. "Dismount," she said coolly, glaring at Lisynia. That relationship would need some mending apparently.

Lisynia sighed deeply, taking the reins into her hand and maneuvering through the mass of people, dragging her horse and her prisoner behind. He exclaimed behind her as one of Xienee's people spit on him. Her mother was right; Xienee's people held no love for the Davegu. She walked to the entrance to the stables, built into the mountain, as the sun began to set.

The Northlanders followed her example, led by Xienee who briefly squeezed her arm as she tied her own horse up with extra rope she had brought. Anger bubbled in Lisynia at the touch, but she focused on untying the sweaty man from her horse's saddle. She jerked the rope toward the wall and lifted the saddle onto a hook. The man groaned loudly, to the laughter of the Northlanders nearby.

She turned around, jerking the rope the man was tied to behind her. Xienee reached for her arm again and she stopped, staring expectantly at the woman in the near absolute darkness. "I'm sorry for earlier," Lisynia said simply, her voice cool.

Xienee shook her head. "I understand why you did it," she whispered, leaning in close to Lisynia's ear. Torvo stared at them from behind Xienee, the little of his face visible etched into a harsh scowl. "But you cannot command me, especially in front of my people."

Lisynia nodded, walking away quickly as Xienee leaned back upright, releasing her arm. She understood Xienee's anger. But that didn't stop her from having some of her own. She dragged the man behind her as he protested quietly, writhing in her grip. As she exited the stable, she pivoted on her heel, pinning him against the wall of the mountain. "Shut the fuck up. We'll talk later. Just be quiet."

He gulped and glared at her with his yellow eyes, proof he was Davegu high class. He breathed heavily, loudly, in the silence as people trickled back outside from the stables. Xienee's form appeared in the darkness, walking toward her swiftly.

She turned to Xienee expectantly, egging her to command her people.

"Follow her," Xienee said to her people, her voice drowning out all the murmurs.

Lisynia nodded at Xienee and turned toward the entrance of the fort. "There are beds for all of us. Up the stairs to the right are the bunks. Find an empty bed and Xienee will give you further directions." How strange it was that just two weeks ago, she was giving this same speech to her own people. A lot had changed in such a short amount of time.

She pushed this thought from her mind and walked toward the entrance, the doors barely visible in the dying light of day. The troops followed closely behind her and her chest swelled at the power behind her. Xienee walked alongside her, shoulders back and head upright as they crossed the threshold into their now joint home.

"I'll talk with him later, take him to the hold," she said to her waiting people as she jerked the rope of the man behind her again. Swiftly, a group of Tevebrisians surrounded him, muffled cries coming from the swell of people.

She let go of the rope and approached Otto, his familiar face standing out from the crowd. She embraced him as people bustled around them, dragging the man to the hold or moving to explore their new surroundings.

"Your mother is in your chambers, General," Otto said, pulling from their hug and gazing upon her with warmth.

"Thank you, Otto," she said, pushing down the happiness she felt at seeing him. She moved past him and looked at the large staircase in front of her. At the top, her mother would be waiting. She had to stop herself from running up the stairs to see her just a few moments quicker.

Her mother waited for her in her room. Lisynia smiled at the sight of her mother, tall and thin, her kind face upturned in a large grin. Her thin blonde hair was pulled into a tight bun behind her head and she wore elegant riding robes, though threadbare and old, they were beautiful. She was beautiful.

"Oh, my daughter," her mother cooed, extending her arms, beckoning her. She fell into her mother's warm embrace, the smooth silk of her mother's dress caressing her face. "You've done so much now. I'm so proud of you." She planted a wet kiss on Lisynia's cheek then pulled away and rested her hands on her shoulders, smiling warmly at her. Lisynia returned the smile, relishing the feeling of her mother's embrace. "How are you doing, Lisynia?" her mother asked softly.

She sighed deeply, staring into her mother's intense brown eyes. "I'm doing alright, Mother. We're preparing for the march on Oshgor now. Me, Xienee, and some of Yidenu's people."

Her mother's face twisted, seemingly far off in thought and she placed her dainty hand on Lisynia's shoulder. "I know why you're doing this, but tell me, why now?"

A heat rose in her body, burning her skin. "They burned the Southern Coalition and that's not even counting everything they've done to our people."

The Queen of Teveban had always supported her war effort, even giving her the dagger that had been passed down in her family for years, the one with the magic to kill with a single slash. Her mother had trained her in the Ancient's magic even though it was forbidden by law and by the king.

Why ask why?

The queen didn't back down, staring straight into her eyes with an intensity only her mother was capable of. "Why?"

"I just told you why!" She pushed her mother's hand off her shoulder, taking a step forward. The heat burned and burned in her body. "They're killing us. Taking us as slaves. For years they've kept us hidden!"

Her mother smiled slightly. "I know, Lis, but why now?"

The heat began to diminish, flowing out of her face as she realized what was happening. Her mother was testing her, prodding her to back up her opinions and her thoughts. It was one of the more annoying qualities she had.

Lisynia chose her words carefully. "There never is a good time for revolution, is there? It's always hard for one person or another. That alone does not warrant our complacency. I won't stop what I've put into motion, Mother, you should know this. I'm doing this for our people."

The queen nodded, her stony face betraying no emotion. "Good. I'm just worried. We already lost Catina, we can't lose you too."

The heat now welled behind Lisynia's eyes, threatening to fall onto her face at the mention of her sister. Seven years had not healed the wound. "I understand, Mother, and you won't. We have allies, we have our magic, training, and the element of surprise. I even brought back a Davegu spy today." She thought back to the man in the dungeon, whimpering, pathetic. Her thoughts strayed back to the words she heard that day in Xienee's camp. "There's something else that I wish to talk to you about, though."

Her mother raised her eyes to meet hers again, glimmering in the low light of the lantern. "What is it?"

"I had an... experience in Xienee's camp. A vision almost. The Ancients spoke to me."

Her mother's mouth fell open and her face whitened. She took a step forward, staring into Lisynia's eyes with a fervor. "Are you sure? They have not reached to us in centuries."

Lisynia nodded slightly, meeting her mother's eyes. Her chest swelled as she thought more about it. The Ancients reached out to *her*. The most powerful beings known to ever exist chose her, of all people, to speak to. A smile built on her face, the corners of her mouth raising as she spoke. "I'm sure of it."

"Which one was it?" her mother said.

Lisynia thought hard about the voice, the words it spoke, the words that had not left her mind since she heard them. "I don't know..." she admitted, her smile fading. The Goddess had given her no name.

Her mother gulped loudly, seeming to resolve herself for a second. "That's okay, love, what did she say?"

Now Lisynia had a question she could answer. "She said we don't have the full truth about our history. There's something hidden in Teveban and things hidden in 'the holds of your oppressors' that would tell us the truth." She stepped forward grasping her mother by the arms.

"That's another reason why I have to do this. We have to know the truth and they might have answers in Oshgor or Dhunviro. The capital of the Davegu Kingdom is bound to have some answers." Her chest rose and fell heavily as she spoke, the nerves of admitting this out loud gnawing at her mind. She had to support her. She had to.

After a long silence, her mother spoke, her voice low and choked. "Do you think that's what Catina was searching for?"

Tears welled behind Lisynia's eyes again and she nodded. "Yes. She wanted to find the truth. Now," she took a deep breath, steeling herself for what she was about to say, "I need to find it."

Her mother's eyes shot up and she prepared herself for the vitriol that would undoubtedly spill from her mouth at this, warnings that it was too dangerous. But it didn't come. She raised her hand to Lisynia's cheek and softly stroked it, her warm touch making her shudder. "My daughter," she said and Lisynia closed her eyes, turning her head away from her. She should've known better than to tell her this. "You will find it. I know it. For your sister, for our people, I know you will. I will support you every step of the way,"

A warmth filled her, quite unlike the warmth from earlier. This warmth was serenity and nervousness and hope and horror. She opened her eyes and pulled her mother into a tight hug. "I will be careful, Mother. Thank you. I love you."

She watched from the main entrance of Ryrie as the night fell. She had something to do now, something important. She thought back to her sister, all her talk of revolution in their bedrooms when the nights were much like this long ago. She took a shaky breath, fear filling her body at what she had to do now.

Footsteps sounded behind her and she quelled her fears as much as possible. A soft touch skimmed across the small of her back and tingles spread through her body. She turned slowly, hiding her face from the light that would betray her fears to him. "Otto," she said, her voice slightly choked.

"General," he said, his voice low and playful as he sounded the word out.

She smiled slightly. Leave it to him to never take anything seriously. He moved his hand to her shoulder, the tingles dissipating as quickly as they came. She wished he would move it back and just hold her through this fear.

But instead, he spoke, "Your mother has been set up with a room and the Davegu is in the hold. Guards are awaiting your orders."

Lisynia took a deep, shaky breath, preparing herself to enter back into the part of her mind she hated the most. The general, the leader, the hardass. "Good," she said, her voice deepening on command, acting the part. "I'll head down right away."

The corners of Otto's mouth lifted a bit as he chuckled under his breath. "Of course, General. Do you want me with you?"

Yes. Oh, absolutely. But that's not what she said. She shook her head and quickly moved away from her only true friend here, the man that knew her best. Lisynia cleared the space between her and the entrance to the dungeon quickly. Several guards stood at the entrance, the reflection of the lantern's firelight dancing in their helmets. She'd doubled the guard presence since the two Lupegi escaped and sent teams out after them to no avail yet. Hanue, son of Tanue, was lost to her at this moment.

With a Davegu soldier here now, she'd have to triple the manpower, just to be safe.

The guards parted in the center, letting her saunter through them, trying to exude an air of confidence she knew she didn't possess. Lisynia threw the door open and stepped down the stairs quickly, desperate to get away from all the eyes watching her—always watching her. Her fingers traced the gems in the dagger at her hip mindlessly, soothing her thoughts as she descended into the darkness.

It was silent.

When the Lupegi had come in, she had approached whimpers and low voices but now only complete silence greeted her. She tried to quell her discomfort, reminding herself of the pathetic nature of the man she approached.

The darkness enveloped her, dim lanterns casting a glow on the stone walls. She moved past the first cell, her eyes slowly adjusting, then the second, then, finally, the third. The one Hanue, son of Tanue resided in. She gulped before making herself visible and put on a cool, stony exterior, one she had lots of practice portraying. Then she moved into view of the cell.

The Davegu man stood still in the darkness, unmoving. His small, sickly yellow eyes were trained on her, watching her intently as she pulled up the chair and sat down in front of him.

They stared at each other in silence for several moments, her studying the man's face. He was gaunt in the face, but his body was quite built, taller than her by several hands. The armor he wore was ill fitting and loose on his body, a sight that chilled her to the bone. How large was the average Davegu that they were going to face in battle? He had stringy black hair, hanging below his shoulders and a large squash nose.

"Who are you?" she finally asked, breaking the silence.

"My name is Molac Kludishav. Davegu diplomat," he said simply, his voice wavering slightly. For being such a burly man, he sure seemed scared of her.

"General Lisynia," she said, gesturing vaguely toward herself. "Why are you in Andyse?"

Molac gulped loudly as Lisynia's eyes focused on his face, watching, waiting. He shifted his weight on his feet nervously. "I'm trying to get a message to Xienee from Queen Meluth."

Her stony-faced act almost dropped at this assertion. What message could the Queen of Davegu possibly have for Xienee? Her heart began to pound, theories running wild in her head. Were her people at risk?

She took a small breath, her fingers tracing the dagger's hilt faster now. "What message would that be?"

The man in front of her began shaking slightly. "It's a warning. The king is going to kill you all."

Anger boiled her body at his words, and she rushed to the bars, pushing her face against them, nose to nose with the man inside. "Is that a threat?"

Molac stumbled backwards, nearly falling off the step in the cell. He shook his head violently as he struggled to maintain his balance. "No. The queen doesn't want war. The king killed the Southern Coalition against her wishes. He's been psychotic lately, turning on his aristocrats and..." he trailed off.

Lisynia backed away from the bars slightly, still keeping her hands firmly wrapped around the cool metal. "I know he attacked the Southern Coalition. They joined us."

"They joined the Northlands?" he said nervously, standing at the very edge of the step. He gulped.

She smiled a mischievous grin. "No. The Teveban."

Molac scoffed slightly. "The Teveban don't exist. They're an old legend, a fairytale."

Her smile grew wider, baring her teeth as she pushed her hands through the bars reaching out for the man. "Are you willing to bet your life on that?"

Her fingertips tingled, a numbing feeling spreading through her arm. Small sparks of power flew out of the tips of her fingers, reaching further out for him in the darkness. Lisynia knew it was a bluff, the sparks would simply freeze his muscles, not cause any actual harm but he backed away quickly, the sparks fizzling out in the air.

His breathing quickened as he gulped loudly. "So, it's true? It's real?"

"Do I look real to you?"

He nodded quickly, hyperventilating now.

Pathetic.

Lisynia chuckled softly. "I think we're going to be good friends, Molac."

Chapter Twenty-Two
Anavi

Anavi's heart pounded in her chest as she ran through the tall grass, her boots catching on the dead strings below. No sign of her brother anywhere. For days. Where the fuck was he? She could not possibly go back to Jovan without Hanue; that was a failure. And she did not fail.

The river that separated north from south ran along the right of her, pounding through the earth like her feet. The sound deafened her, the only thing she could hear except her own ragged breathing.

She slowed her pace, coming to a stop as her legs burned with the effort of running so much. She peered around her, the faint light of a cloudy morning illuminating the world around her. Just grass and water and rocks. No sign of life anywhere. She'd kill it anyway. She'd kill everyone except her brother if it meant getting him back and completing her mission. She knew it wasn't a good idea to bring him here, to separate from him. But The Seven and their missions demanded blood when they wanted blood and who was she to not oblige?

If any of the settlers survived, they would've headed toward the land of the Southern Coalition, just beyond the river. If her brother was alive, he was certainly there, right? And he had to be alive, she knew it, she just did.

Her breathing slowed as she bent down, dunking her fingertips into the rushing water, almost willing it to tell her what it had seen. The shock of cold invigorated her, cooling her burning muscles.

Going south was not a good idea, she knew that. She'd blown her cover to their leader long ago. He would try to kill her sooner than help her. But there was no other choice. If Hanue wasn't dead, he was there. She would go south. Anavi would kill the whole camp to bring her brother back if necessary.

She raised herself up, shaking the water from her fingers and pounced onto a large rock within the river. She wobbled as her feet slid across its wet surface. "Shit," she said under her breath. She thrust her arms out to her sides, regaining a semblance of balance. She looked around, searching the waters for another foothold.

Another large flat rock lay beneath about a fingertip's worth of slower moving water a small jump away. She steeled herself as water soaked into the skin of her feet and jumped, landing on all fours on the surface. The water stung her body at the touch, sending shockwaves of freezing cold through her skin. She pushed from her hands and came back to standing on two feet. She was close to the shore now, closer to finding her brother, closer to getting the fuck out of this wasteland and back to The Seven.

She jumped again, landing with a roll on the shore. Anavi burst to her feet and broke into a run, headed south. Her breath heaved out of her mouth, the cold of the early morning frosting it as she ran. The water of the river soaked her clothes, sticking to her body, to her legs as she ran.

Anavi ran and ran until the sun was fully covered by clouds, darkness cast over the world. She ran until her muscles screamed and her breath came only in short bursts. Her sword hit her leg over and over, with every step, a small trickle of blood running below her pants, mixing with the river water. The world around her transformed from dead, yellow grass to greens and browns as the rushing of the river faded away.

She was going to find him, for Jovan.

But he was gone.

Hot tears built behind her eyes, blurring her vision. Her brother was gone. Gone. Like he never existed. Just like her father that fateful day. She couldn't lose Hanue too; she couldn't go back to Jovan empty handed. She'd failed him once before; she couldn't do that again.

She slowed her pace again as tears spilled out of her eyes. The ground met her knees, cold hard packed dirt digging through her pants. He was gone. She'd failed.

Anavi lowered herself fully to the ground, the dirt siphoning the heat from her body. The tears came silently as they always did.

He was gone.

Pulling her long blouse over her knees, she cradled herself in her own arms as sobs racked her body, drowning her in waves. Pain ebbed through her body, adding to the burning pain of her legs and lungs as she cried into her hands.

The sky above her wailed with her as she sat, motionless, silent, letting her own tears soak her face and hands while the rain soaked her back, each drop a tiny pinprick of freezing cold.

He was gone.

Why did she let him come? She pictured him as a child, a toothy smile on his little face as he came running to her, cute grubby little hands outstretched for his sister. Memories came bursting through her mind—his fear when their father disappeared, the anger when she took over the household, the pride she had when he got accepted to the smithing school in Aethiel. He had made the very weapons she carried with her now. And he was gone. Hanue was gone.

She'd failed The Seven. They told her to keep him safe, to fulfill this mission, and to use it as a training opportunity. And she *lost* Hanue.

Agony poured out of her in the form of screams now, wailing into her hands. "Where are you? Where are you?" She shook violently as her scratchy voice reached her own ears, burrowing into her brain. How was she going to ever find him?

A clang pounded over her screams. Just like the clang of Hanue's hammer on hot metal. She smiled a bit now, the tears still pouring without reprieve. It clanged again. And again. And again.

Wait.

She shot her head up, shaking the tears from her eyes. She pushed off from the muddy ground, rain pouring down now. The clouds blocked every hint of sun around her, the rain obscuring her vision even in midday.

The clang came again, and she forced her shaky hand to her sword's hilt, steadying it slightly. Her blood pumped as she stared through the rain and grass, searching for the source. Multiple figures emerged from the darkness running toward her, black armor blending them into the sky's darkness.

Davegu.

She raised her sword as they approached, steeling herself for a fight. They weren't here for anything good. "What do you want?" she shouted over the rain.

The figures did not answer, instead unsheathing their swords, blades pointed right at her. Her heart dropped. More came into view in her periphery, approaching from the side, swords drawn, bows pulled back. She backed up, her feet moving slowly as she held her sword up. Fuck.

The largest figure in front rushed her. Anavi dropped her sword and reached below her blouse. She pulled her throwing knives that Hanue had custom made for her.

Anavi let the first loose at the figure coming toward her, the blade spinning in the air before landing in his neck, between his breastplate and helmet. He fell to his knees.

She spun toward the right, throwing the second with a gusto that made her arm scream from the effort. He landed in the grass with a slight gurgle.

Anavi turned to face the figures in front of her again. Something whistled through the air toward her. Then, agony exploded in her knee. Her legs gave out beneath her, and she landed roughly in the mud. Pain screamed through her body, emanating from her leg as she dragged herself through the mud, the slimy substance offering no traction. The

Davegu approached her, swords pointed right at her. She was going to die. The arrow in her leg protested her movements as she desperately pulled herself away.

They raised their swords. She closed her eyes, thinking only of The Seven. Her heart pounded and pounded and pounded, the sound deafening her as blood rushed in her ears.

"Hold," the one closest to her said. She opened her eyes, and a man stared at her from behind a helmet, holding one of her knives. Confusion mixed with the pain. "Lupegi knives. She's one of Jovan's. The king will want her alive."

The man twisted his sword in his hand as she reached for her last knife. She'd be damned if they took her without a fight. But a hilt came down on her skull and the world went black.

CHAPTER TWENTY-THREE
RAUNA

"We need to go to The Seven," the boy that came with Gaabi said, his voice rising.

Rauna's patience with him was wearing thin; she drummed her fingers on her crossed arms, Gaabi behind her. Since she had realized Tivea was leaving alone and had decided to join her, the bickering had been nonstop.

"Do you think they protect you? Do you think they'll care? I already said I'm not going, not right now."

He scoffed, throwing his arms in the air as he walked toward the mouth of the cave. "What issue do you have with them? Why not leave? You got a death wish or something?"

Rauna rolled her eyes, glancing at Tivea who sat outside the cave about twenty paces, away from the bickering, having lost patience with the lot of them after about ten minutes. She sat upright, her arms extended into the leaves that littered the forest floor. She ran her fingers along them slowly, her head dipped down to look at her journal. Rauna smiled slightly.

As Hanue cleared his throat, Rauna pulled her eyes away from Tivea and back to him. "You know nothing of The Seven if you think they care about us. You're rich, right? A smith for the Sevensguards? Your sister works for them? Do you truly not know how little they care about us? They're the ones that sent Gaabi here in the first place. They'd rather kill us to hide their failure than actually help us." She crossed her arms over her chest tighter. "That woman out there saved my life over and over. She found Gaabi for me after the men you think are gods sent her to die." Rauna reached her hand back to Gaabi's, pulling her toward her. Her warm body pressed against Rauna's back, just like when they slept in the same bed in that single room. "I need to help her; I owe her that much. And honestly, so do you."

Hanue scoffed again, louder this time. "I don't owe her shit."

"She saved your life," Rauna said through gritted teeth. *Ungrateful brat.*

"No, she saved your sister, I was a side effect," he retorted, a vein in his forehead popping out.

Heat spread through Rauna's body at his accusation. "She saved you and my sister from a death The Seven sent both of you to! The Davegu are attacking her people, and you want to turn a blind eye? Do you really think The Seven will give a shit about any of this before it reaches their gates?" she spat, trying to hold herself back from punching him. This kind of attitude, this nonsensical worship of undeserving men was one of the biggest reasons why she left Aethiel. "I gave her my word and maybe a person's word doesn't mean much to someone that lives in The Seven's pocket like you, but to me, it means the world."

Hanue's face twisted, his fist clenching at his side "Do you understand what's in that mountain? What we escaped from? I'd rather take my chances with The Seven than what's in that fortress."

Rauna dug her fingernails into her arms, trying to calm herself down. She opened her mouth to speak but before she could, Gaabi's voice chimed in. "Both of you, stop it."

Rauna sighed in relief at her sister joining in. "Listen to her, she's smarter than all of us."

"We do need to get out of here, but there's no need to be rude about it." She pointedly glared at Rauna, then Hanue.

"Nevermind, don't listen to her," Rauna said, scoffing.

Gaabi sighed deeply, touching Rauna's hand with her fingertips. "Why do you actually want to stay?" she said softly, her hazel eyes willing an answer from her. "We could just stop in Lasari; I bet Hanue would even agree to pretend he never met us."

Rauna sighed deeply, her eyes wandering back to Tivea outside the cave. She looked so peaceful sitting there, feeling the leaves, like when she cuddled up to her leg when they slept last night, like when she talked about her clorhestas, like when they walked through the woods together to gather water. She couldn't leave her here alone, to suffer, to die at the hands of a Davegu soldier.

"She saved me," Rauna finally said, still staring at Tivea. "I wouldn't have ever found you if she didn't help me." Rauna smiled, turning her face back toward Gaabi's.

Gaabi smiled back.

Rauna continued, "I need to help her find her family too."

"So, you do have a death wish!" Hanue said, breaking the peaceful serenity Rauna felt with his grating, whiny voice.

"Look," Rauna said. She took a deep breath, calming herself slightly. "How about this—I want Gaabi safe and you're right, she's not safe here and she's certainly not safe if The Seven hear about her. But I need to help Tivea." At the mention of her name, Rauna caught Tivea turning slightly toward the conversation, a worried expression on her face. "What if you guys take that mountain path you and your sister took? Wait for me at the top and me and Tivea will look for your sister and find her father. When we all meet back again, Gaabi and I will stay in Lasari. You and your sister never saw us."

Gaabi grabbed her hand, squeezing it tightly. "I'm not leaving you again," she said softly, sweetly.

Rauna squeezed her hand back, ignoring her protests and awaiting an answer from the boy.

He mulled it over for a second, his face twisted in thought. Annoyance crept into her mind. Tivea wanted to leave already. She was waiting for an answer.

Just hurry it up.

Finally, Hanue opened his mouth. "Fine. You find my sister and we all leave. If you take too long, we'll leave without you. I'm not letting Gaabi stay here."

Gaabi spoke quickly, a tinge of anger in her voice. It was the way she always reacted when she didn't get her way, a trait that Rauna found endearing, adorable. "I'm not leaving her, Hanue. I just found her. She's coming with us or I'm not going."

Rauna turned toward her sister, taking her other hand into hers as well. She squeezed her sister's soft hands with her calloused ones. "Gaabi, this is what's best. I promise I'll be okay. I'll be home before you know it." She looked at her sister, trying to convey the love and care and happiness she felt at being able to hold her hands again after so long. "Hanue will get you home safely. You even said yourself that you need to leave. But I don't need to, I need to do this."

Tears flowed down Gaabi's cheeks as she squeezed her eyes shut and for a second the girl in front of Rauna was not her eighteen namedays old little sister, she was the kid that cried every time she left for work, the little girl with messy hair asking when their parents were coming back, the kid that sobbed when they packed up the wagon to move from Aethiel to Lasari. Rauna pulled her into her chest, enveloping her tightly in a warm embrace. She ran her hands over the top of her messy knotted hair, just like she always did when she cried. A sting of guilt pulled at her heart at the idea of leaving her. But Rauna needed to help. And Gaabi needed to be safe.

"I'll be home before you know it. And if anyone asks, you *never* came to Andyse. Ever."

"Mom and Dad said they'd be home before I knew it too," Gaabi said, her voice muffled by Rauna's shirt.

Her words were like a deadly blow to the heart and tears spilled from Rauna's eyes too, dripping into Gaabi's hair as she cried. She'd have to tell her the truth about their parents soon, the reason their mother never came home and why their father never woke up. But that was a box of snakes Rauna was not ready to open yet.

Rauna wiped her face with the tips of her fingers, pulling slowly from the embrace. Gaabi's face was splotchy and red, streaks running down her cheeks. "I promise I'll be alright," Rauna said, forcing a smile onto her face despite the pain.

Gaabi's face twisted into a mixture of anger and incredulousness. "I can't believe you're doing this."

Rauna exhaled sharply, turning her attention back to the woman at the mouth of the cave, a slight breeze blowing her long brown hair to the side, a serene smile on her face, eyes closed, beautiful. "I can't either," she finally said, a smile creeping onto her own face.

The four of them walked through the forest, headed north toward the secret pass Hanue had mentioned he used with his sister. Rauna held Gaabi's hand in her own, the idea of leaving her alone again beginning to weigh horribly on her.

She'll be safe. She'll be in Lupegi. The Seven will never know.

Rauna's eyes kept flitting back to Tivea's figure, slightly ahead of them, walking silently through the fallen leaves, like she weighed nothing at all. Her clothes were dirty and torn, her body shivering under the beaten-up animal hides she wore. Rauna was cold too, the biting wind chilling her to her bones. It was going to be a long walk to Xienee's camp.

Out of the corner of her eye, Rauna caught Gaabi throwing flitting glances toward the boy, her little sister's lips upturned in a small smile.

The boy, Hanue, muttered under his breath, annoyed words and curses of Rauna's stubbornness, words she pretended not to hear. It wouldn't matter soon anyway. And plus, he was getting Gaabi out of here. However unbearable he was, he was doing her a great favor and Gaabi seemed to like him enough. He bumbled through the woods, probably used to the riches of Aethiel streets instead of the mud and muck.

She hated the people of Aethiel, with their posh accents and sneering faces, always looking down at everyone they considered below them and Hanue was no different. An arrogant little brat. The fact he even cared at all about Gaabi, or his own sister, was nothing short of a miracle.

But she pushed those thoughts from her mind as Tivea suddenly stopped, quick enough that Hanue nearly ran into her.

"Sorry," he muttered, an air to his voice that suggested quite the opposite.

"What is it?" Rauna whispered to her.

"We're being watched."

Hanue scoffed again, "How could you possibly know that?"

Tivea turned on her heel, raising a finger to her lips. "The trees told me."

"Oh, you've gotta be kidding me," Hanue said incredulously. "The fucking trees?"

Rauna exhaled again, pinching the boy's arm harshly. "Shut up."

Tivea ignored the slight from Hanue, peering around his head at the woods behind them. Rauna released Gaabi's hand and turned herself, facing the same direction. Behind her, Tivea rustled, pulling the Davegu sword from her belt and pushing it toward Rauna, who took it, her hands growing sweaty at the thought of having to use it. Was she even holding it right? "How far is that pass, Hanue?"

Hanue gulped now, the seriousness of the situation seeming to finally kick in for him. "Far, about a full day's walk. We'll not get there before morning."

Rauna searched the woods, her eyes scanning every log, branch, tree, and leaf, looking for something, anything, to jump out at her. A branch cracked in the distance, low voices barely carrying.

Shit.

Rauna turned quickly to Gaabi again, staring into her little sister's bright, watery eyes. "Go with Hanue, get to the pass."

Gaabi protested but Hanue jumped into action, grabbing her by the waist and ripping her away.

"I'll get her home safe," he said, breaking into a slight jog as Gaabi struggled against his hold.

"Rauna! No, please! Come with us!" Gaabi's voice was raw, the visceral emotion of her pleas punching Rauna in the gut.

As her voice faded away into the forest, Tivea inched forward. Rauna steeled herself, pushing her sister's cries from her mind. The leaves crunched beneath her feet as she stepped lightly onto them. Voices got closer, louder. "The Lupegi prisoners! Come on!"

The sword in her hand became heavy with the idea of a fight but she gripped it tightly, attempting to stop her hands from shaking. As the men approached, Tivea whipped out her journal, sifting through the pages before outstretching her hand and causing a thick wall of vines to burst from the trees, grabbing at the three men as they came within distance. They fell to the vines, whipped into tree trunks as Tivea muttered something under her breath.

Though she had seen it before, Rauna found herself shaking worse than before at Tivea's power on full display.

Tivea breathed heavily next to her, turning to stow her journal back in her satchel. The third man wriggled from the vines that tried to bind him and sprinted toward them, his mouth open in a roar as he raised his sword, heading straight for the distracted Tivea.

Before she could think of what to do, Rauna pushed Tivea out of the way and thrust the sword awkwardly toward the man's stomach. A stray vine whipped around his hand, jerking him to the side and right into Rauna's blade.

He whimpered, clutching with his other hand at the blade running through his stomach. Rauna could not focus on anything except the blood dripping slowly from his wound, his face twisted in pain only a few hands in front of her.

Her legs buckled, her stomach contorting painfully. Slowly, she pulled the sword from his body, the flesh squishing as the blade moved. Rauna fought the urge to throw up.

He was still breathing. He was alive. His eyes still moved. Did she kill him? She didn't kill him. But he was going to die?

Her father's face, drunken and blotchy red flashed in her mind, his hands clawing at her just like this man clawed at the blade.

Her breath heaved in and out of her chest quickly as Tivea finished stowing her journal and shouting erupted from the other two men.

"Run," Tivea said, breaking into a sprint eastward, dragging Rauna away from the bloody scene behind them and the memories she'd suppressed.

CHAPTER TWENTY-FOUR
HANUE

Gaabi thrashed against him as the ground shook beneath his feet. She bit and kicked and punched, sending sharp bursts of pain through his body.

"Gaabi," he said, his voice coming out strained as he ran, tightly holding her against his chest. She gave no acknowledgement of hearing him, her fist meeting his shoulder again. "Gaabi!"

"Put me down!" she half-whispered, half-shouted. "Put me down! Rauna!"

Hanue glanced quickly over his shoulder to the two women behind him running in the distance, men wearing leather armor flailing about in a mess of vines. "She made her decision."

"She'll be killed!" Gaabi said frantically, wriggling her way from his grasp. She fell to the ground in front of him and scampered to her feet.

Hanue thrust his arms out, catching her in the stomach as she let out a sharp gasp. He picked her up again, raising her over his shoulder as he struggled to catch his breath. "Calm down!" he hissed as she struggled to free herself again. "Gaabi, stop! It's alright, it's alright."

Gaabi's energy seemed to fade as her struggles became slower, less painful to his body. After a few seconds she melted into his arms, the weight of her body heavier than before. He sighed in relief and began walking briskly, raising his feet high in the air to prevent them from being caught on the underbrush of the forest floor. Gaabi shook slightly, resolving herself to his hold. He kept walking.

As the light of day began to fade, Hanue reached his hand up slightly, stroking Gaabi's face as she cried. The weight of her suffering pulled at his heart. Anavi came to his mind as he jogged through the forest, listening intently for following footsteps. Where was she? Was she even alive? He thought of her warm voice, her slight chuckles when he presented her with her swords, the sword he lost when he was captured.

The trees around them swayed in the wind, their leaves falling to the ground around him as a strong gust swept through them. The brilliant bright colors of the world around him mocked the feelings of dread in his heart. He had to get Gaabi to Lasari then go to Timestone, traveling alone, his sister missing, probably dead at Xienee's blade. He had to warn The Seven of the happenings here. Getting out of this forest wasn't even half of the journey ahead of him.

As no voices followed them, as Gaabi shook more violently in his arms, as he absentmindedly rubbed his fingers along her face, his thoughts strayed further, back to the dungeon they were in all too recently.

The general, with her pin straight blonde hair and skin that glowed in lantern light. The legend of the people of the mountains, magical, powerful, deadly. The Davegu soldier that hung herself upon capture. The look on the general's face at the mention of his crazy father, one of recognition and pain. And Rauna and Gaabi's distrust of The Seven. What did all of it mean?

Hanue slowed his pace as the light left and turned on his heel. The wall of trees wasn't visible now; how much distance they had made, he did not know. But the sky turned orange around them, the color of the flowers he would always pick in the fields for Anavi upon her return from some random mission to welcome her home.

He let out a small, pained groan at the thought of his sister, her head bleeding on a pike in Xienee's camp.

No, she was smarter than that. She was probably already back to Aethiel by now, getting ready to head to Timestone herself. She had to be. She *had* to be.

Hanue slowly lowered Gaabi to the dead leaves below. His arms ached with the effort of carrying her this far and as he put her down, he rubbed his biceps, trying to get the soreness to dissipate.

"I'm sorry," Gaabi squeaked out, her voice small and raw, barely reaching Hanue's ears.

This was what he needed to snap him back to reality. The trees came into better focus, the sky casting deep oranges on the frost that sparkled on the branches.

"After we lost our parents, Rauna's all I've had. I'm sorry."

He shook his head, lowering himself to the ground with her, sitting cross legged in front of her. He reached a hand out tentatively, raising her face to his. The sight of her face pained him, red, splotchy, raw from the tears. "Gaabi," he said soothingly. "You have nothing to be sorry for. Nothing at all."

Gaabi shook her head quickly, pulling away from his touch. "No, she's going to die just like our parents," she hiccupped loudly, "I should've tried harder."

Hanue exhaled sharply. He couldn't really argue. Rauna had a death wish, staying here with Tivea. The Teveban were a story told to children to get them to behave, a boogeyman in the dark. And they were apparently real, and alive, and here of all places, hunting them. She was going to die.

But he couldn't say that. Instead, he took her hand from her lap and pressed his lips against her soft skin. She cried silently, lowering her head back down. Hanue wrapped his arms around her and pulled her into his chest. "It's okay, Gaabi. She'll be home right behind you."

The pale orange of the sky faded around them, the setting of the sun casting deep shadows over them as the trees danced in the wind. He held her to his body, letting her cry, letting her feel the pain of being ripped from her sister right after finding her. Especially given the hints of the way her parents disappeared. Before he could stop himself, he blurted out, "What happened to them? Your parents?"

Gaabi looked up at him with watery eyes for a second before turning her eyes downwards. "I don't know. Rauna came home when I was really young one day covered in blood and told me Mother was gone. Then, a few days later, Father never came back from the bar." She shivered. "They weren't really that great of people, but they were still our mother and father, you know?"

Hanue mulled this over for a second, thinking back to his own parents, the way Anavi had taken over for their parents too. He sighed. "My mother died when I was barely old enough to remember her and my father went crazy at the loss." Part of him was unsure if crazy was the right word to use anymore after what he had seen himself in the past few weeks. "My sister stepped up just like yours did. And if Rauna is anything like Anavi, she's smart. She's going to come back to you." The idea of singing Rauna's praises like this irked him slightly. He found her nothing short of insufferable. But Gaabi needed it, so he pushed his own feelings down. "She's smart and she loves you like Anavi loves me. She'll be alright."

At the mention of Anavi's name, Gaabi looked up, her eyes flashing with what seemed to be a hint of recognition. She began to shake harder and Hanue's breath quickened, hoping, praying to The Seven that it was a fluke. Anavi was not well-liked in most of Lupegi, and he really wanted this woman in front of him to like him. After a second, Gaabi looked back up at him, her face stoic once again. "Thank you, Hanue. She'll come back to you, too, I'm sure of it."

His chest swelled at the sweet sound of her voice and the lack of anger at his sister's name. Against his better judgment, he let a goofy smile across his face. "Let's get going, find somewhere to hole up for the night."

Chapter Twenty-Five
Lisynia

S eek the truth in me, Lisynia.
Seek the truth in me.
Seek the truth.

Lisynia woke with a jolt, a cold spot drenching her bedsheets. She glanced around her, half expecting to see the figure of the Goddess in the darkness watching her as she slept. The room was dark, only lit by the lantern in the windowsill, crackling all through the night. The sun had not yet risen, and she jumped from her bed, grabbing the lantern to search her quarters.

Lisynia swung it wildly around the room, illuminating her desk, papers strewn across it haphazardly, her chairs for her and her top strategists, her bed, disheveled and messy. But nothing jumped out at her. She exhaled deeply, sweat pouring off her body.

"Just calm down," she whispered to herself, forcing her breathing to slow from the frenzy it was in.

The Ancient's words had come to her in her dreams every night, plaguing her every waking thought, never leaving her mind.

What did it mean?

A knock sounded at the door, and she jumped at the sudden intrusion. "Come in," she said meekly.

The door opened slowly, revealing the messenger boy from before, Ason. His eyes widened at the sight of her, and he just stared for a second. Confusion gnawed at Lisynia's mind at the boy's shock, and only then did she realize how crazy she must look. She glanced into the mirror above her desk, catching a sight of the woman he stared at. Her hair was wild and knotted from restless sleep, a sweat-soaked gray nightgown hugged her body, and a look of pure, unbridled disturbance was etched on her haggard face.

She looked like Catina the last few days before her death, worn out and exhausted. Lisynia sighed, turning her attention back to the boy, pushing down the embarrassment she felt.

Ason seemed to be over the shock of seeing her that way and opened his mouth to talk. "General, Xienee wished for me to send for you," he said, the high pitch of his voice tugging on her heart. He was so young, so very young and all armored for war. She pushed this thought from her mind as he spoke again, "It's time for training."

Lisynia nodded at him. "Thank you, I'll meet you down there."

The boy nodded and closed the door, the lock clicking shut behind him.

Her heart pounded in her ears as she quickly made her way to the desk, looking over the notes and papers from the night before. War plans, paths to get to Oshgor with the least detection, headcounts of her forces plus Xienee's and the few of Yidenu's that had joined the effort. 3,500 strong all together. Her breath shook as it exited her mouth, her hands shaky as they shuffled the papers around. The time to advance on the king quickly approached and, with the voices in her head, she couldn't help but wonder if it was a good idea.

It was. It had to be. She had to do this. Her thoughts drifted from the war plans to the faces of her people, gaunt from years of malnutrition, hiding in their homes when the raids came through. She had to do this.

An anger in her reignited; she grasped the quill and slammed it in the inkwell, splashing ink over her papers and plans. With one shaky hand, she scratched out three words onto a blank sheet of parchment.

Kill the king.

The armor fit her body snugly, made specially for her by Otto from when he used to be Teveban's leatherworker. Her feet made their way down the staircase toward the main foyer of their own accord, as if she wasn't even controlling them herself. A group had already gathered at the bottom of the staircase, a mass about 200 strong, the first rounds of her people to be trained.

Xienee stood at the helm of the group, saying something that didn't quite reach Lisynia's ears. As she got closer, the faces of her people came into view, tired, worn out from the long days and nights in the training grounds outside. Yet another long day sat ahead of them. Lisynia gently nudged her way through the crowd who parted slightly to let her pass as Xienee's words reached her.

"This will be rough—a hard day of intense training. We are going against a force so strong, so formidable, that we have long lived in fear of them. But we will not fail." Her voice was overwhelming, echoing off the stone walls and even though Lisynia knew the way the Davegu fought, Xienee's words still struck a chord of fear in her mind.

Steeling herself, she kept moving, arriving now at the head of the crowd, at Xienee's side. The commander nodded pointedly at her and Lisynia's mind blanked for a second. Her eyes wandered in the crowd in front of her, faces young and old, frail and strong, the faces of a people oppressed, the faces of Teveban. Her eyes settled on Ason, his young face so full of hope, a glimmer in his eyes that hadn't quite been extinguished. She smiled.

"We are going to war!" she shouted, quickly raising her dagger in the air.

Several in the crowd jumped as the others murmured amongst themselves at the sudden volume of her words. "We are going to war, and we will win! They have magics, they have armor, better than ours. They have training and weapons we do not. But do you know what they don't have?" she paused, her eyes searching the crowd. Ason jumped in place a bit, his face eager.

"Us!" Ason shouted, his voice echoing across the foyer.

Lisynia's eyes trained on him and only him. She lowered her dagger, beckoning him toward her. He withdrew from the crowd slowly, the murmurs louder now as the crowd got worked up. He reached her side, and she grabbed his hand, thrusting it into the air with hers. "He's right. They don't have us! They will never have us again. That is what we fight for: our children, our families, our homeland! We fight for each other, every person in this room fights for the person alongside them, friends, family, neighbors. We fight for us, and they fight for nothing but greed! We fight for us!"

Ason chuckled slightly beside her, giddy with excitement. The crowd roared its agreement, the intensity of their cheers tearing into Lisynia's body. Xienee roared next to her, a visceral anger in her scream. Her hand suddenly grasped Lisynia's other one and shot into the air as well.

"We fight for us!" Xienee screamed.

The crowd screamed with her, a cacophony of unthinking, instinctive roars, of pain, of anger, of fear, of rage, of hope.

Hope. Lisynia's chest swelled as she stared at the group in front of her, screaming, yelling, thrusting their weapons into the air. They were going to fight. They were going to find out the truth. They were going to march and scream and win. They were going to win.

She let a small smile cross her face. They were going to win this battle; they were going to learn the truth. She was finally, after all these years, going to know what Catina and Tanue died to protect, the thing she had been searching for all these years.

She was going to finally, finally, get the truth. Either through war, her Davegu prisoner, or that Lupegi boy somewhere in the woods.

Lisynia glanced again at the people in front of her, screaming, ready to fight, and Xienee's hand touched her back. So Xienee had gotten over her upset, it appeared.

The woman spoke softly, leaning in toward Lisynia, her lips almost touching her ear. "The value of a leader is how many people they can get to fight and die for them, and Lisynia, they would die for you."

Lisynia pushed Xienee's hand away with a fervor, her happiness overtaken by disgust at the woman's words. She took a deep breath, quelling the anger that boiled within her. "And I would for them. They are my home, and I am theirs." She turned back to her people, the faces of everyone she'd ever known cheering, their yells echoing in a beautiful orchestra of hope. "I would do anything for them," she said, her voice strained from holding back her rage. "That is the true value of a leader. And you would do well to know that."

The leaves beneath her boots sounded their protest at her footfalls as she moved, a flurry in the air. Her sword hit the dummy again, a satisfying thud reaching her ears as stuffing seeped out of the hole she tore in the burlap.

Lisynia hit it again, harder, her mind consumed with the need to kill the face she pictured on the dummy. The king. She had to kill the king.

She stabbed at the burlap sack that constituted a head, heat bursting through her veins with each movement. She stabbed it again, again, again, a scream building up inside her throat as her mind focused on all he had done. Killing her people, trading them as slaves, working with the Lupegi to keep them down. Killing her twin sister for daring to disobey.

No more.

She was going to kill him herself.

The scream burst from her mouth; it tore at her throat as it exited her body. She stuck her sword through the sack one more time before pulling it. She smiled as she imagined the gush of red that would spurt from his neck.

Breathing heavily, she stepped back from the dummy. The leaves once again sounded their disapproval. Her chest rose and fell quickly, the adrenaline still coursing through her veins. Her arms shook beside her.

A rustling sounded behind her and she stopped. It came from the direction of Ryrie but the footfalls were too heavy to be her people or even Xienee's. Davegu. She had seen their scouting groups, rounding up stragglers in the plains. Blood pounded through her head, and she listened intently. It came again.

They'd never come this close to Ryrie before.

Turning on her heel, she inspected the forest, her eyes moving slowly across the trees. Then something caught her eye, a flitter in the distance ducking behind a tree. She stepped toward it, unsheathing the dagger at her side.

"Show yourself," she demanded. She took a heavy step toward the tree, raising her dagger.

A sudden burst of sound greeted her as a man jumped out from behind the tree, Davegu sword raised in the air aiming right for her head. Lisynia ducked and thrust her elbow up, catching the man below the chin. He howled, stumbling backwards.

She raised herself back to her feet as he took another swing at her, his sword gliding through the air with a vicious speed.

A sharp burst of pain exploded on her arm at the blade's contact, ripping through her flesh. Lisynia stepped backwards, a rage building within her.

Kill him.

She moved toward him with a fury, thrashing her dagger through the air as she advanced. Blood streamed down her arm, coating her hand with sticky red fluid. The soldier backed up, fear glimmering in his eyes.

A smile burst onto her face as her bloodlust grew. She thrust her body at his, knocking him to the ground. With one hand she pulled the sword from his, the blade biting into the flesh of her palm, and threw it to the side. Pulling her knees up, she pinned his arms to the ground. She ripped his helmet from his head, revealing a boy, absolute terror twisting his features.

Lisynia turned the dagger in her hand and rammed the hilt into his mouth. His teeth broke with a satisfying crunch, and he screamed, a horrifyingly gruesome sound. She relished the whimpers that escaped his deformed jaw.

A flow of blood rushed from his mouth, dribbling down his broken jaw. Tears welled in his eyes as he thrashed against her hold and Lisynia's smile grew. He blubbered something incomprehensible, obviously pleading.

Lisynia threw her head back in laughter and then jutted her face right up to his mangled and beaten one. "That's right. *Beg*."

"Lisynia!" a voice called out from behind her and heavy footfalls rushed her way.

She glowered at the man below her and sighed. His eyes flashed in terror as she raised her dagger again and pressed it slowly into his already bloodied neck. He gasped and choked on his own blood as the light faded from his eyes. Red spattered from his mouth as he drew in one last measly, ragged breath. Lisynia pulled her dagger and wiped it carelessly on her shirt.

The footsteps got closer, stopping in their tracks right behind her. "Lisy—" she recognized the voice.

Staring at the blank eyes of her opponent, taking in his deformed jaw and bloodied face, she spoke, "What is it, Otto?"

His hand grazed her back, a firm touch that she found herself leaning into. "Thank the Goddesses, you're okay. A group of Davegu soldiers just tried to storm Ryrie. Took out some guards but no one else.

One had escaped." He took a deep, shaky breath behind her. "But I guess you handled him..."

She sheathed her dagger and raised herself from the man's body. Turning to look at her closest advisor, taking in his appearance. He was sweaty, his blonde hair slicked across his forehead, a look of concern on his face.

A tinge of guilt hit her as she looked over her bloodied shoulder at the broken mess that was once human. Blood trickled from his mouth and neck, slowly dribbling down into the ferns below.

Her thoughts wandered back to the Ancient's words, her awakening this morning.

...In the holds of your oppressors.

She just killed one of them.

She sighed in embarrassment at the fact that Otto had to see this. But she would not apologize for doing what needed to be done.

"Are you hurt?" he asked softly, reaching out for her.

She sighed, finally letting herself calm down enough to feel her wounds. She spread out her hand, revealing a large, deep gash within it. "Only a little bit."

"Goddesses, Lisynia." Otto pressed his hand against the flow of blood from her wounds.

Lisynia raised her head defiantly and glared at Otto. "Enough of that." The Ancient's words still echoed in her mind. "We're taking the Davegu prisoner to the castle tonight."

Chapter Twenty-Six
Molac

It had been over a full day since he arrived in the second cell he had resided in in as many weeks. He couldn't seem to escape the prison walls, no matter where he went. What a laugh his father would have at him now.

But this one was different. He was surrounded by strangers, old legends and myths come alive. His fate was not sealed by an arena match of an insane king but rather by a woman with insane claims and blood-lust in her orange eyes.

He sat in the dark, hunched over in a cold corner where the light barely reached his eyes. He wrung his hands repeatedly, his thoughts running wild.

It was all a lie. Everything he knew was a lie. He thought back to the times he'd snuck from the manor to meet with Asmuto as a young child, the way the boys would hold candles below their chins, their faces dancing in soft candlelight as they exchanged spooky stories of the secret bloodthirsty people living in the mountains, snatching people from their beds to drink their lifeforce and dine on their flesh, peeling it from the bones.

Molac had walked into a childhood nightmare of which there was no waking.

His breathing became unsteady as his thoughts rested on Asmuto, oh what he didn't know. His chest rose and fell erratically as the handsome face of his friend danced in his mind, lit only from below as if the candles from their childhood were still there. The face opened its mouth wide, wide, wider still, razor sharp teeth and bloody gums opening to swallow him whole. Molac jumped, shaking his head wildly to remove the image from his brain.

"The darkness is just playing tricks on you, Molac," he reassured himself, wringing his hands quicker now.

A harsh light stung his eyes as a loud *clang* reached his ears; the door down the hallway must've opened. Footsteps. Someone was coming.

Molac scurried to his feet, standing below the step, staring at the wall beyond the bars, waiting, staring and waiting. He kept fidgeting with his hands, picking at his nails now.

The footsteps got louder, closer, the sound echoing off the empty stone walls. A man came into view from the right, his large figure drowning out the lantern light. He had ashy blonde hair and orange eyes, glimmering in the low light like a simmering fire. Wrapped in the same armor Lisynia had worn, the pieces of leather stretched across his body tightly, barely fitting over his muscles. He held a plate of hot food in one hand, the steam causing the stone bricks behind it to waver.

Molac gulped. Was it his time to die?

No, Meluth had said he had her protection.

But he was never supposed to be doing any of this peasant work anyway.

"The general wishes to see you now," he said gruffly. "Eat up."

The man thrust the food through the bars. It landed with a small thud a few hands away from Molac's feet. Hunger overpowered him as the smell of freshly cooked meat drifted to his nostrils. How long had it been since he'd eaten? Hours? Days?

Molac fell to his knees, shoveling the food in his mouth, barely even chewing before gulping it down like an animal.

The man sneered in disgust at Molac's piggery and Molac's face burned. This was not how an aristocrat should eat. "General, he's ready for you."

Molac paused his eating, chicken bone in hand, listening intently as more footsteps headed his way, quicker but softer than the man's. A chill came over his body. Lisynia.

Her familiar face came into view, glaring down at him. As he watched her sneer, his fists clenched. What he wouldn't give to wipe that superior look right off her face.

But he took a deep breath and raised himself to his feet as she spoke, dropping the chicken leg. "Thank you, Otto. You can go now."

"Yes, ma'am," the man, Otto, said, quickly moving away from the cell and disappearing into the hallway where Molac couldn't see him.

Lisynia stared at him motionless in the glimmering light, her face betraying no emotion. After a long time, she spoke. "Did you enjoy your food?"

He nodded slowly.

"Good," she said. "You need to keep your strength up."

At these words, Molac blinked quickly. What did she have in store for him? As ideas of him strung up by his hands, legs dangling below him or becoming food for the group of barbarians he resided with flew through his mind; she offered no explanation.

The general pulled up the same rickety, old chair, probably older than either of them and lowered herself onto it. "Are you ready to talk, Molac?"

No. No, he was not. But what choice did he have? He nodded slowly. Was it the grease of the chicken leg or the nervousness he felt choking him? His father's diplomacy training was obviously worth less than the dirt the man was buried in now.

Her orange eyes narrowed, and she leaned toward the bars. Molac gulped, holding his ground despite his brain screaming at him to back up, to run, to hide.

"What do you know of us?"

Molac exhaled, stepping slightly forward toward her. "I know that you don't exist," he said, his voice coming out shaky despite his efforts. He cringed at the fear in his words. Maybe that was due to his focus on 'diplomacy' training instead of something actually useful. "But I guess that was wrong."

The general's eyes narrowed more. "What do you know?" she repeated, her eyes so intense Molac could've sworn they bored right through him.

He wrung his hands, feeling all the curves and ridges of his fingers. How much should he tell her? "You're violent, more violent even than the Davegu," he said.

Her eyes flew open and Molac flinched. But she laughed, a terribly high-pitched noise that rattled his bones. "Well, that's true of some; but not all, I certainly am. Do you want to know what I know?"

He drew a shaky breath but couldn't quell his curiosity at the offer. "Yes."

She leaned back in her chair, its fragile legs creaking under the weight. "I know that your people are our enemies. Your king has treated us as filth, slaves, your people as if we are myth, evil stories told in the dark. But we are not that." She took a deep breath, her voice rising in volume, booming in the stone walls. Molac took a step back from the bars, backing deeper into the cold cell. "We are mothers and fathers, we are kindhearted and good. We have been enslaved for hundreds of years by you and the Lupegi to the west. We have been raped, tortured, beaten, and murdered under orders from your king. I've seen the violence you speak of, and I can tell you, it is not our doing. I have seen my sister hang, my father beaten, my friends killed. And you come here and speak to me of violence? What do you know of us?"

Molac's breath came quickly in and out of his mouth. His hands shook violently. She was going to kill him. "I know that you are real."

"We are real. What stories are told of us?"

"Legends," he said simply, his voice barely coming out of his mouth as his body shook. "Stories in the dark."

"Like what?" she hissed, leaning closer to the bars, sticking her hand through them, red sparks dancing between her fingers just like yesterday.

She smiled slightly as Molac took another step back, his back against the far wall of the cell now.

"An old Davegu king and The Seven killed you all to save their people the last time there was peace between the Davegu and Lupegi many years ago. I was told that it was an old story, no truth to it."

"There is some truth to it," she said cryptically. After a few seconds, she spoke again. "I will punish them. And you're going to help me."

The ropes cut into his wrists as Lisynia led him through the forest by a tight lead, cutting open his old wounds. His legs were jelly, protesting his very weight. His eyes struggled to adjust to the darkness of the world as she pulled the rope taut again.

The man to the side of them, Otto, stayed at a distance, his sword halfway drawn as his head swiveled around, peering at the trees around them. He trotted alongside them, his blade catching the light of the moon and shining into Molac's eyes. He grimaced and peered ahead at the clearing they headed toward.

Lisynia slowed her pace as they approached the edge of the clearing, the rope loosening around his wrists. She paused at the very edge, moonlight glinting in her blonde hair, waiting for his shaky legs to carry him closer to her.

A wave of relief washed over him as the moonlight hit his face, a sudden strength returning to his body. He jogged to the woman at the edge of the forest, holding back a smile as the wind blew his hair in his eyes. He wasn't free but, damn, it felt nice to be outside.

"Do you understand what I'm asking of you?" Lisynia asked, her voice low, barely reaching his ears.

He nodded quickly, the instructions drilled into his mind from her repeating them over and over before they left the cell. "We're going to

Teveban. I am to stay close. I am to stay quiet. I am to answer any questions asked. Then I will be free." His voice wavered at these last words and his mind strayed to the idea of getting back to Davegu, to Asmuto, to his manor. He never thought he'd miss the kingdom of blood.

"Good," she said sharply. "Stay close, Otto," she called to the man.

He grunted in response.

They sprinted through the clearing, Molac running awkwardly with his hands in front of him as the other two moved with the grace and agility of well-trained warriors. What had he gotten himself into? His mind strayed to her words in the dungeon.

I will punish them.

His heart threatened to beat out of his chest as he remembered the malice, the visceral rage in her voice. He took a deep breath, steeling himself as they slowed their pace.

"Otto," the blonde spoke, handing the edge of the rope over to her guard. "Take the prisoner, we're being followed. I'll catch up."

Molac watched her closely as her eyes flickered in the pale moonlight. She pulled a dagger from her belt and gripped it tightly. The man jerked the rope quickly and walked forward, Lisynia stepping in the opposite direction, blade raised.

"It'll be easier this way," the guard said, seeming to speak to himself. He turned quickly on his heel, headed toward Molac and his heart threatened to leave his body as the man approached. The man reached his hand out and touched Molac's forehead lightly, a tingle spreading from the spot of contact.

A deep chill spread through his body as he fell to the hard ground.

Fuck.

Molac tried to scream, but nothing came out; he couldn't move, he couldn't think. His eyes, the only thing that he *could* move, flitted around as Otto approached, his boots crunching the leaves beneath his feet. The man bent down, and Molac felt his arms around him and tried again to scream to no avail.

Otto heaved Molac over his shoulder, knocking the wind from

Molac's lungs as he faced the ground, ferns peeking out from beneath a bed of dead leaves. "Sorry," he said simply, "easier this way."

In the distance, there was a loud crashing of metal on metal. Using all the force he could muster to break whatever spell the guard had placed on him, he fought to raise his head. Otto ran, Molac's head bouncing ever so slightly as the man flew over the ground. Finally, Molac was able to keep his head still for a second longer and gaze upon the carnage behind them.

The general stood, covered in blood in the moonlight, three men at her feet. Each one had only one simple cut across their stomach or forehead, but they did not move. The men wore Davegu armor, a fact that caused another chill to shudder through his body. They did not groan in pain, laying still on the forest floor. Molac stared hard at the men and a horrifying discovery reached his mind.

It was the men he had traveled to Andyse with. His commanding officer's scowl was the same in death as it was in life.

Lisynia turned and ran toward him, sheathing her blood-soaked dagger with a demented smile on her face.

CHAPTER TWENTY-SEVEN
TIVEA

Tivea and Rauna crashed through the trees on their way to the open plains. As they approached, Tivea slowed her pace, falling behind as Rauna ran toward the tall grass. Tivea searched for any sign they were being followed, any far-off footsteps or faint crashing, but found nothing. They'd been running for hours. All they could do was hope that they'd left the Tevebrisian men far enough back yesterday.

Heavy breathing met her ears and Tivea looked back toward Rauna who now stood facing her, her expression contorted in pain. Whether it was from the exhaustion of running for so long or something else, Tivea didn't know. Rauna hadn't wanted to talk about the man she'd killed last night when they stopped to camp but Tivea had woken to her crying quietly, scrubbing her hands with a fervor.

"Why did you stop?" Rauna asked, her breath heaving.

"I wanted to talk," Tivea said as steadily as she could, the stitch in her chest worsening with each word.

Rauna swallowed hard, attempting to catch her breath. She put her hands on her hips and Tivea's heart fluttered, struck by the way the sun's light slipped through the canopy of trees and glistened on Rauna's face, highlighting her strong cheekbones and the tip of her lips. Tivea moved closer to her for some reason, focusing on Rauna's face, flushed and sweaty and yet still beautiful.

Rauna raised her eyebrows. "What is it?"

Tivea averted her eyes. "Why did you come? You didn't need to, you had your sister right there, you could've just gone back home and pretended this all never happened."

For some reason, the prospect of an answer to this question scared her and Tivea focused on the leaves that swayed in the wind instead of looking at Rauna.

"Do you know what happens to people that fail The Seven in Lupegi?"

This pulled Tivea's attention back and she shook her head. Rauna's face seemed to harden, her mind far off, someplace else.

"Gaabi failed their mission, and they wouldn't care about the circumstances or the reason why. They never would've sent anyone to find her," Rauna's voice cracked. "Ever. I was injured, a complete mess. You helped me more than I deserved. I have nothing in Lasari; I work at a shitty bar where the drinks cost more than I make in a week. Gaabi's all I have."

Maybe it was because Tivea had always known her own world in Andyse to be closely knit, people helping others mostly without question, but she felt a sense of dread creep into her at the thought of feeling utterly alone, even surrounded by people.

She opened her mouth to speak but Rauna took a deep breath and continued, "I can never repay you for getting Gaabi back to me. But now that she's safe, the least I can do is help you find your father."

Tivea nodded as Rauna seemed to come back from wherever her mind had gone. Rauna's eyes met hers, full of intensity, and Tivea stepped forward slowly, reaching a tentative hand out for Rauna's.

"Thank you," Tivea said, not entirely sure how else to respond. "It's okay if you want to go back to your sister. You don't owe me anything." She smiled shyly at the woman in front of her. "I promise."

Rauna's lips turned upwards with a smile that didn't quite reach her sad eyes. "Hold on," Rauna averted her eyes, "don't say that, I do owe you. And I know you were upset with me for that. I know I'm a lot sometimes and too brash. But I'm not stupid, Tivea. I know you were pissed with me."

Tivea couldn't help but feel a tinge of guilt as Rauna pulled her hand slowly away and turned back to the tall grass of the plains.

"No," Tivea sighed. "I mean yes, I was angry. I was very angry. My home was destroyed, and I was watching out for you instead of looking for my father."

Rauna's sad eyes turned angry now. "Why not say anything then? Why not leave?"

"My father taught me to help those that need it and you and Gaabi needed it," Tivea said slowly, trying to figure out the answer herself. "I wasn't angry at you. More the situation."

Rauna crossed her arms. "Well, you need to tell me if that happens again. I don't like secrets, Tivea. I will repay you for everything you did for me as much as I can. No matter what, I will help you find your father but please don't shut me out."

Tivea averted her eyes now, fidgeting with her fingernails. "I'm sorry."

"Don't apologize, you have no reason to. But if we're gonna keep watching each other's backs, we need to talk to each other." Rauna's fingers reached Tivea's arm, trailing along the furs she wore and Tivea shivered. "I want to help you. Just tell me how."

Tivea fought back a small smile, the touch of Rauna's hand shooting a blissful cool over her. "Alright. Well, let's start by getting to Xienee," she said, turning and pointing to the line of smoke in the distance.

The sky melted into brilliant oranges and pinks as the sun set over the mountains to their backs. A slight breeze swayed the grass, causing Tivea to shiver in her thin clothing. Xienee's camp was just up ahead, the smell of smoke and cooking meat tickling her nose as they approached.

Even from the distance they were at, the camp was vastly different than that of the Southern Coalition. Instead of longhouses, there were small, squat cabins and canvas tents of various sizes, fires crackling loudly along the sides of the path. As Tivea approached the camp, she rehearsed her speech to Xienee in her head.

What would she even say? Especially bringing a Lupegi woman with her, whatever she said would have to be enough to rouse Xienee's frail sense of loyalty to Yidenu or they'd be cut down where they stood.

Tivea walked slowly and low to the ground, the grass tickling her nose. Rauna crouched beside her, both of them trying to avoid alerting anyone in camp of their presence.

"Do you think she's there?" Rauna whispered, leaning in close to Tivea's ear.

Her skin tingled as Rauna's hot breath caressed her ear. Tivea pushed Rauna from her mind, shaking her head slightly.

She searched the camp's edges for any hint of Xienee's presence, the white horse she always rode when meeting with her father, or her advisor Torvo that always accompanied her. People milled about on the path, laughter reaching even this far. But Xienee's large figure and Torvo's long brown cloak weren't among the people she saw.

She squinted, jutting her head over the grass a little more to get a better view. Then her eyes settled on a man. A familiar balding head of long dark brown hair, strong shoulders, and rough features, even visible from here. Tivea jumped to her feet, barely allowing herself to believe it. Her father's right-hand man had made it to Xienee?

"Mych!" She cupped her hands around her mouth, ignoring Rauna's pleas to her to stay quiet. Hope pounded through her veins, her hands shaking at her mouth. The man turned toward her, scanning the grass before his eyes settled on her. "Mych! Over here!"

A group gathered around the man as Tivea jumped in place, trying to keep his attention. Rauna's hands tugged at her clothes, trying to bring her back to the ground. "What are you doing?" she asked in a frantic voice.

"He's part of my father's coalition!" Tivea said, refusing to take her eyes off the man as he stared at her incredulously.

Rauna's hands fell from her body, and she backed up, further into the grass.

Mych said something to the group that had gathered around him and then broke into a run toward her. What a stroke of luck, finding a member of the Southern Coalition alive!

Tivea's body filled with a happiness she hadn't felt in ages, the pleasant warmth radiating from her chest as he approached.

"Tivea?" Mych said, stopping in his tracks as he got a better view of her face. "Oh, Goddesses, Tivea, you're alive!" He broke into a run again, taking her into his arms as he slammed into her. She wrapped her arms around him, tears welling in her eyes. "I thought they took you too, I thought..."

He pulled out of the embrace, his eyes landing behind her. His hand shot to his hip, to his sword and took a step to the side of her.

"Oh, no!" Tivea quickly interjected as Rauna's eyes flashed in fear, backing further into the grass. She jumped in between them, waving her hands at Mych. "No. She's with me."

Mych stopped his hand, his eyes still trained on Rauna. Rauna's breathing got heavier, her chest rising and falling quickly as she stared at Mych with terror in her eyes.

"Who is she?" he asked, his voice accusatory.

"She's with me, she helped me get here. I wouldn't be here without her," Tivea said simply, slowly moving back toward him, pushing down his hand tentatively. Tivea's heart threatened to beat out of her chest as Mych still stared, eyeing Rauna with suspicion.

Rauna swallowed hard behind her, quickly making her way to her feet. Mych lowered his hand from his blade, his face twisting in confusion. "Who is she?"

Tivea turned to Rauna, gently pulling her closer to her, still keeping the woman behind her. She reached behind herself, her fingers snaking into Rauna's clammy ones. Rauna squeezed her hand and Tivea's heart pounded. "Her name is Rauna," Tivea stated simply, hoping he wouldn't ask any more questions.

"That's a Lupegi name," he said, the confusion twisting his face harder. He backed away slightly. "She's Lupegi?"

Tivea sighed deeply, her eyes trained on Mych's hands, watching for any sudden moves. "I know, it's odd—"

"Odd?!" he exclaimed, scoffing loudly. "That's one way to put it, the daughter of Yidenu himself traveling with a Lupegi girl. What would your father think?"

Rauna took a sharp breath as his voice grew angrier, muttering quickly under her breath. Tivea squeezed her hand tighter. Rauna's hand shook within hers, her breathing erratic behind Tivea.

"My father would thank her for keeping me safe!" Tivea raised her own voice, waving a hand in front of his face. "Mych! Listen to me, okay? She's safe, she's not a danger."

He glanced between the two of them, obviously still uneasy but he nodded his head slightly and stayed quiet, crossing his arms tightly over his chest.

"Rauna's a friend. She's helping me find my father."

Shock crossed Mych's face at this, his mouth falling open and arms falling to his side. "Yidenu's alive?"

"He was the last time I saw him," Tivea said, fighting back tears as she thought of her father, beaten, bruised, bloody. "The Davegu were taking him and a few others prisoner from camp. He's not dead."

Mych's mouth hung open at her words and Tivea's heart slowed slightly, tears still threatening to pour out of her eyes. She swallowed hard. He was less angry now at least.

"He's alive," he whispered, mostly to himself.

Rauna's breathing calmed slightly, going back to a steadier pace and she pulled her hand from Tivea's. She spoke from behind her, voice still strained with the remnants of fear. "I'm just trying to help Tivea, Mych. I wish you no harm."

Mych's eyes, less full of anger, now stared at Rauna, an intensity still within them that Tivea could feel even from here. "Why are you here then? I know a Lupegi didn't come across the border just to help Tivea. I bet those stupid fucks leading you don't even know what's going on."

Tivea snickered a little at this; The Seven's incompetence was known far and wide in Andyse. Though their military was way larger and better equipped than Xienee's, they almost always got their asses handed to them by her forces, pushing them off her land. Occasionally, a mission would go better for them than normal but that was few and far between. It was infuriating how unknowing they were of Andyse.

Rauna didn't seem taken aback by this affront to her leaders and stared right back at Mych, the fear seeming to fade into distant memory, replaced by a certain resolve that struck Tivea. "I came to save my sister. She was sent on a settling mission here, the ones that you all kill." Her voice was full of malice and accusation.

Tivea's heart started pounding again, preparing to step in between them.

Mych threw his hands up in exasperation, taking a step back. "Little girl, your sister shouldn't have even been here, on our land, but we didn't kill them."

This piqued Tivea's attention, and she stared hard at Mych, searching for any hint that he was lying. "You didn't?"

"No, we didn't. But enough about that, I don't owe a colonizer an explanation." He shot a look at Rauna of utter disgust before turning slowly back to Tivea and plastering a smile on his face. "Sweetheart, why are you here?"

Tivea's mind ran wild with the fact that Xienee didn't kill the settlers and from her periphery, she could tell Rauna was just as confused, her face contorted in thought. *The Teveban.* They had done it alone. They had killed the settlers and then taken the survivors prisoner. She pushed this realization from her mind, turning to face Mych, focusing on the task at hand. "Where's Xienee?"

Mych's face dropped. "Oh, sweetie, she's gone south. She's not here."

Tivea's stomach twisted painfully at his words. *Gone?* Tivea shook her head in disbelief. She didn't come this far to not talk to Xienee now. Her father's life was on the line. No, she was talking to her. "Can you bring me to her?"

He grunted in the affirmative then jerked his head toward Rauna. "Is she coming, too?"

Tivea turned quickly to look at the Lupegi woman. She was obviously still reeling from the new information presented to her, his mouth slightly agape. "You don't have to, Rauna," she said quietly.

But Rauna's eyes fell on Tivea again and Rauna took a deep breath. "I'm going with you."

Tivea's heart fluttered, and she fought back a smile.

The walking was grueling, not physically but rather mentally as she followed Mych through the plains, back into the forest as night settled over the lands. She wanted to run, to sprint, to find Xienee, her only hope of finding her father now. But Mych's pace was steady and slow as they crossed into the forest. He didn't seem to be in any sort of hurry to save her father.

Tivea sighed, forcing herself to focus on anything else besides her father's unknown fate. He was alive, she knew it, felt it in her bones. But she could do nothing about it from here. Her eyes wandered as the trio stepped over a fallen log. They wandered to the trees, the night sky and its stars, anywhere, in a futile effort to distract herself. When they wandered again, they landed on Rauna's back, her shirt hugging the curves of her body, visible even in the darkness of falling night.

Her heart began to beat faster. Tivea watched, her gaze resting fully on the woman in front of her. Her cream white skin shone in the moonlight, almost glowing. The braid of black hair that fell down her back swayed with her movements and all Tivea wanted to do was reach out, touch her silky hair, feel the heat of Rauna's breath mixing with hers.

Tivea stopped in her tracks, shaking her head vigorously to rid her mind of the thoughts she hadn't been able to stop herself from thinking these past few days. For some reason, all she wanted to do was be close to her, hold her, like they did in the cave for warmth on those cold nights. They'd slept close last night, and Tivea wanted nothing more than to feel her warmth again.

Rauna noticed her sudden stop, turning around to face her. "Is everything okay?"

Tivea's breath quickened as Rauna stepped close to her, her throat seeming to close as her heart pounded in her chest. Concern flashed across Rauna's beautiful green eyes, darkening them. She reached a hand out to Mych in front of her, grazing his back with her fingers.

Now it was his turn to turn to Tivea. Tivea's chest squeezed tightly. They were both looking at her, that same look of concern on both their faces.

"Are you okay, Tivea?" Rauna asked, stepping closer still and outstretching her hand.

Tivea eyed her outstretched hand, begging it to touch her, to hold her. When had this happened? *Why* had this happened? She closed her eyes and took a deep breath.

She swatted Rauna's hand from the air, unsure of what else to do. As their hands touched, a jolt of pure electricity shot through her body, and she shivered. Opening her eyes, the two people in front of her just seemed to have more concern etched on their faces at her sudden movement.

Come up with something, anything.

Her eyes flitted around the forest again, trying to come up with some explanation that wasn't related to the woman in front of her. Finally, she settled on turning to Mych and asking him a question that had been burning in her mind for quite a while. "Where are we going?"

The look of worry dissipated from his rough, scarred face and his eyes darkened. "Xienee is on a warpath, Tivea. The massacre of the

Southern Coalition forced her hand," he shifted his weight like he was uneasy and a chill shot through Tivea, "she joined her forces with someone else."

Dark recognition gnawed at her brain, her stomach dropping. "Who?"

Mych sighed, averting his gaze and swaying in the still air. Tivea turned to Rauna's face, her green eyes wide in fear at Mych's words. *Them.*

"Don't tell me she joined the mountain people," Rauna's voice broke the silence, anger tinged in her words. "They took my sister, held her prisoner. They'll kill me just for being Lupegi. They're savages; they're beasts!"

These words sent Mych into a fury. "You know nothing of this land, girl! You don't know our pains, being constantly looked down on, called savages, deemed lesser by the trash that sits on your pearly white thrones while they send their assassins to kill our leaders, our children, our families!" He took a step toward Rauna, jutting his face into hers.

She did not back down, staring him right in his fiery eyes.

"Mych, stop!" Tivea cried out, jumping between them and pushing on Mych's chest.

He kept going, his voice rising with every word. "Your people killed us for centuries. We're only savage because they keep us that way! They burn our schools and kill our healers. Xienee did what she needed to do when that bastard king attacked Yidenu and you will not judge her for that, not in my presence."

Rauna took a step back, her eyes watering slightly. Whether that was because of his words or something else entirely, Tivea did not know. Mych was fuming, his chest pressing into Tivea's hand as he stared at Rauna.

"I—I'm sorry," Rauna said quietly, her voice barely a whisper. "I didn't know."

"No," Mych spat at Rauna's feet. "You didn't know and yet you still judge us for what we do for survival."

Tivea sighed, turning to Rauna. Despite her feelings for the woman, her ignorance wiped her mind of that truth for the moment. "Our history has only been written by those that wish to exterminate us. Of course, they write us as beasts and savages. It makes us easier to kill if we're not humans in our own right."

"I didn't mean the Andysi," Rauna said, her voice wavering as she took a step back, leaves crackling beneath her boots.

Mych stepped back too, anger still radiating from his scowling face. "'Course you didn't," he muttered, "but those 'mountain people' are victims as much as us. You. Know. Nothing."

Tivea scoffed and pushed Mych back. "Enough, both of you."

A heat that wasn't there before the explosion of yelling gnawed at Tivea's skin, burning her with its intensity. She turned her gaze to Rauna. The woman stood stock still, grief swimming in her trained on the forest floor.

"I'm no fan of The Seven myself," Rauna said, finally breaking the tense silence.

Mych grunted. "You Lupegi are so brainwashed, you worship them. I have trouble believing that."

Rauna's eyes raised and landed on Mych, Tivea still between them. Tivea prepared herself for the screaming match to start back up again but instead Rauna spoke softly. "I don't. Neither does my sister. I'm really sorry, I didn't know."

She turned now to Tivea, holding eye contact. A shiver ran up Tivea's back and her breath hitched. Rauna reached out for her slowly, taking her hand within her own. The words Tivea wished to speak got stuck in her throat and she forced out a choked version of them. "If Mych says we're going to the fortress, I'm going with. That's my best chance of finding my father." Tivea took a deep breath, steeling herself for what she was about to say. "You don't have to come."

Rauna squeezed her hand, and a small smile flitted across her face. "But I will. For you."

Chapter Twenty-Eight
Tovik

Tovik ran his fingernail over the stitching of the sleeve of his velvet robe absentmindedly. The black stone walls that made up the throne room were bare, dull candlelight flickering over the cracks in the rock. Footsteps approached slowly, carefully. They were always coming, closer, louder. Tovik shifted on the throne, raising his head and clenching his jaw.

The curtains were drawn, the lack of light in the throne room concealing the identity of whoever approached, just a shroud of darkness in front of him.

But he knew who it was.

Tovik smiled slightly as the light of the candles reached her cloaked face.

"Meluth," he said, raising his arms to welcome his wife.

She paused her movements, the deep green cloak she wore obscuring her face from his view. The thick fabric swirled at her feet as she stopped, her hands clasped in front of her. She said nothing.

He already knew why she was here.

Tovik raised himself from his throne, taking a large step down the stairs to the woman below. "I'm guessing you have yet another warning for me?"

The cloak over her face shifted as she nodded, silent, still, cold.

Tovik smirked. "Well, speak your mind."

He waited, the air in the room growing stiff, chilled, between them. He scoffed as she stood in front of him, motionless. Heat built in his body, an anger growing in his mind. It was always the same, always. She came here, to him, to the *king* and demanded him to obey her. He had, for far too long, allowed her to make him weak, to double deal behind his back with Yidenu. The aristocrats began to come to the queen instead of the king. And since he had taken his righteous power back from his wife, she came every day without fail to spout the same thinly veiled threats.

"Speak!" he shouted, his harsh voice reverberating off the black stone walls of the throne room.

Meluth did not flinch, still standing in front of him, hands clasped beneath her cloak.

Tovik swallowed hard, the silence growing between them once again. The rage within him got more potent with each passing second and his face twisted as he stared at her, his body shaking with anger.

He flew forward, grabbing at her arms. He dug his fingernails into her thick cloak, his teeth gritted as he jutted his face right up to her cloaked one. "SPEAK, WOMAN!"

Her body stayed still while he held her arms. Tovik's face burned, red blurring his vision as he gripped her tighter still. Raising one hand from her arm, he thrust it up in the air, bringing it back down to her face with a rage. As his hand made contact with her skin, a loud *slap* echoed through the room. But she stayed still.

"You raise a single finger to me again and I will personally be your downfall. Stop the troops, stop your ego-driven desire for control. Stop it all." Her voice came out in a soft whisper beneath the fabric over her face. "You will regret it, Tovik. I promise you that."

"How dare you? I am the king! You have no power here, bitch!"

Meluth unclasped her hands and pressed the tips of her fingers into his chest. Tovik found himself suddenly releasing her arms and backing up as her touch spread through his chest like the cold of deep winter.

She turned quickly on her heel, the fabric of her dress skimming over his boots as she faced the door. Tovik's breath heaved out as she retreated toward the double doors at the end of the hall.

The suffocating hold Meluth put him under, the cold, dissipated from his limbs and he screamed out, "Treasonous viper!"

She paused, her dress swaying from the sudden stop. "You attacked our allies, you subjected the people under your protection to death and torture, you destroyed the peace I was able to foster. You send masses and masses of your soldiers into Andyse to slay anyone they find. You speak to me of treason?" Her voice was low and steady, without a hint of emotion behind her words.

But something struck him about the words she spoke, and he started toward her, hands clenching and unclenching to grab her, to shake her, to show her his strength, to display what happens when you disobey the king. How dare she? How fucking *dare* she? "You took my power from me and made me weak! The Davegu Kingdom needs no allies. You betrayed me, my own wife! I just took my power back from your unworthy hands. This is what happens to your 'allies' when you undermine your king."

Meluth resumed walking, moving quickly toward the doors as he approached. As she flung the heavy wooden doors open and stepped into the hall beyond, she turned back to him as he approached her, heat pulsing through his veins. "Continue on this path, Tovik, and I will show you true power."

The door slammed into place, the *bang* resounding through the air in between him and the exit. He broke into a run now, hot blood pumping through his limbs as he slammed himself into the wood, yanking the door open.

He swung his head wildly, looking down all the hallways that connected here only to be met with empty stone walls and wooden floors streaked with blood from the peasants and traitorous aristocrats that had been dragged through here toward the torture chamber. A man approached from one of the hallways, garbed in the armor of a Kingsguard and Tovik flew toward him, his feet pounding on the wood planks beneath them.

"You, there!" he yelled, his voice booming through the space between them.

The man jumped, quickly standing upright and at attention. If Meluth wanted a display of power, oh, he would show her his power.

"Get me Asmuto in Oshgor."

The Kingsguard nodded slightly, his body shaking from fear. "The queen's general?"

Tovik raised his chin, a sly smile coming onto his face. "No one can disobey the king, not even the queen's dog. He will take Andyse for me. I will show her how powerless she is."

Chapter Twenty-Nine
Anavi

She controlled her breathing as much as she could, the bag over her head making the air she inhaled stale and humid. She wriggled her bound wrists desperately as the horse she was tied to meandered to Seven knows where. The rope bit into her skin, tearing at the tender flesh. It had been a full day now, she figured, her body aching and throbbing in pain as they moved. They must've given her some drug, something that kept her fading in and out of consciousness

Anavi's breathing quickened, pulling the burlap bag into her mouth from the sudden inhale. She spit; the scratchy material stuck to her tongue. She had to get back. She had to.

She moved her leg as best she could, the rope cutting into her thighs as she attempted to gauge the amount of damage done to her knee from the Davegu arrow. A sudden shock of white-hot fire burst through her body. She bit the sack, hard, muffling the scream that threatened to escape. She would not show weakness. She was above that.

But the pain continued shooting its way through her body like a thousand knives all at once and a small groan released from her mouth.

"Shut it," a gruff voice barked from beyond the bag, the person riding the horse she was tied to most likely. "You need to save your voice for your meeting with the king."

She bit back the urge to laugh. She'd had run-ins with King Tovik before—he was weak, a puppet truly. When she'd been imprisoned in Mergrin last year, it was under the Davegu Queen's orders, not Tovik's. Every bit of intelligence The Seven had pointed to him wasting away, getting high, and letting the aristocrats and his wife run amok. At the prospect of meeting the queen, though, Anavi strengthened her resolve and struggled against her bounds harder.

"Stop!" the voice commanded, the horse coming to a sudden stop beneath her. She flailed through the air, the ropes catching her fall as she slipped the solidness of the horse's back. She coughed, hard, gasping for breath as the air from her lungs left. "I said stop!"

Rough hands gripped her arms tightly. Anavi winced at the touch, the pressure on her arms tighter than anything she'd felt before. The light she saw through the sack moved quickly as she was flung into the air, weightless, gasping for air. She landed back on the horse, hard, any bit of oxygen she had knocked from her lungs at the sudden landing. She coughed and wheezed, her body still writhing against the rope, screaming for breath.

"By the Goddesses, you're stupid," the voice said as she thrashed on the horse's back.

Then the man let out a grunt over her struggling and a hard object hit her head. The world went black.

As she came to, a dull, pulsating pain reached out from the top of her head. Groggily, she opened her eyes, the burlap sack now replaced with a black blindfold. She thrashed her hands out, free now from the ropes. Her wrists screamed as she removed her blindfold, her head still pounding. As Anavi lifted the fabric from her eyes, the world around her was dark, the air damp as she gulped it in.

She peered around the dark room, half expecting to see the king himself, just watching. Seemed like something he would do, watch a woman sleep, or in her case, watch a woman knocked out.

But he wasn't there. No one was.

Her eyes adjusted to the darkness slowly as she rubbed the top of her head, her fingers getting caught in her tangled braids. She was in a cell, water pooling on the floor. Basement, she wagered, taking in the gritty room around her. The thick bricks of the blackstone walls extended up to the ceiling. Girthy iron bars kept her in the far edge of the cell, a space so small she could probably stick her feet through the bars with her back against the stone wall. A dark slimy mud served as the floor; it clung to her body as she raised herself gingerly to her feet, ignoring the pain in her knee. She sunk into the ground as the mud gave way and let out a deep groan.

"Shit," she whispered to herself, her leg giving out beneath her weight. She landed in the mud with a splash, the dark substance coating her body.

Anavi sighed deeply, staying on the ground. Her leg throbbed in pain again and a small moan escaped her. She rubbed her thigh, straining her eyes to see the damage to her knee. In the darkness, she couldn't make out much beyond blood—dried, dark blood.

You've had worse.

Her hands shaking from the pain, she pulled at the fabric, sticky with her own blood. It tore beneath her hands. The sight below was gruesome, a deep hole in her upper thigh, congealed, half-clotted red liquid within the wound. A small trickle of fresh blood, dark red, crept down her thigh toward the ground. She gritted her teeth and pressed her shaking hand against the hole in her leg to stop the stream. Her skin burned on contact, sending white-hot pain blazing from her thigh that shot up her body with a malice. Crimson still steadily oozed from her body, climbing between her fingers as she pressed down on her leg.

Taking a deep breath through clenched teeth, Anavi tried to make her mind off the situation—trapped in a Davegu dungeon, wounded, with no way out. She looked up at the blackstone ceiling, biting her lip to prevent herself from crying out as another wave of pain rushed through her leg.

As she stared at the ceiling, trying to avoid feeling the throbbing pulse of her own blood abandoning her body, she let herself daydream of the place she wished she could go back to, The Seven's Hall, a beautiful castle named Salica. Rich and lavish, ornate purple, silver, and white banners decorating the walls, the colors of the Lupegi flag. She still remembered the first time she had set foot in that beautiful hall. It was exactly one month after her father's disappearance, summoned off the streets by Jovan himself.

How was she to know that all these years later, she would be here?

She brought herself back to the reality of her situation, a strange combination of anger and sadness washing over her, taking her mind hostage. Building her resolve, she focused on one thing and one thing only.

She had to get out.

Anavi pulled her hands from her wound, the bleeding having stopped for now and with newly steady hands, tied a piece of fabric from her torn pants over the arrow hole. Now it was time to get to work.

Her hands slapped in the mud, coating her fingers, soaking under her fingernails as she dragged herself toward the wall. Sharp pains stabbed through her leg as she slogged through the mud but Anavi gritted her teeth hard and shot her hand out , grasping the stone brick and pulling herself to her feet as a scream built in her throat

Legs shaking, she stumbled toward the bars. She was going to get out. She had to. She had to find Hanue and get to Jovan and get the fuck out. Get out, get out, get out.

Stumbling through the dirt, she fell into the bars that caged her in. She held herself up with solely her grip on the cold metal.

"Hey!" she said, jutting her face out between the bars as much as she could. No answer.

As her eyes adjusted, she took in her surroundings through the bars. A dark hallway lay beyond the cell, empty besides one motionless lantern in the far corner from her hanging from the ceiling, a faint flickering light around it. There were two more cells between her and the door that way. She turned her head, pressing her face as far through the bars as she could, the cold metal biting into her cheeks. There was one more cell on this side and then a brick wall, marking the end of the prison block.

Anavi sighed, backing away from the bars slightly, her lame leg sliding in the mud behind her.

A voice reached her ears—a man's, soft and worn down. "It's no use. They ain't coming back down here for the likes of us. I've been waiting for the king for weeks."

She pressed herself against the bars again, turning her head toward the cell further down the hall from hers, straining herself to try and get a peek of the owner of the voice. Pressed against the bars, sitting in the mud she made out a slight outline of a man, hunched over in the corner, his knees against his chest. "Who are you?"

The man in the cell laughed slightly, a discomforting sound that struck her to the bones. His shadow moved toward her as he crawled toward the wall that separated their cells, and her heart pounded in her chest. "You really don't know? I know who you are, spy."

CHAPTER THIRTY
HANUE

Hanue drummed his fingers on his arm, tap, tap, tapping his skin over and over, the boredom eating at his mind. He sighed deeply, raising his head again to gaze at the land below them. The forest below was dark and gloomy with the coming of winter. Most of the leaves had been shed at this point in the season, leaving only the decrepit branches below, like a sea of sharp needles. Curled leaves littered the ground, covering the ferns and grass with their death. A breeze thrust up the mountain side toward them, his clothing billowing behind him in the wind.

The unease in his body grew with each passing second as the trees lay still, silent. They'd been here for a full day now, waiting, watching for Rauna at Gaabi's request.

She sat beside him, her hands grasping the rock as she gazed into the woods below, searching for any sign of movement. They had seen a deer, two actually, and some rabbits but nothing more. There was no sign of her sister anywhere in the death down the hill. Hanue drummed his fingers harder into his skin as he stared at the back of her mess of red hair, mulling over in his mind how to tell her it was time to leave.

As his mind struggled to piece together the words, they strayed to his own sister, somewhere in those same woods, alone, cold.

If she was even still alive.

His fingers stopped thrumming against his arm, frozen in the air as memories of Anavi came flooding back.

On cold nights like this in Aethiel after their father's disappearance, she would curl her body around him in the empty alleys between the shops, giving him all her warmth as frost bit at their small bodies like the hungry dogs that roamed the dark streets. She gave up everything she had for him, did any odd job she could just to buy him some extra soup from the kindly barkeep down the road from their old house. Her dreams of becoming an actress like their mother, traveling the land with The Seven's Theatre, were gone the same day their father was gone, replaced with Jovan's promises of reward for killing his rivals.

And here he sat, wanting to leave her, all alone there in the woods.

She never would've done that to him.

Hanue sighed deeply, staring back into the trees, half hoping that Anavi's figure would come up the pass toward them.

But of course, she didn't. The trees stayed standing there, unmoving, undisturbed, unforgiving. One thing was sure though, as his sister's smile lit up in his mind, he couldn't live with himself if they left. Not yet.

Gaabi drew a sharp breath beside him, and he turned his head toward hers. She turned quickly to face him, her face scrunched in fear. He stared down where she was looking as the darkness of night fell on the land below. Several figures walked through the wood below, lanterns swinging in their hands, illuminating the thick cloaks they wore with a soft yellow haze. Guffawing laughter reached his ears as their faces peered up the mountain. His stomach curled.

With one quick motion, he pressed himself flat to the ground, pulling at Gaabi's arm to bring her down with him. Maybe they didn't see them. Maybe the rock in front of them offered enough cover from their lantern light.

But as the laughter moved closer, he didn't bet on it.

Gaabi's breathing quickened and he scooted himself on the cold rock toward her, pulling her shaking body into his arms. "It's alright," he whispered, pulling her hair from her ear. "It'll be alright."

She whimpered, the sound of her terror shooting a pang through his chest. She shook in his arms violently, like a piece of hot metal he'd just struck with his hammer. A muffled cry escaped her mouth; he flinched as it reached his ears.

"Shh, Gaabi, shh!" He pressed his hand against her mouth as the noises from the men below stopped. Had they heard her?

She stared at him in the darkness, her light brown eyes wide in a fear he hadn't seen in them before.

Please, by The Seven, please don't hear us.

By some luck, the laughter resumed, moving away from the rock they hid behind. Hanue slowly released a breath and moved his hand from Gaabi's face, her eyes still wide. Hanue gripped the top of the rock, pulling himself up to peer over it. The woods below were empty again, devoid of life. The men were gone, their voices having faded into the night.

They'd been spared from whatever men those were, Davegu or *other*. At least for the time being. But as he breathed shallowly, as Gaabi rose up from the ground to gaze over the rock as well, only one thing was on his mind, eating at his consciousness.

His sister.

The only family he had left. He couldn't leave her, not here, not now.

He was going back into the wilds of the Northlands. He was going to bring her home. Turning to the girl beside him, he sighed deeply. Her face was curled into a look of terror, of fear and dread, even this close to safety over the mountains. It was only another day's trek through the rocks to get back to Lasari.

"I'm not going with you, Gaabi," he said simply, averting his eyes from her face, preparing for her protests and begging to bring her home. But they didn't come. He opened his eyes slowly, turning to look at the girl sitting beside him.

Her face was no longer twisted in the fear of before, rather, a determination that struck him deeply. "Good. I'm not going back either."

Hanue's jaw dropped, her words hitting him square in the chest as they sunk in. "Why?"

She made her way to her feet, looking down at him as she extended a hand to him to help him up. "You're not the only one with someone you care about. And I'll be damned if I let you go alone. You did say we have to stick together, after all."

Hanue blinked at the girl above him, a small bit of relief spreading through his body. He took her hand in his, pulling himself to his feet and wrapped his arms around her body, tucking her close to him. Her warmth was refreshing, ebbing through his body at every point of contact. He lowered his head to her level, eyeing her full, pink lips. Her breath hitched and she moved her head closer to his, pressing their foreheads together.

It was now or never; they could die before they reached the bottom of the mountain.

He cupped her chin and raised her face to his but before he could steel himself, her hands shot out and pulled him close, pressing her lips softly against his. The warmth was replaced with pure, blissful heat as he hungrily took in her taste, the feeling of her body on his, her lips on his.

Slowly, painfully, he pulled away from her, tracing her lips with his thumb. Her body quivered in his arms and her lips turned upwards into a large, beautiful smile. His own matched hers as he pressed his forehead to hers once again.

He whispered, soft and low, "There's no one else I would rather stick together with."

They made their way through the forest carefully, as silent as they were able to as the cold dark of night enveloped his extremities. Hanue took another step over a fallen pile of leaves and turned, extending his hand to the girl behind him. Gaabi took it, pressing into it as she too jumped over the leaves, desperate to make no sound as they traversed the wilderness.

As she stepped over the leaves, landing softly in the grass of the clearing, Hanue racked his brain. If he were Anavi, with all her training and skill, what would he be doing right now? Where would he be?

No answer jumped out to him. A disappointment filled his body, weighing down his arms and legs. Where do you even start trying to find a person trained in how *not* to be found?

Gaabi's voice broke his focus on his own loss. "Thank you for coming, Hanue."

He glanced at her, the darkness concealing most of her features but in the light of the moon, full tonight, he could make out her fingers, twirling her hair around them. A smile tugged at his lips, and he closed his hand around hers, relishing the warmth of her soft skin. "Of course I'd come."

Now it was her turn to smile, a sweet sight to his eyes. "Do you think they're okay?"

"I don't know," he sighed, turning his back to her and toward the forest they still had to move through to get back to the cave they found Rauna in. "I hope so."

Gaabi exhaled deeply, stepping to his side. "Tell me about your sister. Anavi, right? That's who you're looking for?"

A jolt shot through Hanue's chest, and he froze in place as Gaabi's voice spoke his sister's name. He dropped her hand; his arm falling to his side and took in a shallow breath. Turning away from Gaabi, his throat went dry. His voice strangled; he spoke, "What do you want to know?"

"I don't know, whatever you want to tell me."

Hanue quickly wiped his watery eyes, hoping that the darkness of night provided enough cover so Gaabi wouldn't see his tears. He breathed out shakily, willing his voice to be steady. "Well, she's the only one I have left." He shook his head slightly, tears falling freely as he spoke the words aloud.

Gaabi's hand grazed his arm, her touch soft and welcoming. He fought to not fall into her embrace, to stay strong. For her.

"Our mother died and a few years ago, our father left, driven crazy from grief, I guess. Anavi's taken care of us since." That last part of a bit of a lie, The Seven had taken care of them in exchange for Anavi's loyalty. But he couldn't very well tell Gaabi that, especially considering her hatred of them.

"She seems very important to you."

"She is. I would be dead many times over without her. She's smart, good at what she does."

"And what does she do?"

Hanue felt his face drain of its blood and his eyes darted quickly from Gaabi's face. Lie. Lie. Lie. He had to lie. "Nothing of import."

Gaabi's face twisted in confusion. "Are you sure?"

He nodded, studying her face closely. A hardness swept over her eyes, a far cry from the typical sweetness or the sparkle of one of her good ideas he had grown accustomed to in those beautiful seas of honey. He swallowed, carefully keeping his face straight.

She knew.

"I know who your sister is, Hanue," she said simply.

Hanue gulped, awaiting her anger.

"You asked me before why I don't like The Seven and one day I'll tell you all of it. But there are things about your sister that I don't think you know, things she's done at their request. She's known in Lasari, her anger and rage." She chose her words carefully, speaking slowly as if to avoid upsetting him. Gaabi walked toward him, taking his hand in hers. Hanue's heart fluttered as she pressed her warm lips against his cheek. "I'll help you find her, but I want you to know something; you don't have to be like her."

At her words, something seemed to click in his brain. He'd always wanted to be like his sister, never even considered any other option. But as he looked in Gaabi's eyes, there was a softness, a kindness, he couldn't seem to remember seeing in Anavi, at least not since she joined The Seven.

CHAPTER THIRTY-ONE
RAUNA

It had now officially been days since she left her sister. Maybe, just maybe, Gaabi had given up waiting and had crossed over herself with the help of that Aethiel boy. That's all she could hope for as she traveled deeper into the forest, further from the relative safety of the northern pass she promised to meet Gaabi at.

The mountains towered over her, growing only larger as the trio moved steadily toward them. They moved toward the fortress that had held her imprisoned sister less than a week ago with slow speed but still at a pace that caused her legs to burn from the effort of keeping up.

The leaves crunched beneath her feet as another cramp hit her thigh. Rauna bit her lip, hard, and turned to the reason she was doing any of this to begin with.

Tivea.

Her brown hair shone in the morning light, dancing as they passed under the trees and glimpses of sunlight hit her hair. The light caught her honey brown eyes as well, highlighting the beautiful glimmer in them. Tivea peered up at the trees, running her fingers across the bark of a nearby one. Her lips turned upwards in a small, soft smile. The kind of smile that sent butterflies flying through Rauna's stomach. The kind of smile that made Rauna smile right along with her.

Rauna moved her eyes from Tivea and toward the man in front of them. Mych walked with determined speed as they hiked through the woods—a speed that was becoming torturous to keep up with as the burning sensation in her thighs heightened.

But after her indiscretion last night, she dared not question him.

Tivea jogged beside her to catch up to Mych and tapped him on the back. He turned quickly, hand flying to the sword at his side before he realized who had touched him.

"What is it, sweetheart?" he grunted.

Rauna snickered a bit; this man was never in a good mood apparently.

Tivea stopped in place and Mych followed suit. Rauna sighed.

Thank The Seven, I've got time to rest.

"Tell me more about Teveban," Tivea's soft voice spoke.

Rauna's legs faltered at her words and she nearly stumbled.

"I want to know what we're walking into."

Mych shifted his weight back and forth, obviously uncomfortable with her question. "I don't really know much about them." He took a shaky breath. "There are the legends, of course. But I never believed the people to actually exist. At least until recently."

A heat built in Rauna's chest, spreading outward at a vicious speed and she bit her tongue. He didn't know? He didn't know what he was leading them into?

Tivea had the same reaction, her expression souring. "How are we to know that Xienee isn't dead then? How are we to know we'd be safe there? We heard them talking." She gestured slowly to Rauna. "They hate the Lupegi, want them dead."

Mych's face twisted into a sort of rage and Rauna took a step forward. He spoke, more of a grumble than words. "They're not the only ones."

His eyes shot daggers at Rauna as she approached and the rage within her only built, stronger and stronger. "I said I'm sorry, Mych! I am not responsible for the crimes of The Seven. I'm a fucking barmaid!" She stepped toward him, toe to toe. "I do not wish you any harm. I'd appreciate it if you could kindly return the favor." The night of her mother's death played in her mind. "You don't understand what they do to those that oppose them."

Mych's hand twitched above his sword, his voice suddenly deadly calm. "They consider my *existence* an opposition to their power. I know their hatred better than you."

Rauna's mouth opened, trying to think of something, anything, to shoot back at him. Her mother's death, the Sevensguards that were given free reign of any woman they could get their hands on, anything. But some part of her knew it was in vain. He had a point. But that still didn't mean she had any say in who led Lupegi, it didn't stop her anger. She took a step forward, her eyes narrowed.

Tivea's hands grasped Rauna's shoulders and she stumbled backwards, falling nearly over the woman. Mych's expression was one of pure rage as he stood stock-still, fuming. Struggling against Tivea's hold, Rauna felt vines begin to creep up her arms, holding her in place. Mych threw his head back in laughter before his expression turned to one of fear as vines similarly wrapped his legs in place. He reached for his sword, but a vine burst from the tree behind him and grabbed his hand in the air.

"Both of you, calm down," Tivea said, releasing Rauna to her leafy bonds. "First of all, Mych, how could you hide this?"

Mych glared at Tivea, but his anger seemed to be dissipating given the lack of mobility he now had. Still, the way he was looking at Tivea only stoked Rauna's anger. "Hide what? I'm trying to get Yidenu back as well as you. This is our best chance."

Biting her tongue wasn't working anymore as her mother's last moments hit her mind and words slipped from Rauna's mouth. "And my best chance of death." She thrashed against Tivea's vines. "Can you let me go so I can beat his ass?"

"Like you'd have a chance!"

The vines tightened around Rauna's chest and arms at these words, squeezing painfully. Mych's did the same.

"Stop!" Tivea roared, the loudest Rauna had ever heard her.

She went silent and stopped fighting the vines. Mych closed his mouth and stared at Tivea behind her, his eyes flitting back to her for passing glares every so often. The silence was tense, louder even than Tivea's shout, and Rauna shifted uncomfortably beneath the plants.

"Can you both just stop bickering?" Tivea stepped in between the two of them, Mych's eyes intense and shadowy as he looked at her. "Mych, you should've told us we were going into the unknown and stop antagonizing my..." Tivea took a breath, "...friend," she finished slowly.

An odd feeling of disappointment shot through Rauna's heart. Friend? But she forced herself to push past that. Tivea said they were friends. That was something, right?

As the feeling passed, she glared at Mych gloatingly. Tivea quickly turned to her though and she felt her face drop.

"And Rauna, you don't know shit about the Andysi or what we have to do to survive. Stop being so ignorant and know that when we talk about hating the Lupegi, we mean The Seven. At least, I do."

She whipped back around to Mych.

"Rauna has helped me survive and kept me sane after everything I'd ever known was burned down by the Davegu. Stop blaming her for her leaders."

"If she hates them so much, why doesn't the bitch do anything? Why not put her anger somewhere worthwhile?" he spat.

Rauna balled her fist. Who's to say she hadn't already tried that? Her mother had...

Mych's features contorted as the vines tightened around him again. He coughed and sputtered, spit flying from his mouth. Rauna felt herself smile a bit.

"Fine, fine, can you just release me?" he gasped.

Tivea looked back to Mych, her hair flying through the air as she turned. "Behave," she turned again, facing Rauna, her face stern. "Both of you."

Rauna nodded, wiping the smile from her face. With a wave of Tivea's hand, the vines loosened their grip, falling from her sides. She rubbed her wrists and arms where the vines had bitten into her flesh, the skin tender to her touch. Mych relaxed as the vines retreated from him, winding back into the trees above or wrapping themselves around the trunks.

An anger still simmered in her blood, heating her body but she pushed it down as much as she could and stepped forward toward Tivea's shaking body. "I'm sorry, Tivea," Rauna whispered, reaching a hand out to her.

She took her hand in hers and suddenly, Tivea threw herself toward Rauna, wrapping her arms around her neck. Rauna's heart pounded in her chest and shock replaced the anger in her veins. Falling into her warm body, she embraced Tivea, not ever wanting to let go. Rauna let the warmth of their body mix, a fiery passion burning within her.

This didn't feel like any friend she'd ever had before.

Rauna raised her head from Tivea's shoulders and slowly cupped her chin. Her heart beat faster than she'd ever felt before, but Seven, did she want this. She took in the woman's face, waiting, wanting. Closing her eyes she moved her face toward Tivea's lips.

Mych stepped heavily toward them and they flew apart. Rauna's heart sank, and she cleared her throat, eyeing Tivea from the corner of her eye. She blushed hard as she caught Tivea's eyes meeting hers, a sly smile toying at the woman's lips.

The large man pushed through them and began walking swiftly. "Enough of that, you two. We're losing daylight."

As the daylight faltered, Rauna stared at the back of Mych's fat, balding head. Despite Tivea's warnings to both of them, she still harbored an anger for the man that would not dissipate. Especially after interrupting what could've been...

She stopped herself. It could've been *nothing*. Rauna was leaving as soon as Tivea got within the walls of that fortress. They'd never see each other again. There wasn't anything that could ever happen between them. But she couldn't deny she had been craving her touch since long before Mych had forced them apart.

Rauna shook her head, ridding herself of her thoughts. The Malcier mountains loomed over the trio as they walked steadily through the underbrush of green, orange, and yellow and she forced herself to focus on them as they got ever bigger with each step.

Hopefully Gaabi was over those mountains.

Tivea inhaled sharply, a sound that brought Rauna back to her senses. She ripped her eyes from the mountain tops and turned to the woman next to her.

"We're getting close." She leaned close to Rauna's ear and Rauna shivered at the proximity. "I recognize the woods here, the trees' voices."

A chill shot through Rauna's chest, her heart rate picking up. Everything in her told her to turn, to run, to avoid that place entirely. But as she gazed upon Tivea's face, scared of what was to come, she couldn't bring herself to leave. Not yet.

Rauna slowed her pace as they approached the mountainside. She searched the woods for something, anything that confirmed her suspicions that they were not alone here.

Sure enough, a slight rustling reached her ears, and her breath hitched in her throat. Without thinking, she reached out and grabbed Tivea's arm tightly. Tivea stopped in place, stumbling as she came to a stop.

"What is it?" Mych asked, his voice loud and booming.

Too loud for Rauna's comfort. She fought the urge to shush him.

But he shut up anyway, the rustling getting louder. Rauna's heart jumped into her throat, blood rushing in her ears as it got closer, louder.

Mych turned and stepped toward the women, drawing his sword from his hip. "Stay close. It might not be them."

Rauna searched the trees frantically trying to pinpoint the source of the noise, but it was to avail. As it got louder and louder and louder, she gripped Tivea's arm tighter, tighter, tighter. Out of the corner of her eye, Rauna caught Tivea wincing and she loosened her grip.

Tivea's hand caught hers as she moved it away, gripping it just as tight. "Don't let me go," she whispered, fear in her voice.

Rauna smiled, sliding her hand into Tivea's fingers and a calm came over her mind at her touch. "Never."

The rustling got closer and Mych backed up, raising his sword. "Who's there?"

A boy, no older than sixteen, emerged from behind a tree clad in leather armor, thick wool pants on his legs and a sword at his side. His face was young, but his eyes had a certain hardness to them, a look Rauna was well familiar with from her time in Lasari. He approached them with his hands up. "I was going to ask if you were friend or foe, but she recognized you before I could."

Rauna felt confusion bite at her mind, her eyes once again scanning the woods for a human presence. Then, out from behind a thick tree, a woman appeared. "Thank you, Ason."

She was tall, several hands taller than Rauna or Tivea, almost towering over Mych himself. An older woman, maybe mid-forties but a terrifying one, nonetheless. She had short brown hair, chopped off messily at her shoulders and clothed in furs and leather.

Tivea squeezed her hand tighter, and an unease came over Rauna.

Mych bowed his head, lowering his sword. "Commander Xienee."

The woman smiled and it sent shivers down Rauna's spine. She fought the urge to run once again, harder to ignore this time.

Xienee spoke, her voice loud and overpowering. It was no wonder that she was the most feared person alive to so many. "Mych, it's good to see you. I trust you to come with friends?" She shot a glare at Rauna, singling her out from the other two.

Rauna lowered her eyes.

"I did," Mych said simply. "Yidenu's daughter and... her friend," he said the last word with a bite of malice that caused a heat to build in Rauna again.

Xienee walked closer. "Yidenu's daughter, you say? I figured she was dead." She grasped Tivea under the chin, raising her head to look her in the eyes. Rauna heard Tivea gasp slightly, and the heat only built. "You must be Tivea?"

"I am," Tivea said, her voice steady. "I need you to help me get my father back."

"Yidenu's alive?" Xienee asked simply. "No issue, that'll be done. Tell me though, who's your *friend?*"

Rauna raised her head quickly, turning to Tivea with a pleading look in her eyes.

Lie, please, lie

Tivea seemed to hear her silent pleading and responded without skipping a beat. "A survivor from my father's camp."

Mych shifted in unease in front of her and she glowered at him, warning him, begging him, to stay silent.

"Strange," Xienee reached for Rauna's chin now. Her skin flushed at the firm touch of her calloused hands. "She has the look of a Lupegi. Same coloring as a head I have decorating a pike at my camp."

Rauna gulped.

Xienee dropped Rauna's chin. "But nonetheless, the daughter of Yidenu has arrived." She turned to the boy behind her, Ason. "Take them inside and tell Torvo to gather my people."

The boy nodded and turned his back, walking toward the mountain. Rauna took a deep breath, eyeing Xienee's face for any indication that she was in danger here.

Mych stepped toward Xienee and her hand flew to her side. Rauna backed up and accidentally pulled Tivea with her.

"Sorry," she muttered, eyes still on Xienee's sword that her hand rested on.

Tivea chuckled slightly and squeezed Rauna's hand. A cool calm came over Rauna, spreading out from Tivea's touch on her skin.

How am I going to leave?

Mych spoke, his voice grating, "Do you want me coming in with her, Commander?"

Xienee extended a hand to Mych's. "No, I believe we'll be okay. Come back in a week. The plan still holds for the march."

Mych nodded and retreated from view; Rauna didn't dare to take her eyes off Xienee, her heart still pounding in her chest, a sinking feeling consuming her. March? Who were they marching on?

Did she even want to know?

As Mych walked away, his footsteps faded into the distance. Xienee turned back to the women and Tivea squeezed her hand again.

"Is your friend joining us, Tivea?"

Tivea turned her head to Rauna, her face flushed. Rauna weighed her options in her mind, but the answer was already set in stone before they ever met.

Her sister needed her.

Rauna raised her head, trying to exude an air of confidence in the face of Xienee, in the face of leaving behind the woman beside her. Her voice still shook as she spoke. "No."

CHAPTER THIRTY-TWO
LISYNIA

Only a few short weeks ago, Lisynia had been here, gathering her armies, leading them out through the sewers like they were nothing more than rats instead of a fighting force to be reckoned with. Now, she was back.

She stared up at the walls, all too familiar with the feelings and memories that would come within their walls. It was the same every time.

But this time, she came bringing someone in, not sneaking them out. Maybe that would make some difference in her thoughts.

Otto walked in front of her, carrying Molac over his shoulder like a sack of potatoes. Lisynia looked beyond them, focusing on the wall, searching for Lupegi or Davegu soldiers. By now they had to know their slave population was dwindling.

But as she searched the turrets, no one was present. Maybe they were too busy with their war on Andyse to notice the Teveban population shrinking in a matter of weeks. If one good thing came out of that tragedy, it was that.

Lisynia jogged forward, passing Otto as they approached the sewer grate. The smell assaulted her senses just as it always did but now was not the time to move slowly.

She pulled at the grate, the grinding of the metal making her cringe. Beckoning Otto, she ducked within the tunnel once again and pulled the grate back into place behind him and the prisoner.

"Come on, hurry," she hissed, moving quickly through the liquid as it splashed up her legs. She tried not to focus on what it contained. There were more important things right now.

How close was she to finding out the truth? Finding what Catina had died to protect?

What old knowledge would this prisoner lead them to?

Otto splashed behind her as they moved through the tunnel, the darkness of the underground swallowing them whole.

Molac grunted and squirmed on Otto's shoulder, his spell wearing off. Lisynia paused her movements. "I've got it this time."

She focused again on her breathing, in and out, in and out, in and out, and pressed her pointer finger firmly against the forehead of the bound man. The magic flowed through her body, white sparks flying from the point of contact and he became still again.

Lisynia panted and Otto's face stared at her in the darkness, concern on his features.

She nodded at him, swallowing hard. "Back to it."

He turned, facing the pinprick of light visible at the end of the tunnel. Breaking into a jog, Lisynia made her way in front of them, her hand flying to her side, where her dagger rested in its sheath.

Her legs burned from the effort of running crouched down, but she did not stop. She couldn't stop. Not when she was this close to the answer that had eluded her for years.

The tunnel widened, the grate above them spilling light into the dreary hole. With another splash, Otto appeared behind her.

"Shh!" she pressed a finger to her lips.

Sounds of a scuffle echoed from above, shadows passing the grate quickly. A woman screamed, her voice high-pitched, raw.

"Please, no, please!" the woman pleaded with some unseen foe.

Lisynia lurched forward, grasping the grate's metal bars and pulling roughly.

"What are you doing?" Otto whispered urgently, gripping her arm.

"What I have to." She wrestled free of his grasp and pulled the grate from its resting spot. Lisynia jumped into the air as the woman screamed again, her fingers catching on the rough stone. She pulled herself into the street, not bothering to check her surroundings. She had to help. If not, what was she good for?

Springing to her feet, she took in the scene in front of her. An old woman, her face frail and wrinkled, struggled against the hold of a man wearing the Lupegi colors on his arm. He had his back turned to Lisynia, but the woman's face dropped at her sudden appearance. She raised a finger to her lips again and whipped out her dagger.

The Lupegi man growled something inaudible and twisted the woman's arm. Lisynia burst into a run, raising her dagger as she approached. A *snap* resounded through the empty street, the woman's arm cracking under his grip.

Lisynia's rage only intensified, and her feet pounded against the cobblestone. The man turned now, facing her. He dropped the woman to the ground, and she whimpered, clutching her broken arm.

"What the—"

Lisynia didn't give him time to react. She threw herself at him, slashing at his skin. Fury blinded her, the only thing she could see was his blood, pouring from a wound to his arm.

She backed up, flicking the blood off her dagger as he reached to draw his sword. Lisynia felt a smile spread across her face as a blackness crawled from his wounds, stringing along his limbs like vines. He gasped, screaming as it spread and stared at her in horror before falling to the ground, unmoving.

Lisynia rushed to the woman, stowing her knife back in its sheath. "Can you walk?"

The old woman stared at her in awe, eyes flitting between her and the crumpled man at her feet. "Yes."

She hoisted the woman up by her good arm. "Good. Get out of here, go to the physician and get that arm set."

The woman nodded, tears still streaming down her face. "Thank you, Princess."

Lisynia took a step back. No one had called her that in years at this point. The title seemed foreign, belonging to a girl she used to know, a girl she never was. She composed herself and stepped back to the woman, patting her on her good shoulder. "Call me Lisynia, ma'am."

The old lady nodded again, walking off into the dark street. Lisynia watched for a moment then turned to the body she had left in her wake.

Blood poured from his arm, running between the cobblestones like a river. He was crumpled in a mess on the ground, eyes glassy and wide.

She fidgeted with the gemstones in the hilt of her dagger, a faint smile settling on her face as she stared at the body of the Lupegi soldier. After she was done with the Davegu, she was going to come for them. He was just the first but, by the Goddesses, he wouldn't be the last.

Something rustled behind her, and she pivoted on her heel. Otto pushed Molac's limp body up the manhole, his face skidding along the ground.

She ran over, grabbing Molac's arms and lifting his face from the cobblestones. "One more push."

Otto grunted, obviously displeased with her. But he obliged, pushing on Molac's legs one last time. Lisynia hoisted the man by the arms and fell backwards, his body landing on top of hers on the ground. A pain exploded in her skull.

She groaned, lifting her head as much as she could and feeling the back of her head. Sticky liquid coated her hair, the deep color clinging to her fingers as she pulled them back. Lisynia pushed Molac off her. He landed in a lump next to her while Otto rushed over to her.

"Are you okay?" he asked, his voice frantic as he pulled at her arm to lift her up.

She winced, the wound from the Davegu in the forest burning at his touch. Still though, something about his touch invigorated her.

Lisynia pushed his arm off hers quickly and made her way to her feet. "Yeah, I'm okay. It'll take more than a bump to the head to take me down."

Otto laughed slightly but his eyes betrayed a pain she hated to see. Was he upset she pushed him away?

She ignored the look in his eyes, pushing her own feelings back. Gesturing to the Lupegi soldier bleeding in the street, she spoke, "Let's get that body out of here."

After shoving the soldier's body into one of the grain barrels, always empty now, Lisynia led Otto to a hidden back entrance to the castle that her sister had shown her long ago. As they made their way through the castle's tunnels, Molac still hoisted over Otto's shoulder, they approached the exit, a painting in the hallway right outside her father's quarters.

Molac stirred as the magics began to wear off again. Paralysis only worked for so long and damn, did it take it out of the caster too.

She fidgeted with her dagger, waiting for her strength to return. Lisynia could feel her body weakening every time she touched a finger to Molac's forehead and this time it hadn't returned quickly.

They approached her father's room in the castle, and she knocked.

It had been months since she had seen her father, since she decided to avenge Catina and moved the first group to Ryrie. He never supported it; her, Catina, or their mother's desire for freedom from the Davegu and the Lupegi. He saw it as too dangerous, too risky, even after Catina's execution. How would he react now?

She didn't know what she expected, truly, but as the door opened and her father pulled her quickly into a tight hug, it wasn't that. She stiffened in his arms as he waved Otto inside, closing the door tightly behind him.

"My daughter," he said, his voice wavering. "Oh, my daughter."

His hand moved to her shoulders as the shock of her father's sudden affection wore off. Her eyes scanned over him, taking in all the changes over the past six months. King Lesino was a large man if not a little wizened by age, his back hunched slightly and his muscles less pronounced than she had remembered him but he still exuded an air of confidence. His orange eyes darted over her face and Lisynia felt a slight pang rush through her chest as she gazed upon the royal mark of Teveban, the orange eyes said to be a gift from one of the Goddesses, sent down in the family that held the most favor. It was a mark Lisynia shared and Catina once had as well, a mark that had always cast her as different, dangerous to the foreign soldiers that crawled through the streets.

Her father squeezed her shoulder and turned to Otto, seeming to just now notice the man splayed across his shoulder. "What is this about?"

Lisynia sighed, her nerves shaking her. "Father, we need to know about Catina."

Her father's eyes shot back to her, wide and open. "What? No. No, I don't talk about your sister. You know this."

Of course.

She bit her tongue, fighting the urge to call him a coward to his face. He let the Davegu and the Lupegi steal their people, take his daughter's life, and still insisted on allowing it to happen, demanding to work with them instead of against them out of fear of retribution.

"Father," she said, fighting to keep her voice steady. "I just need to know where her and Tanue were. The tower? Outside the walls? Where were they?"

"Why?" He crossed his arms. Her mother always said she got her stubbornness from him. Now it was just a question of whose resolve would win out.

It had to be hers.

"Please." She turned up the sweetness, trilling her words. "Please, I just want to know what happened to my sister."

The king shifted uncomfortably then walked to the door and opened it, swiveling his head down the hallways. He slammed the door and locked it, the bolt sliding into place in the silence of the room. He turned back to Lisynia with sad eyes, tears building up.

"She heard an old saying of the Lupegi and Davegu from that man." He put his finger on his chin, scratching at the hairs of his beard as he thought about it. "In the tower, the Teveban bemoan, something like that."

Molac stirred again, his eyes flashing as Lisynia turned her head. She fought back a smile; he knew something. She steadied her face, turning back to her father.

"I told her not to go, that the tower's off-limits." His voice quivered. "But she didn't listen and Tovik's guards caught her and Tanue and..." His voice cut off as tears spilled from his eyes. He didn't need to finish the sentence. The story ended with her hanging and Tanue gone, like he was never here to begin with.

As he buried his face in his hands, Lisynia turned to Otto and gave a curt nod. He returned her nod and walked toward the door, pressing a finger to Molac's forehead again to still him. Lisynia's attention focused on her father, the man she grew up seeing as strong and just, then upon her sister's death, weak and stupid and now, as he cried in front of her, he was pathetic and sad.

She refused to be like him.

The tower of the castle she was raised in was grimy from years of sitting in solitude, unused. It was forbidden to enter that wing of the castle, even for the royal family, even for her father, the king. Of course, that hadn't stopped Lisynia from using the rooms within to train her magics and fighting prowess. Or for her sister before her from searching for something hidden within it.

As she pushed the aging stone door open and headed down the hallway to the staircase beyond, dust clouded her lungs like a low smoke spit out by an ancient fire. She focused on the feeling of it choking her lungs, trying her best to not dwell on her father's warnings.

She followed Otto closely, Molac in between them, blood from his face dripping behind them. Her heart pounded as Molac walked with a slight limp, slowing them down. They had to hurry.

Lisynia quickened her pace in the dark hallway, ignoring the flood of thoughts and memories she would rather keep buried regarding her sister's life... and death. Then to her father, the sight of him sobbing and shaking. All of it was tied to this tower.

She took a deep breath, the dust flooding her lungs, coating her nostrils with its grime.

If there really were secrets to be found within Teveban, they were here.

Molac tugged at the rope around his hands, the end of which was held by Otto. Otto grunted and stumbled, nearly falling to the ground as he grasped the rope tighter.

Jumping forward, Lisynia caught Otto before he fell, pushing him back to his feet. As her hands touched his back, the thoughts of her sister faded away, replaced by thoughts of the man in front of her touching her back, holding her close.

She shook her head, quickly pushing that out of her mind. She couldn't be distracted. Not even by him.

Otto muttered a thank you, his voice smooth and calm despite the danger they were in here. Lisynia envied his ability to stay calm in every situation; it was a trait he'd had since they were kids and one that she herself had never possessed.

The trio kept walking deeper into the darkness, their path only lit by the small windows casting streams of early morning light into the hallway. Molac was slowly gaining more control over his body, the limp lessening.

As they approached three doors, Otto stooped down, releasing Molac to the floor where he slumped over, exhausted.

Lisynia nearly laughed at the sight of the man, all crumpled and weak from her magic. But before she could, Otto tapped her shoulder.

His breath heaving in and out of his mouth, Otto whispered, "He's so goddamn difficult. Did we have to bring him?"

Lisynia's mind shot back to the Ancient's words. "Yes. I think he recognized that saying my father mentioned."

Otto pursed his lips, the light from a window above barely illuminating his face.

Molac stirred, still refusing to raise his eyes to theirs.

"We have to hurry," Lisynia said, growing impatient from the events of the night. "We march in just two days, and it'll take a whole day to get back."

"I know, Lisy. We'll get back in time. In the meantime, your mother is keeping the troops in line."

But she was already on the ground, tugging at Molac's dirty clothing to raise him to his feet. He grunted and groaned, swatting her hands away.

"Get up, asshole."

Otto sighed behind her, joining into the fray. He hoisted Molac to his feet and struck his back with a hard pat. "Come on, man. Make this a bit easier."

Molac only groaned. "What do you want to know? What did I get dragged halfway across Andyse for?"

Lisynia jutted her face into his, pulling his greasy hair back from his face. "What stories do you tell of the hidden knowledge in Teveban? I know there's something here."

Molac grumbled, swatting at her hand again as he rolled his yellow eyes. "Nothing."

Lisynia felt the familiar heat of anger begin to bubble within her chest. She raised her knee and kicked him in between his legs. He doubled over and she pulled at his hair again. "I've heard parts of the poem. 'In the tower, the Teveban bemoan'."

Molac's eyes flashed with recognition as he clutched his jewels, fear in his eyes. "Never heard it." His voice was shaky and high-pitched.

Lisynia raised her hand and opened it. Focusing again on her breathing, sparks flew from her fingertips, a burning sensation traveling up her arm. "You're a bad liar so I'll give you one more chance. Paralysis isn't the only thing I can do."

Another bluff but as his eyes widened, it seemed to have paid off.

Molac's breathing quickened. "Fine. The rhyme goes like this:" he said, the light of the sparks glinting in his fearful eyes, "In the tower; the Teveban bemoan; an ancient power; behind the stone."

Lisynia smiled, dropping her hand. "You hear that, Otto? *Behind the stone*," she said, turning to him with giddy excitement like they were still kids, just having found his mother's stash of sweets. "It's in the walls."

CHAPTER THIRTY-THREE
MOLAC

The woman in front of him was crazed, running her hands frantically across the walls of the corridor. Molac watched her with little interest, his eyes focused instead on the man between her and him.

The guard from the mountain prison he resided in just yesterday stared at him, his eyes dark with suspicion.

They had been searching the walls to no avail for several hours now, the light of mid-day pouring through the windows, highlighting the dust that floated into the air every time one of the three moved.

"Lisynia," the man warned, not taking his eyes off Molac's. "Are you sure he's not lying?"

Lying? How dare he?

He was an aristocrat, not some common peasant.

Molac shoved his bruised ego down as he returned the man's stare. He swallowed quickly, bile rising in his throat at the thought of the woman's anger turning back to him. His hand absentmindedly clutched his crotch and his damaged goods.

The general spoke now, "He had no reason to. We'd kill him."

Molac squirmed at her words. He thought back to the queen's

words, her promise. How she didn't know the truth of what he would get into.

The general spoke again, turning back toward him and the guard, Otto. "There's nothing in here. Next room."

Otto gave a curt nod, the guard's eyes lingering on the general after she pivoted and began walking. Molac smirked, looking toward the woman himself as she moved away from them. He traced her curves, hidden slightly by her armor but there nonetheless, as they swayed while she walked.

Despite all her... less than savory qualities, she sure was something to look at. Without thinking, he spoke to Otto, "Once you're done with her, let me have some fun too."

Otto's eyes fell away from the general and onto Molac. His heart dropped. "What did you just say?" Otto said, his voice dangerously level.

Molac gulped. "Nothing. Sorry, it was nothing."

Otto tugged at the rope around Molac's wrists especially hard. "That's what I thought."

The rope burned as it rubbed against the bruises and cuts from the last time he was bound, making him wince.

"You ever talk about her like that again, you won't have only her anger to worry about."

Molac grimaced. He sure was bad at staying out of trouble.

He stumbled along behind Otto as they began walking, his arms and legs still unnaturally heavy from the paralysis spell they threw him under.

He couldn't put it out of his mind, even now, the spell. Magics was a known thing in Eterin, sure. The magics of The Seven of Lupegi was well known, even throughout Davegu. In Davegu, the battlemages like some of Asmuto's foot soldiers were basically an ill-kept secret. He had even traveled with them. Then in Andyse, stories of plant mages, people that could talk to animals. Magics was known.

But not any kind that can freeze a man in place. Or kill with one swipe to the arm like she did to that Lupegi soldier earlier when she thought he was still in the sewer.

His unease grew as they traveled deeper within the tower's corridor toward a large stone door at the end of the hallway.

It was magnificent, the gray stone bordered with a large arch of dark wooden planks, intricate, old carvings within the wood half faded away by now and covered in dust.

How long had it been since someone was down here last? He didn't even know if he wanted to know.

The general approached the door, her hands flying over the stone surface as if looking for a secret hidden within.

Molac moved slowly, as slow as he could while Otto yanked him forward but something about the door gave him chills that spread from the tips of his fingers to his stuttering heart. He gulped as Otto gave him more slack, distracted by the door himself.

"I think it's warded," the general proclaimed to no one in particular, stepping away from the door with her hands on her hips. "But it's worn off a bit. I can probably get through it,"

Molac scoffed. Warding supposedly was ancient and powerful magics, the magics of the Ancient's priestesses themselves from the days when the Goddesses involved themselves in human affairs. He had thought their magics to just be legend, old stories from those few devout followers that still remained, like the crazed leader of the Southern Coalition, Yidenu. Warding was as stupid to believe in as blood magics.

"What makes you say that? The Ancients are just old legends," he blurted out, before he could stop himself.

Both Otto and the general turned to look at him, their eyes wide in surprise. The general took a few steps forward and Molac instinctively flinched, preparing for another one of her outbursts toward him.

But it didn't come. He opened his eyes. She smiled as she approached with a grim sort of sly smile that made his skin crawl.

"The Davegu really are a faithless people, aren't you?" she cooed, placing her hands on her hips again. "Didn't you say the same thing about us?"

He gulped, giving her a slight nod as she moved toward him. She moved one hand toward him and he flinched again. The general grabbed his chin and squeezed his face, sending a dull pain through his head.

"The Ancient Goddesses are real, Molac," she said, squeezing his face tighter, her fingertips digging into his skin. "They live."

It took hours. Hours in which Molac sat frozen against the far wall from the general and the guard. The rope sat limp at his feet, having been discarded while the two Tevebrisians attempted to break through the apparent warding over the door.

While he sat, one thing kept eating at his consciousness, gnawing at his mind.

They live.

It was horrendously similar to the way Yidenu had promised retribution in the dungeon. He shifted uncomfortably, nestling himself further against the wall as it scratched into his back through the thin shirt he wore.

The Ancients were a legend, just tales of powerful immortal women that didn't really have anything to do with real life. They didn't exist; they were simply something that people decided to pray to to absolve their own responsibility for their life.

At least that's what Davegu taught him.

But they also taught him that the Teveban were a myth and look where he was now, in their kingdom. They taught him aristocracy meant he was special, protected. He didn't feel protected now.

He shifted his weight again as the general groaned in the distance. He turned his eyes toward the direction the Tevebrisians stood and watched as sparks once again flew from the fingertips of the woman while she pressed her hand against the stone.

The sparks fizzled out and the stone stayed still, unmoving.

Molac scoffed under his breath, tearing his eyes from them. He fidgeted with the rope around his wrists, running his fingers along the rough fibers.

Then a yelp reached his ears. He shot to his feet, teetering as he attempted to regain his balance. His shock at the sudden noise morphed into an odd combination of horror and awe as the great stone door slid open of its own accord.

Inside was musty, probably not having seen the light of day in centuries, and reeked of heavy alcohol, stains and burn marks spilling out from a door to their side.

But the general didn't seem to mind; she went to work immediately. Her hands traced every stone brick, looking for any signs of weakness.

Molac drummed his fingers along the back of his hand, the only place he could reach with his hands still bound and scoffed as the general and her man moved in a frenzy.

What was important enough that they'd risk their lives for it coming back?

Or more likely, why were the Teveban stupid enough to come back? They got out of the kingdom they claimed oppressed them so badly. Why come back?

As his thoughts wandered to all the violence he'd seen: the group he traveled with mowed down, the Lupegi soldier in the street, the way they treated him, he thought back to the tales told in Davegu.

Bloodthirsty, stupid people.

That's what the Teveban were. Bloodthirsty and stupid, just like the stories said.

He turned his attention back to the general as a squeal escaped her, ringing in his ears in a way that made him cringe.

"There's stains on this one, old blood stains," she said excitedly, the happiest Molac had ever seen her.

He jutted his head out, looking around her. She stood in front of a brick on the bottom of the wall, pointing at it to Otto.

Lisynia dropped to her knees.

I'd love to see her like that more often.

Molac snickered to himself at his thoughts, watching as she grunted and pulled the brick from its resting place. Her body blocked his view of the interior, but she grabbed something and shoved it into the pack she wore at her side.

His blood ran cold as he thought back to the poem.

An ancient power; behind the stone.

His breathing quickened, thinking back to Asmuto, to Dhunviro and Oshgor, to the queen, to the people the general was going to march on soon enough. If she had just found that 'ancient power', it only could mean one thing:

They were fucked.

So much for restoring his title.

Chapter Thirty-Four
Tivea

Tivea shoveled the meat into her mouth with a fervor. This breakfast was the first good meal she'd eaten in weeks. The people sitting around her in the great hall of Ryrie, Xienee's people, were either too polite to say anything about her lack of manners or simply decided not to since word of her life these past weeks had spread through the fortress.

All the suffering, the sights she couldn't get out of her head, the fear and uncertainty. All of it still haunted her despite people's reassurances that she was safe here.

Tivea paused her consumption as a boy walked up to her, standing right in front of the table she sat at. She looked up from her plate, ignoring all the stares she garnered from the people around her. The boy was young but clothed in armor nonetheless, like everyone else here besides her.

It was the boy from the forest, the one that was with Xienee. He smiled at her, revealing a gap in between his teeth. It appeared almost as if his adult teeth hadn't quite grown in yet despite being about sixteen namedays old.

Tivea swallowed the mouthful of food and smiled back.

"How are you settling in?" the boy asked, pulling out the chair across from her.

She sighed, mulling the question over in her mind, deciding if she wanted to answer truthfully or not. "Fine, I guess," she lied, averting her eyes.

The boy cocked his head. "Is that the truth? I know when I first came here a few weeks ago, I felt very out of place."

Tivea looked up, her eyes falling on his young face. "I don't know. It's weird being here to be honest." Her stomach sank as she gazed upon him. He was so young and yet here, preparing for war. "Why did you come here?"

The boy chuckled slightly, his laugh high-pitched and childish. Tivea cringed again, trying to avoid looking him in the face. She'd had enough sadness these past weeks. But then he spoke. "I came here for the same reason as the rest of the Teveban. Freedom."

At his words, Tivea found herself looking at him again. His face was hard, a hardness she had only seen in the leaders of the Coalition before, Mych, her father, and all the others that had war touch their lives. What had this boy gone through?

She dropped her fork, looking him directly in the face now, her interest piqued. "Freedom?"

The boy sighed before he spoke, his voice low as he leaned in toward her, like he was scared of Xienee's troops hearing him. "My mother was killed by Davegu soldiers for keeping books." He sniffled. "She taught me to read. It's illegal in Teveban except for the royal family and only allowed for them so they can read the edicts from Davegu and Lupegi. I'm one of the only ones here that knows how besides the general. I teach a class and run messages because I'm one of the only ones that can, thanks to my mother. They took her hands off in front of me before they..." he paused, looking away.

Tivea felt her stomach turn at his story and found herself at a loss of words.

"I'm sorry," she said, the only thing she could muster herself to say. Even most Andysi knew how to read and write. Maybe she was wrong about the Tevebrisians. Maybe her mother truly was right. She moved her plate to the side, ignoring the grumbles from the man next to her. Tivea reached over the table and took the boy's hand into her own. "I'm so sorry."

The boy sniffled, turning away as he wiped his tears with his other hand. "It's just life in Teveban. The general is trying to change that. That's why I'm here."

Tivea squeezed his hand, her thoughts falling back to the night she watched her world burn, her father taken away by Davegu soldiers, a shell of himself. She thought of her own mother, a woman of magics and kindness, killed by something that she still didn't know to this day. What would she do if she saw them die in front of her like this boy had?

She pushed those thoughts from her mind as best she could, tears beginning to well in her own eyes. She swallowed hard, her throat tightening.

Leaning toward the boy, she whispered. "I watched my father get taken by the same people that did that to your mother. I can't say I understand your pain, but I understand why you're here. You're doing good by her, and I hope you know that."

The boy nodded, his eyes still glimmering. "Thank you. Your name is Tebea, right? I'm Ason."

Tivea laughed slightly, a feeling blooming that she hadn't felt in a while. Happiness.

"Tivea," she corrected. "It's nice to meet you, Ason."

The rest of breakfast passed without many thoughts of her mother, or her father, or Rauna. Instead, she focused on the young boy with the shaggy blonde hair. She told him of her life, before the attack. She told him of her mother, his father's laugh, and pulled out her journal to let him read something new again, his eyes growing watery as he traced the neatly written letters in awe. He told her of his life, the things he had gone through, the pain he had suffered, and she found herself once again at a loss of words, something in him held onto hope for a better future.

Even while Ason spoke of horrors and atrocities, there was an undeniable sense of hope in his stories. Her thoughts drifted back to her father, his idea of working with the enemy, working with the Davegu diplomatically to maintain peace after her mother's death. Hearing what Teveban had been through was proof enough that King Tovik would never allow peace while he lived.

Ason moved to get up, grabbing her fully eaten plate from in front of her. "I'll get that for you."

Tivea smiled, getting up from the long table. "Thank you."

The boy nodded and walked away, leaving her alone once again. She looked around cautiously, watching as people similarly got up from the tables in the mess hall and exited in a large archway opposite from where she had come in.

She used the exodus to finally calm her mind enough to take in the intricacies of the fortress. It was old, the stone aged and worn. A thick layer of dust covered every surface above a level that could be easily reached. The large tables they ate at were equally old, the wood half-rotted in some places. This place was old, older than anything else she had seen before. She twirled her hair around her finger, eyes gazing every which way.

As she twirled her hair, her thoughts shot back to her father.

Your mother used to do that.

Tears stung at her eyes, and she pulled her finger from her hair, wiping desperately at her face instead. She'd been here less than a day; she couldn't break down in here, in public, in front of everyone. She wouldn't.

She looked around the hall again, searching for something to distract herself from the physical pain that ebbed through her body at the thought of her father. Her eyes settled on Ason, coming back out from the large archway. He smiled as he approached and raised a hand to wave at her.

Tivea smiled slightly, her eyes still blurry from the tears, and returned the boy's wave.

He jogged to her now, his leather armor squeaking as he approached. Tivea raised a hand to her mouth, stifling a laugh.

"You're still here?" he asked, a wide smile on his face.

"Where would I go?" she asked, turning to begin walking with him out of the hall. "I don't know where anything is."

"That's true, I guess," he said, his smile still not fading as they exited the mess hall. "Come on, I'll give you a tour."

Tivea's smile faltered as she looked over the banister at the foyer below. A crowd was gathering at the entrance of the fortress, Tevebrisians and Andysi alike. She approached the wooden banister closer, gripping the railing as she peered over.

Ason joined her, standing at her side. "What do you think it is?"

"I don't know, I was about to ask—"

A loud horn sounded, interrupting her words. Xienee came through the large double doors that served as the entrance and bellowed, her voice echoing up the walls of the foyer as they reached Tivea's ears. "Boys, we found them!"

Her heart pounded and she gripped the railing tighter, her knuckles white from the strain.

Rauna.

She watched intently as people spilled through the doors after Xienee, two people carried over the soldier's shoulders, blood dripping onto the floor from their faces. One man and one woman.

Her heart dropped and her legs went weak, her fingers tightening around the guardrail to keep herself upright. Ason looked over to her quizzically, his brow furrowed. Her heart pounded in her ears, her vision blurring as she attempted to make sense of the sight in front of her.

It wasn't Rauna.

It was Gaabi and Hanue.

Chapter Thirty-Five
Anavi

As she paced the small cell back and forth, back and forth, jolts of pain shot up her leg. Anavi groaned as she took another step, a fiery agony shooting up her thigh.

"Will you stop that already?" the man from the cell next to her called out from the darkness. "I'm exhausted."

"I'm sorry, your highness," she spat back sarcastically, still pacing. "I didn't realize you were okay with dying here."

There was a rustling from the next cell and the man responded with a voice that was stronger, louder. "I'm not, but fucking your leg up more won't help anyone."

She paused her movements, standing with most of her weight on her good leg as her knee throbbed. "I don't see you doing anything about it."

"That's cause I'm not advertising it, spy."

She scoffed. What did he know about escaping a prison? Old fuck like him had probably never been to a prison before in his life.

But yet, he knew who she was.

All the time they'd been in here together and she still didn't know who he was. Every time she asked, he changed the subject or simply went silent. She resumed her pacing, moving her bad leg awkwardly to avoid putting too much weight on it.

Another jolt shot through her, and she stumbled, reaching out for the wall to steady herself.

"You keep fucking up that leg, we're never getting out of here."

She closed her eyes, taking a deep breath as anger choked her. "What the fuck do you mean 'we'?"

The man laughed, a sound that only amplified the grip anger held on her body. She balled her fist and pushed it into the rock wall, relishing the biting feeling of the stone against her skin.

The man spoke again, "You're not getting out of here without help, girl, not with that leg."

Anavi gritted her teeth, pressing her fist deeper into the stone as a trickle of blood flowed down her fingers from its roughness. "What, and you propose I let you help me? The man that won't even tell me his name?"

"Yes."

She didn't know how to respond to such a simple answer and her mind went blank, the anger dissipating slightly. Anavi pulled her fist back from the stone and pressed her fingers into the wounds it left, relishing the sting that came with it.

"What is your name, old man?"

"If you really wish to know, spy, I promise you won't like the answer."

Her mind wandered as he said this. There were plenty of people she wouldn't like to be trapped in a prison with: all the widows of the people she killed for The Seven, the children of the men that whispered of uprisings, the fathers of those whose children she'd beaten into submission. The list was endless.

"That's not really a high bar for me," she said, trying to ignore the sear of pain that enveloped her thigh with her movements.

"Do you wish to know?"

"How many times do I have to say yes for you to answer?"

Her patience with his games was wearing out, the gnawing feeling of annoyance chewing on her mind. Her leg gave another protest, and she stumbled again.

She thrust her arms out as she fell, the mud of the cell floor oozing between her fingers. Her breath heaved and she lowered herself to the ground and sat against the wall she shared with him.

"Are you alright, spy?" the old man asked, his voice seeming to show genuine concern.

Great, now he thinks we're friends.

"Yes, I'm fine. Are you going to answer me or not?"

"I think not yet," the man responded. "Not after you just lied to me. Give yourself some rest."

Anavi's patience dissipated quickly, and she balled her fists again, squeezing the mud in her hands. Her leg screamed in protest as she made her way back to her feet, storming over to the wall that separated their cells. "I didn't lie."

The man responded quickly, his voice booming so loud it seemed to shake the walls. "Yes, you did, spy. Take a break, give your leg the rest it needs."

Anavi stepped back, her leg throbbing beneath her weight. She wobbled, her leg shaking horribly before she fell again, flying toward the ground.

She landed roughly, the force sending shockwaves through her arms. Tears threatened to spill as the blood poured from her wound, reopened. Anavi turned in the mud, sitting on her bottom now and pressed her dirty, muddy, hands against the spot above her knee that throbbed painfully.

He was right. She wasn't getting anywhere like this.

She spoke dejectedly, her voice wavering slightly. "Fine. I'll rest," she said, "but only if you tell me what your name is."

The man sighed deeply, the sound carrying well through the hallway to her. "You're Anavi, the spy."

"I know who I am," she said, gritting her teeth as another jolt shot through her, blood spilling over her fingers. "Who are you?"

"I nearly killed you," he said simply. "I am Yidenu."

Chapter Thirty-Six
Hanue

It was cold. That's all he could focus on. It was cold in the dungeon.

The winter seemed to have arrived early down in the cell he now resided in. As he slowly moved toward the wall that separated his cell from the others, his bloodied fingers froze into icicles. He had already taken note of his injuries; all minor, scrapes and cuts on his arms and legs. But for some reason beyond his knowledge, the people that brought them in seemed to be under a no-kill order. They didn't even draw their weapons.

Still, the pain ebbed through his arms as he moved to stick his hand awkwardly toward Gaabi's cell. His voice came out with a croak. "Gaabi?"

A rustling met his ears, probably as she moved in her own cold cell. "Hanue, I'm here."

He breathed a sigh of relief, his breath misting in front of his face. He turned and pressed his back against the cold stone wall that separated them and curled into himself as best as he could. His mind wandered to the forest he was in just hours ago, the daylight shining through the trees.

They had come as a group ten strong of Andysi and Tevebrisians and snatched Gaabi from his arms.

Even now, he still couldn't protect her. And they certainly couldn't escape again, their captors would be prepared for another try at Gaabi's trick with the keys.

He turned to the bars that held him within the cell and squeezed his hand through, twisting it awkwardly to touch the freezing metal bars of Gaabi's cell. Her fingers twirled into his, her warm touch sending heat through his body as she grasped at his hand.

"I'm scared," she murmured, her voice muffled slightly like her mouth was covered by her shirt.

He sighed deeply, his breath freezing again in front of his eyes as he shivered. "I know. I am too."

His thoughts strayed to that Davegu soldier that was brought in with them the first time, the crack her neck made when it broke from her hanging herself. They'd surely not let him and Gaabi escape again. Was that the only way to get out of here now?

"We never should've come back. We should've just left like you wanted," Gaabi said softly, her words choked. "We didn't even find Rauna or your sister."

Her pain pained him, hitting his chest like a brick. As her words sunk into his brain, each syllable strengthened his resolve.

I will not let her die here.

That was the only thing he could focus on, the girl in the cell next to him, crying into her shirt. She was too kind, too good, to die here.

She would not die here. He would get her out if it was the last thing he ever did with his life.

Even if he never left this cell, she would. She would find her sister and live happily, far away from this hellhole. He would do anything to make that come true.

He squeezed her hand, thoughts straying to her lips on his, the way he failed to protect her when they came from the woods, the feeling of her fingers intertwined in his, the pain she undoubtedly felt at the loss of her sister again.

"Gaabi, I'm going to get you out of here, I promise."

She sniffled, her fingers squeezing his tighter. "How could you possibly say that?"

Hanue sighed, his mind wandering back to several weeks ago, the first time he saw her. Her red hair was messy, covered in dirt, her wounds extensive. She looked so helpless, and he had promised one thing when she leaned on him that day. He would protect her. And now, he wouldn't just protect her, he cared for her, in a way he'd never felt before.

He took a deep breath, sticking his fingers further into her cell, as much as he could and grasped her hand tighter. "From the moment I saw you, covered in blood and dirt on the ground, I knew one thing; I would protect you with everything in me."

She gasped and his heart pounded as he awaited her response. He heard her crying stop and his heart sunk at the silence, gripping her fingers tighter still.

"It's alright, Gaabi. I promise it's alright."

"No, it's not!" she burst out, pulling her hand from his grasp.

He retreated his arm, his heart sinking deeper into his stomach as his throat closed.

"Nothing's okay. And you don't have to protect me, Hanue."

"What's wrong, Gaabi?"

"I already have a 'protector'. I have my sister, and I have myself. Right now, I need you to stop worrying about saving me and start working with me to keep away from whatever fate they have in store for us. I care about protecting you too."

Hanue nodded, embarrassment taking hold of him. "Alright. Then let's figure it out together. But not right now," he said quietly as a soft sound echoed through the hold, like a door opening. "Someone's coming."

Gaabi went silent. Hanue pushed off the ground and raised himself to his feet shakily. He flicked at the bars, sending a metallic *clink* through the hallway. If they were coming down here to take them again, maybe he could annoy them into taking him first.

Footsteps approached quickly, as if the person making them was running for some reason. The light of the lantern flicked ominously as a shadow grew on the wall and his heart pounded, threatening to leave his chest.

"Hey!" he shouted, trying to quell his fear as Gaabi's cell remained silent.

The shadow grew and grew and grew, becoming more detailed as the footsteps got louder.

A woman came into view. Passing Gaabi's cell and reaching the front of his. His blood ran cold at the sight of long hair flying in the air, his eyes struggling to adjust to take in the person in front of him.

"Hanue," a familiar voice said.

He blinked in confusion, approaching the bars as Gaabi gasped.

"Tivea!" Gaabi's voice burst out, a slight clang following her voice as she pressed herself to the bars of her cell.

The woman nodded as she came into focus. Long brown hair, tan skin, soft features. It was her.

"What are you doing here?" Hanue ventured, his voice shaky as he twisted his head around to search for another person. Then a thought he hadn't considered came to mind, an anger building within his chest. "Did you tell them where to find us?"

"What? Why would I?" Tivea shushed him, raising a finger to her lips as her eyes flitted toward the direction she came. "I can't be down here long. I got my friend to let me down to talk to you. How did you get caught?"

Gaabi reached her hand through the bars, grabbing Tivea by the shoulder with a grimy hand. "We got caught in the forest. Where's Rauna?"

Tivea's face twisted in pain and Hanue's suspicion faded slightly as she spoke. "I don't know. She was headed to find you."

Hanue gasped, taking a step back at this assertion. He peered through the bars and saw Gaabi gripping Tivea's shoulder with a fervor, pulling her toward her.

Gaabi's voice was more level-headed than he expected. "You mean she's not here with you?"

Tivea shook her head, her features twisting into a look of anxiety Hanue had never seen on her before. "She's not here."

Hanue took a deep breath, stepping forward toward Tivea and Gaabi. He was far from a fan of Rauna. She was stubborn, arrogant, rude and her decision to stay in Andyse was nothing short of stupid. But the fact she wasn't with Tivea, was traveling the forest alone with no idea where her sister was, was far from what he would wish on anyone.

He asked one question. "Where is she?"

CHAPTER THIRTY-SEVEN
RAUNA

The frigid air bit at Rauna's skin as she moved through the forest with a speed rivaling the birds flying above her head. She was almost there. Almost to her sister after days apart.

Her thoughts strayed as she ran. The woman she left behind smiled in her mind, her face warm and inviting.

No.

Rauna would never see her again. It was no use focusing on her. Now she had to focus on her sister. She picked up her pace, pushing tree branches away from her face.

Her breath heaving in and out of her body, Rauna approached the pass, the meeting point, and she turned her eyes upwards, searching the mountain for any splash of red on the rock face.

But there wasn't one. Rauna slowed to a stop, shivering as another gust of wind blew down the mountain, throwing her hair every which way.

Where was she?

Confusion and panic tugged at her mind as she started moving again, climbing on her hands and knees upwards toward the slight plateau she expected to see them on.

Maybe they're hiding.

But something about that didn't seem right. Something felt off about this, chilling her to the bones as her hands grasped at the rock, dragging herself upward. Her fingers screamed in protest as they seemed to freeze into the rock itself, pulling at her skin. But she pushed that from her mind. That didn't matter. None of that mattered. The only thing that mattered was her sister.

With one last pull, she collapsed onto the cold, flat rock of the plateau. Scrambling to her feet, her breath froze as it exited her mouth, a crystallized mist in front of her eyes. She moved quickly, searching behind the boulders and crevasses for any sign of her sister or the boy she left with.

But there was nothing. Nothing, except for a small burn pit behind one of the rocks.

Either they had left or...

Stop. You can't think like that.

But either way she was gone.

Her breathing quickened, her body shivering wildly as the wind roared through the plateau again. Her mind ran in every direction. She's gone. She's gone. She's gone.

Rauna's stomach turned, her heart pounding as she flew across the plateau, searching every crack in the mountain once again.

But she was still gone.

She shook, whether from the cold or the fear, she wasn't sure. Rauna moved quickly to the edge of the flat spot, looking down the mountain from where she had come, hunting for a sign of her sister anywhere. Her eyes settled on a clearing in the distance, the grass and ferns rising in tufts, as if there was struggle beneath the trees.

Rauna pounced into action, scaling back down the mountain with a fervor, the pack thumping against her back as she moved. War was coming to Andyse and now her sister might be caught up in it yet again. As her feet hit solid ground, she quickly pivoted and began running to the south, to the clearing. She moved with a speed she never had before, her heart banging against her ribs as she ran.

The ferns and grass grabbed at her feet as she made her way through the forest, shoving branches and limbs from her face as they tugged at her hair, scratched at her face. She crashed through the trees, coming up to the clearing.

As she entered the open expanse, her eyes shot to the ground. The grass was torn up, deep footprints in the mud below from heavy boots.

She panted, her thoughts running wild as she searched for anything else within the clearing that gave any answers as to what happened here, any blood, or broken teeth.

A glimmer of red caught her eye. On the ferns at her feet, speckles of half dried blood were splashed onto their leafy surfaces. Rauna gulped, her mind going to the worst possible outcome of the scuffle here. But as she searched the foliage nearby, she didn't see any other specks of blood or running red in the mud.

Either way though, her sister was gone and this scene fresh.

She was taken. Rauna raised her hands to her head, her mind escaping her.

Rauna raised her head and lowered her arms, turning back toward the south. Her feet moved swiftly without her input, like a part of a different person.

She crashed through the forest again, headed back to Ryrie. *I know who took her.*

Rain hit her bare arms hard, feeling more like stones than raindrops with the torrential downpour that covered the treetops with water, sending flurries of wet dying leaves onto her.

Her hair stuck to her face as she ran, her shirt clinging to her body as it soaked with sweat and rain. But she didn't care. Just like that night she left Lasari to find her sister, she would find her now, no matter what.

Water splashed up her legs as she traversed the woods, puddles and small streams of running water twisting and turning her every which way. Darkness began to settle over Andyse, slowly blanketing the world in the sightlessness of a forest night.

Rauna ran, spitting rainwater from her mouth as she moved. She pushed through the trees as they cut her arms, her legs, her hands, her face, blood running with the rainwater down her body, the touch of the wood leaving a stinging sensation on her wounds.

Her legs burned as they pounded into the muddy ground. She pushed on, ignoring the fact that she could barely see as the clouds overhead blocked out the moon. She shivered slightly, the blood pumping through her body not enough to keep her warm as the temperature dropped steeply.

But she couldn't stop. She wouldn't.

As she crashed through the woods, a light greeted her eyes in the distance, flickering as tree limbs swayed in front of it.

Ryrie.

She forced herself to move faster, quicker, ignoring the exhaustion making her limbs heavy and tired. There was no time to stop, not now when she was so close.

Rauna burst through into the clearing, her eyes crazed as she searched the stone face of the mountain for a door, any entrance into the fortress.

A crack of lightning lit up the sky, the thunderous boom that followed shaking the ground. She wavered in place as she readjusted her balance.

But the quick flash of bright light had done its job, illuminating the door just for a second. She forced her tired legs to move toward it, one last burst of energy propelling her.

A man yelled from behind her as she reached the door. She didn't hear what he said but as the familiar sound of a sword being drawn behind her rang out in the night, she reached for the handles, desperately begging any god that would listen to hear her, to let her in.

And miraculously, the doors swung open, and she burst inside, another boom of thunder sounding behind her.

Light met her eyes blindingly and a rough hand grabbed her from behind, pulling her back. She wrestled away from the grip on her arm and sprinted into the warm light of the inside.

"Where is she?" she screamed, her voice cracking as the sound ripped through her throat. "WHERE IS SHE?"

The guards around her moved quickly, grabbing her by her arms, their grip digging into her skin. She fought and thrashed as swords were drawn, pressed against her skin, streams of liquid coming from the points of contact.

Rauna screamed again, not even feeling the blades biting into her skin. As a crowd started to gather, she saw one face in the crowd that she recognized—a tan woman with brown hair, tied back in a neat braid over her shoulder and a look of shock and horror on her pretty face.

Tivea.

Chapter Thirty-Eight
Lisynia

S he clutched the leather pack and the books within with a vice grip as rain tore through the air. The entire way back to Ryrie, she had refused to loosen her hold, even for a second. Lisynia hadn't even dared to open the books, not until she was in the safety of her quarters with her mother.

They were close now and as the rain picked up in intensity, Lisynia moved quicker, eager to finally get to read the books so long hidden. And eager to sharpen her sword for the march tomorrow.

Otto quickened his pace, Molac dragging behind by his rope bonds. Her childhood friend's hand skimmed her back as they walked, nestled perfectly in the small of her back and she fought a smile from appearing on her face at his touch.

Instead, she forced a frown onto her features and turned to him, barely able to see him between the downpour of rain and darkness of night. "What is it?"

He smiled as he turned to her, or at least that's what Lisynia could gather he was doing as a flash of lightning lit up the sky. "Just wanted to walk with you."

The smile she fought so hard to keep buried spread onto her face in full force at his words and she slowed her pace, his hand pressing into her back harder now. "How's the prisoner doing?"

Otto chuckled slightly, the sound of his melodious laugh widening the smile on her face. "He's grumpy. But he always seems to be, so no big issue there."

Now it was her turn to let out a laugh. "He's a very grumpy boy, isn't he?"

"I can hear you," a voice called out from behind them and Lisynia raised her free hand to her mouth, stifling her laugh.

Another strike of lightning burst through the sky. She turned back to Otto, her stomach twisting as the reality of the situation set in. "It's a big day tomorrow. We have to get home and get the rest of the plans in order, make sure all the weapons are clean and sharp. We need to check everyone's pack, we need to—"

"I know," Otto said with a chuckle, raising his hand to her cheek to wipe rain drops from her skin. "Don't worry, I'll be right there with you the whole time." As his calloused fingers skimmed across her skin, her stomach turned, her smile once again widening as her skin begged for more of his touch.

Don't think like that.

She quickly pushed his hand away, swatting at it like a bug on a summer's day. She couldn't want his touch. Not when they all might be dead within days.

Her stomach twisted again, this time considerably less pleasant than before as her thoughts strayed to the Davegu soldiers she'd killed, the wounds on her arms and hand. Images of Ason, Otto, her mother and father all dead and bleeding from wounds she was helpless to treat flashed in front of her eyes.

"We're going to fight like hell against that bastard king and we're going to win, Lisy. I know how you get in your head. But we're going to win," Otto said, moving his hand to scratch the back of his head.

Lisynia tore her eyes from him as they walked, focusing her eyes ahead, toward Ryrie. "Well, one thing you said is right, we're going to fight like hell."

There wasn't any other choice.

As they approached Ryrie, the sun had fully settled beyond Andyse, blanketing the world in the dreary feeling of a rainy night. Her feet sloshed in the mud as they climbed up the hill toward the fort's entrance. Molac had been groaning behind her the entire way while Otto walked stoic and calm at her side.

Despite everything to come in the next few days, Otto's presence was a welcome and calming one. He always knew how to keep her calm, the only person that could.

A strange noise reached her ears as she took another step through the muck and her interest piqued. It was a mixture of the chatter of angry people and the sound of raindrops hitting metal. She raised her eyes to the mountain to her side, peering through the canopy of empty branches and her eyes caught the light in her bedroom, lit.

Something was happening at Ryrie.

She turned to Otto, her eyes wide as her heart beat hard in her chest. She whispered, moving close to his ear. "There's something happening in the fortress. I'll kill the prisoner, if it's his people, he's just going to be a liability."

Otto nodded but his face betrayed his unease with this idea. "Do you have to kill him?"

She didn't answer. Of course, she did. He'd outlived his usefulness. What better idea was there?

Lisynia grabbed the rope from Otto's hands and pulled it taut, moving her hands up the rope toward Molac. As she approached, his face twisted into a fear she'd seen before, from her people when they were taken by the slavers or when the raids pulled them from their homes. A pang shot through her.

Be better than them. Her mother's old adage played in her head.

She pulled the dagger from her side with one hand, still holding the rope tightly with the other. A wave of guilt washed over her body as he whimpered, raising his hands up as much as he could.

She held the dagger above her head, preparing to bring it down on his neck but something within her stilled, her hands trembling beneath the weight of what she was about to do.

He flinched away from her, his eyes closed tightly. His body trembled almost as bad as her hand and Lisynia lowered her dagger.

She sighed, her thoughts urging her to do it, to kill him but as another sound reached her ears from Ryrie, she balked at the thought of bringing the dagger down.

Her hands moved of their own accord toward the ropes that bound him. As she sawed at the rope, the prisoner opened his eyes wide, the yellow irises focused on her movements with a quiet intensity.

"Wh—" he said.

"Get out of here," she pulled the rope from his hands, dropping it to the ground, "hurry, before I change my mind and drop you where you stand."

Molac took a deep breath, his eyes still wide, so wide they seemed to pop out of his head. He nodded slightly, unsure, and moved slowly away from her before turning around and running into the forest, his feet sloshing through the mud as he retreated.

Otto walked behind her, his footsteps reaching her ears beneath the sounds of chaos at Ryrie and she tore her eyes from the direction Molac disappeared into, heading south toward Davegu.

"We have to get to Ryrie," she said simply, pivoting on her heel and pretending not to see the look on Otto's face—a look of confusion and... was that pride?

She pushed her own hesitation from her mind and began walking swiftly toward the source of the noise which had died down now, barely detectable.

Otto jogged up to walk with her. "You let him go," he said simply.

Lisynia nodded, already regretting her decision. "I did. He helped us. And I should try to keep my word."

"I'm proud of you." Otto nodded in the corner of her eyes as the rain slowed. "I really am. I remember when you used to threaten my life when you lost hide and seek as kids."

Lisynia shot a look at him, pretending to be deeply offended. "I would never."

Otto snorted. "Lisy, you know you did. But now, that strength and determination is going somewhere other than brandishing a fist at your friends. I'd follow the Lisy walking next to me now into far more than just the Davegu Kingdom."

Lisynia let a small smile play on her features, trying to figure out what he could mean by that. But the sounds of Ryrie were growing louder, and she pushed forward.

They came up to the fortress to a group of people, Andysi and Tevebrisian, standing outside in the rain, staring into the trees in every direction. Lisynia quickened her step, walking to the front of the group. "What's the meaning of this?"

She moved her hand to the journal within her pack and gripped the leather tightly, her rage building at the lack of an answer. She opened her mouth to shout again.

A strike of lightning hit nearby, making her jump, her mouth closing quickly and a familiar voice entered her mind. Her skin crawled as it hummed, drowning out the rain and muttering of the people in front of her. Every hair on the back of her neck stood up, her vision fading as the humming grew louder, a melody she couldn't quite make out. The world went dark, and her body became weightless, the ground beneath her feet disappearing.

The humming grew ever louder, and she couldn't hear anything else, see anything at all in the unending darkness.

The shadowy woman stepped out from the darkness again, her head covered in a blinding, glowing red. Lisynia's skin burned as she approached, slowly, methodically. The woman reached a hand out to

Lisynia's chin, her touch both soothing and painful as every cell in her body attempted to scream.

"I will have you soon, Lisynia."

She woke in a pool of sweat, frantically looking around for the woman, the Goddess that just stroked her skin. Her flesh still burned as she sat up straight. The woman was not there, instead another familiar face met her sight.

Strong features, brown eyes, dirty blonde hair.

Her mother.

Her hand moved slowly along Lisynia's arm, grazing the wound from the fight with the Davegu soldier and Lisynia flinched. She peered around the room and was met with her quarters, the same dim light of the lanterns, the same desk with papers strewn over the top of it, the same four-canopy bed with red curtains.

She turned to her mother again, grabbing her hand as the woman moved it to stroke her face.

"What happened, Mother?"

Her mother's eyes went wide. "You're awake?"

Annoyance tugged at Lisynia's mind; couldn't she tell she was awake? "Yes."

"I'm sorry, honey, you were thrashing and talking while you were out. I wasn't sure if you were awake. Otto's come by every few hours to ask for you."

Lisynia's face dropped, her mind frantic now. She dropped her mother's hand, her chest heaving as she panted, anxiety filling her chest, strangling her heart.

The march, the king to kill, the people outside.

What happened?

"What do you mean?" she asked, moving to get out of bed, to figure it out herself.

Her mother caught her and pushed her back on the bed.

"Mother, how long was I out for?"

"A few hours, honey," her mother responded, pulling her hair from her eyes and pressing her lips to Lisynia's forehead. "Do you want to talk about it?"

Lisynia shook her head, pushing her mother away again. "What happened?"

"I don't know, Lisynia. I was hoping you'd be able to tell me," her mother said, moving her hands once again toward Lisynia's face, stroking her hair with one while the other caressed her face. The feeling of another human being touching her, holding her, brought tears to Lisynia's eyes, pinpricks of heat burning as she thought back to the last moments she remembered.

The woman with red. Touching her.

Claiming her.

"All I remember is coming up to Ryrie and..." Lisynia inhaled shakily. "Otto caught me as I fell. The Goddess came for me again, Mother. She came back."

"Calm down, child. You're safe," her mother soothed, her voice low and quiet. "What did she say?

Lisynia felt a tear slip down her cheek and she fell into her mother's embrace, sobs wracking her body as they jolted through her. "She said she'll have me soon. What does that mean?"

The queen didn't answer, just holding her tightly. Lisynia wiped furiously at her face, fighting back the overwhelm that threatened to seize her body. Now was not the time to be crying. Now was the time to prepare for war.

Her mother tightened her hold on her, wrapping her arms around her head and pulling her into her chest, like she used to do when Lisynia was young. At this, the sobs she'd been withholding crept back up and it took everything in her not to give it to their draw.

"I need to get my troops ready, Mother."

"You need rest."

Lisynia raised her head, pulling herself from her mother's embrace. "Will you at least tell me what happened before I arrived? Everyone was outside and staring into the woods. Why?"

"There was a woman that burst in. Your guards took care of it, like you trained them. She ran off into the woods, but she'll be dead soon enough." Her mother's face bore a warm smile, a sight that erased any doubts from Lisynia's mind like it always did. "And the scouts brought in that Lupegi boy and a girl."

Lisynia nodded. Hanue, son of Tanue, was back in her grasp. Any more information she could've gotten from Molac could certainly be pulled from the boy instead. Her thoughts strayed back to the woman, before she passed out. Just the idea of her touch sent shivers down Lisynia's spine. But still something beckoned her to the feeling, drawing her to the Goddess that had come alive without warning when she touched the books.

The books!

"Mother!" Lisynia said frantically. "Where's my pack?"

Her mother removed her hands from Lisynia, bending down. Lisynia shivered at the sudden lack of warmth, the cold of winter hitting her with full force as her mother rustled with something on the ground and lifted herself back up, her long bell-sleeves obscuring the thing in her hands from view.

Lisynia's heart slammed against her ribs, the feeling almost painful. But as she stared at her mother's hands, something in her calmed.

A wave of soothing cold passed over her body. Not the type of cold that's painful, uncomfortable like the winds of a harsh winter, but rather the cold of slowly lowering yourself into a cool mountain stream.

Her eyes focused on her mother's hands as the woman set the contents on Lisynia's lap. The cold grew stronger, more serene and as her mother's hands moved away, the ancient journals came into view.

Old and leather-bound, half rotted from centuries in the dirt behind the wall of the tower's basement. But as she stared at them, there in her lap, the woman's voice came back to her, less terrifying now and more tranquil, kinder.

I will have you soon, Lisynia.

The books seemed to call to her and Lisynia tentatively reached a hand out, skimming her fingertips over the top of the smooth, cool leather.

"Thank you, Mother," she said simply, her voice as steady and smooth as the cold that had settled over her. "We need to get ready for the march." She grabbed the journals, moving out of bed quickly as her mother protested. "Tell the guards to prepare the prisoners for movement. I'm not letting them out of my sight again." Lisynia pulled the drawer in her desk open, shoving the journals inside and covering them with random papers and plans. "When I leave, make sure no one touches these journals."

Chapter Thirty-Nine
Anavi

The silence between them was deafening as it had been since the reveal of the man's name.

Yidenu.

She was in a dungeon, a prison, with Yidenu of all people. She still remembered it clearly as day and in the darkness of the cell, it was all she could focus on. Anavi twisted her hands, fidgeting with her fingernails as she tried desperately to think of anything else besides that night; her first mission.

Her first mission was really a two-in-one, a test of her loyalty to Jovan and the rest of The Seven. The first arm was in Teveban, the nature of which nearly destroyed her. Then the second was to Andyse, and while she completed the mission, her distraction nearly got her killed.

She breathed in deeply, the stale air of the dungeon filling her lungs as her mind forced her to relive the first mission she ever did for The Seven. After training and learning from The Elders themselves, Jovan, the head of The Seven had pulled her aside right after her training session one night years ago and told her she wouldn't be going home that night. He had something for her to do.

Upon Yidenu revealing his name, she had muttered excuses, the same ones she'd given herself for years; she had to, there was no other choice, it was a criminal that committed treason against The Seven, if she didn't, someone else would. But they fell flat.

Of course, they did.

She killed his wife.

She wouldn't apologize. Apologizing was admitting weakness; that's what Jovan always told her, drilled into her in her lessons with him. And she never had, not once since that lesson, to anyone.

Jovan's word was law. When an immortal, all-powerful being tells you, warns you, not to admit defeat or weakness, you didn't and she lived by that in everything she did, at least after that night.

That night would haunt her for the rest of her days.

Her breathing was shaky as she stood up from the ground, forcing her mind elsewhere, away from that night in Andyse.

Escape. You need to escape.

She clung to that idea, pacing once again, limping with her bad knee. She prepared herself for Yidenu's rage at her movements. But it stayed silent. Agonizingly silent.

After making her fifteenth lap, she spoke, her voice a far cry from the typical strength it carried; it was weak. *She* was weak. "It had to be done. But we need to escape. That needs to be done."

Silence met her words.

Then a rustling and the strong voice of the Commander of the Southern Coalition of Andyse boomed through the cell, echoing off the walls. "You never have to do anything you don't want to; that's an excuse of the immoral and weak. You chose the path you walk, Anavi, and nothing will change that."

His words cut through her typically stoic demeanor like a knife, like he had just stabbed her instead of yelled at her and she felt an unfamiliar burning sensation behind her eyes. She wiped desperately at her face and her hands came away with hot liquid on them. Tears.

How odd.

She sniffled slightly, steadying her voice before she responded. He was wrong. It needed to be done. "We need to escape," she said simply.

Yidenu sighed. "They really did a number on you. But you are correct."

She buried her confusion and pressed on, stepping toward the wall that separated them and pressing her hands against the stone. "You've been here longer than me, how do you say we do it?"

"How's that leg doing?"

"Fine." She fought back an anger that built in her, squeezing her hands into fists. They needed to escape, and he was worried about something as stupid as that? Ridiculous.

"Well, spy, they're planning something. Something that will take them from Oshgor where we're being held. That's when we move."

"Do you always speak in riddles, old man?" she said, moving away from the wall. "At this point, I'll do it myself."

"And you'll die."

"Then I die in service of The Seven, as I lived."

He sighed again but silence fell over the cells afterwards. She resumed her pacing, ignoring the pain that shot through her thigh as she moved. There were more important things to focus on now. Like the fact that, if Yidenu could be trusted, something will be bringing soldiers away from Oshgor soon.

Anavi didn't know what that something was and not even a little part of her cared. She had to make her move and make it quick.

She still had a brother out there and a mission to report back to Jovan.

Chapter Forty
Molac

As Molac exited the forest, slamming through the final burst of tree branches, his breath heaved in and out of his chest. He didn't stop running. He couldn't.

The general could change her mind at any time, send her troops after him and he would be dead before morning light.

His feet moved swiftly over the plains, the grass poking through the thin trousers they had clothed him in, scratching against his lower torso.

Why had she let him go? Why not kill him where he stood? His mind went back to the moment she cut the ropes on his hands, the look in her eyes. She was going to kill him mere seconds before and, while he was glad she didn't, something within him was suspicious of the sudden act of kindness from a woman like her.

She thought she was better than him, treated him like trash, ruled with an iron fist over his life for the past few weeks.

As his thoughts dwelled on everything that had happened, all the insanity of the last few weeks, the stitch in his chest grew in intensity, a sharp pain in his side.

But he kept moving.

He ran south toward the river, toward the Davegu Kingdom, toward his home.

But was it even his home anymore? They had lied and lied and lied. About Teveban, about the Ancients, about everything. His father had always told him, warned him, to have contingency plans, to know that the aristocracy was not a secure position. But Molac had never expected how much of his life was truly insecure. How was he to possibly face the people that had lied through their smiling mouths about everything outside of Davegu?

For the longest time he thought that the way things were in Davegu was the only way, the only truth. He was a coward. the Goddesses were a crutch people clung to, the Teveban were old stories, the Davegu armies were the most powerful in Eterin, the king was powerless to do anything without the aristocrats' approval. Everything was fake, wrong, untrue.

And no one would believe him, even if he got back in time to warn the king against coming into Andyse with his armies. Knowing crazy, old Tovik, he'd probably just send Molac back into the Cruor for daring to question his judgement.

But he had to try.

His feet pounded against the grass, flattening the dead plants with a *crunch* as he moved and his thoughts strayed to Asmuto, the only one that had ever been truthful to him.

Asmuto was the man that had the most knowledge of Andyse given his history with Yidenu. The king would make him and his foot soldiers lead the assault.

He's going to be the first to die.

Molac shook his head violently, trying to throw the thought from his brain but it only strengthened. His best friend, only friend, was going to die if he didn't stop this from happening.

He had to stop it. He had no choice.

Molac slowed his pace as the stitch in his side grew, enveloping his whole chest.

"Fuck," he said, winded and placing his hands on his knees. He paused for a second in the darkness, his body slowly edging out the pain in his chest.

A cold breeze blew, freezing against his exposed skin, biting into his flesh like knives.

"They couldn't have given me warmer clothes first?" he muttered, raising himself back to a standing position.

He started running again as the breeze strengthened into large gusts. He had to keep moving or at this rate, he'd freeze to death before he got there.

As he approached the river, headed southwest toward the single bridge into Davegu from Andyse, something in the distance caught his eye, glimmering near the edge of his sight.

He slowed his pace again and focused on the lights, straining his eyes in the dark.

The reality hit him like a brick, and he stumbled backwards in horror.

Molac raised his hands to his hair and clutched at it, shaking his head madly.

No.

A large mass of small fires moved in the far distance, bobbing up and down in the night sky. They flickered in and out of sight, carried by black spots in the distance that his eyes barely registered as people. The line went back all the way out of his sight, hundreds and hundreds and hundreds of people marching. The earth seemed to shake beneath his feet as his legs threatened to give out beneath his weight. It had to be a force greater than 3,000 strong.

This was it. The Davegu army had come. He failed to stop the king.

They had no idea what they were walking into.

And now they were all going to die.

As Molac approached the line of soldiers, his horror did not dissipate. Laughter and roars screamed out from the line, men and women jesting and boasting amongst themselves with no idea of what was to come.

He ran.

His breathing squeezed out of his body a meager amount, his chest seemed to be closing in on itself.

He kept running.

Sweat poured down his forehead despite the cold as people, faces, came into view.

Still, he ran.

A murmur reached his ears as people began to notice him, pointing at him, raising their weapons from the side of their campfires.

Molac slowed his pace, raised his hands and gathered as much oomph into his voice as he could muster, his heart pounding as one soldier nocked an arrow, raising their bow to be pointed at his chest. He squeezed his eyes closed, shaking his hands in the air. "Don't shoot! My name is Molac. I'm here on a mission from Queen Meluth!"

His chest heaving, he waited for the inevitable, the pain that would precede a hopefully quick death. But it didn't come, and he opened his eyes.

A man wearing leathers shoved through the line of soldiers toward Molac. As the man passed the soldier with his bow up, he pressed the weapon down and pushed the soldier holding it. The soldier stumbled at his touch and landed hard in the dirt.

Molac's heartbeat quickened in his chest, his hands shaking at his sides as the soldier tramped toward him. But the man raised his helmet, and a familiar face met his eyes, a friendly face for the first time in weeks.

Asmuto wore a large toothy smile on his face. He extended his arms to Molac and Molac let out a laugh.

He fell into Asmuto's open arms, not even caring enough anymore to keep any sense of decency expected of a Kludishav. He raised his head, pressing his lips to Asmuto's. The peasant soldiers could have a show, it didn't matter anymore. "You have no idea how much I missed you," Molac said, tears burning behind his eyes as he pulled away. "Oh, Asmuto, I missed you."

CHAPTER FORTY-ONE
TIVEA

Tivea moved quickly as the dawn peeked over the horizon. Its light would be calming if not for the fact the people that had taken her in were marching to war as soon as she got back, possibly sooner.

She jumped over a fallen branch, landed on her feet, and listened to the trees.

As the wind whistled through the leaves, they corralled her into a pathway south, the path winding and erratic but short. A new fervor came over her and she moved toward a clearing ahead, her feet pounding against the floor of crunchy leaves.

"Rauna!" she hissed, her voice barely a whisper. "Rauna, are you here?"

No answer.

Her breathing quickened as she came into the clearing, searching for the woman on the ground, just within the woods, hidden behind a tree somewhere. Her eyes settled on a spot in the distance, something black sticking out from behind the tree, close to the ground. She broke into a run across the clearing, the trees chattering around her.

Tivea turned around the tree and Rauna came into view, dried blood in streams down her arms and neck, her breathing shallow and eyes closed. Her skin was pale, paler than usual with a yellow pallor to it. Falling to her knees, she pressed her hands against the woman's wounded neck.

"Rauna!" Tivea said, shaking the woman slightly. "Rauna, please!"

No response.

Tears streamed down her cheeks, her panic building as Rauna didn't wake, her head falling to her shoulder. Tearing a piece of her shirt, her bloodied hands wrapped Rauna's neck with the fabric, her vision blurred from her tears.

Think, think.

The knapsack she brought with her had still had her mother's journal within its confines. And as her hand skimmed the leather bag, an idea came to her.

The bark she had given Rauna to help with her ankle wasn't the only thing of use in that journal. Her mother's healing potions. That was her last chance of saving Rauna. She lowered Rauna into her lap, her body cold like the late fall breeze. Tivea swallowed hard, trying to quell her panic as she pulled the journal from her pack, sifting through the pages.

There had to be something in here, there just had to be. The pages flew in front of her eyes, her mother's scrawling that usually brought her only comfort just building the panic within her.

She couldn't lose Rauna, she just couldn't.

As her shaking hands approached the end of the journal, something caught her attention, a potion that her mother had created herself, the recipe written in neat handwriting on the yellowed pages.

As she read the words, her mind going faster than her eyes, a swell of hope swept over her and a smile burst across her face. It was a healing potion, the healing of wounds using plant barks.

"If I can do this," she said, a weary smile on her face as she pressed her hands against Rauna's face, "I can save you."

Rauna did not respond, only moaning in pain as Tivea slid herself out from beneath her body and gently set her head down on the ferns below.

Tivea burst into action. First ingredient was oak bark, ground, and Tivea turned her head wildly before settling her eyes on a tree in the distance, large and strong, and oak.

She dug her fingernails into the bark, pulling at it as it bit into the tips of her fingers. She pulled a piece off the tree and snapped it in her hands, pressing the meat of her palms into the bark, grounding part of it.

Her anxiety grew as Rauna coughed, the sound hoarse. Tivea had helped enough of the elderly at camp pass peacefully to know what it sounded like when someone was dying.

The next ingredient, stream water where the blue algae blooms. Her feet again moved on their own volition toward the small mountain creek winding through the clearing. She scanned it up and down for any indication of the blue algae in the book and her eyes settled on a rock in the distance, blue streams of plant growth beneath the water level.

She rushed over to it, Rauna's harsh cough growing louder, rougher. Tivea dug through her knapsack and grabbed a vial from her pack. Her trembling hands dipped beneath the surface, plunging her hands into the freezing cold of the coming winter. She thrust the vial from the water, throwing that and the bark into her knapsack.

The next ingredient as she read it on the weathered pages, blue algae. She grasped at the rock, pulling the strands of algae bloom from its smooth surface and throwing that into her pack as well.

Rauna coughed again harder and Tivea turned, her chest heaving. She rushed over to the woman, her face growing paler by the second and wiggled below her head again, reading the journal's instructions.

Combine the ingredients.

She fiddled with her knapsack, pulling the ingredients from the depths of the leather. Tivea cupped her hand and poured the stream water into her palm, mixing the algae and bark with her finger as Rauna shifted, groaning slightly in her lap.

Come on, come on.

Her breath came out of her body in bursts as she hyperventilated, the warm air misting in the cold winter breeze that trickled through the trees. With her free hand, she traced the words in the journal, the water shaking in her cupped palm.

One last ingredient.

The tears of one that cares for them.

Her heart sank in her chest, her stomach twisting in her body. Gaabi was the best option, of course, but how was she supposed to get to Gaabi from here? She was locked in the dungeon. There was no way Tivea could get there and back in time before Rauna slipped away from the world.

Her heartbeat pounding in her ears, Rauna shifted in her lap again, a coughing fit racking her feeble body. She was going to die.

The one person she had left, the woman she had come to care about in a way completely foreign to her, was going to die. Without ever knowing her sister was safe, without ever knowing how Tivea felt, without living the good long life she should.

Tivea's eyes burned, blurring her vision as she watched the woman she traveled with all these weeks fade away in front of her, her coughs growing weaker and weaker with each moment. As tears streamed from her eyes, falling down her cheeks, she blinked them away.

Wait.

She moved her hand carefully up to her eye as another tear slid out, landing in the mixture she had in her hands. With her other hand, she pressed on Rauna's forehead, stilling the barely breathing woman.

Would it work? She didn't know. But there was no other option.

She pushed Rauna's body into an upright position, pulling her lips open and slammed her hand against Rauna's mouth, forcing the mixture down her throat.

Her eyes shot back to the journal, and she muttered the hastily scrawled words on the page. "With this potion, may the Goddesses heal the wounds, may they bring them back to health for me."

Tivea's eyes wandered back to Rauna's face, her hasty breathing growing deeper.

Rauna coughed again, harder this time, the potion flying from her mouth. Tivea grasped at her head, pressing her palm against her mouth, forcing it down her throat, her hands shaking slightly. She couldn't lose her, the one person in her life now that saw her for who she was and not what she could do for them. Her mother, her father, they were all gone and Rauna was the only one left now.

Rauna shook violently and then went limp, only upright by Tivea's hands.

Tivea watched Rauna's wounds intensely, waiting, hoping against hope that this would work. It had to work.

Rauna's eyes fluttered open, the beautiful deep greens of the forest staring back at Tivea. Tivea sighed in relief, tears still spilling from her eyes, slipping down her cheeks. Pressing her forehead against Rauna's, she laughed slightly, the sound coming out choked from her sobs.

She opened her eyes, still holding Rauna's head and looked at the wounds on her neck as they rapidly healed, leaving only large scabs across her pale skin.

But the bleeding was stopped, and she was awake.

She was alive. Against all odds, she saved her. Against all odds, Rauna was alive.

CHAPTER FORTY-TWO
LISYNIA

The morning sun woke her with a start as it poured through the windows into her bedroom. Today was the day, after all the work she'd put in, after all the pain and suffering she'd endured, after all the strange things she couldn't explain, it was finally the day she'd been waiting for. The day she'd get answers.

She rose from her bed quickly, jolting her mother as she moved, waking her up. Her mother roused, staring at Lisynia with tired eyes.

"What is it?"

"It's time, Mother. After all these years of you training me for this moment, it's finally time."

Her mother quickly made her way to her feet as Lisynia moved toward her armor stand, grabbing the leather pieces and strapping them quickly to her body.

"I'm so proud of you, Lisynia."

Lisynia smiled at her mother's words and turned to face the woman, taking her soft hands into her own calloused ones. "Thank you, Mother. I couldn't have done any of this without you. Or Catina."

Her mother's smile turned sad at the mention of her sister and Lisynia grimaced at her words, regretting them already but her mother quickly erased the pain from her features. "Of course, my daughter. You have done so much in your young life and I'm in awe that I raised daughters such as yourself and your sister."

Lisynia's smile grew, tears building behind her eyes at her mother's words. She squeezed her mother's hands in hers and stepped closer, pressing her lips to her cheek.

She turned back to her armor, throwing it over her body quickly. "I had Otto make up some armor for you as well, Mother," she said. "Down in the armory."

Her mother nodded and the women made their way out of the bedroom, Lisynia's mind running wild. After all this time, after all these years, today would decide the fate of her people. Today they marched to Oshgor. Today she would decipher the words of the Goddess or die trying. She pivoted on her heel as they entered the hallway, stealing one last look at the room that had been her home for months.

She might not ever see it again after today. But this needed to be done.

She met with Xienee first, sending her mother ahead to the mess hall. As she entered the quarters she had set the commander up with, she was met with a frenzied woman, a far cry from her typically cool and collected demeanor. Xienee moved among her quarters quickly, flying over plans strewn about the room.

Lisynia cleared her throat, making her presence known and Xienee turned toward her, noticing her for the first time.

"General," she said, straightening her back. "Are you ready?"

"Yes," Lisynia said simply, lying through gritted teeth. Was anyone ever ready to lead their people to what may be their deaths?

"Good. Plan still holds then?"

Lisynia walked into the room, closing the door tightly behind her. Xienee threw on her own armor in the meantime, the pieces old and worn. "You know I could've gotten my smith to make you new armor, right?"

Xienee looked up from buckling her chest piece over her torso and smiled slightly. "But it wouldn't be mine. I'd look like a Tevebrisian, not a Commander of Andyse. You aren't the only one with an identity to be proud of."

Lisynia returned the smile, lowering her eyes slightly. "Of course. And yes, the plan still holds. You and your troops will travel ahead of mine on horseback to scout the forest near Yidenu's old camp and Teveban will follow you on foot through the plains. We'll join together at the river ahead of Oshgor."

Xienee nodded, sitting down on her bed to tie her boots, her sword laying across the blankets next to her. "By this time tomorrow, the king will be dead and both of our people will be free of his scourge."

Lisynia nodded, walking closer to Xienee. As the woman finished tying her boots, Lisynia offered her hand to her. She eyed her with a sort of suspicion before accepting her help and they shook hands as Xienee came to her feet. "Then onto the real prize. The Seven."

Xienee released a hearty chuckle. "Those fucks don't stand a chance against the likes of you, General." Lisynia blanked, her hand still grasping Xienee's and Xienee offered more words in response to her confusion. "I saw what you did to that Davegu kid in the woods. It was a good kill, brutal. I like that about you."

Lisynia chuckled slightly, thinking back to the soldier in the woods when she was training, the fear in his eyes. It hadn't even registered for her that he was a kid, young. But as her mind focused back on his face, his broken teeth and displaced jaw, a wave of horror washed over her.

She pushed the boy out of her mind, but Xienee wouldn't let her forget, sensing her hesitations. "You'll have to be prepared for that. Tovik enforces mandatory military service for anyone over fifteen name-days except their highest aristocrats. There'll be more on the battlefield today. My people are already wary of you, given your..." Xienee paused, for once choosing her words carefully. "...episodes. You can't afford to show mercy, General. Mercy is weakness in a fight for survival."

Lisynia mulled this over in her mind. Xienee's people didn't trust her. A tinge of anger ignited in her stomach but part of her knew they had a point. She'd passed out at Xienee's camp and then again yesterday in front of her own fortress. It's not like she had told anyone besides Otto and her mother *why* that was happening to her. Xienee was unfortunately right; she could not afford to show mercy, not if she wanted to keep her alliance. She'd killed a child before, in the woods. Could she do it again?

As Xienee grabbed her sword, patted her on the back and exited the room, Lisynia settled on an answer.

For her people, for their freedom, for their safety, for their lives, she could do anything.

As she entered the mess hall, Xienee having left Ryrie with her forces right after their conversation, Lisynia's people stared up at her, leaving their breakfast untouched on their plates. All of them, right in here, ready to follow her into possible death. Very few would stay behind to hold down the fort, the rest would either win or fall within days of now.

How bizarre it was that this is where life took her.

Lisynia cleared her throat as they looked at her expectantly. She picked faces out of the crowd, Ason, Otto, her mother. As her eyes moved over the people in the mess hall, her mind went wild. They might all die today. They might all get wiped out of Eterin after years, centuries of pain and suffering at the hands of the Davegu and Lupegi. They might never make it back to their families.

She could very well watch them die today.

Or she could very well watch them win.

The largest force that should be guarding Oshgor would be 2,000 and, at 3,500, Lisynia's forces dwarfed that, even with inferior weapons and hastened training.

Her throat squeezing in on itself, Lisynia spoke, trying her best to quell her nerves and the nerves her people certainly felt as well. "We all know what today is. We all know what it means to march on King Tovik and his armies. We know the stories and the tales they tell of that bastard king. But we know something they don't. We're coming. And we're strong!" Her voice got louder, clearer as she spoke, the words barreling out of her mouth before she could think of them. "We have a strength that that king can't take away, one that no one can! The spirit of Teveban lives within us, the gift passed down for generations from our ancestors and, by the Goddesses themselves, we will win! We will prevail in this and all things because they beat us, raped us, stole us away from our homelands but they have not broken the spirit of Teveban that lives in every one of these people among you!"

The crowd roared, cheering and yelling, banging their silverware on the tables in raucous applause. A righteous anger filled her body at the sight of so many people, so many of *her* people ready to fight and die for those around them.

They shouldn't have to.

But by the Goddesses, they would.

"For Teveban!" she screamed, waving them up from their seats with her dagger.

Her army jumped to their feet. "For Teveban!" they screamed back, grabbing their weapons.

Lisynia pivoted on her heel and turned toward the exit of Ryrie, her people pouring out behind her in a cacophony of cheers and the clanging of metal. She made her way down the stairs toward the exit and turned around one last time; her people and Xienee's lined up ready to start the march. They were leaving, they were marching.

They would win. They had no other choice.

Chapter Forty-Three
Rauna

Her breathing was shallow as she moved through the forest. The woman next to her struggled against her weight, Rauna's arm resting on the woman's shoulder as they moved.

As clarity returned to her, the world around her started to make sense, the memories of last night flooding through her mind. She turned her head, causing a deep pounding within her skull, like someone had just hit her with a hammer, but the woman helping her came into view slightly.

Rauna smiled. She was beautiful, even dragging her through the woods, she was gorgeous. Long brown hair caught the early morning sunlight, revealing hints of red in the strands and her face, though twisted from the effort of moving two people at once, had soft features, full lips, a hooked nose and beautiful brown eyes that matched her hair.

The woman paused her movements, noticing Rauna was awake judging from the looks she kept shooting over to her, and lowered Rauna to the ground, resting her against a tree.

"You're awake?" the woman said and her voice, her face, seemed vaguely familiar.

"Are you real? You're so pretty," Rauna said, her words coming out slurred. "Am I dead?"

The woman blushed, her face coming into full focus now as consciousness slowly dripped back to Rauna's mind. Embarrassment took hold of her. The woman was Tivea.

Rauna stuttered over her words as Tivea looked away, still blushing. "Oh, Tivea, oh my, I'm sorry."

Tivea giggled slightly, the sound like music to her ears and Rauna fought the urge to reach out for her. Tivea turned back to her and spoke, "You don't have to be sorry, Rauna. It's okay. You're sweet and very much not dead. You were close to it when I found you though."

Rauna nodded, blushing now herself and her mind wandered to the night before, the blades cutting into her, the fear as she ran through the woods, the feeling that came over her when she saw Tivea.

The fact that Gaabi was gone.

Her head still pounding, she shot to her feet. "Where's my sister?"

Tivea hushed her, pulling her slowly back down to the tree. "You're injured, Rauna. Rest a bit. We're headed back to get her right now."

"You mean she's still there?" Horror washed over her like the rain last night. "She's still in the dungeon?"

Tivea's face fell a bit, her mouth twisting down into a deep frown. "I couldn't get her out before I came to look for you. I thought you were going to die."

Rauna shook her head, lowering her face into her bloody hands as tears began building behind her eyes. "Why did you save me?" she asked meekly.

Tivea went silent for a few agonizing seconds but then Rauna felt her soft hands pulling at her own, taking them away from her face. Tivea cupped Rauna's chin, her touch soothing, calming as the warmth from her hand spread through Rauna's face. "I saved you because I care about you."

Rauna shook her head again. "No, I can't do this, I need to get to Gaabi."

Tivea sighed but obliged, raising herself to her feet and then extending a hand down to Rauna. Rauna took it, her body screaming in protest as she pulled herself to her feet. She let out a small groan as every cell in her body seemed to burn from the effort.

"Be careful," Tivea warned, "I don't know if the potion I used will work again."

Rauna ignored her, pressing herself further to her feet. She took one step, and her legs wobbled beneath her weight, threatening to give out from under her. She stumbled as she moved through the woods, her legs shaking with every step she took.

Tivea's hands grazed against Rauna's back, an action that sent shivers through her spine. "You don't even know where you're going."

"I've gone this far, haven't I?" Rauna said through gritted teeth, "I'll find her. Even if I have to tear this world apart, I'll find her."

"Rauna, you don't have to tear the world apart. I'm coming with you."

Rauna paused, turning to look at Tivea, the kind, gracious woman that had put up with her shit for long enough, saved her ass over and over. "But your father?"

Tivea sighed. "That's where I'm going next. The Tevebrisians are marching toward Oshgor right now. I'll join them after you get Gaabi back."

Tivea paused her movements and Rauna turned to look at her. Her face was full of worry or was that fear? "What is it?" Rauna asked, her voice soft as she reached her hand out to Tivea's.

Tivea sighed and turned away, like she was embarrassed of what she was about to say. "After we find Gaabi, I'd like you to come with me, maybe."

Rauna smiled. Maybe by now she should know it wasn't a good idea. But what was truly left for her in Lasari? The Seven would never allow a day's peace for her and Gaabi, especially given the fact they knew about Teveban. She took Tivea's hand in her own and grazed her other hand across her cheek. She was warm to the touch and her skin soft. Rauna could stay here forever, holding her close, feeling the warmth of her body, and never grow tired of it. Tivea turned her face, her eyes flitting back and forth from Rauna to the forest floor as Rauna spoke. "I'd follow you anywhere."

They made good time, even considering Rauna's injuries, and soon enough they were at the entrance to Ryrie, the large wooden doors towering over them. She stared in awe at the fortress in the sunlight. It was a marvel, honestly, the bricks barely noticeable unless you were looking for them, the door hidden around a corner of the mountain made with deep rich wood that matched the trees.

And somewhere within those confines was her little sister.

There were no guards stationed outside, most of the fortress was probably on the warpath right now with Xienee and her people. Perfect time for a jailbreak.

Rauna pulled the Davegu sword from her belt and walked forward but Tivea grabbed her shoulder.

"You're injured. Let me take care of it."

Rauna nodded but her patience was growing thin. Every second they wasted out here was one more second closer to Gaabi being out of reach forever.

She watched as Tivea moved into the clearing, raising her hands from her sides, palms facing toward the sky. The forest came alive around her, rustling and creaking from all directions. Vines snaked from the trees into the clearing and wrapped around Tivea's arms like they had a life of their own. Tivea shot her hands forward, the vines thrusting toward the door, whipping through the air like arrows. They wrapped quickly around the door's handles, squeezing tightly around them. Tivea pulled her arms back and with a loud creak, the handles flew off.

Rauna's eyes went wide as the vines retreated as fast as they had come, her chest heaving at the display of power.

Glad we're on the same side.

Rauna raised herself to her feet and ran forward, following Tivea into the fortress's walls.

As they entered, two soldiers turned, shouting amongst themselves. "Intruders!"

Tivea raised her arms again and the vines shot around Rauna's feet. She lowered her sword, watching as the vines crept past her and up to the guards, pinning their arms, their legs as they desperately hacked at the plants to no avail before they were completely immobile.

"Sorry," Tivea said sheepishly, doubling over. Rauna ran to her, catching her as she fell to the floor, the vines losing their grip.

Rauna held Tivea up, throwing her arm around her shoulder and raising her sword again. "We don't wanna hurt you. I just want to know where the dungeon is. Fighting is not worth your life."

The face of the man she'd killed days ago flashed in her mind, the blood pouring from his wound. Rauna's stomach twisted at the thought of having to kill again. It was a bluff but as Tivea slowly lost more and more of her consciousness, it was the only tool Rauna had. For Gaabi, Rauna would kill everyone that stood in her way. One of the soldiers struggled free and approached, Rauna's head pounding with blood.

Fuck, fuck, fuck.

The soldier was young, just a boy, and as Rauna looked at his features, she recognized him as the boy from the woods when she dropped Tivea off.

"Ason," Tivea mumbled next to her.

"Ason!" Rauna called out. "Please I don't want to hurt you."

The boy approached still but he did not draw any weapons. Instead, he took Tivea's other arm and wrapped it around his shoulder, waving the other guard away as he stared on in confusion. "I saw it on Tivea's face when those prisoners came in, they mean something to her, to you, don't they?"

Rauna nodded, unsure if this was a trick or not. But what choice did she have?

The boy averted his eyes, his voice small and sheepish. "They took the prisoners with them. The general wanted to keep them close since they'd escaped before."

Her breathing quickened and she gasped, doing her best to hold Tivea upright while her world fell apart. Her sister, gone, marching as a prisoner to a battlefield. It was the very thing she entered Andyse to stop and here it was, happening again, no longer a pawn for The Seven but a pawn for people Rauna understood even less than the secretive Lupegi leaders.

Her breathing quickened, the gray stone walls coming closer to her with every inhale. Her sister was gone.

A newfound strength came to her as she spiraled. Rauna straightened her back, calming her breathing as much as she possibly could.

Her sister was gone.

And she was going to find her. Just like she found her in Andyse, she'd find her in Davegu, she'd find her anywhere.

Chapter Forty-Four
Hanue

The cart swayed beneath his feet as he stood on the tips of his toes, face pressed up against the crack in the boards, trying to get a view of the outside. Splintered wood dug into his cheeks, stinging slightly with every move of the cart.

The outside was just woods, forest, and people. Oh, so many people. He counted in his head, mouthing the words, his heart dropping more with every number he muttered.

Twenty, twenty-one, twenty-two, twenty-three, twenty-four.

Each person was clad with leather armor and armed to the teeth, swords, arrows, and daggers glinting in the sunlight. He sighed, lowering himself to a sitting position in the cramped cart. His knee bumped into Gaabi's as he sat down.

She held her face in her hands, shaking her head slightly in the darkness, the light coming from the crack in the boards the only light they could see by. Hanue reached out, stroking her soft cheek with his calloused hands.

She looked up slightly and embarrassment flushed his cheeks; he quickly pulled his hand away. He was a blacksmith with calloused, dirty hands daring to touch a beauty, a genius, like her. But her hand reached out and grabbed his chin, turning him back toward her.

She was smiling, a sight that made this whole situation better, or at least tolerable. Gaabi's tear stained cheeks were bright red and her eyes raw and bloodshot from her cries. But, by The Seven, the sight of her quickened his heart. She was so beautiful, that smile sending a fluttering through his stomach.

Her fingers traced his chin, and he leaned into her warm touch, pressing his cheek against the palm of her hand. She lifted his chin, raising his face to hers and pressed her soft lips against his. Sparks flew through his body as their lips connected.

She smiled against his mouth and the fluttering in his stomach increased, his lips turning upwards into a smile. Gaabi pulled away slowly, still tracing his face with her delicate fingers.

"I can't let you be the only one that makes a move, can I?" she teased, the light from the crack in the boards glistening in her honey brown eyes.

Hanue smiled, lowering his eyes as heat burned at his cheeks. "I guess not. There's no one else I would rather be in this cart with."

She giggled slightly, a pride filling his chest at her laughter. "I'm glad we're in agreement on that." Gaabi pulled her hand away from his face, her features contorting into sadness as she spoke and he reached up, grabbing her hand with his.

He ran her fingers along the creases in her palm, bringing it to his lips and leaving small kisses on her wounds. "It's okay to be worried," he said. "I am too. But you're not alone. I won't let anything happen to you."

She smiled slightly, a sad smile and twisted her fingers into his. "I'm glad you're here but I can't stop thinking," she bit her lip, turning her eyes downwards, "what happened to my sister, Hanue? She should've been here by now."

Hanue sighed, squeezing her hand slightly. "I'm sure she's fine. Probably looking for you right now."

Gaabi scoffed, throwing her head back against the walls of the swaying cart. "That's what I'm worried about, her following us." She shook her head slightly. "She's always been so... protective of me, since even before our parents. It's infuriating honestly. Feels like I don't have a life of my own sometimes. She'd burn down the world without a second thought."

Even though Hanue barely knew Rauna, he could certainly understand her being overbearing.

Hanue's thoughts strayed to his own sister, a feeling he couldn't quite place coming over him. Would Anavi do that for him? With all her missions and quests she was sent on by The Seven, she hadn't been home much in years. But she cared about him, right?

Maybe she was on her way right now to find him. She had to be.

But as a shout erupted outside of the cart and they moved quicker over the ground, he wasn't so sure.

He turned back to Gaabi, trying to push his sister from his mind but Gaabi's words stuck in his brain.

You don't have to be like her.

His thoughts were interrupted by another shout and Gaabi flinched. Hanue pulled her closer. "If her pigheadedness has kept her alive this far, it'll certainly keep her that way. But right now, just focus on me." He tightened his grip on her hand as she shook. "We'll find a way out of this, I promise. Between your smarts and my unending optimism, we will figure it out."

Despite the situation they found themselves in, Gaabi chuckled slightly. "Sounds like a deal."

CHAPTER FORTY-FIVE
ANAVI

She was still as she waited in the prison cell, listening for anything above her head that said that her captors were gone. She hadn't heard anything in almost a full day now, but it didn't hurt to be careful. A guard still came to bring her and Yidenu breakfast this morning. Someone was still here. And that was their way out.

Yidenu hummed to himself in the cell next to her, the same melody he had been humming for hours now, over and over and Anavi fought the urge to snap at him to shut up.

But that wouldn't do her any good whatsoever. She needed him to get herself out of here, no matter how much she hated that fact.

Finally, she spoke, her voice coming out strained from the hours of silence. "So, when do we get out of here?"

Yidenu's humming stopped, and Anavi strained her ears harder to hear him. "When they bring the lunch, spy, we've been over this. Do they not teach you patience in your training?"

Anavi scoffed, turning her head toward the direction the soldier would walk to deliver the bowls of bland porridge to them. Of course, Jovan taught her patience. What she wouldn't give to show this asshole what else Jovan taught her.

"Don't you know that time is of the essence?" she said calmly, imagining her blade sinking into his back, right between his shoulders. "We can't afford to wait."

"You got a better plan then?"

Anavi quieted, anger seething within her. She had things to do, she couldn't stay locked up in here forever. The Seven were waiting on her report and she was going to get it to them. That's what she did, that's what she would continue to do. All that mattered was The Seven.

As her mind jumped between The Seven, the mission that brought her here, the plan to get out of this dungeon, all of it, her thoughts focused on one person and her anger nearly boiled over as she clenched her fists.

How did she forget about her brother? Sweet, innocent Hanue somewhere out there doing who knows what? If he was even still alive.

She slapped herself, hard, her ears ringing from the sudden hit. She hit again, and again, and again, her skin stinging with each blow she delivered to herself.

Yidenu's voice rang out of the dark, barely reaching her ringing ears. "What the fuck are you doing?"

She didn't respond and brought her hand up to her face again, relishing the sting that shot through her cheek, her fingers. Anavi moved her hand downwards, to her arrow wound and pressed her thumb against the wound, reopening the fresh scab over it. Blood streamed slowly from her wound, coating her fingers and she pressed harder, biting back a scream that tried to escape her throat.

She failed the mission, she still had no idea what was going on here despite her best efforts, she got herself locked up in a Davegu cell, and she forgot about her brother. She needed to be punished and if Jovan wasn't here to do it himself, she would do it for him.

"Anavi!" Yidenu shouted out as the scream finally erupted out of her mouth. "Stop!"

Something in her stilled at his words and she pressed her palm against the wound, trying to stop the bleeding from her thigh. The blood oozed around her fingers.

She cocked her head, watching the flow of red that seeped over the back of her hand.

"What was that about?" Yidenu asked, his voice tinged with concern.

What a weak emotion for a man of his power to betray.

"I fucked up my mission," Anavi stated, the blood beginning to slow its pace. She brought her hand up to her mouth and sucked the hot liquid from her fingers.

"You're a piece of work. I didn't know they had that impact on people."

Anavi felt a slight bit of confusion at his words but didn't respond, instead listening for the door to open down the hallway, the sign it was time to go and get out of here.

She waited in the dark, hand pressed against her wound for a long time before she heard anything. Yidenu did not hum anymore, instead sitting in silence like her.

Then the door creaked and she whistled slightly, warning Yidenu it was time and raised herself to her feet, pressing her weight against her good leg. Anavi hobbled to the bars of her cell and judging from the rustling from Yidenu's cell, he did the same.

The guard came around the corner, clothed in the typical Davegu armor, chainmail and steel helmet despite the fact he wasn't off fighting any wars.

But he would still die today.

The guard approached Yidenu's cell first, two trays of food in his hands and as he came within distance, Anavi shot her hands through the bars, grabbing the guard's legs.

He tumbled forward with a shriek and Yidenu's hands caught him by the neck. Anavi watched with a glee building in her stomach as Yidenu's hands tightened around the guard's neck, choking sounds escaping the man's mouth beneath his helmet.

His hands struggled, moving back and forth from swatting at Yidenu to trying to wrestle free of Anavi's grip but it was to no avail.

Slowly, surely, his movement became less erratic, the sputtering of a man dying quieting as his arms fell to his side. Yidenu held tight to the man's neck with one hand and snaked his arm up the guard's torso to the keyring on his belt with the other. Anavi watched his old, wrinkled hands carefully, the first look she had gotten of him in years.

A cool feeling came over her, chilling her to the bones as she focused on his hands, covered in sunspots, and his typically tan skin pale from lack of light in the dungeon.

She remembered when those hands were wrapped around her own neck, trying to choke the life out of her. If Yidenu had plans to kill her, she would win, just like she did back then.

Even the most well-trained Andysi was no match for an assassin that had taken an oath to The Seven, even a weakened one.

Yidenu grasped the keys, pulling them up to his cell's lock and Anavi dropped the guard's legs, his body falling limp to the ground of the dungeon.

The cell door next to her squeaked open and Yidenu came into view in front of her. He was noticeably smaller than she remembered, his muscles weakened from age and imprisonment. Meanwhile, she had only gotten stronger. Killing him wouldn't be an issue.

His hair was gray now, only speckles of the original brown visible, glinting in the lantern light. His beard was full, over-grown even, and more wrinkles than before decorated his face. He smiled at her, showing off his yellowed teeth and held up the keys, jingling them in front of her.

"Before I let you out, I know what you're thinking," he said.

Anavi snapped back to attention and stared at him.

"I'm not going to kill you, Anavi. Years have passed and you were just a kid when you killed her. And you spared my daughter, never told The Seven about her. I'm guessing there's still a little bit of humanity left in you somewhere. To get out of here, we need to work together and that won't work if we're constantly looking over our shoulders."

Anavi nodded but her rage built with his words. He was weak, oh, so weak.

But there was some truth to his statement; she never mentioned the girl to The Seven. It was a mistake that would soon be rectified.

Yidenu unlocked her cell, opening the door slowly, releasing her back into the world. "We have to trust each other, Anavi," he said, extending a hand to her. "Can you try to trust me?"

No. But she could lie.

They made their way up the stairs side by side, Anavi refusing to let him get behind her lest he go back on his word. Andysi liked to do that, so she'd been told. As they entered the doorway into the rest of the fort, Yidenu took the lead, walking swiftly down the hallway and peeking his head out around the corner. Anavi's leg pulsed in pain with every moment she made, despite the fact the bleeding had stopped.

She gritted her teeth and jogged up to Yidenu. "How do you know your way around?" she hissed into his ear as she approached him.

He did not turn, still focusing on the hallway around the corner. "I used to come here to meet with Asmuto, one of the king's generals. Before he turned on my people."

Anavi's mind registered the words he spoke, but she was focused on his neck, how easy it would be to jump on top of him and choke the life out of him like he did to the guard. But something within her stilled as he moved forward, beckoning her into the hallway.

"They usually kept prisoner belongings in the armory. It's just down this hall."

She followed him closely, the hallways long and winding as they turned every which way in the blackstone building. They approached a large wooden door and Yidenu pushed on it tenderly. It flew open without restraint, revealing armor stands and weapon storage beyond. Her heart pounded in her chest at the sight, and she fought the urge to jump within the room and grab everything she could. Davegu weapons may be inferior to the Lupegi versions but as she traced the jagged, sharp edges of the swords, she fought back a smile. In her hands, even that sword could be deadly.

Yidenu moved into the room, swiveling his head back and forth as he crept forward. Without turning, he beckoned her in behind him and she obliged.

She looked around the room, weapons and weapons and weapons, picked clean. The Davegu soldiers were certainly doing something right now given how slim the weapon choice was. Her eyes caught a chest in the corner of the room, and she limped over to it, her leg sending jolts of pain as she moved.

She bent down, her knees hitting the floor, sending another shockwave of heat through her at the contact. Anavi ran her fingers along the chest, a simple wooden box with a lock on the lid. Turning around she called for Yidenu. "Do you still have the keys?"

He lifted the keyring from his belt and trotted over to her. He tried one key, then another, then another and none of them worked. Anavi felt the rage within her grow, and she grabbed a knife from a nearby table, thrusting the blade into the lock and twisting it, hard.

Anavi pressed all her body weight against the hilt of the knife and the chest popped open with a satisfying *crack*.

Lifting the lid, she gazed upon the materials within. Her knives and swords and other weapons. She grabbed at the interior, pulling her weapons from the chest. Anavi stood, tying the sword's sheath around her waist and tucking her knives in their spots within her boots. Yidenu followed suit, his hands bringing a sword and one dagger from the interior.

Anavi's eyes moved to the chest again as Yidenu suited up armor onto his body from nearby. Several knives and swords were still within the chest. "Who else was kept here?" she asked.

Yidenu sighed, a look of pain crossing his face at her question. "Others from my camp. They killed them quick."

Anavi blinked at him as his face twisted, seemingly thinking of his people's death. His eyes glistened with tears and Anavi cocked her head.

How strange.

She pushed that from her mind and moved past him, still walking with a slight limp. "We need to get going."

CHAPTER FORTY-SIX
MOLAC

As he walked through the camp, following Asmuto closely, his mind stayed stuck in Teveban, the dark echoey hallways of the tower, the sound of the brick being dragged from the wall, and the general's promise to him in that cell. The promise to kill the king.

He watched the Davegu army closely, men and women of all ages, children to elderly, here, weapons at their sides and armor on their bodies to retake Andyse in the name of the king. He was too late to stop it, so now he had to watch as the fire rained down. The people around them all laughed and joked amongst themselves, smiling faces everywhere. If that woman's promise held true, there was an army marching on them right now and they were none the wiser. The general had taken down five men in front of him, by herself. He shivered as he thought of what a whole army of those people could do. Maybe there was a reason that they were locked away, maybe keeping them hidden and downtrodden was the one thing he could agree with the king on.

He tapped Asmuto on the shoulder, flinching away as the man turned on his heel. Molac opened his eyes again, quickly, hoping

Asmuto didn't notice his fear, but Asmuto's face was scrunched in concern. "Are you okay, Molac?"

Molac sighed deeply. What a complicated question. He moved to shake his head, but his body didn't obey his command, still frozen in fear. "No," he admitted.

"What's going on?"

Molac's voice failed him, and he found himself unable to speak. He stared at Asmuto, a sense of severe dread filling his body as he stared at his best friend, his locs tied back into a ponytail behind his head giving Molac full view of his face contorted into a look of disquiet. Molac's eyes traveled Asmuto's body, heavily armored and muscular, such a far cry different from the way it was when they were kids, when Molac was the daredevil, the favorite, the heir to the Kludishav name, and Asmuto was the scared little boy hiding behind him in rags, coated in dirt. Now, he was damaged and Asmuto was a top-ranking general in Tovik's army.

At the thought of the king, Molac found his words returning to him. "Where is the king? Didn't he want to travel with his army, show off those fighting skills he's so legendary for?"

Asmuto eyed him pointedly, but humored Molac's change of subject. "The king is 'attending important business elsewhere',"

Molac rolled his eyes and Asmuto chuckled slightly.

"He came to me to go above the queen. Tell me I had to kill the prisoners and fight the people I've been working to make peace with for years," Asmuto said spitefully. "He's a coward."

Molac's heart sank at the word, even though it wasn't directed at him. Asmuto must've noticed the change come over him because he wiped the disdainful expression from his face and placed a hand on Molac's shoulder, squeezing it slightly.

Molac took a deep breath, placing his hand on Asmuto's as his thoughts strayed back to the General of Teveban. He shivered. "I have something to talk to you about."

Asmuto squeezed his shoulder again and then his hand was gone as quickly as it had come. "I have work to do, can it wait for later?"

Before Molac could protest, insist on the importance, Asmuto turned quickly, walking back through the camp, keeping an eye on his troops. Molac was alone, again.

He swallowed and turned around, leaving Asmuto to his work and headed back to the tent Asmuto was kind enough to offer to share with him. As he walked through the camp, jeers met his ears; now that Asmuto wasn't with him, people were comfortable mocking him openly. His name was already known far and wide as the crazed man that ran up last night half-naked.

Great.

Sighing, Molac made his way to the tent in the distance, weaving in and out of the sea of people itching for a fight. He wouldn't give it to them, he wouldn't. He was better than that. He was an aristocrat; this army was nothing more than peasants.

But as something hit him in the back, knocking him forward with a painful start, he swiveled quickly, his eyes settling on a woman, laughing and hitting the soldiers around her as she pointed at him. "I told you I could hit the coward!" she jeered to the others.

Molac's eyes fell to the ground, to a piece of spare firewood. He bent down slowly, picking it up from the grass and rushed forward with a scream, raising it high in the air.

His body slammed into hers, both of them falling to the ground and she rolled around, screaming in his ears. Hands grabbed at him, but he pushed them off, pinning the woman to the ground below them. He brought the firewood to her skull, over and over and over, the hot blood hitting his face, the scent of copper filling his nostrils. With every hit he delivered, his eyes burned more and more. Blood sprayed his face as she went limp beneath him, but he didn't care, he didn't stop.

I'll show them a coward.

Screaming erupted around him and the firewood was pulled from his hand by someone he couldn't see. Something came down on his head, sending a pounding sensation through his skull and the world faded away.

When he came to, he was in the tent he'd shared with Asmuto the night before, his head throbbing, a knot forming on his forehead. The canvas betrayed no light from beyond it. Molac moved to press his hand against his head, but something stopped his and as he looked down, his panic grew. He was bound—again—his wrists tied together in front of his torso.

He thrashed against the ropes and the canvas lifted at the entrance, revealing Asmuto.

"What were you thinking?" he spat, pacing back and forth in the small tent.

Molac sat up as best as he could, jutting his wrists forward. "Release me."

"No, Molac, I can't. You killed one of my soldiers. She's dead!" Asmuto glared at him. "I have people calling for your death, man!"

"She attacked me first!" Molac said indignant, his voice coming out shrill.

"I don't care who started it, you've sown distrust in my ranks and the king is keeping a very close eye on this mission!" Asmuto threw his hands in the air, standing over Molac, a towering figure. "Do you know what he'll do to everyone here if we don't take Andyse for him? Do you think any of us truly want to be here?"

Molac stopped struggling and glared at Asmuto incredulously. "Why are you helping him?"

Asmuto pinched the bridge of his nose. "He wants this land, by any costs necessary."

Molac felt a heat build in his chest. "Then you're going to die. There's more in these lands than a few backwards tribes!"

The tall man let out a curt laugh. "Like what? Those legends we used to tell in the dark?"

"Yes!"

"Oh, Molac," Asmuto said, bending down to his level and pulling his knife from his belt. He cut the binds around Molac's wrists and stared him in the eye. "Those are ghost stories, a boogeyman. Being here alone drove you crazy but I promise, it's fake."

"What happened to the men I was sent with, then? I watched them die, Asmuto," he said, pleading with his friend to understand, to listen. "Those legends are real! They're real and they're coming!"

"I can't do this." Asmuto walked back out of the tent, leaving Molac alone again.

"They're going to come! And we're all going to die!" Molac shouted, stumbling over himself, crawling after his friend. "We're all going to die here!"

CHAPTER FORTY-SEVEN
LISYNIA

As the sun began to set over the forest, the Tevebrisians approached the edge of where the dead grass of the plains met the devoid trees of wood. Lisynia hesitated as she reached the last tree. With one step, she was making a choice there was no going back from.

But part of her knew there was already no going back.

Gingerly, she extended her leg, pressing her booted foot into the crunchy grass of the plains and took a step out of the woods. Then another, and another, one after the last, moving toward Oshgor quicker with each step she took. This was the start of a war for freedom and liberation and by the Goddesses, she was going to fight for her people until her last breath.

Her heart pounded as she walked briskly through the grass, the sounds of the army behind her reaching her ears, the chatter of people that had never been this far from their walled city in the mountains before this moment. Her heart jumped in her body, thrumming against her armored chest with a fervor.

The plains ahead of her were devoid of life, not a single blade of grass rustled as the still air stifled Lisynia's breath.

She walked deeper into the unknown, heading south toward Yide-nu's old camp. They had to get there to camp tonight before they moved further south into Davegu territory tomorrow.

By tomorrow night, she would know the future of her people.

The thought struck her like a fist, and she took a deep breath, begging the Goddess to come back, to help, to at least tell her which one she was, what name she went by. But there was no answer. The Goddess came when she wished to, it seemed.

A rustling reached her ears as she walked, and Otto jogged up beside her. Her heartbeat slowed at the sight of her friend.

"General," he started, a playful tone in his voice like always. "Did you ever imagine this as a kid? Leading an army to kill the king?"

Lisynia sighed, taking in his features for what may be one of the last times. "No, I didn't. Catina was always the revolutionary. I was a scared little princess girl that hid under her covers when it rained."

Otto chuckled slightly, placing his hand on the small of her back again. "Look at you now, all armored, angry and powerful with an army behind you. You're not the buck toothed knock-kneed girl anymore." He paused for a second, running in front of her and walking backwards so he could face her. She let out a fake laugh, her thoughts elsewhere, but Otto smiled, his face growing more serious. "She'd be proud of you, Lisy. She would be so proud of you."

Lisynia tried to hear his words, to feel them. But something within her couldn't believe his words. There was a very real chance none of them would ever make it back home, just like Catina when she left that night to go to the tower.

She shook her head and Otto retreated to her side, his hand sliding down her arm to her hand. "You've got this, Princess. All these people here, every one of them, is here because of you."

Lisynia pulled her arm from his grasp quickly, her focus on the thing in the distance, three specks moving quickly through the grass. She shot her up arm, motioning to the army behind her to stop and strained her eyes in the direction of the movement.

Her heart sank. People.

The Davegu were closer than she thought.

"Stay here," Lisynia hissed under her breath, stepping forward quickly and drawing her dagger from her belt. "Davegu scouts."

Her feet moved quickly through the grass. She half-stumbled, half-ran toward the specks moving in the distance, coming more into view now.

There were three of them, their backs turned to her as they headed south toward Davegu lands, all armored and armed.

And she was going to kill them.

She pressed her fingers into her mouth and whistled, grabbing one of their attentions. He turned around, waving the others on. The others moved quicker over the plains, retreating from her.

She chuckled slightly. For being such renowned warriors, the Davegu really all were cowards judging from her recent experiences. Between the prisoner and these men running from her? Pathetic. A swell of hope that she could actually take the full army rose in her chest.

"What are you running from?" she mocked, her voice carrying over the plains. "Are you scared of me?"

She gripped her dagger in her hand as she approached the one Davegu that stayed behind. He was big, bigger even than her and wore the chainmail of Davegu foot soldiers, the metal rippling over his chest as he moved toward her.

With her other hand she grabbed at her sword from her side, drawing it with a *swish* as it cut through the air. The man was right in front of her now, raising his sword.

She swung her sword out toward the man as he ducked below her blade. Lisynia moved quickly, her dagger corralling him just where she wanted him.

He brought his sword down, the air whistling next to her ears as she rolled away from the blade's edge. It landed in the dirt right where she was standing, sending a puff of dust into the air. Her heart pounding in her chest, she grabbed at the dead grass, taking a fistful from the earth and thrust it into the soldier's face. He backed up, swinging his sword toward her again and she jumped back, landing on her ass in the scratchy plants below.

Scrambling to her feet, she swung her sword toward his side again, making contact with his metal armor with a resounding clang. He doubled over, stumbling backwards slightly as he swung his blade wildly. She pressed her sword against his, eyeing the blade that came so close to her face with a shaky breath.

Calm down.

She breathed in deeply, in and out, in and out and her strength returned to her, she pushed against his sword, sending him on the defensive. Her hands shook from the effort of holding him back and she jumped to the side, sending him flying forward.

She turned, dropping her sword and jumped on his armor-clad back, sending him to the ground, a cloud of dust shooting into the air as he landed.

On his back, Lisynia thrust the dagger into his armpit, where the armor didn't reach. He screamed, writhing beneath her and thrust her off him.

But it was too late for him. The dagger would take him soon, the magics imbued in the blade would spread through his body quickly.

Lisynia breathed deeply, making her way back to her feet as the man crawled away from her, his good arm gripping at the ground. He stopped, his arm convulsing. Then his legs, then his whole body shook, and he screamed again, his fingers feebly tearing at his armor as the black tendrils of magics crept through his veins.

She smiled at his pain, watching as his movements slowed, then stopped. The screaming died out as quickly as it had come and she fell to her knees in front of the man, her hands searching his armor for any weapons she could take from him.

Suddenly, his hand shot out and grasped her wrist. Her breathing quickened as she wrestled away from his grip desperately.

"Who are you?" he asked, his words slurred as his eyes glazed over.

She stopped wrestling against his hold and his fingers tightened on her wrist, biting into her skin. "Why don't you ask your king?" But she was amused. "You're going to die," she said simply. She pulled her wrist from his hand as his arm went limp, falling to his side.

As he let out one last shaky breath, Lisynia sighed, pulling his sword from his hand.

She turned her attention to the others, now specks in the distance as they ran, too far for her to catch.

The Davegu would know they were coming. But she smiled. They didn't know what they were going to be facing.

CHAPTER FORTY-EIGHT
TIVEA

Rauna and Tivea moved quickly through the forest, heading south toward the Davegu kingdom. Tivea's heart thrummed against her chest, a metronome she timed her footsteps to as she moved over the foliage of the woods underfoot. Her head ran wild with fears, hopes, pain, and confusion.

She was headed into a warzone with a woman she met only weeks ago, a battlefield they had no standing in. Her father's imprisoners pitted against those holding Rauna's sister. Though she tried not to think about it, to put it out of her mind, she couldn't help but think that at least one of them was going to be met with bad news.

And then there was Rauna. Tivea turned her eyes to the woman running next to her, the Davegu sword she gave her in that cave weeks ago held tightly in her hand. She was up, moving, *running* when just this morning, she had been dying in Tivea's arms.

She had saved her, a bittersweet thought given the ingredients of the potion. Somehow in a couple short weeks and a few life-threatening scenarios, she had come to care for the woman running alongside her and that was nothing short of terrifying given the situation they were in.

Even if they got her father and Gaabi out alive, what was the likelihood they'd survive themselves? At the thought of watching Rauna die, blood pouring from some unseen wound as she laid in the grass, unmoving, bile rose in Tivea's throat.

Tivea slowed her pace, shaking her head to rid that image from her mind, her legs burning from the effort of running and Rauna slowed too, stopping a few feet in front of her.

Rauna turned to look at her. "Why are you stopping?" Her voice was full of agitation, impatience and still, Tivea couldn't help but smile at her.

Goddesses, I care too much about this woman.

Rauna stared at her expectantly, drumming her fingers along her crossed arms in the dying light. Tivea's heart fluttered just looking at her and her smile grew.

Say something.

Tivea waved her hands in the air, gesturing to the setting darkness. "We need to talk about this, Rauna. We're going into this just armed with your sword, my clorhestas and nothing else. We have no plan. We don't even know what's happening there, Ason didn't have much information. We're no use to Gaabi or my father dead."

Rauna sighed, walking closer to Tivea. She reached for her and Tivea's breathing quickened, wanting just to reach out and grab her, pull her in close, tell her the truth of why she stopped.

She almost lost her once. She couldn't deal with that again.

But that was stupid. Rauna didn't care about her like that. She came to Andyse for her sister, and she would leave for that same reason. It was unreasonable to expect anything else from her.

Rauna's hands grazed hers and Tivea took a deep breath, trying to calm her heart's relentless fluttering. Her touch was warm and soft—all Tivea needed to be sent over the edge.

Tears streamed down her cheeks and Rauna's face changed from agitation to confusion, pulling Tivea into her chest and wrapping her arms around her. Tivea froze in her arms, stiff as Rauna ran her fingers through her hair. The tears came stronger now and she fell into the woman's embrace.

Tivea buried her face into Rauna, listening to her heartbeat thump beneath her ribs, steady despite just running for miles.

"I can't lose you too," she whispered, her voice muffled from Rauna's shirt and Rauna's movements paused.

"What do you mean?" she asked, pulling away from Tivea and staring at her with those beautiful green eyes.

Tivea gulped, her own pounding heart the only thing she could hear now and studied Rauna's face, searing it into her memory.

Just in case.

As she opened her mouth to speak, something cracked in the woods nearby and Rauna's neck snapped toward it, tearing her eyes from Tivea.

Tivea's eyes followed Rauna's, searching the woods and Rauna raised a single finger to her lips. She stepped back from the woman and shifted her focus to the forest around her, willing the trees to listen to her commands.

Her eyes shot open as the image came into her mind, the trees pointing to a man hiding behind a tree. "There's someone else here," Tivea whispered.

Rauna gave a curt nod, raising her sword at her side, the dying light of day glinting off the blade through the canopy of the trees.

Tivea focused on the trees to the south, the direction the man was in, searching for his body sticking out from behind any of the trees. But nothing reached her eyes, not a dead leaf out of place. Then a flash of deep green blurred her vision, nothing and everything all at once. She took a step forward, moving toward the light. It almost beckoned her, like nothing else mattered.

A whizzing zipped past her ears and then her chest exploded in a burst of red-hot pain.

Tivea tumbled backwards, landing on the ground hard, staring at the empty branches above her as jolts of pain screamed through her body. She couldn't hear anything, just saw Rauna run forward out of view, her mouth stretched open in a silent scream. Tivea's hands clawed at her chest, grasping at something wedged within it. Her heart screamed, beating faster than ever before and as she brought her shaking hands in front of her face, breath heaving out of her body, they were coated in deep red liquid.

Chapter Forty-Nine
Rauna

Rain barreled toward the direction the arrow had been shot from, a heat building within her as her feet trampled over the dead leaves. Tree branches smacked against her face, cutting into her cheeks, ripping open the scabs and scrapes on her skin, but she was going to find whoever shot that arrow and kill them herself.

As she passed a tree, her heart thumping in her ears, a flash of black in the corner of her eye caught her attention. She turned on her heel, her feet sliding over the ground as she changed directions.

The man came into view, wearing black chainmail with a red tunic over the top of it, running from her. Davegu.

She sped her movements up, pushing her legs to move faster, to catch up to the man running in the woods. Her grip on the sword tightened as she pushed through the branches.

Her chest swelled running through the trees, heat biting at her fingers. She caught up to the man and barreled into him with a roar, knocking the breath from her chest.

But she didn't care.

She swung the sword at his chest, the blade heavy and lanky in her hands. He pushed her back, the sword's edge glancing off his armor and he scampered to his feet again, running into the woods.

Rauna sat on the forest floor, watching as his figure disappeared among the trees, gone from her sight.

She failed. Her hands shook as her rage calmed. She'd been ready to kill, she'd *wanted* to kill him. He would've been the second person in three days that met the end at her blade. Before, with the man in the vines, he was after Gaabi, and no doubt would've killed her soon after. But this man was running away.

As she tried to make sense of her anger, of the rage that seemed to boil just below the surface of her shaking body, her heart sank as the image of Tivea, shot with the man's arrow laying on the ground came into her mind, the way she fell to the ground playing over and over. Guilt consumed her, the feeling physically painful in her chest as it tugged at her. Rauna didn't even stop to check on her before she left. The wave of horror that washed over her was nearly debilitating, but she forced her body to obey her commands and get back to her feet.

Rauna gripped the sword again with trembling hands, rushing back in the opposite direction toward the woman lying in the underbrush.

Her body came into view, blood streaming from her chest onto the dying plants below and Rauna's breath hitched. She fell to her knees, crawling on all fours to Tivea.

Blood covered her chest, soaking the animal furs she was clothed in with crimson red liquid, her hands clutching at the arrow within her breast, pale and trembling. Heat filled Rauna's eyes, and she pressed her hands around the wound, Tivea's blood coating her hands, oozing between her fingers. She fought back the bile rising in her throat as Tivea choked back a cry of pain.

She's dying. She's dying and I left her alone. I left her.

Rauna's eyes blurred, water building in the corners. She pressed the woman's chest harder, willing with everything in her that the bleeding would stop, and she would be okay.

Tivea's voice, small and feeble, reached her ears, strained as she lifted her head slightly. "Go find your sister."

Rauna shook her head wildly, one of her hands flying to Tivea's face, stroking her cheek with bloodied hands. "No, I'm not leaving you."

A small smile that jerked at Rauna's tears came onto Tivea's face and Tivea's hand met hers, holding her hand against her face.

Rauna smiled slightly, refusing to believe what was happening in front of her eyes as Tivea's skin paled. "I promised you I wouldn't let you go, remember?" Rauna choked out, fighting to keep her voice steady. Tivea nodded slightly, gasping for breath and Rauna felt the tears spill onto her cheeks as she spoke. "I left you once already, that was plenty enough time for me to regret it with every fiber of my being. I won't ever do that again. You're stuck with me."

Tivea laughed slightly, a look of pain crossing her face at the movement and Rauna fought the urge to break down into a sobbing mess. She couldn't, she had to stay strong for Tivea.

"I promised you I'd help you find your father too; do you remember that?" Rauna asked, her thumb rubbing the side of Tivea's face. "You're going to see him again; you're going to make it through this."

At those last words, a determination clutched her body, her arms moving without her direction. She wiped the tears from her eyes and shoved the sword into her belt. They were so close to the edge of the trees. All she had to do was get her there, get her back to her father at least one last time.

One last time.

Her heart tightened at the thought of that. But she didn't stop her movements, standing up and then bending down, taking Tivea into her arms. She carried her over her arms, Tivea's face nuzzled up to her chest, blood still slowly seeping from her wound. She would get her there, she would not let that man take this from her, not when she was this close to seeing her father again.

Rauna walked carefully, making sure not to shake the woman in her arms too much, and headed toward the edge of the forest, swiveling her head for anyone following them.

If it was the last thing she did with her life, Rauna was going to stay with her until she saw her father again. Rauna was going to get her sister back and get Tivea to her father.

Tivea would not fail now, not if Rauna had any say in it.

Chapter Fifty
Molac

The dim light of the sunset came descending onto the world outside the tent, easing the interior of the canvas into deep reds, the only other light being the single burning candle on the table to his side. He had not left the tent since his fight earlier with Asmuto and he had no desire to step outside, to face the truth of the impending battle to come.

He knew in his heart that the general was on her way to them at this very moment, her armies marching behind her with a strength he dared not even imagine.

Asmuto had kept him vaguely updated. They'd stopped for the night to make camp. And to prepare.

Two scouts had arrived a few hours back, telling of an army marching toward them at this moment. They said it was Xienee's people, that the third in their group was taken down by an extremely talented Andysi.

But Molac knew better.

His brain focused on one thing as the silence chilled his body: they're all going to die out there.

He shook his head wildly, trying to force the thought from his mind, to stay hidden from it all. His thoughts strayed to the queen all those weeks ago, sending him on this mission. He was so proud, the feeling of comfort and ease of his movements as he traversed into Andyse. He was an aristocrat with the queen's blessing. He was going to restore his title, he was going to be a hero, not the coward boy of a fallen family.

Little did he know it would be his death.

He wondered where the queen was now, if she was still waiting for his report or if she was huddled up somewhere with King Tovik, the two damned leaders of Davegu finding solace in each other for what they didn't know were to be their last moments. She seemed to hate the king but women were fickle things. Despite his father's aggression and the pain he inflicted, his own mother had never hesitated to seek him out during the times her sickness made her weaker than usual. Meluth was probably clinging tight to Tovik right now, having abandoned all her morals and decency; just like his mother did.

Something rustled outside the tent, a shadow on the canvas, large and wide. His heart thrummed against his ribs, and he pulled his legs tighter against himself.

One hand snaked to the side table next to him, toward the sword that laid across the wooden surface. His fingers grazed the hilt of it as the shadow grew, headed toward him.

He wrapped his fingers around it, hoping that it would pass him by.

But a hand lifted the flap slowly, his breath hitching in his throat as the entrance widened.

Molac jumped to his feet, grasping the sword tightly and raising it at his side. He crept toward the entrance, his legs shaking beneath him. A man entered the tent and Molac swung the sword at the bulk of him.

He froze right before the blade made contact, his hands shaking under the weight of what he almost did. The man was Asmuto.

He raised his hands, quickly taking a step back. "Whoa, whoa, Molac, what the fuck? You going to kill me now, too?"

Molac's trembling hands dropped the sword and made their way to his own head, clawing his nails into his skin.

He was going crazy with paranoia.

"What's going on, man?" Asmuto asked, slowly pulling Molac's hands away from his face. "You're acting insane. This isn't the kid I grew up with."

He didn't have to say the rest; this isn't the boy I used to love.

"You don't understand," Molac said. "They're coming."

Asmuto sighed, shaking his head. "This again? Is that why you attacked my soldier? Why you just nearly killed me?"

Molac shook his head in a frenzy, dread consuming his thoughts. "They're coming, Asmuto, I'm telling you, we have to leave."

Asmuto flung his hands in the air. "You think I don't want to? I can't disobey a direct order from the king, no one can, not even the queen."

"You have to if you want to live, Asmuto!" Molac said, flying across the tent and grabbing Asmuto's arms tightly. "You have to."

Asmuto's face twisted in anger, and he pulled his arms from Molac's grasp, staring at him incredulously. "He'll kill me himself! I'm not like you; I didn't grow up in a fancy house with servants, you know this! This position is all I have, Molac. I cannot abandon it," Asmuto raised his voice. Then he went silent, closing his eyes tightly and redoing the tie around his locs. He opened his mouth to speak again but a man burst into the tent before he could.

Molac turned to the man, his entire body shaking. The man was clad in typical foot soldier armor, chainmail and heavy boots, far different than Asmuto's light leather armor or Molac's plain clothing. His eyes were wide, and fear seeped from him, almost palpable in the air.

"General," the man spoke, turning to Asmuto. "There's something outside."

Asmuto shot a quick glare at Molac, a look that Molac understood as him saying they'll talk later and exited the tent. Molac flew behind him, gazing upon the plains in the distance.

Fires crackled in the dark distance, growing closer with every second. And a sound, oh, fuck, *the sound.*

March, march, marching boots, that shot through his body with each step they took in the distance, seeming to shake the very earth he stood on. The clanging of metal, the shouts of voices far off, warped by the distance and the volume, becoming something otherworldly and grotesque. He turned away from the sight in the north, looking toward the forest to the west as the dread that had been building in him since he arrived flooded his body.

His stomach dropped. Fires burned at the edge of the forest, people dancing around them in the distance, their figures only pinpricks as they jumped and walked.

No, no, no.

He turned to Asmuto; his friend's jaw tightened, a vein in his forehead pulsing as he stared ahead to the north. "That doesn't make any sense," he whispered, his voice shaking as the fires got ever closer and the sound got ever louder, "Xienee doesn't have a force that large."

Molac tapped Asmuto on the shoulder with a shaking hand, pointing to the forest. Asmuto turned his attention toward the fires to their side and his face paled, his whole body tensing.

"That's Xienee," Molac said before turning back to look at the army marching toward them from the north. A chill ran through his body as they approached, the light of the fires growing stronger, more sinister. "That's the general."

Asmuto's next words came out barely a whisper. "They've got us surrounded."

CHAPTER FIFTY-ONE
ANAVI

They approached the River Crossing fort, leaning low to the ground to avoid the steady watchful eye of the tower they approached. A light shone from the top of the brick spire, a man's laughter carrying down to her ears and she pressed her body closer to the ground.

Yidenu moved swiftly through the grass on his hands and knees, Anavi following close behind. She lifted her eyes to the sky, brilliant colors of red and orange in the sunset and she thought back to the old Lupegi saying her father told her as a child, the first time her mind had drifted to him in years.

"The Lupegi have an old saying about this," she whispered to the man in front of her without thinking.

He didn't even turn around to respond. "I don't care about your folk traditions, spy."

"You should," Anavi said softly, not even sure if he could hear her. "Deep red sky means bloodshed is nigh."

The corners of her mouth lifted into a smirk as she stared at the crimson colors, fading away from her sight quickly as darkness descended upon the world. There was a war coming, the sky hadn't been this dark in years, not since she killed the rebel leader in Estia. And before that it had only been this shade of red on the night of her first mission.

The man in front of her turned his head, staring deep into her eyes in the descending dark. He raised a single hand and beckoned her forward.

Begrudgingly, Anavi obliged. Getting into a fight with him here was not smart. She needed to wait until they crossed the river ahead to kill him to avoid the eyes of the man in the tower lest he kill them both. The grass scratched at her hands, the air around her turning cold as she approached the old man.

"We need to wait until the guard change to move further. He'll see us," he whispered looking toward the watchtower in the distance, "just stay close."

He pressed his hand against her back as the light circled around toward them, pushing her to the ground. Anavi's hands grasped at the grass, pulling it from the ground at his touch, a fury building within her.

She took a deep breath, trying to calm her rising rage. Closing her eyes, she focused on the feeling of the grass beneath her, the cold winds that streamed across the top of her body. She stayed pressed against the cold dirt for several minutes, unmoving.

Yidenu removed his hand from her back, rustling in the grass next to her. She opened her eyes and saw him pull himself into a crouch, whistling for her to follow, the signal they had decided on in the dungeon.

Anavi raised herself up, eyeing the tower carefully as the light flickered silently in the distance and began moving across the plains, headed north toward the river.

Her leg throbbed as she moved, upset with her for her awkward stance. Anavi gritted her teeth and pressed forwards, ignoring the pain that built with every step. Now was not the time to slow her pace.

The sounds of the rushing river reached her ears as it roared through the land, and her smile grew on her face. Yidenu raised himself to his feet now, turning around and offering his hand to Anavi.

She sneered, raising herself awkwardly to her feet as her leg trembled beneath her weight. "I don't need your help."

In the darkness, she couldn't see Yidenu's face well but enough of the moonlight glinted off his features for her to see it contort into something like sadness.

He lowered his hand to his side. "We're coming up to the river. It rushes hard this time of year so stay close."

"I know how to cross a river, old man."

"You don't know how to cross this one, little spy."

Anavi limped toward the river's edge, ignoring his words. She was a warrior, the top spy of Lupegi, who did he think he was telling her she didn't know how to cross a river?

It was wide, the bank in the distance about twenty paces away, and white water rushed over the rocks beneath it. They'd have to swim; the bridge to the east was out of the question—the guards in the tower would easily see her.

She steeled herself, dragging her leg behind her through the grass. Anavi dipped her boot into the water as Yidenu walked up behind her.

"Be careful," he warned.

That was enough to send her rage spilling out and she dove into the river, the cold water surrounding her on all sides.

The currents threw her into the rocks, sharp bursts of pain exploding through her body as the world around her spun, blurred by the rushing waves. Anavi thrashed her arms out, desperately trying to swim to the shore as her body pounded into the boulders and water filled her lungs.

She couldn't see anything, everything around her just black as her hands clawed at the water to no avail. The roar of the river swallowed her and she gasped, fluid filling her lungs.

Panic spiked in her body and she screamed beneath the waves, twirling in the water as her body slammed against a sharp rock. Her mind repeated one thought as the river beat her into submission: she was going to die. She was going to die.

The world around her faded, her sight failing as she gasped for breath, only getting a lungful of water in return.

Something grabbed at her, and she thrashed against its hold. But it didn't let go, pulling her through the waves as her vision blacked out completely.

She opened her eyes slowly. The stars above her were gorgeous, glimmering in the night sky. Anavi coughed, hard, rolling to her side, water exiting her lungs with force as she choked on it. It burned her throat, the foul taste of muddy water the only thing she could focus on.

Wait.

She sat up quickly, her hands flying to her face, her chest, her legs. The river roared next to her, droplets spraying her wet face.

She was *alive*.

Then a voice rang out, sounding like it was off in the distance. She turned her head, her body weak and trembling, the cold of the night air setting in.

"I told you to be careful," it said with slight amusement.

She wasn't sure how to feel as she made out the man in front of her. Yidenu.

"Why did you save me?" she asked, an unfamiliar feeling growing in her chest. She couldn't quite tell what it was but, by The Seven, it was uncomfortable.

Yidenu's face came more into view, a look on his features that told her he didn't know why he saved her either. "I didn't even think about it, I would've done it for anyone," he finally said.

She shifted uncomfortably, checking her body for all her blades. Anavi staggered to her feet, stumbling as a pain shot through her legs.

Yidenu's hands rushed out, catching her as she stumbled. She swatted his arms away but the feeling in her chest did not dissipate.

As she turned her eyes upwards, staring at the man that saved her life, she put her finger on it.

Gratitude.

Anavi scoffed, trying to quell the growing feeling but she couldn't. Something in her felt indebted, thankful for his help. It was not a feeling she was comfortable with, especially considering soon she'd kill him and tell The Seven about his daughter. In the end, the whole family would fall at her blade. That's how it had to be.

An assassin should not—could not—have gratitude for her prey.

She shook her head, limping away from Yidenu, trying to rid the emotion from her mind.

Something in the distance caught her eye. Deep orange light flickering in the north, at the edge of the horizon, right in the path of her way back to The Seven, back to her brother.

Yidenu gasped as he arrived next to her, raising his hand to his mouth. "My daughter..." he whispered.

Anavi limped forward, the intensity of the fire growing in the distance, getting closer to them. Slowly she raised her eyes to the horizon, little slivers of red still streaking through the darkening sky. "Deep red sky means bloodshed is nigh."

CHAPTER FIFTY-TWO
HANUE

The night's chill shot through Hanue's body with every breath he took. The darkness had fully settled over Andyse now and he strained his eyes, urging himself to see more than a few feet in front of him.

Gaabi laid across his lap, asleep but still fitful, her legs twisted awkwardly against the edge of the cart's walls. His hand stroked her soft face absent-mindedly in the darkness, his thoughts elsewhere.

He could've gotten them out of here, gotten Gaabi to safety if he hadn't gone down the side of that mountain to find his sister. Anavi could handle herself, that's all she'd ever done since their father disappeared. But instead, he came back to the woods and got him and Gaabi caught up in a war they had nothing to do with.

He sighed, the air misting in front of him as cold bit at his fingers. The cart jumped, the wheel going over a rock outside and he winced, his head hitting the wall he rested against.

Gaabi twisted in his lap, a scream coming from her mouth at the sudden jerk and he bent down, kissing the top of her forehead. "Shh, shh, it's okay, I'm still right here. I'm right here."

Her breathing was ragged and stilted, coming out in gasps. His hand traced her chin, her skin warm to the touch. The corner of Hanue's mouth lifted a bit as she settled back down in his lap.

"Thank you," she muttered out, her fingers interlacing with his.

At least he still had her.

As she settled back into a restless sleep, he focused on the sounds outside the cart, the hushed voices and boots slapping against the ground as they moved, the neigh of the horse that pulled the cart and the crackle of the torches. There was a pit in his stomach that would not dissipate.

There was no way out of this. They were going to die, either at the hands of the Davegu or the hands of Lisynia herself. There's no way the general of the legendary Teveban would let them escape again. She was always nice enough when they talked but he had seen first-hand with the Lupegi mission what she could do.

His eyes burned as he thought of his home, his true home from before Anavi's service to The Seven. The little two room house they'd lived in before their parents left, his forge at the manor, the sword he made for Anavi now lost to him forever. He should've known better, should've listened to Anavi that the wilds of Andyse were no place for him. But he wanted to impress The Seven, wanted to prove he had a place, a worth, in this world. He never fit in with the higher classes of Aethiel he and Anavi had been thrust into; he'd always been deemed lesser.

A tear slipped down his cheek as the cart swayed. He bent down, wrapping his arms around the woman laying across his lap. She was lesser, at least to The Seven, to the higher classes, but with her, he felt like he belonged, and she was worth more to him than any of The Seven's missions or the fancy manor. If he were to die, he would die protecting her. He would die truly himself.

The voices outside the cart got louder, more pronounced and the cart stopped moving. He scooted along the bottom of the moving prison and pushed Gaabi behind him. She stirred in her sleep but did not wake. His heart pounded, and the voices grew louder still.

"Calm, men, prepare to advance."

His breath hitched and he scrambled to his feet, leaning over Gaabi to press his face to the crack in the boards. An army was in front of them, men lining up for battle in the distance.

So, this was it. This was where he was going to die.

CHAPTER FIFTY-THREE
LISYNIA

Cold air gnawed at her fingertips, making them numb and stiff as she clutched the reins of her horse and rode to the front of the line. The darkness of night blanketed the world around her, the light of the torches casting deep shadows on the faces of the people in front of her, the faces of the people she was going to kill.

Their line built up across from her, preparing for her army's assault, and she felt the corners of her mouth lift in a smile. Lisynia's eyes turned to the west, toward the mountains and the sight of Xienee's people just at the edge of the forest.

Shouting erupted in the distance as the Davegu realized what was happening. One army at their side and another in front of them.

Perfect.

The plan worked; they were trapped.

The Davegu had to fight on two fronts, the northern and the western. They would not retreat. She knew that; the Davegu were very proud of that fact. And that would be their undoing.

"Light the signal fire," she said to Otto who had been at her side the entire march. "Xienee's in position."

Otto nodded and turned on his heel, running off into the darkness toward the large bonfire. Lisynia trained her eyes on the men in front of her, a force much larger than hers, sure, but as they scurried around their camp, she could nearly taste their fear.

The fire caught quickly to her side, spreading heat to her face and she heard a collective roar from the west. Xienee's army came charging out of the trees in droves, running toward the Davegu camp.

She turned to the people behind her, her archers. "Fire!"

Arrows loosed from behind her, whistling through the air as they flew above her head. The Davegu in the distance moved quickly, their own archers sending back arrows toward them but they couldn't seem to decide whether to aim for her or Xienee. People next to her darted from side to side, dodging the arrows as they came down onto her forces. Her breathing quickened and she tried her best to block out the screams from the man hit next to her, falling to the ground with an arrow in his leg.

Lisynia exhaled, bringing her hand down again to signal another round of archers right as Xienee's forces slammed into the Davegu on the side, clanging metal and screams cutting through the night air toward her ears.

Several fell from the Davegu line, screams bursting into the night sky as fires from their torches blazed. Otto appeared beside her, jumping onto his horse.

He reached a hand for hers as arrows fell from the sky, landing in the dirt with deadly force. "Ready, Lisy?" His voice was less playful now, more serious than usual. He squeezed her hand.

At least he was here, a source of calm.

She gave his hand another quick squeeze. Lisynia couldn't shake the feeling that the moment she let go of his hand, she'd fall and not be able to get back up.

"Ready," she said, steeling herself for the charge. She raised her sword in the air, and roars sounded behind her. "NOW!"

The rumbling was the only thing she could hear, the rumbling of hundreds of men and women, her people all moving as one as she kicked her feet into the ribs of the horse beneath her. She jutted forward, leaning into the animal as she tucked close to it. Her mind was empty, the reality around her not quite processing yet despite trying to force herself to know the truth.

Lisynia turned her head to Otto, his horse running alongside her as screams and yells filled the air. She wagered a look back, staring at her people, weapons in hand, running into war.

This was it. This was the catalyst of all their struggles.

As they slammed into the Davegu line, she burst up from the horse, swinging her sword at the people below. Her sword cut quickly, one, two, three soldiers falling to the ground as her horse bucked into the air.

All the sound faded away as a rage filled her body, her body shaking violently as her sword cut through their forces.

She swung her head around, a blade cutting into her shoulder with a sharp pain. She screamed, a sound that didn't quite reach her ears as it entered the world. Everything was gone, the fires of the fallen torches spreading through the grass, people fighting in the darkness, blood spilling on the ground below, none of it seemed to register with her.

Lisynia's vision found the soldier standing behind her, his body shaking, without even a helmet. He was young, his first battle no doubt.

But none of the Davegu were innocent.

They were *all* complacent.

She jumped from her horse, walking toward him through the fire that burst around her, the heat stroking her body as blood streamed from her shoulder. He shook his head, his sword trembling in his hand. The corners of her mouth lifted into a smile as she stepped over a body, the blood from his wounds squishing beneath her boots.

Lisynia raised her sword high in the air and slammed it down, the boy's sword falling from his grasp as his hands flew to his neck, his eyes glazing over. She kicked his chest, sending him flying backwards with a scream as she turned on her heel, her sword meeting another in the air. Lisynia struggled against his strength and pushed her other hand out, touching her finger to his forehead.

He fell away at her touch, landing in a clump in the grass. Raising her sword above his body, his eyes darting around in terror, she slammed her sword into his chest. Hot blood sprayed her face as she twisted the blade, his ribs cracking beneath her force.

As she pulled her sword from the man's chest, she gazed upon the battle, people wearing chains and leather and furs fighting and screaming and dying in the light of the fires. Arrows whistled through the air, people falling back as they made their homes in chests, arms, legs, and heads.

Another wave of Davegu soldiers approached from the south, their figures outlined by the orange light of the raging fires and she steeled herself for the onslaught to come, her fingers gripping the leather hilt of her sword with determination.

The battle was far from won. She'd only stop when the king himself was begging her for his life.

CHAPTER FIFTY-FOUR
RAUNA

Rauna's arms grew heavy as the sight in front of her grew more gruesome. But she refused to stop, to allow the fear that shook her to her bones to keep her stilled as Tivea lay dying in her arms. It was like the woman she was only a few weeks ago had died the moment she stepped over the mountains into Andyse. Her world was no longer filled with Gaabi's singing or the dull monotony of working at Bottom Mountain. Now, her world was life or death, her world was blood and fire, her world was Gaabi and this woman in her arms; there was no longer space for failure or doubt.

Rauna was going to get Tivea to her father and save her sister. There was simply no other option anymore.

Tivea's groans assaulted her ears as she shifted in Rauna's arms and Rauna tore her eyes away from the fiery battle commencing in front of her and turned her sight downwards.

She was growing pale, the light of the distant raging fires the only thing Rauna could see Tivea's sallow complexion with. Her brown hair was messy, disheveled, with dead leaves stuck in the muddy strands, a far cry from the neat braid she wore when she first bounded over the forest floor toward her. She was shaking, dried blood caked onto her fingers and chest over her torn animal fur clothing. The arrow stuck out awkwardly from the woman's chest and as Rauna's eyes fell upon it, her heart dropped.

Rauna didn't believe in the Goddesses, but the fact Tivea was still breathing shallowly in her arms was nothing short of a miracle.

Her palms grew sweaty, her muscles burning from the effort of carrying Tivea all this way and she swallowed hard, raising her eyes to the mess of people and death in the distance.

Her sister was somewhere over there, somewhere scared and bound, if she was even still alive. As screams serenaded her ears in an orchestra of death and pain, as arrows flew from both sides, barely visible in the darkness of night besides the glint of the fire on the metal tips, she took a deep breath.

She came here to save her little sister and now to save the trembling woman in her arms. And she was going to do that by any means necessary.

Rauna shifted Tivea in her arms, freeing one hand as much as she could while Tivea groaned softly, her head rolling back as she let out a slight cough. Rauna's heart thudded against her ribcage painfully as she ran her hand awkwardly toward the sword tucked into her belt, her arm shaking beneath Tivea's weight.

She traced her fingers over the hilt of the sword, pulling at it as her breathing quickened. Her mind flashed back to the man's face as her sword hit his stomach, the red blood that poured from his gut. As Rauna removed the sword from her belt, she shakily held it up, pulling Tivea back into her arms, the way she used to carry Gaabi to bed. She'd kill again. For Gaabi. For Tivea.

Rauna raised her eyes to the sight in front of her again. The battle grew louder, a horse galloping from the fray toward the forest. Rauna skirted to the side as it approached, and her body ran cold.

Large gashes ran along the side of the horse's white hair, deep red blood seeping from the wounds with every step it took, landing in the grass below. Rauna watched it as it went by, crashing into the woods away from her, leaving a trail of red liquid on the ground behind it.

She gulped, turning back to the battle in front of her. There was only one way to save Tivea, to save Gaabi. On the edge of the battle to the north, she could possibly go through unnoticed, if the people were too distracted by their own fights to notice her.

Tivea's breathing grew raspier, wheezing as the air exited her lungs.

She had no choice.

Rauna had to go into the crashing of blood and metal and violence in the distance.

She swallowed hard, pushing her overwhelming fear down and tightened her grip on the sword held awkwardly in her hand.

She took a step forward.

CHAPTER FIFTY-FIVE
MOLAC

There's nothing to be done.

That was the one thing he could think as he huddled behind the thin canvas of the tent, his legs pressed into his heaving chest. He grasped at the skin of his shins, kneading it as the screams grew louder, closer to him and the fabric wall he was using for protection.

There's nothing to be done.

He had tried, he had warned Asmuto, he had begged him to leave, to run away from all of this with him like they ran from the shopkeepers in Dhunviro after stealing bread as kids. But it was too late, or Asmuto was too scared, or any other combination of factors that would now lead to both of their deaths.

Light from the fires roared behind the canvas, the deep shadows of people fighting, people dying, people taking their last breaths decorating the fabric from all angles.

Molac shook his head, closing his eyes tightly. This wasn't real, this wasn't real. It couldn't be.

But the screams and cries didn't dissipate with the closing of his eyes. It *was* real.

With his eyes still squeezed shut, he rocked back and forth on the floor of the tent, grass poking through his pants sharply. He muttered under his breath something incomprehensible even to himself, the ramblings of a man half broken.

Was he going crazy?

Would he die insane in a mess on the grass of Andyse?

Was this it?

"No," he said quietly, biting his teeth into his knee as he spoke. "No."

He raised his head from his knees, loosening the grip he held himself with. Molac's breathing was shaky, coming out of his body in bursts as he tried to calm himself down. He reached his hand to the sword to his side, pressing his fingertips into the leather wrapped around the hilt. The fire's shadows were stronger now on the tan burlap, the fighting growing closer with every breath he took. His fingers snaked around the hilt of the sword, and he rose himself slowly to his feet.

Molac took a deep breath, trying to force himself to be calmer, more collected as another shriek burst through the clanging of metal and crackling of fire. He gripped the sword tightly, his knuckles going white as he raised the blade.

He had no training, no idea what he was doing. But he killed once, no, twice before.

And for his honor, his friend, his queen, he would do it again.

CHAPTER FIFTY-SIX
ANAVI

The screams pounded into her body with each utterance of pain and grief from the frenzy of flames in the distance. She fought back a grimace as she and Yidenu approached the clashing of metal and fire.

Yidenu moved quickly over the grasslands, headed straight for the battle like a madman. He held his sword in his hand as he ran in front of her, his head twisting wildly as he looked for something in the mass of death in the distance.

Anavi almost laughed. Almost.

Something about his desperation as he moved past her stilled the amusement that bubbled through her at the sight of him. She limped forward, trying to catch up to him as he ran toward nothing in particular. The orange light of the flames shone in his brown eyes as they grew wider, more anguished.

She took a deep breath, her usual ideas of the weakness, the fragility of emotions fading away as his chest heaved in front of her. Anavi moved her hand upwards, touching his shoulder ever so slightly with her calloused hands. The feeling of another human being's touch, one of someone she wasn't currently trying to kill, was alien, as foreign as the prison they had just escaped together.

"Yidenu," she said, her voice still harboring its usual sharpness, but something within it was toned down, not quite as harsh. "What is it?"

He ignored her for a second, pushing her hand from his shoulder as the screams grew in intensity, ringing in her ears.

It was only a matter of time before they were seen. And she was not safe from either party involved, the Davegu or the Northlanders. She pulled at the man again, turning him back to her.

"What is it?"

His eyes met hers. "My daughter. My daughter is somewhere in there," he threw his arms in the air wildly, peering over her head toward the people fighting in the distance, "I know it."

Yidenu gasped slightly, his eyes focused on something in the distance. Anavi turned quickly, grasping her sword from its sheath.

A woman was traveling through the far end of the battle in the north, carrying something heavy in her arms, a person. She had dark curly hair, the color of night itself. She moved slowly toward the north. Anavi focused her eyes on the woman as much as she could as Yidenu took off running toward her, moving with a speed she'd only seen when people were running for their lives.

Anavi broke into a sprint, or at least as close as she could get to one as her leg seethed from dull, throbbing pain. She hobbled behind Yidenu as he approached the woman. A swarm of people flooded around him, metal glinting in fire. Yidenu disappeared into the mess of people.

He was going to die.

She sped up her movements, something uncomfortable within her telling her, begging her, urging her to not let him die.

Her sword met soft spongy flesh, ripping through the mess of people as Anavi moved forward, blades slashing around her in every direction. There was nothing that mattered, nothing at all, besides getting to the man that saved her life.

Yidenu came into view, his face twisted in anger as he spun on his heel, slamming his sword down on everything that approached him. She paused, the pure skill of this old man hitting her as he let out a scream that burned through her ears. Yidenu was rumored to have once been a fearsome warrior, but Anavi had figured age would've caught up to him by now.

Her breath hitched in her throat. He moved with vicious speed, his sword cutting into person after person after person. Anavi was a warrior herself, but he fought differently than her, a desperation, a visceral need to survive seemed to have taken him over.

It was terrifying.

Anavi steeled herself, gripping her sword tighter as she thrust it into the back of one of the men attacking him, wearing Davegu armor. As she pulled her sword out from the man's back, he crumpled to the ground.

Yidenu nodded at her, kicking the last man in the chest as he broke into a run again, headed to the black-haired woman in the distance.

CHAPTER FIFTY-SEVEN
TIVEA

The numbness consumed everything within her, the cold icy grip of the air around her seeping into her limbs as her arm swung back and forth with Rauna's movements.

Tivea's vision was blurry, a grayish-white spreading ever so slightly from the edges of her sight. She tried to breathe normally, to bring herself back to the present. She focused on the warmth of Rauna's body, her arms holding her, the orange light in the distance she couldn't quite place.

As she stared above, at the darkness of the night sky with its flitting stars, the face of the woman carrying her came into view. She was panicked, her eyes wide with horror and her mouth downturned into a tight frown. Even at this sight, Tivea couldn't help but let a small smile form on her own lips as she used the last of her fleeting energy to nestle her head against Rauna's chest.

Rauna's eyes shot downward, and she breathlessly spoke as she ran. "I've got you. You're going to be alright, I promise."

A lie it was and Tivea knew it.

But something within her was done fighting, all this death and pain and suffering. Tivea softly closed her eyes, her thoughts disjointed and odd as she relived the past month in her head. The burning of her home, the people she had to hurt, the people she was never able to save, the kidnapping of her father...

The kidnapping of her father.

Her eyes shot open again and Tivea coughed hard, a tightness in her chest growing rapidly. Rauna's eyes met hers again and the bouncing of running stopped. Rauna's eyes tore away from hers, focusing on something in the distance and Rauna softly lowered her to the ground, the grass poking into her back as she lay on the earth, staring at the stars above.

"Tivea," a voice called out, vaguely familiar. She smiled as it rang out again. "My daughter, my blossom!" Her old childhood nickname, said in the voice of the man she'd been searching for gave her a comfort that replaced the cold of the night air with the warmth of a tight embrace from her father.

Rauna's voice rang out, far off and distant. "Who are you?"

The other voice responded, closer now. "That's my daughter, who are you?"

A gasp reached Tivea's ears as the stars circled around her vision. Rauna spoke again, her voice hushed, barely audible. "*Yidenu*?"

CHAPTER FIFTY-EIGHT
RAUNA

Rauna stared at the man in front of her, the world of pain and death and fire around her fading from her mind. Her breath hitched as he moved toward her, bloodied sword in hand, his long gray hair and tattered clothing slick with red liquid. There was a large gash in his stomach that he clutched at with one hand. Rauna raised her own sword, stepping in front of Tivea as her heart pounded in her chest.

The man did not stop, pushing past her as he made his way to the woman lying on the ground behind her. As the shock of seeing him wore off, she swung her head around and watched as he dropped to his knees, kneeling in front of Tivea as her chest rose and fell shallowly.

Rauna swallowed hard as she moved toward Tivea. The man was stroking her hair, the bloody sword laid in the grass next to him.

"My daughter," he whispered and as Rauna approached him, sword held out near his neck, the truth of the situation seemed to really set in. A bittersweet feeling swelled, tugging at her heart as tears on his wrinkled face shone in the light of the distant fires.

She had gotten Tivea to her father. She had completed what she promised to do. But what would happen to Tivea now? Rauna stared at the woman's face, doing her best to block out of the gruesome sight of the arrow within her chest. She grew paler by the second, her golden-brown skin a pasty color and her lips chapped and broken.

The man, Yidenu, looked up at Rauna as she lowered the sword from his neck. "What happened to her?" He clutched Tivea's limp body in his bloody hands, his voice shaky and cracking.

Rauna swallowed, opening her mouth even though she didn't have the words to describe this, certainly not to Tivea's father. The sight of his grief, the tears on his dirty cheeks, the pain in his voice, all panged through her heart as she stared blankly at him.

It was strange, seeing a father that cared about his children like this, considering her own experience with hers.

But Rauna pushed that down as she looked up from his face, the utter despair on his features too much for her to look at. A woman approached in the distance, limping slightly as her figure was high-lighted against the fires of the battle to the south. Rauna swallowed hard, raising her sword and Yidenu gazed up at her before turning to look in the direction she faced.

"It's okay, she's with me," he said slowly, the voice of a half-broken man. His shaking hand reached out, pressing her sword down toward the ground. "Tell me what happened to my daughter. Who are you?"

Tivea coughed, the sound barely audible over the screams and crashing in the distance in the south. Rauna lowered her eyes from the sight in front of her, the woman approaching rapidly, and dropped to her knees, gazing once again at the first woman she could truly call a friend, a confidant, a person she connected with besides Gaabi herself.

Rauna pressed her hand to Tivea's cheek, colder to the touch than she had ever felt a person before, and pain choked her as she struggled to find the words to explain. "My name is Rauna." Her voice was shaky and squeaky. She stared at Tivea, life seeming to fade as fast as the blood streamed from her wound. It was no use lying to him. Tivea was going to die and Rauna would probably be soon after her. "I came from the Lupegi province. Lasari. I was looking for my sister. Tivea saved my life more times than I care to admit these past weeks, saved my sister too."

At the mention of Gaabi, the pit in her stomach grew. She was going to lose everyone, she was going to lose Tivea, she was going to lose Gaabi. All for a war she wasn't part of. All because leaders of Davegu and Lupegi were fueled by greed and hatred made them think they were better than Gaabi, better than Tivea, better than anyone that didn't share their hatred. It was that philosophy that took her mother and would now take her sister and the woman in front of her.

"The Seven sent my sister here to attack Xienee. Tivea helped me find her; Tivea helped me save her. Tivea saved *me*." Tears burned behind her eyes, the first show of emotion she had fully felt in hours. "I wouldn't have survived a week without her." All the time before this felt unreal, distant. But it was real and as Rauna ran her fingers along Tivea's cold, pale skin, they struck her like a blow.

She had failed.

She had failed to protect anyone; all the work she had done to get her sister into Valetu, to save her, all the work she had done to get Tivea to her father safe, to prove she could do anything for those she cared about, it was all a failure.

Rauna looked up at Yidenu, the tears falling freely from her eyes now. "She just wanted to find you. I tried to help, I really tried. I'm so sorry, I'm so so sorry." Rauna stared at Tivea as her breathing became shallower and slowly lowered herself to press her lips to her forehead.

Yidenu looked up at her, pain flashing in his eyes. "She takes after her mother with that. Her mother helped everyone she could, regardless of the cost."

Before Rauna could ask what he meant, Yidenu extended one wrinkled hand to her, his bloodied palm cupping her chin as he stared into her eyes with an intensity. "But child, you didn't fail. You got her to me. And if she's like her mother, she's not going to die today."

CHAPTER FIFTY-NINE
LISYNIA

L isynia slammed her sword through everything that moved, a rage burning through her mind as she slashed and stabbed into the mass of flesh in front of her. Swords clanged around her, the sound of metal meeting metal rattling through her bones. She screamed, the sound foreign and far off as she thrust her blade through the back of yet another soldier.

Otto came into view as she pulled her sword from the man, and he crumpled to the ground. His blonde hair was streaked with blood and mud, his face contorted into a grimace as his sword pressed against another, pushing the soldier back.

Lisynia jumped forward with a frenzy, her feet clearing the body of the man she'd just felled. She swung her blade toward the Davegu soldier's side, the blade cutting into his torso with ease, a squishy feeling accompanying the burst of resistance that shot through her arms.

The soldier screamed, backing away from Otto as he clutched his side and Otto swung his weapon around, cutting clean through the man's neck. Lisynia watched with an odd sort of joy as his head fell to the ground and turned her eyes back to Otto, adrenaline pumping through her veins.

Otto cracked a small smile, and she felt one cross her features as well. They were winning. A strange part of her wanted to jump into his arms, to press their lips together, to feel the heat of his body, the strength of his hands. For a brief moment, she allowed herself to picture their lives together after the battle was won.

As she looked at him, a thrill came over her, her vision blurring as thudding sounded in her ears, like the sound of a thousand horses galloping through her mind. She burst her hand out, grabbing Otto by the arm as the feeling intensified, the sound growing louder, closer, stronger.

Otto's hands grasped onto her waist, his sword dropping into the grass below. Everything moved in slow motion as it faded from her view, the fires, the people, the death, the blood, the sounds of clanging and screams. A panic set into her mind as she fell, landing hard into Otto's arms.

She stared up at him, his mouth moving but no sound coming out and her eyes grew heavier and heavier as the thudding pounded through her brain.

"She is coming."

Lisynia's eyes shot open, the thudding gone from her mind as the voice's words echoed in her thoughts.

She is coming, she is coming, she is coming.

Lisynia thrashed out at Otto, jumping backwards from him as he stared on in horror. She turned her head wildly, taking in the violence around her, the blood spilling on both sides, the fires raging through the battlefield, the blood that trickled in pools around her boots. Then she turned to the distance, the south. A ball of green light floated through the air, bright and blinding as she stared at it.

Lisynia gasped, the light growing closer, stronger, pulling her toward it. As it approached in the sky, a collective silence settled over the battlefield, all eyes turning upwards as if drawn to the sky for a reason unknown.

Green flooded her vision, it was everything and nothing. As she watched, an arm, pale and white extended from the light and flicked its wrist. A loud *boom* shot through the world, the ground beneath her feet shaking, shaking, then disappearing as she flew through the air.

Her arms shot out in front of her, grasping for something, anything to clutch onto before she thudded to the ground, the air from her lungs disappearing as the green faded as quickly as it had come, replaced with the dust of a world torn apart.

She is here.

CHAPTER SIXTY
RAUNA

Rauna's breath heaved out of her body in bursts as she attempted desperately to regain air in her lungs. Her arms were limp and numb, tingling painfully beside her as her eyes stared at the smoke-filled night sky. A ringing in her ears blocked out most of the screams, making them distant, muffled.

She pressed her arms into the ground beneath her, clawing at the dirt and grass as it planted itself under her tingling fingers.

As she slowly sat up, there were only two things on her mind: Tivea and Gaabi. Her breathing quickened as her blurry eyes scanned the clouded ground nearby for any sign of Tivea. She sucked a breath in between her teeth, dust coating her mouth. Dread filled her body, weighing down her limbs with its intensity.

Calm down.

Rauna's hand shot to her chest, pressing her fingers into her breast as she attempted to slow her breathing.

Go over what happened, figure it out.

A blinding green light, then weightlessness and finally the cold, hard bed of the earth beneath her.

Her body screamed in pain as she attempted to make sense of

anything that just happened. What could've done that? What happened?

By The Seven, what happened?

Her body shaking, dull pain thudding through her flesh, she pulled herself onto all fours. She had to find them. Dust clogged her eyes, her nose, her mouth. She coughed, wiping her hand against her mouth. Each movement she made was an effort like no other, the pain, the ache eating at her muscles.

"Tivea? Gaabi?" she croaked out, the ringing in her ears making it barely audible. "Tivea!"

The world was just soot, soot and dust, nothing else. Her heart sped up, thumping through her ears, mixing with the ringing.

Nothing was visible through the dust and smoke and Rauna coughed again.

Then, hands.

Hands on her shoulders, hands on her arms, pulling her back. Hands touching her face as she screamed, attempting to view anything through the cloud of gray. Hands shaking her as pain shot through her body.

She swatted wildly at the air with one hand, the other skimming over the ground searching for something, anything to use to strike at the hands. As she gazed upwards, a face came into view, and she paused her movements.

Tivea's mouth moved silently in front of her, her face coated in dirt, grass strewn in her tangled brown hair. Confusion gripped her as she stared at the woman's face. Tivea shook her again, her eyebrows furrowed as her mouth formed another word Rauna couldn't hear.

There's no way she was alive, no way at all. She was dying, shot through the chest with an arrow. Rauna raised her hand, pressing her fingers against Tivea's arms and to her shock, solid, warm flesh met her touch.

"Tivea?" she said, her voice barely audible over the ringing and the muffled screaming.

Tears streaked through the dirt on Tivea's face as her lips turned upwards into a smile and she nodded.

Her fingers trailed along Tivea's arm as Rauna shook her head, refusing to believe the feeling of the woman, the sight of her face, any of it. Tivea's hands moved to Rauna's face and she softly caressed Rauna's cheeks, her hands warm and soft. Then she moved them to Rauna's hands, pulling upwards on Rauna's arms.

Her legs shaking beneath her weight, Rauna made her way to her feet, a dull ache bursting through her body. She held Tivea's hands with the tightest grip she could, refusing to let go of her lest she disappear again, and this was all a dream.

Tivea's mouth moved again and this time Rauna could slightly make out the words she spoke. "Come on, hurry, we have to find my father."

Rauna stumbled with her direction as Tivea pulled her through the cloud of dust and dirt, gripping her hand as tight as she could muster. "How?"

Tivea turned back to look at Rauna, her honey brown eyes flashing with concern. "I don't know," she sighed, stopping in her tracks for a second. "All I remember is you and my father and green and then after the explosion, it's like everything, all my strength, all my life, came back to me."

Rauna blinked at her, the words not fully registering in her mind.

Tivea pulled at her, her arm twitching. "Come on."

CHAPTER SIXTY-ONE
TIVEA

She heard nothing, just a slow, overbearing hum. All she saw in the distance was green, that same green that overwhelmed her sight and invigorated her dying body just minutes ago. As it grew in the background of the field of people raising slowly to their feet, screaming, crying, blood and bones and fire and pain, she trained her eyes downward.

Something about it beckoned her to it, the green cloud of smoke and ash seemed to reach into her very mind, pulling her inward with every step she took. Rauna muttered behind her as Tivea slowed her pace, trying to force the ache for that cloud of green from her mind. Tivea could not hear the words she spoke, but she knew what questions she was asking.

How did she survive?

How was she the only one on her feet after that explosion?

How did her wounds heal so quickly?

Tivea had the same questions and not a single answer to any of them, so she ignored Rauna, holding onto her to prevent her body from pulling her toward that deep green in the distance.

She had a mission, a goal, and she was not going to fail, not this close to completing it.

Tivea searched the ground for her father and her eyes settled on a man splayed in the field. As she moved toward him, her head tried to jerk away from her father on the ground to look back to the green. Her chest heaved as she squeezed Rauna's hand, her touch, her warmth, the only thing grounding her to the moment, to the horror of it all.

Rauna pulled her to a stop, grasping at Tivea's shoulders to gaze upon her face and Tivea watched Rauna's wide eyes and her tensed jaw. "What's going on? Are you alright?"

Tivea pulled from her grasp, falling to her knees as her body jerked uncontrollably. It took everything in her not to raise herself to her feet and run toward the light. Rauna's hands pulled at her as Tivea's breath heaved out of her body in quick gasps.

Finally, a noise reached her ears, breaking through the monotonous thrum she heard. "What's going on? Tivea, just tell me what's going on. Are you alright?" Rauna's voice was pained, an intensity in it that she'd only heard when they first met, when her only goal was finding her sister.

Tivea gritted her teeth and let Rauna pull her to her unsteady feet. She forced her eyes back to her father nearby. His head turned, his face bloodied and shrouded in darkness. But it was him, it was her father. Her arms and legs twitched out of her control as she moved forward, Rauna still holding her shoulders to steady her.

The call of the green strengthened and a scream built in her throat. Tivea bit it back as she fell to her knees again, her mind invaded, focusing only on the ball of light in the distance that cast its glow over everything.

Her father turned his face to her and tears built quickly in her eyes. He struggled to his knees as she fought the pull, the urge, the visceral *need* to be in the green. He smiled, his face glowing with green light, and gave her a slight nod as the first tear escaped down her cheek. His mouth opened and even from the distance she could tell the word he was forming. "Go."

Forcing her eyes to stay open, to stay focused on her father's smile and Rauna's hand on her back, a scream tore through her throat, thrusting her head upwards toward the sky.

Her head jerked from the sky above to the green in the distance, sending a sharp pain through her neck. As she stared at the green, as it enveloped her mind with its pull, a figure came into her view. The world around her faded away as she stared on, powerless to move, to scream, to do anything at all but watch.

Her heart pounded in her chest, thrumming against her ribs as tears slid down her face out of her control. The figure, surrounded by green and only green became clearer and a sense of dread filled her body, taking hold of everything she was and anything she would become.

She screamed again.

CHAPTER SIXTY-TWO
HANUE

Coughs burst out of his body, dry and rough as the dust choked him. The world was dark, his eyes betraying nothing of his surroundings. He was on his back, something sharp digging into his skin below him. As he groaned and moved to sit up, sharp, white-hot pain stabbed through his back.

Fuck.

He sat up, gritting his teeth as his body let him know its displeasure with his movement. Wooden planks and boards slipped from his lap onto the ground. "Gaabi?" he croaked.

A slight moaning, exactly like those when he first found her, reached his ears from nearby and he crawled through the dust toward it.

"Gaabi?"

"Over here." Her voice was feeble and weak, coming out strained.

Hanue moved as quick as he could toward it, the fires in the distance the only light he was privy to as the cloud of dust hovered over everything.

His eyes slowly adjusted to his surroundings and something hit him; they were out of the cart. The world around him was dirt and grass and ashes; the world was fire and smoke and screams. But the world was no longer just the cart.

How that happened, what caused that explosion, what that blinding green light was, he didn't know. But thank The Seven, he was free.

Hanue had to move, soon, before the soldiers screaming and groaning in the distance were able to come to their senses enough to start picking their swords back up. This was his one chance, his only chance, to get Gaabi out of here and into safety.

He moved quicker now, the grass stabbing into his palms as he crawled low to the ground, as smoke filled his lungs. He had to find her. He just had to.

He looked around wildly, his eyes finally distinguishing parts of the world as the dust began to settle. Bodies were strewn in front of him, deep crimson blood seeping over the ground onto the brown grass, swords and metals haphazardly sticking out from the ground where they fell from desperate hands. Then, in the distance, just up ahead, red hair, almost buried with the gray dust that covered everything.

His fingers digging into the dirt, he thrust himself forward as the mass of red hair became a full body, limp on the ground. "Hey, hey, hey, I'm here," he whispered, throwing himself toward Gaabi's body. He pulled her into his arms, his body screaming in pain with the exertion. He gritted his teeth. "Gaabi, I'm here. I'm going to get you out of here."

Running his trembling hands over her face, he wiped the ash and dust from her eyes. She coughed, doubling over as the world around cleared. Her brown eyes opened slowly, then widened as she raised a trembling finger, pointing to something behind him.

His heart pounded as he clutched her in his arms, holding her tight to his chest. Hanue turned slowly, toward where she was pointing, and his eyes could barely register what he saw.

In the distance, over a field of barely moving men and women, deep red bloodstains, glinting metal, and roaring fires, a single woman stood in the middle of a cloud of smoke, an aura of blinding green around her, obscuring her head from view. She was the brightest light, brighter than the still burning fires of war. The green grew brighter and brighter and brighter as Gaabi coughed and clutched at him, as his heartbeat pounded in his chest, as the screams grew louder still.

What the fuck?

CHAPTER SIXTY-THREE
MOLAC

The blinding green stole Molac's vision as he stumbled to his feet, the moans of his fallen countrymen bursting through his ears as they moved to raise themselves or ran blindly through the field. The fighting was done for now, replaced with bodies strewn over the land around him, bleeding, groaning, calling to their mothers.

Molac raised his hand to his eyes as he took a tentative step toward the light and he gasped as the figure of a woman became visible, the green beginning to fade. She stood tall in a flaming field of people laying on the ground, bleeding with broken limbs or crawling around like ants. She was tall and thin, snow-pale skin contrasting with her dark green dress that billowed around her as if a great windstorm swirled around just her.

His legs shook as he thought back to the words of the general in the tower only a few days prior, the warning Yidenu had given Asmuto in the dungeon; they live, they will make you pay. Molac fell to the ground, his knees hitting the dirt with a force that sent shockwaves through his trembling body. Squeezing his eyes shut, he shook his head.

This isn't happening.

As he opened his eyes again, the woman did not disappear, instead raising her hands to the air as green hung still in the area around her face, obstructing it from view. People in the distance started to raise themselves to their feet, faces filled with shock and awe.

He tore his eyes from the sight in front of him, searching the land nearby for any sign of Asmuto... or his body. But a loud *clap* sounded through the air and his head was thrown back to facing *her* like she herself had pulled his gaze back. His breathing quickened as he shook harder, tremors running through his body.

A soft laugh burst into his ears, pounding into his very mind. He raised his hands to his ears, trying desperately to block it out but it still sounded, louder and louder with each passing second. The people around him opened their mouths in screams that didn't reach his ears and he joined them, his scream lost under that loud, pounding laugh. Something about it seemed vaguely familiar, like he had heard it before in a dream and his anxiety grew.

The woman raised in the air, seemingly held up by invisible forces as she floated above the ground. Molac watched in terrified awe as she pointed her hand at the Davegu, at him. "You fight for a king that doesn't care about you; you fight for a truth that is a lie. These people are not your enemies. Be not afraid. Lay down your weapons."

His eyes wide, Molac watched as the people around him dropped their swords and bows, arms shaking, screaming as if the weapons themselves had burned their hands.

The woman spoke again, "Good." Her voice was suddenly kind and soothing in a way that sent chills running up his spine. "Now let's meet the real enemy."

He couldn't shake the feeling that something about her, in some way, was familiar.

Chapter Sixty-Four
Lisynia

Lisynia fought against the hold that she seemed to be placed under, trying to reach out for Otto a few feet from her, her sword on the ground next to her, the dagger on her belt, anything at all, but she found herself completely unable to move her body despite her efforts. It was as if she was frozen in place, as if she was placed under her own paralysis spell.

Her breath exited her lungs in quick, short gasps as her heart pounded. The woman in green in front of her was not the Goddess that had been talking to her, claiming her, leading her, but everything within Lisynia told her that this floating woman was an Ancient, one of the Sisters of whichever Goddess Lisynia had become privy to.

And if it wasn't Lisynia's Goddess, she knew this could not mean anything good.

The woman twirled slowly in the air, her head still concealed by the cloud of green smoke as her dress flowed softly around her legs.

Lisynia bored her eyes into the back of Otto's head of ashy blonde hair in front of her, willing him to overcome the hold of the Goddess and wake her, to tell her this was all just a dream.

But Lisynia knew better. This was no dream.

The Goddess stopped turning in the air, lowering herself to the ground. One of her pale white arms extended from the cloud of smoke and raised a thin finger, pointing toward Lisynia. Her heart sped up now, her stomach jumping into her throat as she choked back her fear.

The strong voice of the Goddess spoke, echoing through the field. "You. Come here."

Lisynia squeezed her eyes shut, the murmuring of Davegu and Tevebrisian and Andysi soldiers all pounding into her ears. She prepared for the inevitable, whatever this being would subject her to.

A familiar voice screamed through the silence, piercing into her heart. Lisynia's eyes flew open.

Otto was no longer by her side, his warmth ripped from the nearby air, instead he clawed into the ground in the darkness, dragged by something unseen toward the Goddess in green.

A desperation came over Lisynia as he screamed again, raw and powerful and terrified as he moved further away by the second. Rage and fear and pain mounted in her body, boiling her very blood as his eyes shot up, meeting her quickly blurring ones.

Everything hurt, everything screamed, everything overcame her as the Goddess ripped Otto from the ground and raised him into the air with one hand like he weighed nothing at all.

The world went silent, the people from all sides frozen in place just like her.

Tears ran from her eyes, and she tried to yell, to call out, to move, to do anything at all to prevent the only person in her life that *knew* her from being put through whatever that woman would do.

As her anguish built, stronger, stronger, stronger, the spell seemed to crack, and her stifled voice reached fruition as she forced the words from her throat. "Leave him alone!"

The Goddess stopped her movements, holding Otto up in the air by the collar of his armor as his feet kicked and choking sounds reached her ears. The woman laughed softly. "My child, I'm giving you what you've wanted for these last years. The king will die tonight. Death requires life. Blood requires blood."

Confusion gnawed at her mind at these words but as Otto screamed again, the Goddess turned away from her and thrust her other pale hand around his neck.

Tears blurred Lisynia's vision as the Goddess released the stilling spell from her and dropped Otto roughly to the ground. He choked and coughed in front of her, the only sound she could hear.

"Please," she sobbed, her pleading falling on uncaring ears.

Otto stared at her with a sort of sadness she'd never seen in him before. Lisynia shook her head. He was not giving up, he couldn't. His strained voice struggled out from his body as he sobbed. "I love you, Lisy. It's okay."

As these words sunk into her ears, the tears flowed freely down her face, hot and heavy and she shook her head again. This wasn't how she wanted this to go, this wasn't how she wanted to hear him say those words.

She wanted to shout it, to scream it, to beg for his life. *I love you, too.*

Otto was pulled from the ground again, his whimpers reaching her ears with horrific clarity as he thrashed and twisted in the air, the Goddess's arms outstretched below him. He screamed, a blood curdling sound that seared into her mind.

Lisynia fell to her knees, hitting the ground hard as her eyes stayed glued to the sight of her only friend in front of her, the man she could finally admit she loved too, thrashing in the air, begging for mercy.

CHAPTER SIXTY-FIVE
ANAVI

Anavi watched the scene unfolding in the distance with an intensity, not daring to look away, not even for a second. The mysterious enchantment that had fallen over her after the explosion had dissipated, leaving Anavi free to move, free to leave. But something about the green woman and the man flailing in the air in front of her kept her stilled. The Seven would want to know about this, *need* to know about this.

Out of the corner of her eye, the glow of green light highlighted the man she entered Andyse with, Yidenu, being pulled to his feet by two women, the two women he had run to before the explosion. Their faces were upturned to watch the sight in front of them, eyes wide and shining with green light.

Surrounding the woman in green were all the forces that had been fighting, killing each other just moments ago, and Anavi recognized some of them as they stared in awe and horror. People from the Northlands, Xienee in the distance, Davegu soldiers, and quite a few, including a blonde woman that had cried out when the man in the air was raised up, that she couldn't quite make out from this distance.

No one fought, no one clamored to help the man screaming like his blood was being boiled inside his body; everyone on all sides just seemed to watch. Just like her. Anavi was an assassin, not a savior.

The woman in green started chanting, her voice reverberating like it came from the air itself, something ancient and visceral as it pounded into Anavi's bones and her heart thrummed in her chest.

The man thrashed harder now, screaming still and Anavi watched, entranced as the green light glowed on his skin. His skin began to stretch, his very flesh seeming to melt as the woman's chanting grew louder, rougher. The shriek that exited his mouth was unlike anything she had heard before as she watched his skin clump and fall to the ground, exposing muscle, tendon, sinew in a mess of red and white.

Anavi fought back a cry from escaping her own throat as the sight became more gruesome, chunks of flesh and blood dripping from the air to the ground with soft squelching sounds.

Screams erupted around her as people clamored, running into the distance, into the trees or toward the river.

The chanting got ever louder. The flesh melted from his bones as if liquid, red blood squirting from his body. Bile rose in her throat.

She was no stranger to blood, to death, to suffering, fuck, she liked to inflict it herself, but this was unlike anything she'd seen before.

The man thrashed and thrashed, somehow still moving as his bones became visible, glowing under the light of the green that cast over everything. Clumps of muscle and blood and organs dropped from his carcass, landing in an ever-growing wet pile of his own body below him.

And then he went silent.

Anavi fought to calm her breathing, her chest rising and falling quickly below the armor she wore, armor that seemed much too thin as a cacophony of screaming and clanging surrounded her. People flew by her, bodies fleeing in a great exodus, abandoning their weapons, their fellow soldiers, everything.

The fires of battle roared in the distance, the sound of crackling flames and breaking bones filling her ears as the brutalized carcass of this man bent and contorted, the bones seeming to lengthen and change in front of her eyes with a flick of the woman's wrist.

Anavi had never believed in the Goddesses but this woman in front of her, bathed in green light and floating in the air next to the skeletal remains of what used to be a man...

Her heart pounded against her ribs painfully as her breath quickened, misting in front of her eyes in the cold air of winter. Her eyes still locked on the bones as they grew and changed and popped and snapped, a far-off voice reached her ears from her side. "Are you gonna help us, or what?"

Anavi turned in the direction the voice came from, toward the women and Yidenu next to her. People sprinted every which way, blocking her view as they passed, but sure enough, one of the women, black hair slick with sweat, stared at her, flames dancing in the reflection of her wide, crazed eyes.

Yidenu came into view and Anavi found herself stepping toward him, his bloodied, wrinkled face nearly unrecognizable as dust covered every bit of his skin.

She had to go back to The Seven, tell them of the Goddess, the deaths of battle, the mysteries she had yet to unravel but still, something within her pulled her forward, toward the man that saved her life. She stepped slowly at first, then quicker, quicker, as she wove between the fleeing bodies and tried desperately to block out the sound of the breaking bones and screams that filled the air.

As each person passed, she quickly glanced at them, searching for her brother among those running for their lives. She brought him here, she brought him into this death and forgot him, *left* him.

The Seven would not accept her returning without him. Jovan wouldn't.

Anavi would not fail him like that.

But as she reached Yidenu and the women, she stayed back, raising her head to peer around the Goddess, trying to make out the shapes of people in the distance, to let the green light shine on their faces, to shine on Hanue's.

Chapter Sixty-Six
Rauna

The mass outpouring of people was like watching ants flee the water that would flood through the streets of Lasari after a heavy rain. Pounding footsteps surrounded her, people running past her, away in the distance, anywhere they could scramble to get away from the hellish scene the battle had devolved into. Few still stood, watching, heads raised to the woman and the body and the screams and the flames, including the woman that Yidenu said was with him. She'd stopped just shy of being of any actual use.

Rauna clenched her fist and squatted down next to Yidenu and Tivea. Though her breathing was shallow and her body trembling, her sister was still somewhere among the fire and weapons and death. Rauna could not possibly leave, her feet firmly planted into the ground.

Tivea crouched next to her as Rauna did her best to quell her fear and avoid looking at the harsh green light and what occurred under its gaze. Tivea was shaking, clutching with one hand at Rauna's arm with a vice grip and her other wrapped around her father. The woman she traveled with, the woman that should by all accounts be long past dead, was twitching and shivering in the cold and her father, Yidenu, murmured hushed words into her ear, holding her tightly to him as tears choked his words.

The chanting of the woman in the distance, the woman in green, the woman floating in the air itself, got louder, harsher, more guttural and despite her best efforts to search the lines for her sister, Rauna found herself raising her eyes to the distance again.

The light swallowed everything in her sight, everything except the body of that poor man, skeletal and cracking in the air as it twisted. The woman thrust her hands into the air again, again, again, forcing her magics into the bones of what was once a man and Rauna watched in horror, her body completely frozen as the flesh and blood and skin and hair grew back around his bones.

Rauna's legs shook beneath her own weight as she struggled to stay upright, struggled to keep herself from dry heaving at the sight. And the sound, oh, Seven, the *sound*.

It was so loud, the sound of a man brutalized. As a body built back around his reddish, bloody bones, grotesque, gurgling screams escaped from his half-formed face. Bones cracked and popped; muscle grew seemingly from thin air.

Rauna couldn't take it anymore and dropped to her knees, keeling over as she spat liquid from her mouth, heaving.

Her fingers dug into Tivea's clothing, twisting around the furs she wore as Rauna squeezed her eyes shut.

This isn't happening, this isn't happening.

Then the chanting and the cracking and the popping and the squelching stopped, like it never happened at all. Rauna gingerly opened her eyes and the sight before her in the distance caused her head to go light, her eyes blurring black.

The man in the air was no longer the young man in his mid-twenties with blonde hair and armor of leather from before. Instead, the man was old, wizened and gray, a thick beard over his wrinkled face that green light seeped into. The woman of green lowered the man to the ground, laying him on the grass below her. He wore nothing at all, nothing except a single crown on his head, bright gold with deep orange gems interlaid within it that shone in the moonlight. He looked confused, pulling himself into a sitting position and bringing his knees to his chest.

The Goddess smiled, her teeth blindingly white.

A hush fell over the people that remained watching and Tivea twitched harder next to her, her breathing erratic. The hush turned into a murmur, then a scream, then finally, a shout.

"THE KING!"

Tivea grumbled something, her voice grating and gruff as if her body had been possessed by something other than the kind woman Rauna had come to know. "The king."

Tivea ripped herself away from Yidenu and Rauna. She raised herself to her feet, twitching as she moved, and walked toward the green. Rauna lurched forward, trying to catch her, fear and worry suffocating her. "Tivea!"

But Tivea sprinted away and Rauna landed hard in the grass behind her.

CHAPTER SIXTY-SEVEN
TIVEA

The world was gone. All that was left was the call of the Goddess in front of her. Tivea's feet moved without her direction, sprinting forward, chills shooting through her body with each step she took, enveloping her in a blissful cold.

It was silent as she approached, the sounds of battle and terror and pain around her all faded, leaving only a soft humming coming from the Goddess she sprinted toward.

Tivea's heart fluttered in her chest, the fear of before, the pain of nearly dying, the worry and the dread and the anxiety all floating away, lifted from her shoulders as the pleasant sound of melodic humming overtook her. As she approached, she thought only of the Goddess, the pleasant deep forest green that surrounded her, the exact color of Rauna's eyes, the color of the forest in midsummer, the color of home. She was meant to be here, the green she'd been seeing in the corner of her eye, the humming she'd hear before falling asleep, this was why.

She took a deep breath, breathing in the air of a crisp summer breeze as her hair flew in front of her eyes with her movements.

Then she saw her, the Goddess herself.

Her face was almost blurred, like looking through the reflection of the water, but Tivea knew her. Her warm-toned skin, the color of acorns, kind deep brown eyes, her long dark brown hair, the same color as Tivea's, worn in a braid over her shoulder. The woman smiled; her *mother* smiled.

The bliss of before was quickly replaced with a deep longing, pulling her forward.

Tivea's heart pulled her faster than her legs could move, tears of joy filling her eyes as her vision blurred. She let out a soft cry as she reached the woman she had longed for all these years. Tivea fell forward, landing at her feet, clutching at her mother's pale orange dress.

Her mother reached one hand out, stroking Tivea's cheek with a warm, soft, touch. Tears slipped freely from her eyes now, cutting a path down her burning cheeks.

A hand cupped her chin, lifting her gaze upwards and her mother's other hand held out a small dagger, old and beautiful, deep green gems in the hilt; it seemed like something she had seen in a dream before. Tivea reached a tentative hand out, grasping the ornate dagger in her hand.

"You know what to do, my child. You know what needs to be done. This man deserves it, this is why I healed you."

Tivea nodded, moving her watch from her mother's kind face, just as she remembered it, to the man lying on the ground nearby. Tovik. An anger unlike any other filled her body, heating her blood, forcing her to move toward him.

This man, this pathetic excuse of a human being, had killed her people, burned her home, kidnapped her father, sent his men to chase her through the woods. He was violence. He was destruction. And he was going to die.

His eyes flashed in fear as his chest heaved, clutching his knees close to his chest. Completely naked, completely unprotected. She'd lived in fear of this man her entire life and here he was...

Utterly pitiful.

Tivea raised herself to her feet slowly, every step toward him feeling like it was way too long coming as she stepped over the bloody remains on the ground. Her hand raised in the air, the blade clutched above her head. She did not shake; she did not twitch.

She smiled.

As if in a trance, she watched from outside her body as she slammed the dagger into his chest. Tovik coughed and clutched at her, his touch feeble and weak as blood pooled around the entry wound, his sickly yellow eyes glaring at her with a combination of fear and pure, utter hatred. He spat at her, hot blood landing on her face.

At this, she leaned in close to his pain ridden face and shoved the dagger in deeper. As he stilled, Tivea released her grip on the weapon and stumbled to her feet.

She stared at the body in front of her, his naked chest coated in his own blood, dagger jutting out from his ribcage. And worst of all, black tendrils spreading under his skin from the wound. Now she shook, slowly at first, then all-consuming as the weight of what she did hit her like a blow to the chest.

She killed a man. She took a life.

Tivea raised her hands in front of her eyes, blood coating her palms, his blood. The tears built in her eyes quickly and she fell back from the body as they began to fall.

Her mother drifted to her, cupping her chin with her soft hand again. Tivea pressed her cheek into her palm, shaking her head wildly as sobs racked her body, her breath hitching in her throat.

"Mother—"

"Shh," her mother said soothingly, "hush, my child."

Tivea clutched at her arm, clinging to it for dear life.

"I am not her."

Tivea raised her eyes to her mother's face, confusion gnawing at her mind. What did she mean? "No, no, I'd know you anywhere."

But as she watched, her mother's kind face twisted, changing in front of her eyes. Her gentle gaze replaced with a horrifying sight of empty eye sockets, blood gushing down pale skin from the holes in her face. Her mother's soft orange dress was now a deep green and her brown hair now pitch black, matching the midnight sky. Gone was the kind, sweet face of her mother, replaced with a monster.

Everything hit her at once as her head swam. She was never her mother, that was an illusion. One to get her to kill the King, one to get her to the Goddess's side.

"No, no." Tivea shook her head faster, as if willing it to not be true. She killed a man; she *killed* a person!

She rocked back and forth as the Goddess released her chin. "You did good, my child. You did good."

Chapter Sixty-Eight
Molac

S hock. Horror. Fear. An overwhelming urge to run. As he stared at the body in the distance, the figure of the Davegu king himself stiff, unmoving, coated in blood, Molac trembled.

Move.

And so, he did. Molac ran from body to body, people streaming past him as he searched for Asmuto among them. The king was dead, killed by that girl in the distance at the request of that ever so familiar woman in green.

A Goddess.

The thought of that power, that hold she exerted over everything within him led him to no other conclusion. The explosion, the blinding green light, the voice that pierced through his skull—she was a Goddess, one of the Sisters. Yidenu was right.

The general was right, they live.

He had to get out of here, had to leave. If they weren't already fucked before, they were certainly fucked now. But he kept searching the bodies and the faces that passed him by. He wasn't leaving without Asmuto, not now.

Molac stumbled as another fleeing man pounded past him, running his shoulder into his back. Molac scoffed but kept his search going, trying in vain to ignore the pain of fear that seeped into every cell of his body.

"Who's the coward now, assholes?" he shouted after the retreating Davegu.

As his chest heaved and anger pulsed through his body, a voice reached his ears. "Molac?"

Turning on his heel, Molac found himself face to face with the man he was searching for. Asmuto was covered in blood and dirt, his leather armor torn and muddied as he helped an injured woman to her feet, her hands clutching at her stomach as dark red blood seeped between her fingers. Oddly, Asmuto seemed to have a concentration of blood on his mouth. But Molac didn't focus on that and ran toward him. "We need to get out of here."

Asmuto's face twisted in annoyance as he looked at Molac. The woman to his side groaned. "No shit, man," he sighed. "The king is gone. I'm not following a dead man."

Asmuto paused for a second to throw the woman's arm around his shoulder as Molac peered around him anxiously. Molac crossed his arms. Couldn't he hurry the fuck up? She was as good as dead anyway.

"I like Yidenu, always have. We were friends," Asmuto said, his voice strained as he waved one arm in the air signaling to any others nearby to fall back if they weren't already. "Tovik made us do horrible things to him. And now the king's dead."

At this, Molac raised his eyes to the horizon once more, staring at the fading green light in the distance and the naked king's body on the field. As it faded, Molac caught eyes on the figures beneath the smoke. The king's killer, a small woman with brown hair and torn clothing at the feet of a much taller woman wearing a green cloak, black hair running down her back.

It hit him at that moment, and he stumbled back, his fear reawakened. He fought the urge to run, to hide, to abandon Asmuto and leave it all behind. He pulled Asmuto's hand from the injured woman, pulling him away, pulling him toward the river, toward Oshgor.

Molac turned to look over his shoulder as Asmuto protested and stumbled behind him, wriggling his hand to break free.

The familiarity of the woman's voice, the green dress, the black hair. The power she seemed to have over others...

He'd seen it all before, *felt* it.

The woman in green was the queen herself that came to visit him in Asmuto's quarters all that time ago. Queen Meluth, the Goddess.

CHAPTER SIXTY-NINE
HANUE

He clutched Gaabi's hand in his as he moved quickly over the bodies and skimmed around the edge of the still-burning fires from dropped torches. Gaabi had caught sight of her sister in the distance after Tivea ran from the sidelines, disappearing into the green light in the center of the field.

Now they just had to get to Rauna without dying.

His heart beat heavy in his chest as he moved, stealing quick glances at the two women and the dead man that laid behind them. Gaabi stumbled in front of him, dragging him forward.

Rauna's eyes were turned toward Tivea, her arms working to lift the man next to her. Her curly hair was raggedy and matted with sweat. Streaks ran down her dusty face where tears had slid from her eyes.

She was right there, he just had to get there. Gaabi sidestepped an unmoving man laying splayed out of the ground, blood oozing around him into the dirt. As Hanue skirted around the man, Gaabi turned back to look at Hanue. Her hazel eyes were watery and bloodshot from her tears, her other hand pressed against her mouth.

"Are you alright?" Hanue ventured out, running his thumb along the side of her hand.

Gaabi nodded to the affirmative, but her face told a different story as another choked sob escaped her. Hanue pulled her closer to him, wrapping his arms around her trembling body. He raised his head, pressing his lips once again to her ashy forehead.

"You're okay. Your sister's right there, okay?" he said softly as she nuzzled into his chest. He had felt powerful before, at his forge making weapons for the Guard, when The Seven sent him here with Anavi, and as he looked back at that, he couldn't help but feel foolish. Here, holding this woman in his arms, getting her out of here alive, that is the most powerful he'd ever feel. "I'm going to get you to her, I promise."

A shuffling behind him drew his sight away from her and he turned quickly, ducking down to grab one of the many weapons that littered the battlefield where people dropped them.

His fingers clenched around the hilt of a short sword and he raised it up, pushing Gaabi behind him as he turned to face whatever approached, his breathing quick and urgent.

Three figures moved toward him and Gaabi gasped, moving forward toward them. When the light shone on the faces of the two closest to them, he lowered the sword.

Rauna shuffled toward them, an older man at her side. The man's arm was thrown over her shoulder as they approached with slight stumbles. "Gaabi!" she called out.

Hanue tucked the sword into his belt and ran forward. As he met them, he ran to the man's other side, throwing his free arm over his own shoulder. "What happened?" he asked breathlessly.

Rauna didn't answer, instead grasping with her free hand at Gaabi as they collided into each other. Choked sobs and disbelieving laughs sounded from the women as they clutched at each other. Hanue felt a small smile begin to tug at his mouth, bittersweet almost, as he watched them.

Hanue cleared his throat, forcing down the sadness that plagued his mind at the sight of Rauna and Gaabi embracing while his sister was still out there, somewhere, away from him.

Biting his tongue, he tried to focus on anything else, anything at all.

The Goddess and Tivea there in the center of the field, the mass exodus of fleeing soldiers, the coppery scent of blood that assaulted his nostrils.

They had to move.

Then the third figure, the one that was walking behind Rauna and the man, came into view as he gazed at the carnage of the battle.

Hanue gasped as the light shone on the figure's face. Her features were slick with blood, her braids dripping with sweat. She walked with a slight limp, her sword held tightly at her side.

Tears welled in his eyes, not the tears of pain or fear or sadness that he had become accustomed to bearing these last few weeks—these were tears of disbelief, of hope, of happiness.

He swung his body out from under the man's arm and ran, barely even paying attention to the gasps sounding from behind him, the screams of pain and dying fighters, the way the grass poked at his scrapes and cuts.

He found her, in all this chaos, he found her.

Without thinking, without waiting, he called out. "Anavi!"

CHAPTER SEVENTY
ANAVI

A shape came running at her through the grass, large, with a glint of metal at its side. Anavi's hand flew to her own side, wrapping quickly around the hilt of her sword. Then a voice cut through the screams and the commotion of people.

A voice she recognized. "Anavi!"

The shape in front of her took form and she blinked, not daring to believe the sight in front of her eyes. A man, dirty and dusty with bloody cuts decorating his skin ran toward her. Anavi pushed herself forward as much as she could, a fluttering growing in her chest.

"Hanue?" her voice came out strangled, muffled.

Her brother crashed into her; Anavi wobbled on her one good leg as the force of his body hit hers. His arms wrapped tightly around her and slowly she removed her hand from her sword, wrapping her own arms carefully around him.

Anavi raised one hand up to her eyes, wiping the hot tears from her face while the other clutched at the trembling man in her arms. "Hanue."

She stared straight ahead at the crowd that Hanue came running from. That woman with black hair held Yidenu up and another woman with red curly hair stood next to them, staring over in their direction.

Hanue's shaking body moved away from hers and he stared down at her, a bright smile on his bloodied face, tears slipping down his cheeks. He chuckled and Anavi felt a tug at the corners of her mouth. His fingers slinked into hers and he pulled her toward the group.

Anavi stumbled behind him, still not believing this was real. Her brother, her naive little brother, survived not only the wilds of Andyse but a battle without her help?

Fake. It had to be fake.

A trick of her weary eyes.

But his hand grasped hers and she moved over the grass. The woman with red hair smiled at their approach and the other woman turned slowly to face them. Her face was less trusting, hardened almost, with a scowl on her features and a flicker of anger ignited in Anavi's chest.

Gritting her teeth together, she pulled her hand from Hanue, her eyes boring into the black-haired woman's green ones. Hanue turned to look at her and a flash of confusion passed through his irises. "What's wrong?" he said, his voice wavering.

Before she could answer, more screaming erupted from nearby and she whipped her head toward the source.

As her eyes skimmed over the carnage, a woman came into view. She was on her knees, closer to the Goddess than most and her face was twisted into an expression of horror, grief, pain unending.

The woman screamed again and, for some reason that escaped Anavi, the sound was vaguely familiar, like she had heard it in a dream in years past. Squinting her eyes, Anavi took a stumbling step toward her, blocking out Hanue's questions and the red-haired woman that slowly made her way over to her and Hanue in Anavi's periphery.

"So, this is the famous Anavi?" she asked.

Anavi didn't answer, instead staring at the woman. The green light and the clouds of dust still hanging stiff in the air blocked her view of the woman in the distance but slowly, her eyes came into focus.

Her heart quickened as the woman screamed again. Tears glinted off her cheeks, glowing in the light of the fires. Her face was bloodied and beaten, splotches of red over her pale skin. Blonde hair stained with blood and dirt was pulled back from her face.

The woman's eyes almost shined orange...

Anavi stepped backwards involuntarily, a shock of pain jumping through her leg when she put pressure on it. She knew this blonde, orange eyed woman. She *knew* her.

As the pieces all clicked together in her mind, a chill ran through her bones. She turned on her heel as fast as she could, heart pounding in her ears as blood pumped through her muscles.

She moved quickly, ignoring the pain that screamed through her leg. Hanue and the red-haired woman embraced in front of her. "Hanue, we have to go," she said, her voice strained as the blonde woman behind her screamed again.

He shook his head, face twisting in confusion as he pulled the woman in closer to him. "What are you talking about?"

Arguing was worth nothing now. Anavi thrust herself forward, grasping at the red-headed woman's curls and yanking her head back. She squealed in pain, but Anavi didn't care, her ears overtaken by the sounds of the ghost behind her.

She threw the woman down to the ground as shouts broke out from the black-haired woman in the distance.

"Anavi, what the fuck?" Hanue said, his hand meeting her chest and pushing her back from the woman on the ground. "Why would you do that?"

As Hanue moved to help the redhead to her feet, the flicker of anger and fear in Anavi's chest now turned to rage, pure, red-hot rage. Anavi's hands grasped at Hanue, pulling him to his feet as the black-haired woman yelled, running over to them, sword drawn.

"I said, we have to leave," Anavi said, pushing Hanue forward, her fingers gripping his arms with all the strength she could muster. "When we came here you promised to listen to me, so fucking listen."

He protested and struggled against her hold, hitting at her arm as he thrashed. His voice, his shouts, covered the sounds of the screams of the woman behind them but her shrill screeching still played in Anavi's mind.

She had to get to Jovan; she had to get Hanue out of here. He was a witness, a necessary one.

That blonde woman on her knees behind her was a ghost, a haunting of her past. One Anavi was not going to confront. She was dead, gone a long time ago, gone with Anavi's own father that day in the hidden mountain kingdom all those years ago.

Catina.

CHAPTER SEVENTY-ONE
LISYNIA

Numb. That was all she felt as hands pulled her back. Numb. Her eyes stayed focused on the sight in the distance, the two women over the king's dead body and Otto's clumpy remains.

She'd failed. Failed to protect her people, failed to protect the one person she thought would always be there, failed to kill the king. She'd failed everything.

He loved her. And she never told him she felt the same.

A whimper escaped from her mouth without warning as her eyes seared the sight into her mind of the man she once knew now simply a pile of flesh and blood on the ground. Lisynia let the hands pull her back, her body heavy from the weight of her loss. Her feet stumbled over bodies and bodies and bodies, her people, Davegu, Andysi, all identical in death. Cold and bloody and glassy-eyed.

A voice reached her ears, muffled, unintelligible. Then a face, familiar and harsh as it pressed into her view. A hand met her face, a sharp blow that exploded through her skin.

Lisynia blinked, the face coming into view, the voice becoming clearer, sharper, urgent. The hands shook her violently. Xienee's face met her eyes. "Lisynia! Come on, it's done. The king's dead, we have to go."

Lisynia stared at the woman in front of her, her ally, her sister-in-arms, despite the times they hadn't gotten along before. Tears built in her eyes at the sight of her, the scowl and fear and urgency etched on her face. Xienee's hands grasped on Lisynia's arms, moving her with force toward the forest in the distance.

Despite the pain and the grief and the anger she knew she should be feeling, Lisynia felt nothing. She allowed Xienee to pull her away from the Goddess, away from the pile of flesh that was her only friend, away from the body of the naked Davegu king that lay on the ground, built from the bones of Otto himself.

Otto was sacrificed to kill the king. And Lisynia didn't stop it. She didn't even kill the bastard herself.

Her eyes stayed locked on the body of the man she'd lived in fear of for years as Xienee roughly pulled her further and further by the second. All the times she'd imagined his death, she'd imagined it to be a glorious fight, a righteous struggle for her people's future and retribution for their past...

It was none of those.

The tears flowed freely down her face now and Xienee stopped manhandling her, stepping in front of her, blocking the consequences of her naivety from her sight. The woman's mouth moved noiselessly; the world silent in Lisynia's ringing ears. Then Xienee pursed her lips, and a sharp pain burst through Lisynia's face.

She exhaled sharply, raising her hand to where Xienee's hand had met her wet cheek.

"Pull yourself together!" Xienee's strong voice burst in Lisynia's ears. "You call yourself a general? You *can't* shut down. Do you see what's around us? They need a leader, Lisynia, they need you."

Lisynia raised her face again, trying her hardest to prevent the tears from spilling. She darted her sight over the battlefield and a pit built in her stomach.

Bodies. Bodies everywhere. Blood everywhere. People running or trying their best to flee with the injuries they had sustained. The Goddess still stood in the very center of the carnage. Davegu forces were gone, retreating in the distance toward the southern river.

Her people and Xienee's people ran recklessly around her, tending to others, crying, standing frozen just like Lisynia, eyes glazed over in shock.

She was no leader. She did this to them.

CHAPTER SEVENTY-TWO
RAUNA

She grasped at Gaabi, holding her tightly to her as her sister screamed into her chest. Rauna watched the disappearing figures heading toward the mountains through slitted eyes, heat burning through her veins. She'd never put it past an Aethiel brat to do something vile but throwing Gaabi to the ground and running off with someone that wouldn't even lift a finger to help?

Her grip on her sister tightened and she bent her neck, pressing her lips against Gaabi's ashy forehead, the taste of dirt filling her mouth. "We need to move, Gabs."

Gaabi's fingers gripped into her arms harder and Rauna pulled away. The Goddess still stood in the middle of the field, less and less people out in the open as the seconds passed. Tivea was shaking at the feet of the green woman and a pang shot through Rauna's heart. After an agonizingly long time watching the figures in the distance, she tore her eyes away from them and started moving toward Yidenu.

"Quickly, come on," she said, pulling her sister toward the man with one hand and placing her other on the hilt of the sword at her belt. Gaabi didn't fight her for once, just crying softly, her resolve seemingly broken by Hanue's departure and the death surrounding them.

Rauna clenched her teeth and moved closer to Yidenu. As they approached, his features came more into view, staring at the center of the field, at the Goddess, at his daughter, green light causing the blood on his face to shine a grotesque brown color over his skin.

As they reached him, Rauna released her hold on Gaabi and threw Yidenu's arm over her shoulder again. Why he trusted her, she was not sure. But as her eyes moved back to the discomforting sight of Tivea at the feet of something eldritch, ancient, and powerful, she resolved herself to at least save Tivea's father from meeting the same fate as so many others did tonight.

Yidenu's head rolled slightly, only half-conscious from the explosion and the wound that steadily dripped blood from his stomach. He groaned. "Where's my daughter?"

Rauna took a deep breath, choosing to ignore this question, at least until they were further away and the stench of death no longer followed them.

Her heart pounded in her chest as she dragged Yidenu over the grass, Gaabi's soft footsteps behind her. Her muscles burned from the effort of holding a man twice her size up over her shoulders. She took a deep breath, turning slowly toward the forest in the distance.

They just had to reach the safety of the trees. There they could regroup. There they could figure out how to get Tivea back. There Gaabi could heal Yidenu's wounds. There they would try to make sense of the chaos they'd all just lived through.

Just reach the forest. Just. Reach. The. Forest.

Rauna moved slowly, exhaustion tugging at her limbs as the adrenaline of the night began to wear off. She blinked and shook her head, trying to rid her mind of the fog.

Something rustling behind her snagged her attention.

In her shock, Rauna twisted on her heel, hand flying to the hilt of the sword at her side. Yidenu fell to the ground behind her, and she shoved Gaabi backwards harshly.

As her eyes attempted to adjust to facing the green light again, her heart screamed in her chest, her gaze searching for anything heading toward them.

A large figure approached them, cloak obscuring the shape of the person. But they were tall, and a glint of metal flashed in their hand. A sword. Rauna's throat went dry and she swallowed hard, trying to quell the fear ebbing through her body.

"Who are you?" she called out.

No answer.

The figure got closer. A brown hood obscured most of his face from view, leaving only the lower half of his face visible, dotted and lined with old scars and new blood. In his hand he held an Andysi sword dripping with red.

Her grip on her sword tightened and she stepped forward, trying to ignore the voice in her head telling her to run.

The cloaked man slowed his pace and lowered his sword, his neck jutting to the side as he peered around Rauna. "Yidenu?" came a gruff voice.

Rauna cocked her head, still not lowering her own weapon and a groan reached her ears from behind her. She threw her other arm out to her side to prevent Yidenu from stepping toward the cloaked man. "Last chance. Who are you?" she asked again.

A rough hand pushed her arm down and Rauna turned her head. Yidenu stood next to her, stepping forward toward the cloaked man, his hand clutching his stomach wound as blood seeped between his fingers. "It's okay, girl," Yidenu said. "Hello, Torvo."

At the sound of this name, the cloaked figure bowed his head. "The commander will be pleased to know you're safe," Torvo said simply.

Yidenu laughed. "Glad to see she's grown a conscience," Yidenu grunted out, his voice unsteady. He teetered slightly and Rauna jumped forward, catching him as his legs gave out, her own legs trembling from the effort.

Torvo did not seem phased by this display and turned quickly on his heel. Walking briskly past them, he waved one hand to beckon them. "Come with me."

Rauna breathed heavily and turned her head, looking one last time at Tivea in the distance...

Gaabi's fingers slinked into hers and her head shot up. Gaabi's tear streaked face brought a calm to her and a hint of a smile tugged at Rauna's face. They couldn't go to Lasari, not anymore, not with Hanue and his sister telling The Seven what happened tonight. She clasped her fingers around her sister's hand and heaved Yidenu up again.

She moved toward the forest, Gaabi and Yidenu in tow, following the cloaked man into the unknown of Andyse.

CHAPTER SEVENTY-THREE
TIVEA

The Goddess's fingers stroked her cheek once more, Tivea recoiling at her touch. "Be calm, my child. You have much still to do."

Tivea squeezed her eyes closed, trying to push the soft voice out of her head to no avail. As she opened her eyes again, she swallowed hard, pushing down her rage and pain and disgust and all the other emotions that fought for dominance over her. Drawing in a shaky breath, Tivea did her best to not let her eyes wander to the woman's face again.

The pale skin, the blank expression, the hollowed out bloody holes where eyes should be...

It was all too much. Instead, Tivea stared at the body, the carcass of the king that laid next to her. His blood was drying now, coating his chest with sticky red, the black tendrils staining his pale skin. It was odd how frail he looked in death.

In the death I caused him.

Tears flowed from her eyes quickly without reprieve even as she tried to fight them.

The Goddess cupped her chin again and raised Tivea's head in a gentle motion. Tivea did not fight it, anxiety flowing through her body. "Look."

She turned her gaze to the distance, to the direction the Goddess pointed with one slender pale finger.

The trees of the forest stood tall over the field of blood-stained grass and dead bodies. Pinpricks moved toward the trees at various distances from where Tivea sat at the Goddess's feet. As she strained her eyes, searching the movement in the distance for any semblance of familiarity, her heart jumped in her chest.

Four figures. One shorter woman with long curly red hair, one raven haired woman, the third figure's arm thrown over her shoulder as they stumbled forward, following closely behind a man in a brown cloak that billowed behind him as he walked toward the trees.

Gaabi, Rauna, her father, and Torvo.

Without thinking, Tivea raised her head to look at the Goddess and cringed as those sightless bloody eyes stared back at her. But there was a smile on her pale pink lips revealing pure white teeth stained red from the blood that ran down her face into her open mouth.

"Do you wish to go, my child?" the Goddess said.

Tivea nodded, a flicker of hope rising in her chest.

"Then go to them," the Goddess said simply, raising herself into the air, fading into the smoke with every second. "But don't worry. I will find you again, Tivea."

Tivea stumbled to her feet, her heart pounding as blood rushed in her ears. She did not look back at the body, she did not look back at the Goddess, she did not look back at all.

Her feet moved swiftly, her strength returning. Grass tugged at her boots, bodies lay strewn motionless, bloodied, dead, all over the field. She weaved in and out, skirting around the pools of blood, the swords scattered haphazardly.

The hope in her chest built and built and built, drowning out the fear, the pain, the dread of the night.

As she approached the figures, she called out, "Father!" It came out choked and breathless, but the figures stopped moving. "Rauna!"

Rauna's back tensed and slowly, the raven-haired woman turned, an expression of surprise on her face. "Tivea?"

Her father's face flashed in recognition. "Blossom?"

Tivea sped up, her pulse racing in her veins. A breathless laugh slipped out of her mouth and tears spilled. Reaching her arms out, barely daring to believe the sight in front of her face, Tivea's fingers grazed Rauna's arm.

Warm, solid. Real.

She threw herself at them, grasping at Rauna's curly hair, her father's calloused hands, anything and everything she could. They were real. It was real.

As she melted into the embrace of Rauna and her father and disbelieving laughter spilled out of her, the pain and the fear and the events of the night fading from her mind slightly.

Slightly.

Tivea cocked her head as her father's arm pulled her close to him and eyed the direction she had run from.

The green was gone, the Goddess gone, like they never existed at all. The only hint they ever existed was the naked body of the Davegu king laying splayed out in the distance, gold crown glittering in the moonlight, the dagger gone from his chest, like it never even existed.

A feeling of dread began to creep through her body, and she squeezed her eyes closed, pressing herself further into the warm embrace of her father's arms.

But the events of the night, the destruction of her life, didn't leave her mind, pounding through her head stronger and stronger and stronger.

The dagger, the dead king, the Goddess with her mother's face.

And her words.

A chill shot through her body as the words played in her mind once again in the same cold detached voice as the Goddess.

You still have much to do. I will find you, Tivea.

The king was dead. The battle was over. But she knew that the war had just begun.

Acknowledgments

I have always wanted to be an author. Since the day I realized books were written by other humans, this has been my goal.

This book has been in my mind for years. It started as just some quick ideas and quotes here and there but quickly grew into something more. Writing this book was the most healing thing I've ever done in my life. It gave me an escape, a place to go when the real world became too much for me.

I cannot thank the people that supported me in this journey enough. From the first teacher that ever supported my dreams, the wonderful Ms. Stagner, to my friends that always pestered me get it finished so they could read it, to my wonderful partner that pushed me to follow my dreams, I couldn't have done it without you.

This book saved my life, however cheesy that is to say, and gave me a place to explore all the darker parts of humanity in a setting removed from my day-to-day life (even though this book quickly became my day-to-day life).

I want to thank my wonderful editor, Mallory Day, for her help getting this book to be the best possible story it could be. I want to thank my friends among many others, for pushing me to never give up on this story and giving me amazing advice.

Thank you to all my beta readers, ARC readers, and everyone that supported my journey in getting this book written and published. I found a wonderful community of great people and I am so grateful everyday for your help and support.

Help an author, leave a review :)

Leaving reviews on books by independent authors like T.M. Baylor helps with visibility and making sure that the books reach as many people as possible. It also helps other readers make an informed decision on whether they would like to read!

If you're at all willing to, leaving a review on any of your favorite book review sites would be much appreciated!

About the Author

T.M. Baylor (also known as Torren) is the author of dark fantasy books that feature hidden aspects and themes of the human experience. Torren has had a passion for writing and crafting stories since childhood. Her debut novel, A Forgotten Legend, is the first of a series called The Secrets of Eterin. She currently lives in Pennsylvania with her partner and their dog.

When not writing, Torren enjoys spending her time outdoors or curling up with a good book. A lover of everything dark, morbid, and macabre, Torren enjoys reading horror and dark fantasy in her free time.

TMBAYLOR.COM